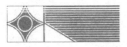

PURPLE
AMERICA

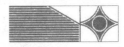

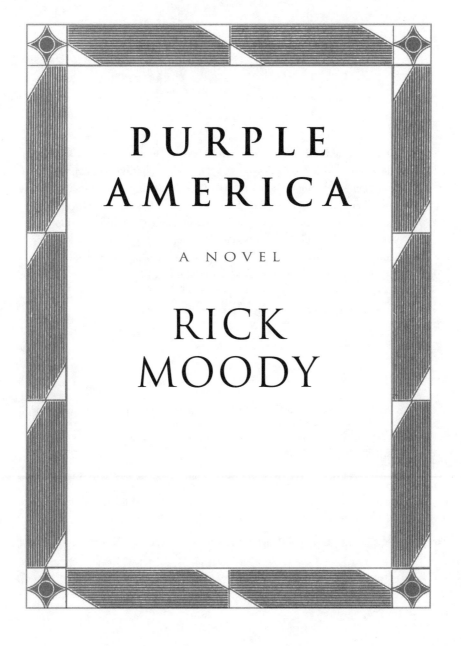

PURPLE AMERICA

A NOVEL

RICK MOODY

LITTLE, BROWN AND COMPANY Boston New York Toronto London

Some medical facts and intuitions from Jessica Dunne and Laura Iglehart. Exit wounds with the selfless aid of Sandu Berschadski. Designs by 3-D Construction. Support from the MacDowell Colony and from Michael Sundell and the Corporation of Yaddo also hereby acknowledged gratefully, as well as my indebtedness to my generous colleagues Michael Pietsch, Nora Krug, Donald Antrim, Stacey Richter, Jeffrey Eugenides, Charlie Smith, and national treasure Melanie Jackson. Bearing up and shouldering of great burdens by my mother — no relation to Billie Raitliffe — by the rest of my family, by the staff and patrons of the Star Burger Deli, W. 46th Street, and by the object of my affections, Amy Osborn.

First Edition

Library of Congress Cataloging-in-Publication Data

Moody, Rick.
Purple America : a novel / Rick Moody. — 1st ed.
p. cm.
ISBN 0-316-57925-4
I. Title.
PS3563.O5537P87 1997
813'.54 — dc21 96-48781

10 9 8 7 6 5 4 3 2 1

MV-NY

Published simultaneously in Canada by Little, Brown & Company (Canada) Limited

Printed in the United States of America

For M S M

I

Whosoever knows the folds and complexities of his own mother's body, *he shall never die.* Whosoever knows the latitudes of his mother's body, whosoever has taken her into his arms and immersed her baptismally in the first-floor tub, lifting one of her alabaster legs and then the other over its lip, whosoever bathes her with Woolworth's soaps in sample sizes, whosoever twists the creaky taps and tests the water on the inside of his wrist, whosoever shovels a couple of tablespoons of rose bath salts under the billowing faucet and marvels at their vermilion color, whosoever bends by hand her sclerotic limbs, as if reassuring himself about the condition of a hinge, whosoever has kissed his mother on the part that separates the lobes of her white hair and has cooed her name while soaping underneath the breast where he was once fed, whosoever breathes the acrid and dispiriting stench of his mother's body while scrubbing the greater part of this smell away with Woolworth's lavender soaps, who has pushed her discarded bra and oversized panties (scattered on the tile floor behind him) to one side, away from the water sloshing occasionally over the edge of the tub and choking the runoff drain, who has lost his footing on these panties, panties once dotted with blood of children unconceived, his siblings unconceived, panties now intended to fit over a vinyl undergarment, who has wiped stalactites of drool from his mother's mouth with a moistened violet washcloth, who has swept back the annoying violet shower curtain the better to lift up his stick-figure mother and to bathe her ass, where a sweet and infantile shit sometimes collects, causing her both discomfort and shame, whosoever angrily manhandles the dial on the bathroom radio (balanced on the toilet tank) with one wet hand in an effort to find a college station that blasts only compact disc recordings of train accidents and large-scale construction operations (*he should be over this noise by his age*), whosoever selects at last the drummers of Burundi on WUCN knowing full well that his mother can brook only the music of the Tin Pan Alley period and certain classics, and whosoever has then reacted guiltily to his own selfishness and tuned to some lite AM station featuring the greatest hits of swing, whosoever will notice in the course of his mission the ripe light of early November as it is played out on the wall of the bathroom where one of those plug-in electric candles with plastic base is the only source of illumination, whosoever waits in this half-light while his mother takes her last bodily pleasure: the time in which her useless body floats in the warm, humid, even lapping of rose-scented bathwater, a water which in spite of its pleasures occasionally causes in his mother transient scotoma, ataxia, difficulty swallowing, deafness, and other temporary dysfunctions consistent with her ailment, whosoever looks nonetheless at his pacific mom's face in that water and knows — in a New Age kind of way — the face he had before he was born, whosoever weeps over his mother's condition while bathing her, silently weeps, without words or expressions of pity or any nose-blowing or honking while crying, just weeps for a second like a ninny, whosoever has thereafter recovered quickly and forcefully from despair, whosoever has formulated a simple gratitude for the fact that *he still has a mother,* but who has nonetheless wondered at the kind of astral justice that has immobilized her thus, whosoever has then wished that the bath was over already so that he could go and drink too much at a local bar, a bar where he will encounter the citizens of this his hometown, a bar where he will see his cronies from high school, those who never left, those who have stayed to become civic boosters, those who have sent kids to the same day school they themselves attended thirty years before, whosoever has looked at his watch and yawned, while wondering how long he has to let his mother soak, whosoever soaps his mother a second time, to be sure that every cranny is disinfected, that every particle of dirt, every speck of grime, is eliminated, whosoever steps into a draining tub to hoist his mother from it, as if he were hoisting a drenched parachute from a stream bed, whosoever has balanced her on the closed toilet seat so that he might dry her with a towel of decadent thickness (purple), whosoever has sniffed, lightly, undetectably, the surface of her skin as he dries her, whosoever has refused to put his mother's spectacles on her face just now, as he has in the past when conscripted into bathing her, as he ought to do now, though in all likelihood she can only make out a few blurry shapes, anyway (at least until the cooling of her insulted central nervous system), whosoever wishes to prolong this additional disability, however, because when she is totally blind in addition to being damn near quadriplegic she faces up to the fact that her orienting skills are minimal, whosoever slips his mother's panties up her legs and checks the dainty hairless passage into her vulva one more time, because he can't resist the opportunity here for *knowledge*, whosoever gags briefly at his own forwardness, whosoever straps his mother's bra onto her, though the value of a bra for her is negligible, whosoever slips a housedress over her head, getting first one arm and then the other tangled in the neck hole, whosoever reaches for and then pulls the plug on the radio because the song playing on it is too sad, some terribly sad jazz ballad with muted trumpet, whosoever puts slippers on his mother's feet, left and then right, fiddling with her toes briefly first, simply to see if there is any sensation there, because her wasting disease is characterized by periods in which *some* feeling or sensation suddenly returns to affected extremities (though never all sensation), and likewise periods in which sensation is precipitously *snuffed out*, whosoever notes the complete lack of response in his mother when he pinches her big toe, and whosoever notes this response calmly, whosoever now finally sets his mother's glasses on her nose and adjusts the stems to make sure they are settled comfortably on her ears, whosoever kisses his mother a second time where her disordered hair is thinnest and takes her now fully into his arms to carry her to the wheelchair in the doorway, whosoever says to his wasting mom while stuttering mildly out of generalized anxiety and because of insufficient pause for the inflow and outflow of breath, *Hey, Mom, you look p-p-p-p-p-pretty fabulous t-t-tonight, you look like a million b-b-bucks,* whosoever says this while unlocking the brake on the chair, whosoever then brings the chair to a stop in the corridor off the kitchen, beneath a cheap, imitation American Impressionist landscape that hangs in that hallway, just so that he can hug his mom one more time because he hasn't seen her in months, because he is a neglectful son, because her condition is worse, always worse, whosoever fantasizes nonetheless about lashing her chair to a television table on casters so that he can just roll her and the idiot box with its barbiturate programming around the house without having to talk to her because he's been watching this decline for two decades or more and *he's fed up with comforting and self-sacrifice, the very ideas make him sick,* whosoever settles her in the kitchen by the Formica table and opens the refrigerator looking for some mush that will do the job for this evening, some mush that he can push down her throat and on which she will not spend the whole night choking as she sometimes does, so that he will have to use that little medical vacuum cleaner thing, that dental tool, to remove saliva and food particles from her gullet, tiny degraded hunks of minestrone and baby food, whosoever trips briefly over his mother's chair trying to get around it on the way to the chocolate milk in the fridge and jams his toe, *shit, shit, shit, sorry, Ma,* whosoever then changes his mind and fetches out a six-pack of the finest imported beer that he brought himself from a convenience store in town, and pops open one can for himself and one for his mother, whosoever then dips into his mother's beer a weaving and trembling plastic straw, whosoever then carries this beverage to his mother and fits the end of the straw between his mother's lips, exhorting her to *drink, drink,* whosoever then tilts back his own head emptying a fine imported beer in a pair of swallows so that he might move on to the next, whosoever then hugs his mom (again) feeling, in the flush of processed barley and hops, that his life is withal the best of lives, full of threat and bounty, bad news and good, affluence and penury, the sacred and the profane, the masculine and the feminine, the present and the repetitions of the past, whosoever in this instant of sorrow and reverence, *knows the answers* to why roses bloom, why wineglasses sing, why human lips, when kissed, are so soft, and why parents suffer, *he shall never die.*

Hex Raitliffe. And if he's a hero, then heroes are five-and-dime, and the world is as crowded with them as it is with stray pets, worn tires, and missing keys.

2

His mother's voice, Billie Rait-
liffe's voice, as she hears it now, as she hears herself through the
dense matter of her physique, *Hey there, cut it out,* as the beer
pours from her mouth and down a dish-towel bib and through the
bib to the front of her housedress, soaking through its drab beige
design, *Hey!,* her voice is faint and inscrutable, she knows, in the
autumn of these neuro-pathogens, full of mumblings and susur-
rings, imprecisions, nonsense, phonemic accidents, nonsyntactic
vocalizations, unfinished thoughts and sentences; her voice is delivered at an improbably slow velocity, and with evident exertion.
She knows. She sends no message but pathos. Her son doesn't
understand, for example, that the can of imported beer, mostly
emptied upon her now, and trickling along the linoleum floor toward one baseboard, is of no interest to her; her son doesn't understand that she doesn't care for beer any longer, as she never much
did, feeling that beer is the beverage of the disadvantaged, not at
all the choice *in her day,* when the basement was full of the pine
crates in which collectibles arrived with their dusty exteriors, *the
wine of the Great Depression being in her opinion the finest, the
wine of the Bordeaux region of France reaching a state of unparal-
leled accomplishment during the thirties.* The straw falls from her
pursed lips, topples out of the can, and cartwheels across her lap,
before splashing to rest in the beer pooling by the side of her chair.
Her son doesn't understand. He glares at her and carries the empty

to a to-be-recycled carton of reinforced cardboard by the back door, and begins again to rummage in the refrigerator. The reason she has summoned him here, having sent home the nurse, Aviva, for the weekend, is among the sentences so far not fully expressed. She is aware of this — as her son, nervously trying to trim a fingernail with his teeth (*Don't hang on the door of the refrigerator, please,* she wants to say), slams the door of same and then lurches out of the kitchen, returning with a bottle of bourbon from the bar in the pantry. Her son tries to anticipate her needs, to preempt her need for words, to eliminate a language based on need, and thus *to eliminate language* (and with it this drama of anguished communication). He reformulates all the conversation into simple yays or nays. *You d-d-don't want the beer? Are you comfortable? Are you warm enough? D-do you want another light on? Kind of d-dark in here, M-m-mom, isn't it? Do you need to be changed? The nurse t-take you out today?* However, even this simple, binary information system is faulty and replete with misunderstandings. Because her replies, mere probabilities of meaning when you get right down to it, are mostly formulated through *micro-gesticulations,* a semantics of the faintly conveyed message — the half-closed eyelid, the pressing together of chapped or drooling lips, the head cocked slightly to one side, or the epiglottal choking sound — those communications still permitted by the encrusted linkages of her nerves. This is the foundation of her language now, she is well aware, and therefore it's *the language of mothers and sons,* the language of love between the Raitliffe generations, anyway; all recollections, beseechments, expressions of tenderness, along with her more mundane requests and importunities, must begin with this semantics of gesticulation. Which is to say that speech, for her, is soon going to be a thing of the past. The speech act will follow, into the gloaming, her handwriting, her perfumed thank-you notes, love letters, her journal entries, her business letters, even her signature, that florid and legally binding evidence of self. Her speech will vanish as these things have vanished. But as Hex spoons a few ounces of applesauce into a teacup for her, *My God, applesauce is tedious beyond belief,* the constraint of silence is more than she can bear, suddenly, she just can't relax, and from inside of her she tries each muscle, each of her smallest appendages, the knuckle of a toe that had once been painted lavender, a fingertip that once tickled the ivories. In the lockbox where she is located, she focuses all remaining intention on her *arm*, thinking, feeling, *Dear, there's something I need to tell you. Could you please settle down for just a minute so that I can explain something to you? Could you please stay clear-headed long enough to have a conversation? There is something troubling I need to ask of you.* She feels this arm moving, she's sure of it, but when she looks (through trifocal glasses), she can see that it is stationary, this arm is stationary in her lap, white downy fuzz upon alabaster flesh, this flesh wrapped haphazardly, loosely upon the ulna. No muscle to speak of. She tries to reach for him, for her son, but the arm, like the other, sits in her lap, left hand holding the spastic right. The left side of her where all the remaining movement has been warehoused can still travel a couple of centimeters to and fro, maybe an inch, but it seems today, when she really needs it, to drowse and idle. When Billie catches her next head cold or cold sore or is bitten by her next mosquito this mobility will — if the past is any guide — abandon her as it has elsewhere. That's how the disease works. (Here Hex Raitliffe sneezes ominously and then looks distractedly around him for a tissue, a strand of mucus yo-yoing from his nose. He staggers to a dish towel, head tilted back, scours his upper lip, and then returns to the applesauce.) This exertion, though, and the transient paralysis caused by the bath, leave her exhausted, too tired, and she doesn't know if she will be able to get tongue and teeth and breath around the simple magic of a few consonants and vowels. The alphabet is all hairpin turns and pyrotechnical displays. She thinks: If there is in her no evidence of any *perceptible* language, who is to blame for that? If perception is required for language, well then, it's a pretty faulty design. Inside her, language dances on. As does memory. What a rich store of memories she has, outside of what might be heard or seen — as Hex fixes himself a drink — what a dance of feelings at the sound of the ice hitting the bottom of the tumbler again. Her son is like his father, as so many sons are, she thinks, and this association leads her astray, this association collides with the present and then darts off parallel, and she follows the past, as she is free to do, until suddenly she comes up short two years ago. *To when they gave her a gift.* Her son and her second husband, it was Christmastime, and they had given her the gift, bought her *a notebook-style computer, Dell Corporation with PCMCIA Type II slot and Yamaha YM262 twenty-voice synthesizer and Mediavision pro audio studio,* as Louis, her husband, had described it, *to be bundled with Microsoft's popular HandiSpeak software,* mostly portable, mostly wireless, a new prototype, a wireless technology, so that the notebook could sit on top of the tray table on her chair and broadcast the message back to the desktop system (situated on her antique rolltop). What did the facsimile voice sound like? The voice of HandiSpeak? The three of them, she remembers, in the tableau around the Christmas tree in the drafty, poorly lit living room, ceilings too high, tree overdecorated, overtinseled (by Hex), the three of them pulling the ribbons from *the gift,* well, Louis and Hex pulling the ribbons from it, herself simply watching, heavy cables and obscure plugs and cords snaking out from under hastily and poorly folded wrapping paper, little seraphic elves dancing on a purple field, pine needles and stray tinsel strands dusting the surface of the black and gray plastic casing as they dusted all the surfaces in the living room. Hex and Louis looked at her for approval, and because back then, two years ago, she still had a little bit of a nod left, *she nodded noncommittally,* and her husband goaded on her son as if he were still a boy and not in his middle thirties, *Go ahead, boot it up,* and Hex did as he was told, turned on the monitor, shreds of plastic tape still affixed to it like sutures, all the gleaming red operating lamps illumined, there was the Windows *desktop,* appearing on the monitor like a reassuring first gasp from an infant, and then the HandiSpeak pointer, with its stylized index finger and rolled-up sleeve. Before them, on the screen (Louis rolled her closer so that she could see) in an ornate computer font — Garamond Antiqua — were the twenty-six letters of the English alphabet, as perfect and simple as atoms must have seemed when Democritus (she thought) imagined them, those simple little squiggles of which arguments were formed, those squiggles that divided houses and united them, that were arranged into the words intoned over baptisms and deaths. Those letters taken from her by her illness. Hex used the mouse apparatus, the ergonomically designed joystick requiring *an absolute minimum of mobility* on the part of its hapless user, and clicked on the alpha of the HandiSpeak alphabet:

> a aback abandon abase abate abbreviate abdicate abdomen abduct aberrant abet abhor ability abject ablaze able abnegate abnormal aboard abode abolish A-bomb abominate abort about above abrasion abscess abscond absent absolute abstain abstract absurd abuse abusive abysmal accelerate accent accept acceptance access accessible accident accommodate accost accretion accrue accumulate accurate accursed accuse ace ache achieve acid acknowledge acme acorn acoustic acquisition acquit acre acrimony acronym across act action activate active actor actual actuary acute adagio Adam adamant adapt add addict address adequate adhere adjective adjoin adjourn adjunct adjust ad-lib administer admiral admire admit admonish adolescent adore adorn adornment adrenaline adulate adult adulterate adultery advance adventure adverse advertise

This forest of *a*-words beautiful and strange as he scrolled through them. Words *were* civilization! And as she gazed on them, on her lost society (though it was obvious that the HandiSpeak's vocabulary had been culled from one of those inferior college dictionaries), she was, of course, *speechless.* Her son eased the joystick through the list, looking for *le mot juste,* the perfect arrangement of euphony and content, and he settled finally on one, designating with the pointer the word **adore.** Then he selected the edit menu and designated *Go.*

— Adore.

Adore, the Yamaha YM262 twenty-voice synthesizer's *disembodied woman's voice* called out from the pile of space junk and wrapping paper on the Oriental carpet in the living room, the disembodied woman's self-assured and yet clinical voice sang out, as though there were a fourth person in the room, an unexpected, overstaying holiday guest. The voice, as Billie recollected it, was like nothing so much as the voice of *science,* the voice of technological advancement, the voice of lasers and digits and particle colliders, of ultra-high-frequency transmissions. A woman's voice as men would design it. There was a perfume in the room of dying pine. A rich smell. And there was candlelight. An intimate little fire in the fireplace. And then there was this voice. Louis and Hex circled around her trying to gauge her response. They were expectant. Hex knelt by the computer and clicked on *return* twice more: *adore, adore.* The enormity of the machinery was apparent to Billie Raitliffe at last, what science could manage, which, in her case, amounted to using fifty pounds of microchips and motherboards and plastic chassis to enable her to croak out a few meager remarks in a prefabricated woman's voice, not her own voice at all, which had been rich and full, with vigorous laughter, ample melody — *her voice was gone.*

She had been a talker. She had been able to put the awkward at ease; she had been able to comfort children; she had been able to sweet-talk truculent shopkeepers. But her voice was gone, was consigned now to the netherworld of widowed socks and earrings. She began to cry, in the living room, and her tears were of the specifically disabled sort. They came without pounding of fists or oaths, they simply fell, like summer drizzle, no sound accompanying them, just their erratic progress along her cheeks, *W-w-we tried to make sure it was a w-woman's voice,* Hex said, tripping over a coil of patch cords as he made his way to her side, and then Louis said, *Billie, honey, you have to make an effort, you can't just let this happen the way you're doing; we love you, but you have to make an effort. This will help you hang on to your independence, don't you see? Don't you want that? Don't you want to be able to get around in daily life? I know you do. We know you do. We were thinking about you, honey; we want the best for you, and we got the best, top of the line, the most advanced model. Just give it a try.* And Hex said, *If it was up to me, Ma, I would have gotten you an Urdu voice, or a T-T-T-tibeto-Burman voice or something, but you can add extra voices, Ma, just the way you can add extra t-typefaces for your computer. We g-got an upgrade kit, right there with the software.* But it wasn't the woman's voice — that husky, dental assistant's voice — that put another nail in Billie's pine box. That was just the *perceptible* part of it. The relentless predictability of disabling traumas was beyond words, stretched out around her, fore and aft, hemmed her in. So why speak at all? *I will not,* she said, *I will not use it. I will not.* And those words *were* properly transmitted. Louis Sloane, her husband, and her son, Hex, they heard her, though they didn't want to. It put a damper on the rest of Christmas Day. When Aviva tried to feed her, at the dining room table — a morsel of goose speared on the end of a tine — she kept her mouth clamped shut tight. Like an unruly brat. And since then *the gift* had sat unused, its backlit, active-matrix screen blinking, waiting for the moment when the affections and recollections of Billie Raitliffe's life would be gobbled by it and converted into the ones and zeroes of a 16-bit sound card. Well, as time passed, she did use it occasionally, grudgingly. There was the telephone message. She always wondered why people didn't hang up on it: *Hello, this is Billie Raitliffe of Flagler Drive in Fenwick. I am temporarily unable to speak with you. My assistant is available, however, if you would care to call again in the early afternoon. Have a wonderful day.* But mostly it was unused, her doppelgänger, though the household current continued to circulate through it (the current originating at the generator up the coast, at the utility where her husband, Louis Sloane, was plant manager). Mostly, her double was silent, that is, until yesterday. Thursday. Which was when Aviva wheeled her up to her desk, and helped her work out the text of her telephone call. She was summoning her boy. Her middle-aged son. Her only child. The son now raising the stainless steel tablespoon of applesauce toward her mouth, tugging down her chin with one hand, his face close to hers now, the broken blood vessels like a contour map around his nose and under his eyes, his head shorn of all but a faint shadow of his rich chestnut hair, his chin, disgracefully unshaven, with its mix of strawberry blond and gray hairs, his awkward eyeglasses, from the nineteen-fifties (she guessed), his bloodshot eyes, oh, what has happened to him! How had he begun so suddenly to grow older? When he speaks at last, when he emerges from distraction to notice her and to see in certain *gesticulations* the fact that an urgency is upon her now, *What is it, Ma? What's wrong? Is there something you want t-t-to say?,* when he presses his probably unwashed ear, clotted with wax, presses it close to her lips, close enough to graze her lips, *then* she begins to feel the reservoir of panic in her, the panic that is like a second inhabitant in this loose-garment body, the panic that is never distant, the panic she mostly manages to put aside, but which is now swelling in her like a miraculous pregnancy, *Oh, Dexter,* she says to her son, whispering the words as best she can, a minute elapsing before she can complete the thought, in the stillness of the kitchen, at the beginning of night, with autumn announcing winter, *your mother is in a marvelously big parcel of trouble. Oh, Hex, I am alone.*

3

An ordered linearity of events, a sequence in which his mother then tells Hex that *Louis has left,* her husband has left, has abandoned the premises, has fled, has absconded, has done as so many husbands have done before — husbands from antiquity, husbands right up to the present — has kept his own counsel, or discussed his plans only in secret with like-minded absconders and adulterers, and then packed in secret, or not so much in secret, since he might easily have packed in the open, in his separate bedroom, with his disabled wife laid out flat in the master suite, or on her hospital cot downstairs, he might have drawn the blinds and packed, pausing in the midst of organizing a stack of extra-large boxers only to go look in upon his wife and *turn her,* thereby ensuring against bedsores, he might have kissed her upon closed eyelids, returning to the open suitcase (royal purple) to cram his sock garters deep into a pair of loafers, repacking again the folded and starchy dress shirts (fresh from the dry cleaners), piling upon them a number of pastel-colored cardigans, sweater season having just now begun, sitting on the suitcase in order to close it properly, remembering not to forget the folding aluminum suitcase cart — an orderly sequence of events in which betrayal is followed by recognition, in which Hex Raitliffe's mother tells him that *her husband has left,* and Hex, concussed by the information, falls lifelessly into a chair at the kitchen table and massages his gray eye sockets with stubby fingers, in which past is ineluctably followed by present, *this sequence necessarily unravels at this spot.* In the gravitational field of crises, you just don't get one thing after another, one event causing the next. So when Hex seizes his mother's shoulders in the kitchen, illuminated only by the streetlamps outside on Flagler Drive, *Jesus, why d-d-don't we shed some light on the subject, huh, Mom? Now, t-t-tell me again what you just said, okay?,* when he switches on the ancient fluorescent bulb over the range, he realizes that, in a way, he *already knows,* has already suspected, was already pacing and worrying, though not really gifted with insight into the chaos of domestic relations. *Go and look . . . go ahead,* his mother whispers, and he does. Or does he fix another drink first? Before walking through the vaulted chambers of their stone manse, empty and dilapidated, walking through it for the first time in months, before coming to that godforsaken computer, that information storage and retrieval appliance, does he, before this, take his mother by the shoulders and say, *What is it you're t-t-trying to t-tell me?* Is this how he will remember the sequence later? He makes a quick survey of his mother's condition. Her chair is braked, the house is quiet, the golf cart traffic eases occasionally past their address, and there is a distant and reassuring sound of surf. His rental car, which seems to him to be *leaking fuel* in some way, is parked in the drive. And again, for a second, he gets caught upon the stupendous hurt of the crime. Think of it in sequence. His stepfather returning Wednesday night from work as usual; his stepfather dining, say, upon pork chops and applesauce and asparagus — preparing them for himself; his stepfather loading the dishwasher (overfilling the detergent cup), managing even to grind beans and to prepare the Swiss automatic coffeemaker, to set the timer so that on Thursday morning, when Aviva will arrive, Billie's *half-decaf/half-regular* will be awaiting her. Then, after lugging his large suitcase down the attic stairs to his bedroom — large suitcase as opposed to the overnight or garment bags — Sloane begins *to pack.* Is this how it goes? A number of such possibilities intersect — some invented, some true, some *both invented and true* — and these intersections appear and vanish in Hex as he sets out through the pantry toward the living room. Which is to say that a long story begins here, with Hex — who usually avoids his mother, her husband, and *the mausoleum* they inhabit — installed at home, going through the house turning on lights. This is his project, anyway, and the first thing that happens, in the pantry, among glass cases filled with crystal, with holiday finery (mostly dusty and unused), beside the silver chest, is that he stumbles over an old velvet stool. *P-pal, you are into some d-d-d-deep shit, you are into some serious long-t-term nursing here.* Limping, as he goes. Taking his time. The past gathering around him.

He was seven when they moved here from the city, away from the predations of what used to be called simply *Town* — the ghettos, the crime, the immigrants, the other classes — when they moved here according to that *theory of paradise,* that theory of the fifties, when they moved here to Fenwick, Conn., to Flagler Drive, to rhododendrons and roses and geraniums and magnolias and dogwoods of spring all lit up in his new yard. Opulence! He was seven, the school year had just ended. A pair of moving trucks with a half-dozen axles each were parked in the turnaround, and friendly, agreeable movers were unloading his mother's Shaker armoire, setting it at the end of a trail of antiques that led across the gravel driveway to the front door. 1959. The car door swung shut. His nanny and his mother each took one of his hands, and he stood at full attention in front of the great, forbidding portal to this idyll. Brass gargoyle door knocker. His mother lifted up his blundering hands to touch the face of it. He pounded. And clamored to turn the doorknob too. *So, as you passed through the main entrance and into the foyer,* as his mother might have said, you came first upon the Pilgrim-era New England portraits she had collected back then, portraits from antique stores and flea markets. Most of them gone now, or mislaid, because Lou Sloane seemed to feel confused, as Hex did himself, by the fact that these people were not actual relatives. *Well,* his mother had explained, *my parents would never have commissioned portraits themselves. And a portrait has such a warm, personal aspect, don't you think?* Yes, the portraits were the point of origin on that tour, and his mother as she led, as she held his hand, was beautiful and blond and her lips were painted brightly, this was *before the cane,* the long period of the cane. She was strong enough then — she was able-bodied — to kneel and pick weeds in the landscaped island in the turnaround out in front of the house. She was strong enough to take him in her arms and actually carry him part of the way through the premises (in the same direction he travels now). Past portraits of *Esther Miller, Gentlewoman and Friend to Those in Need, 1840,* pictured there in the first year of the Mormon Exodus, and *Beloved Moses Trask,* past the pewter candlesticks *forged in the shop of Paul Revere,* which stood on a butter-churning table once housed at the Button Gwinnet Museum. His mother was strong. And she led now to the left, across the long, narrow rug that decorated the foyer, a dark Persian design from the mid-nineteenth century, which picked up the colors in the stucco plastering. His mother and her designer, Mavis Elsworth (Mavis trailed behind them), spoke in this language of ornament. This rug *brought out the iron balustrade* that led up to the open landing on the second floor, where a second weaving from the same period hung upon the wall. *They were working toward a union of opposites,* the design team, in the matter of color harmonies. His mother stopped momentarily to address him. *Hex, darling,* she'd said, *this is your new home.* Of course, they were trying to coax him out — he wasn't stupid — and they had been trying for weeks. They were trying to soften the blow of relocation. It was all double-talk. His rightful home, as he well knew, was the Upper East Side of Manhattan, New York City, and the hills, shrubs, open fields, and statuary of Frederick Law Olmsted's Central Park. Where, even if the kids were always trying to steal his muffler and taunt him with it, he was a little feudal lord in a dream of old New York. Those toughs had been his friends. What was he doing here? In the sticks? This skeptical city kid. In the library. (You go through the foyer to the left. The library with its dark oak paneling.) *All this wood,* his mother told no one in particular, *all this paneling came from trees lost in the hurricane of 1938, a real humdinger of a storm. Fenwick, you see, was mostly under water — all this, the country club, the beaches, the marshes, everything. There was tidal erosion, you know, and then the river overflowed, too.* The mighty Connecticut River, that is, whose estuaries and marshes formed the spot where this coastal village had been settled and incorporated. His mother stood in the library and raised wide her arms as if to describe the resplendency of natural disaster. The volumes in the library then (Hex recalls now, pausing here to switch on lamps with shades of the deepest red leather — their light muted, somber) antedated this storm, dated back to the proud early period of American letters: Whittier, Longfellow, Cooper, a dusty, unopened edition of Emerson. These decorative books iterated an enduring literary philosophy, but exactly whose philosophy it was was unclear. Mostly when Hex was in the library he thought of storms, not ideas.

Then there had been the enormous painting that hung on one wall above the bookshelves, a spotlight trained upon it. Where the ceiling was vaulted. Now his mother drew his attention here. Oil on canvas. Four feet by eight feet. From the Scottish school of the late nineteenth century. *Brush strokes restrained, and yet celebratory.* The painting featured — against a backdrop of plow horses, rolling hills, and abundant sunshine — the kind of rosy, fat, congenial children his parents had believed that Hex himself would be. These trompe l'oeil children, these cherubim, had geraniums in their pudgy fists. They were forever trapped in the best part of a colorful spring day, gamboling, rassling, embracing. *They* never stammered, and were therefore never subjected to imitation stammerers. They never had to strain for words. They were the inhabitants of the *ideal of rural paradise.* No surprise, then, that Hex showed much more interest in his father's felt-lined gun case, just below the painting. Yes, his father loved guns, and now had plenty of room to collect them. Here in Connecticut he had filled out his collection, and had even left his Winchester side-by-side twelve-gauge outside the case. It leaned against the wall in the porch, where it would always sit while he was alive, so that he could, if needed, fire salvos at intruders or local pets. (But the library is empty of books now, Hex the dawdler notes, and the porch likewise, the winterized porch, is devoid of the hothouse blossoms and tropical climbers it had once nurtured. All readers have moved on from this place. His mother's double vision makes reading difficult. And Louis Sloane? He's a skimmer of techno-thrillers.) From the library, in those bygone days, his mother, his nanny, and Mavis

Elsworth walked through the porch and out the screened entrance to *the swimming pool.* They took in the patio, the pool, and the vista: not a hundred yards away, the shoals of Long Island Sound. The physics of those gentle waves against this peninsula, the very respiration of nature. How those waves comforted. In the distance, the country-club golfers and their caddies ambled along the front nine behind the house. It was so treeless, so flat in Fenwick that you could see golfers even on the fairway most distant raising their drivers — as if to mock the ire of spring electrical storms. And best of all, better than all the luxury thus far described, better even than the swimming pool, was the landscape design feature to which the youthful Hex Raitliffe now hurried. The goldfish pond! With its mutant carp! Carp the size of whales! And on that first day, that original day, this was where he found his dad lounging. Sitting on a rock beside the pond. His *actual* dad. The old man, with his quizzical smile. His *real* dad. Allen Thomas Raitliffe. With a shaker full of those flakes, sating the whales, scattering a layer of orange dandruff across the goldfish pond, an enigmatic smile upon his face. *See this, whippersnapper? This will be your position of great responsibility. You are going to be the feeder of fish.* The immobilized carp drifted to the surface, their sucker mouths engulfing the nutrient-enriched parchment that sustained them. His father loved all of it. His father was in a great mood, loved everything, skittered excitably from one demonstration of privilege to the next. Allen Raitliffe pushed the creaking patio furniture up around the pool. Pointed to spots for the women. His mother, Hex remembers still, wore a knee-length skirt (lavender) so that her calves were exposed — shapely, with a little knot in back from her heels. Hex, gazing upon his mom, upon her physique, would have liked *to eat those calves,* seize them and devour. But he was distracted from his fantasy by Allen. His dad had plans. As the ladies were seated and comfortable, Allen Raitliffe stripped off his own lime green permanent-press shirt, stepped out of his loafers, and then decisively eased himself into the shallows of the swimming pool, where he thumped his chest and whooped for his wife's benefit. Then: he reached out his arms for his boy. *Okay, let's go, Dexter.* Oh no. Hex was not a swimmer, though, because of summers in the city, had never swum in the public swimming pools, *absolutely not*, his experience with immersion amounting to no more than the occasional dunk at the shore on Long Island. He was frozen, paralytic. *Please, no thanks, nope.* And it was clear his mother wasn't going to intervene. Yet his dad, with swimming trunks billowing around him, stood on the lowest step *beckoning*. His dad's hands were furry on the backs; they were grand, substantial hands, and Hex trusted them. Kind of. Trust was a new thing he was trying out. He wasn't entirely sure about it. Nonetheless, he attempted to heed its call. With the abandon that comes with trust, and without taking off his patent leather shoes (*Oh, Allen, not with his shoes on!* his mother rising up off the lounger), Hex hurled himself off the ledge of the pool and into his father's arms. He arced out above the blue ripples, legs bicycling through the air underneath him, arms flapping, and plunged gracelessly in. His father caught him, or most of him, and, chuckling, set him, drenched, upon the topmost step of the pool. Half above, half below. In the backdraft of his own waves. Now it was time for another practical lesson. Patiently, Allen Raitliffe demonstrated the way in which his son might hold his nose, pinch shut his nostrils to avoid compromising the sinuses in any way, and immerse his impressive little head (male Raitliffes with their proportionally large heads) in the watery deep. Hex, according to the imitation that is a crucial part of the sinister progress of families, clamped shut his own freckled nostrils and toppled over sideways, off the steps, into the shallow end. They all had a good laugh! *I now pronounce you a citizen of the countryside,* Allen Raitliffe said, fishing Hex out, kissing him on the crown of his head, and then standing him beside the pool on the flagstone. *Welcome, young Dexter, to the kingdom of the good life.* And Allen Raitliffe, who had a post-baptismal towel folded by his shirt and shoes, reached for it — for his son, but Hex, trailing chemically treated water and grit from the patio, his dress shoes squeaking as if he were a flatfoot, a G-man, would not have himself dried. He was too excited. Instead, *he made a run for it.* To his new house. As he flanked the side, away from the patio, alongside the poplars, *he came next to the dining room and then to the back door that led into the pantry,* and in this way Hex, the middle-aged Hex, also manages to put off visiting the inner sanctum, the centermost room in the house, the living room. He emerges into the pantry again (his mom is still there in the kitchen — she hasn't gone anywhere), glances in at the dining room table — seats twelve — at the polished bronze chandelier, the Victorian gilded mirror, and then *goes around again,* the way he came, back to the foyer, and up the main stairs. Following, you see, his original tour of the house step for step — the young Hex dashing up the main stairs, his mother's formerly bemused expression becoming rather stern as she followed, from the pool to the pantry through the foyer to the second floor. He was tracking water all through the house! *Hex! Come here this minute! Right now!* Tears stung his eyes. He couldn't control his feelings. He didn't care if it was beautiful. *He didn't want to live here.* And on the second floor, his lungs heaving with the effort, he came up short in front of the master suite. The door was open. The movers were setting down the armoire. Canopied master bed (long since sold off) in silk and velvet, all enclosed in draperies. A phalanx of adults trailed him, now, including Mavis the designer, who had been tacking up wallpaper swatches in the hall when he passed. He kept moving. Dashing under the arms of a mover. Past the guest room, where the corpulent Lou Sloane would, years later, sit upon his Samsonite luggage, past the attic stairs, where, at the terminus of the corridor, he came at last to his own room. Here he was at the end of the day, at the end of the chase. He whimpered. He put his shoulder into the door, sticky in its frame, and it gave. His parents right behind him. Reaching for him as he passed through that threshold. Then — Oh! Oh! That impossibly large bedroom! That empire of play! The colors inside were astounding. It was a carnival. Where a symphony of brights and mutes tastefully adorned the rest of the Raitliffe House, Flagler Drive, Hex's room was a *carnival,* a place where all rules of interior design were suspended, where all was childlike excess. *The thundering oom-pah-pah of the primaries.* And the toys. They were *really* trying to butter him up. The hand-carved and hand-painted clowns, seafarers, military men, mummers from animated films on the walls, all the colors in that room, they mimicked the showoffy autumn in the Northeast. He would never feel alone there! Among the pillows and comforters and stuffed animals! Mobiles over the bed! There was even a light *under the bed,* to drive out spooks and hasten the passage to Nod. These were the best simulations of companionship that money could buy. By the end of all this, this three-and-a-half-hour drive out from the city, this trauma of relocation, this chase and chastisement and renewal of affections, boy, he was ready for a nap. So his mother shooed them off — shooed away her husband and the entourage — tucked Hex in, and left the door behind her imperceptibly ajar. *And his consciousness narrowed to a point.*

But today, this day of infamy, as the modern Hex completes this circular tour of his childhood, as he completes his prolonged series of delays by sitting on his old narrow bed, with his refusal to face what is in front of him, sleep, unfortunately, is *no option.* There's nowhere else to go in the house but the living room. He's going to have to read the note. From Sloane. And so twenty minutes after setting out he at last heads down the front stairs, makes the left into the library and the right into the doorway of the living room. Which at one time featured the mahogany couch-with-end-tables, the carved Brunswick Craftsman–style pool table, the inlaid music cabinet with Victrola, the rosewood love seat and parlor set, the imitation British pub–style bar with Waterford crystal low- and highball set, the early Magnavision monochrome television receiver, the floor-model French birdcage with stuffed parrot, and more; here there had been a whole history of his family as rendered by Mavis Elsworth: *My clients, the Raitliffes, had their roots in the Midwest, and though they had a frontier spirit, a rugged, foot-on-the-footrest type of spirit, they were concerned with re-creating the New England stylings of their adopted region. We combined, then, authentic Pilgrim-era antiques with fine reproductions. I'm personally not interested in an original if it's not functional, and the Raitliffes shared this pragmatic style. We looked for furniture that could be used to entertain and that would withstand the punishment of children. The Raitliffes were eager participants in the acquisition of these New England antiques and I often encountered the both of them at auctions. I even bid against them on occasion and found them to be informed, decisive collectors. The living room of the*

*Raitliffe house, with its high ceilings, paneling, and muted earth
tones, presented some difficulties for a decorator looking for tasteful
decorative fabrics. It was a big house and the budget was not limitless; nevertheless, Mrs. Raitliffe expressed a very adventurous desire, a modern desire, to work with radiant colors. Especially colors
in the purple family.* Purple, most of all, in the living room, in fact.
But now this hue is vestigial, leftover, a mere trace of the era that
prevailed here — in the time before faded convertible couches and
medical equipment. Now the living room has taken on the aspect
of a clinic. There is the extra wheelchair, for example, with its tibial
restraining straps (during the early months of paraplegia her legs
seized and trembled uncontrollably); there is an oxygen tank with
plastic mask; and there is cardiological apparatus — a home EKG
monitor (since the steroid treatments she has struggled with arterial blockages). The eidolons of Hex's childhood are scarcely visible
in the therapeutic glare of the present. From standing lamp to
standing lamp, Hex compulsively switches on lights. The pool table
is gone, the bar mostly empty (Lou Sloane was no drinker). The
stucco walls are a decade past their last appointment with the
house painters. But most of all it's the adventure of the old place,
the *adventure of country life,* that is gone now. Hex's discomfort is
expanding, as he thinks about it. His discomfort lists across decades, from his first scamper through the splendid corridors of his
childhood home to this disconsolate trudge down the staircase to
the living room — he can tell it's going to be *one of those weekends
when everything g-g-goes all to hell, he doesn't want any p-p-part of
it,* and he can see that the computer is on, its color screen blinking,
the unraveled sleeve of the HandiSpeak pointer signaling at the
bottom of a message, *What's the file name, anyway, DearJohn?* He
stops at the bar, refills, *freshens,* and then seats himself at the
computer, feeling a bad catch in his breathing, *Holy shit, what
k-kind of a g-g-guy* — a computer message, not even a handwritten
message, not even a face-to-face notification, no, *on the computer,*
and not on Sloane's own computer either, but on his mother's
computer, the one they gave her for Christmas. Sloane *knew* she
wouldn't use it. The message here, in this spot, only because of the
symbolic freight of situating it here. Sloane knew, moreover, that

she couldn't read well anymore. He was banking on the fact that Billie would hit *Go*. So that the dental assistant woman, calling out in the language of follow-up appointments and reminders to floss, that voice of digits, which rendered the complexities and struggles of human psychology in either-ors, dialectics, that voice could now proclaim the verdict on fourteen or fifteen years of marriage:

Dear Billie,

If you think this means I'm angry, then you're right. If you think I have come to a time when I can no longer care for you, you're right. I hope you will come to your senses and live out your remaining time with a little bit of effort. I can't watch you retreat from life this way. Your poverty has tired me out.

L.

4

———————————————— I'm going to t-t-take his life.

Hex's voice precedes him through dining room and pantry. It's his stammer that nudges Billie from recollection. That's what the accursed message on the computer is about, anyhow, how there's only the one *here and now,* how she spends too much time away from it, away from this mathematics of the empirical and veridical. She's slipping out of the quantifiable, in her chair, in the kitchen. She'd grown accustomed to the idea that these difficulties with Lou, these spats and disagreements, were just the little troughs of all the betrothed; she relied on the fact that decorum would take the day; she even believed, after first gazing upon *the note,* that Lou would get a good night's sleep at the Tides Motel, think better of all this, and turn up back at the house with, say, a crockpot of clam chowder (New England style), prostrating himself. But now that her son has seen the letter its factual status has become, well, somewhat reliable. And she's afraid.

— I'm going to hunt him d-down, son of a bitch, I'm g-gonna find him and torture him. B-b-boy, I never liked the guy to begin with, Mom, I could see that right from the start. I never liked him. I always thought there was something f-f-f-f-fishy about him, even at the wedding, M-m-mom. There was something off about his b-b-b-behavior even at the ceremony. I mean g-guys with *p-p-p* —

And here her son's stammer gets the best of him for a moment, as he waves a printed-out copy of the offending document, and his face winds up as though there's a rear molar about to be extracted. As the seconds pass, Hex is frozen, the *p*'s clogging the exit. This, she thinks, must be what the passions look like these days: shaved head and secondhand tweed sack suit and French-cuffed dress shirt, all smartly tailored, and the syntax choked off. When the exertion becomes embarrassing for both of them — *who knows if he'll ever get it out* — Hex does what he used to do as a boy. He strikes himself. He reaches out with his left hand (he's a lefty), and reddens his own cheek, until his opinions are shaken free —

— *p-p-pocket calculator all monogrammed, for godsakes,* he's a guy with a goddam monogrammed p-pocket calculator . . .

At which she becomes irritated herself:

— Just a second . . . hold on there . . .

— And giving slide rule lessons to his —

— What business is that of yours? . . . Her words like a mush, a consommé of talk. — Can't you —

— W-w-w-*what?* Hex shoves one of the chairs from the breakfast table up next to her. — Ma? If we're g-g-going to . . . You'd better start by trying to p-p —

— I don't ask you . . . about . . .

She means to ask him about his girl, his paramour, Barclay or Gillian or Carrington — some Christian name that no girl outside the city limits would ever have — who is startlingly absent, and this perhaps accounts for his gruffness. But then she can't bring herself to ask, because the girls are often absent after a time, and he is always pining after them, the ones that will enable his soul sickness of love. She was a fine, well-turned-out young woman, and now she is gone.

Irritably, by way of supporting the hypothesis, Hex kicks the chair to one side and begins pacing the room, hastens to the breakfast table, stirs the half-eaten bowl of applesauce. He's stuck again. Blushing. The *p*'s. He slaps himself.

— *Pronounce your words,* Hex says at last. — You'd better start p-p-pronouncing your words. Don't you want the rest of this?

— I don't . . . care for applesauce. *Dunwannapulllshhhhh,* somewhat plausibly. The words are onomatopoetic. Perhaps their soundalike quality is enough to convey sense. — I didn't even feed

you applesauce . . . when you were young, I don't think . . . it has
the . . . necessary minerals, in fact, for a . . .

— I can't understand you, he says.

— I don't want to argue now, she says. Could we discuss this . . .
gently? Because your mom . . . is hurting. We'll have plenty of time
for tangling later —

— Okay, b-but I think you should try.

And what is it he doesn't understand, she thinks, that so pro-
vokes him that he has a sort of caged expression? Is it *what* she's
saying or simply that it's she who is saying it?

— Dexter, she says, I can't make this any clearer, I'm afraid
(*cnnnmkkssssclrrrfrd*), this is how I . . . well, you *know* . . . you'll
simply have to listen . . . and I need . . . I need to ask . . . you
something important —

— Wait, he says.

And before she can get any further with her initiative on subjects of family responsibility, mortality, etc., before she can address
these things, Hex sneaks around behind her, stamps on the foot
brake at the back of the chair, and begins to steer her forward
across the kitchen. The lights with their ergs throw a strange
flindering of shadows over her as she's wheeled through the pantry,
the foyer. Hex is changing venues. He says nothing, and maybe
there isn't much to be said. Except this: if she gets two or three
years out of herself, it will be tremendous good fortune. More
likely, in the next year or so — well, she doesn't even want to think
about it. On the bright side, there will still be recollections and
daydreams. The two of these indistinguishable. Daydreams of
what? Of company, of reaching out, of asking her son how *his
business is going, or is he dating* (since Gillian or Carrington or
Barclay left), daydreams of sticking around long enough that she
might recognize a grandchild, *child of a child,* an urchin playing
with blocks, nestling beside her on her sickbed, if Dexter would
only reproduce! And recollections of ardor, of the crouching and
pouncing and laughing with her respective husbands, of long dinners and hands held — these routine acts of imagination will be
hers *to invent and falsify and to cram into time in such a way that
they'll make spaghetti out of time,* these recollections will be what

she'll have left, and she will furl herself into them, these memories, for example, of Cadillacs snaking up to the church, disgorging adorable little boys and girls, sprinting, Hex, a couple of years after they arrived in Fenwick, with his clip-on tie. Or the girls with their corsages, skipping upon the flagstone walkways to Grace Episcopal Church, on the brick path where some cad, some young ruffian (it was perhaps the Nelson boy), seized Hex by the neck, as she watched, the other mothers and fathers also watched, Brian Nelson's pale hands making thumbprints just beneath Hex's Adam's apple, saying, *Raitliffe, why are you so fat, anyway?* and Hex trying to stammer out a reply but getting caught upon the words, breaths damming his rejoinder, *Raitliffe, you sausage!,* her own boy stunned and motionless, on the lawn, reaching out his hands to her, to Billie, where she was heading for the chapel, walking up to the chapel for goshsakes, in some understated tweed skirt, ankle length, and deciding, *no, the thing to do was to do nothing,* even if they should push him down and grass-stain his summer suit, she couldn't be there to intervene every time, she had to permit *principles like injustice and boorishness to make their marks on him a little bit,* that's what childhood was, had to permit a boy of nine to learn nine-year-old things and to reach out to her, crying, and to watch her go into the chapel, leaving him there. Oh, why did she do that? She'll never again feel half so guilty.

— Look, I don't want to make this d-d-d-difficult, Dexter says, wheeling her into the living room now, that nexus of American socializing, back to the damned computer. Well, of course. The things you avoid become your allies.

— If we have to talk this out, he says, — I m-mean I think that's what we're agreeing we ought to be doing, right? I mean, so I can know exactly what happened, what you want to do, all th-th-that stuff. What legal stuff we have to undertake. What p-p-p-powers of attorney. Who's going to be d-d-deposed. You're going to have to t-type into this goddam thing and I'll just read it off so we d-don't have to listen to that v-v-voice talk her trash. So just d-do this for me, okay Mom? So we c-c-can expedite the p-p-process?

. . . Recollections of Allen Raitliffe will be the sustenance of her decline. She'll give in to the precipitation of memories of her son and his father — Allen, who didn't fit under ceilings or into automobiles, around whom other men were so uncomfortable, his fierceness stretched about him like the plains and lakes of his old Midwest. Capable of such fits of rectitude that Hex's derriere was blue where Allen had paddled it, though there was also a fatherly passion for straightening things out, *Dexter, I am sorry, son, I know you don't have any reason to forgive me now, but I will hope that you can forgive me later.* Round, rotund even (just as Hex was as a boy), over six foot, with barrel chest, with garish turquoise belt buckle. He ate enormously, drank more, kept a bell by the table where he could ring for seconds. He made the fortune in the mining business after the war, uranium mining, sold out for a bundle, and after that he made no effort to curb his appetites, except maybe on Sunday, when he was ravenous for *the spirit*, for the polished, shellacked interiors of the church, for instruction in the finer ethical questions. So they woke their boy and took him to sit with the affluent kids of Old Saybrook and environs, the Chafees and the Wards and the Walker girls, the Snyders, the Sutherlands, the Morses. Allen and she took young Dexter Raitliffe to church, the nine-year-old fat boy with the stammer, and he was educated there in the Gospels, like it or not. And he didn't like it. Hex would sneak in at dawn on Sundays and turn off their alarm clock, or feign illness, and it seemed therefore that he attended church only on the weeks in which Mrs. Skillings, Sunday School instructor and harridan, would pass around candy corn or chocolate Santa Clauses or marshmallow Easter bunnies, those commercial lures that went with theological indoctrination: *Okay, now listen up while you're eating your sweets, boys and girls, to the story of the birth of the baby Jesus. In the season of Advent we're going to be discussing that wondrous event, just as it is in the first four books of the New Testament, anyone know what they're called? The Gospels, that's right, and this very first book of the New Testament is called what?* "When His mother Mary was engaged to Joseph, before they came together she was found to be with child from the Holy Spirit." *Do you all understand that? Okay, I'm not going to bother with the biology, better ask your mom and dad, see how it goes on:* "Her days were completed to give birth and she bore her first-born

Son, whom she wrapped in swaddling clothes and laid in a manger, because there was no room for them at the inn." Anyone know what a manger is? Perhaps Hex raised his hand, though he was infrequently called upon, because of the lag associated with his answers, and instead Brian Nelson, the torturer, shot up his hand, twisting and writhing in his chair — evidently he knew what a manger was. — Oh, Mizz Skillings, me! Here! And then shouting out his answer. — It's a stable. It was there, in Sunday School, that Billie and her husband began to understand the dimensions of Hex's difficulties. As Billie recalls it, the children were invited to illustrate this momentous fib about the manger: *Behold I announce to you good news of great joy that will be for all the people.* And the Walker girls were fashioning ornate finger paintings of the Annunciation, cribbed from Daphne and John's coffee-table art books — finger paintings in which Mary was keening in front of a gigantic angel. And little Brian Nelson was contributing something along the realistic lines, a lovely crude rendering of poor little Jesus, shivering in a stable surrounded by livestock polluting his bed, sows rooting through vegetable ends, and Mary's difficult labor, placenta, and afterbirth, Joseph standing off to one side passing flagons of wine to a confraternity of toothless farmers who'd been crisscrossing the plains stunned by the sight of the first ever arc lamp, a distempered cow in the manger shuddering, foaming at the mouth, Mary hemorrhaging, *a fine myth, of course,* but nothing like the picture Hex drew, which he brought home later, and described: *Jesus c-comes again, Mom, in N-new York City, he wants to live in N-new York City, that way he can g-get rid of the b-bad guys in the streets, all k-kinds of bad guys. See, he's a p-policeman, Mom, and he works all the time, and one d-day there are these b-bad guys trying to escape from Jesus, he's ch-chasing them and stuff. Oh yeah, and his p-p-p-parents found him in a h-hotel near the airport, lying in a b-b-basket, b-because there were no rooms at all the hotels in N-new York City, all full, and so he grew up in an Irish p-p-part of t-town, really far away from everything, and he's p-p-part Negro and Italian, his d-dad makes cheeses and stuff, and he chases b-b-bad guys, he chases them because they shoot people and they don't know the G-g-g-g-golden Rule, and he's gonna k-k-k-k-k-kill them, so he shoots one of them through the heart and this g-g-g-g-guy is d-dead. This b-b-bad g-guy lying on the street. There are his wife and b-babies all c-c-crying over him and he's all b-b-bloody. And the other two g-guys are g-getting away and Jesus c-can't c-catch them b-because he d-doesn't want to h-hurt anyone accidentally with his p-p-p-p-p-p-p-police car. So he chases them for a while and then he g-gets out and ch-chases some more, running after them, b-but one of them gets away, and the other one, Jesus b-breaks the man's arm so that he'll learn a lesson. The guy's sitting there with a b-broken arm and screaming, AHHHHHHHHHH!, and Jesus flies off, b-but he c-c-c-crashes —* That's quite enough, she told him, *that's plenty.* But her husband found it amusing, imaginative, wasn't concerned at all, seemed to get a good kick out of it, that is, until they got the call from Mrs. Skillings, implying that their boy, was, well, *having trouble,* in the eager, supportive environment of Sunday School, though in truth she, Mrs. Skillings, found him occasionally thoughtful and cheerful, well, but he couldn't seem to get along with the other students. And this was a problem. He was also having trouble in school. So Allen decided to go the following week to talk to her, to this Mrs. Skillings. The Sunday after he first took Dexter hunting with him, up into the woods, up to Amenia, to instruct Dexter in the use of the .22 caliber rifle. And it was clear when they came home on Saturday night, that Hex, his hair windblown, his cheeks dusty rose, was infatuated like his dad with the destructive power of guns. Against this backdrop, the next day, Hex went with his dad to talk to Mizz Skillings. He would have gone anywhere with his dad. When Billie woke, her husband and her boy were already dressed and cooking — eggs with Tabasco sauce, oatmeal with maple syrup, Canadian bacon. Allen was in midsentence: *You are a ladykiller, fella, and don't forget it. They'll fall at your feet. Your day will come. They'll want what you have. Don't worry about the lean years.* Billie showered and primped, and when she was ready, the two of them were out in the coupe, motor running. She climbed in back. Allen prepared himself for the confrontation with the woman. *So what is the problem with this Sunday School teacher? Is she teaching you anything at all?* To which Hex replied with a nervous shake of the head. And so Allen began to get a little irritable, although up to a point willing to be polite, he was just going down to give Elaine Skillings a hello, to say that this was our boy, Dexter, that he stammered, yes indeed, and he was a little overweight, he was even a little obtuse, but he was our son. We had no other. But on the way there his resolve came undone: *If she was a damned Sunday School teacher, she could well use a few Christian virtues like understanding and forgiveness, instead of complaining about her charges, if she wanted repetition in her job, maybe she wanted to work a radioactive glove box someplace, if that's what she wanted, but if she was an Episcopal Sunday School teacher, well then she could practice her goddamned religion instead of complaining about how a boy who only needed some personal attention wasn't fit for her candyass class,* Allen hollered, but as far as Billie could tell from later accounts, a conversation with the Skillings woman never took place. They went down the stairs, the two of them, the Raitliffe men, Allen stooping under the heating ducts, Allen in all likelihood smoldering with a certain impatience, a molten quality in his eyes, as though he had seen disagreeable things. They descended the stairs into that dungeon where the heresies were being purged, and Allen peppered Hex with contentions, things like, *Well, maybe she's right, maybe Mrs. Skillings is right and you aren't applying yourself. How should I know? Why don't you prove it to me, Dexter, if you want me to argue your side of the controversy. So tell me, for example, who the Pope is. Do you know who the Pope is?* Hex shook his head again, *no.* Allen stopped. Ran his hand through Hex's hair. *Well, it's not important anyhow. He's an Italian guy . . . with an art collection. Don't pay any attention to that.* There was a skip in Allen's gait as he thought of the next question. *Trinity?* he said suddenly. *What's the holy Trinity? Do you know what that is?* And then her husband, Billie Raitliffe's husband, leaned against the edge of a filing cabinet in the hall there, as if to take a moment to think through the correct response to such a question. It was a plain, gray filing cabinet that housed old church bulletins, backdated sermons. And Allen lurched against it. He, the boy, was turning over the question about the Trinity, the sound of the choir upstairs (where she herself, where Billie was throwing a dollar bill into a brass offertory plate), the choir was hitting the high note of some madrigal, and downstairs the metal of the filing cabinet was buckling a little bit. *Ah,* Allen said. The initial surprise coming from him. What was his dad doing? Hex wondered. Was it a prank of some kind? A further test of his grasp of these questions? Was this the answer to the question about the Trinity? *Something's not . . . Hey, stay here for a second, okay?* his dad said. And then Allen Raitliffe fell onto the floor; all the equilibrium went out of his body — as though his insides had pitched suddenly. He tipped over. Fell from where he leaned against the filing cabinet. To the floor. He moaned once. It was his head. He held tightly on to that enormous head. *Oh boy,* he said, *I really don't feel too well. Dexter, do you think you could just jog down there and alert . . . uh, Mrs. Skillings for me? Think about that question I asked you, though . . . Take your time. It's not a trick.* And then he began to bleed. The blood was medieval and generous. Where could blood come from so precipitously? *And why so much?* He wasn't injured or sick. Just bleeding. From the eye? From behind the left eye? Allen held his hands up to his eyes and the effluvium ran down, cascaded along his sleeves, until there was a kind of a stigmata look to his palms, and he shuddered, and his body emptied, from this *aneurysm,* and Hex didn't fulfill his father's last wish (that he should fetch Mrs. Skillings), *rooted to the linoleum* in that corridor; and a lifetime of psychiatry wouldn't undo the fact of this immobility. Oh, her poor son. Hex was trying to say something to his father, was desperate to say something, but, under the circumstances, the chances were slim. Time was not limitless. *Hex,* his father said, calling his son by the nickname, a name Allen normally disdained though it was easier for their boy to pronounce. It was his last word, to be complete on the subject, for as the runoff continued, as Allen arrived at his own panic in this imbroglio, at the terrible disappointment, not to mention acute physical discomfort. He understood his diagnosis. He knew how much blood he was losing. How many seconds had passed? He was puddled everywhere. Hex fell upon his father, hugging, crying. The screech that at last issued from the boy never did amount to a word. Hex was a boy finger-painted with his father's blood, in a poorly lit corridor, in a suburban church, whose fervent wish — that his dad was going to be okay — would not be granted by the limited omnipotence of the church. Then Elaine Skillings emerged into the corridor, instructing the kids, *Stay in the classroom, please,* and Allen was unconscious now, drifting in coma, the sound of a door with a glass window slamming shut, the fearless Brian Nelson closing himself and the rest of the kids into the room and hiding with them under the table, the service upstairs grinding to a halt for the sound of commotion, recognizable in the still awe of the Eucharist, Elaine Skillings's heels on the linoleum, taking Hex's hand, dragging him off the body, saying, *Come on now, dear,* running upstairs with him, blood on herself now, too, her dress speckled, and then at the rear of the chapel, pulling open the doors, as though the era of martyrdom had come again to the Protestants, an apocalyptic look to her, at the point at which she, Billie Raitliffe, herself entered the story, turning from Eucharistic prayers to face her poor boy, *Oh my God, she had never seen . . . Oh my Lord, what is all this blood?,* knowing without being told that her own good fortune had been exhausted, and then that long black minute, almost eliminated from recollection, the moment in which she stepped from the pew and passed from knowing of Allen's death to being its witness, by his side, *her husband was gone,* actually he lived for a day or two, though unconscious, and she was watching the proceedings from some exalted or angelic aerie, watching herself from this distance as she covered her eyes, keening, the gurney clattering down the stairs behind her, the firemen with their gurney, footmen of ill, and then thinking, *Where is Hex? Where is Hex?* Alone with Allen one last minute. His face resigned, exhausted, his arms flung out. She rose when lifted by others to find that Hex was upstairs with the minister, of all people, who couldn't have realized that her son's religious instruction was just now coming to its abrupt conclusion, *that he had just received all the theology he would ever need,* that he would never again set foot in a church, that he would avoid pews, sacristies, clerestories, antechapels, naves, narthexes, and altars of churches, that he would refuse all instruction from churches. They removed her husband, her comatose husband, to linger in New London, in the hospital, and she went to find Hex, who was

just then asking the rector *who the Pope was.* Under the circumstances, the priest had no reply.

That's one memory Billie has.

— Take your time, Hex says, now, in the living room, wheeling
her up to the joystick, to the electronic apparatus. — No rush,
plenty of time. Although I do want to g-get something to eat eventually. But take your t-t-t-time, okay?

5

I-95 would be the best road out of town for Lou Sloane. That massive artery would be best, as he leaves, in his cream-colored Cadillac, with show tunes on the stereo, windows open, the breezes of autumn blowing through the car, blowing around the empty Styrofoam coffee cups littering the leatherette interior. I-95 was the road he selected, in fact, according to an itinerary mapped some hours earlier, when, through a kind of automatism, he decided to *leave the state*. What better road? Those six lanes of interstate are the avenue of choice for those who sunder themselves from habits and routines and head out on the road, avoiding the car-pool lanes, turning the radio up, and singing (tunelessly) — these Americans, bending the rules a little as far as open container restrictions go, paying no heed to restrictive speed limits, passing on the right, *these rugged individualists,* who at the end of a long tussle have concluded that marriage is a confinement, these guys who are convinced that there's a part of the good life hidden from them, a patch of contentment so far denied, *the pursuit of happiness being written into the original national documents for godsakes.* The road for this guy has to be the interstate, I-95, the road northeast, with its array of McDonald'ses, state troopers, tractor-trailers (and amphetamined drivers), I-95, a vast democratizer given away for free by our government after the war to open civil defense routes in the event of enemy attack, I-95, *be sure to bring along the picks and shovels,* the northeastern pavement that goes anywhere worth going. The fact of the matter is, though, that the interstate is always being repaired, every fifteen damned feet, or seems like it to Sloane, who is at this moment finishing his last lunch ever in coastal Connecticut, at Arlene's Surf 'N Turf: *fried fish medley,* featuring calamari, shrimp, simulated crabmeat, and scrod in a heavy breading — and sides, in waxed paper cups, of slaw and tartar sauce. *Cement dividers and the merging traffic and troopers everywhere,* they've been repairing it all the way from New York City to Boston, two hundred and fifty miles, never finishing it, just leaving battalions of construction guys out there with their hardhats, backhoes, flagmen standing nonchalantly in the passing lane, they're always there, back and forth from Pelham to Lowell, day after day, during rush hour or in deepest night, one section repaved as, elsewhere, a bridge collapses and the crews are rushed in. I-95 is a damned parking lot, if you want to know the truth, full of angry members of the working classes in their uninsured low-riders, *you hear it every day,* Sloane thinks, you hear it from the traffic helicopters, from the all-news stations, *Stay off of I-95.* And as he ruminates thus Lou — who crumples his paper napkin, pushes it to the center of his plate, and who then repairs to the gents' to recomb his lacquered white hair and to clean his tinted glasses — Lou couldn't possibly imagine that his stepson, his stuttering, overdressed stepson (who is leaving New York City at this very moment in his leaky rental) *has recently faced the same problem* with respect to I-95, and has arrived — like Lou — at the very same unavoidable conclusion. Sloane, however, while gazing at the antimatter Lou in the foggy rest-room mirror, believes the elegant solution is his alone: *He's going to have to take U.S. 1.* At least part of the way. At least till New London. Then again from Groton for a half hour or so. U.S. 1, *the Boston Post Road,* the oldest road in the country, relic of the colonies, stretching from New York up to Boston, and then beyond, winding through the state of Maine, along that rocky coast and through the North Woods, through logging country, before vanishing into the Canadian hinterlands. The Boston Post Road, where the warring private postal systems — which antedated the federal monopoly — hotfooted it through Indian turf, delivering to the Pilgrims. Now, three hundred years later, it's a road entirely given over to a strip shopping center, from beginning to end, from Fordham to NYC where the kids buy marijuana or harder drugs — all the way to the Auto Mile of Norwood, near Foxboro Stadium, where there are more car dealerships per acre than anywhere on earth, dozens of them, with their unctuous, bowtied sales staffs. The Boston Post Road stands for franchising and transit and especially that combination of the two — auto sales — which caters to those Americans inclined to abandon and to never look back. Sloane thinks, *Well, darnit, if I have to take the Post Road, I'll just take the Post Road, maybe until Kingston, and then I'll get back on 95. Can't be all blocked off all the way up the coast.* And he completes the rituals that follow his lunch (washes his hands twice, dries them carefully on the scrolling towelette), and returns to his table to obsessively figure his tip — fifteen percent on the nose. Sloane knows his mathematics. He is preoccupied with the tip, moreover, because payment at the register (a requirement at Arlene's Surf 'N Turf) will bring him close to the proprietor of this establishment, to Arlene herself. He's been eating at the Surf 'N Turf for probably fifteen years and a certain knowing kindness exists between himself and Arlene. She knows, for example, about his termination at *the plant* — the Millstone Nuclear Power Station subsidiary of Coastal Power and Light, Inc. — because gossip at Arlene's is not unusual, especially Millstone gossip, and she may even know of his most recent address, the Tides Motel (of Niantic), but he doesn't care to discuss it with her, or with anyone else he might meet this afternoon. He hopes she'll continue to observe this polite silence as she has so far. Still, he's nervous. But because Lou is large, sad, taciturn, and habitually wears amber-tinted dark glasses, he encounters no difficulties. Lou finds, as Arlene spindles his check and runs an age-spotted, nail-polished hand through her maroon hair, that she has other things on her mind: *Lou,* she says, *listen, my granddaughter comes home four in the morning last night.* She makes change automatically. She doesn't count back. *I don't care how old she is! Not in my house! Not in my house!* Shakes her head ruefully. Lou smiles, but is otherwise mute, because strategies of evacuation are still calling to him. For example, before returning to the office, he needs to make one more stop, to settle up, at the Tides Motel, the dive where he has often caught some winks over the years — for late-night safety tests (spot checks of the feed-water systems, backup coolant arrays, runoff valves, emergency drills for Codes One, Two, and Three — coolant loss, emissions, and core damage), and because of the occasional night shift in the control room. He likes to keep a hand in. On these occasions, Sloane has always favored the Tides. For reasons of convenience, but also because Sloane appreciates repetition. Reliably moth-eaten blankets, starchy sheets, the sound of Route 156, the lapping of the Sound on the hull of a dinghy moored somewhere nearby, seagulls circling overhead. Lou likes repetition. *Why else would he have stayed fifteen years with a woman who could no longer walk, talk, make love, or even eat without his feeding her? Why the hell would he have stayed so long if not because there was some stupefy-ing comfort in it?* As he passes the gumball machine and the ciga-rette vendor, there's a tightening in Lou's chest. He's having palpitations, again, and he presses one thumb against the other wrist as he ambles into the parking lot, leans dully against the car, and waits it out, the arrhythmia of desperation. The sun is on the way down. The parking lot is full. American cars. It'll be better when he's out on the Post Road. Lou climbs into the car, guns it, and starts back across town. Across Waterford. To the motel. Seven traffic lights. Waterford is organized like all disappointed shore towns. Union, the avenue that divides the waterfront and the inte-rior. The amber of afternoon is reflected here, on his left, upon the choppy Sound. He passes the post office, the video arcade, a host of motels, mostly shuttered in the off-season, marinas with their seacrafts up on stilts, the chamber of commerce, and then he's out of town again heading southwest, into Niantic, to where the Tides Motel overlooks the water. Out by the beer distributors. Here, Sloane parks in front of room #3, home away from home, and walks back over to the office, where he finds Pranav K. Chanapur-thi at reception stiffly watching a talk show on a tiny, shrill black-and-white set. *Pranav, how much?* Lou had intended to stay one night only, if necessary to accomplish the odds and ends of his last day. Thursday was to have been the night. That had been Strategy

A. But on Wednesday, Sloane had been overcome by *some unex-plainable event of the human heart,* some paroxysmal remorse, including (again) palpitations and shortness of breath, *while changing Billie's disposable undergarment.* Like this. He was watching television with his wife of fifteen years. Urine leaking from her onto the floor of the library, leaking out from beneath her dress, as they watched a videotape of the Kirov ballerinas. Aviva had not, apparently, fixed Billie's diaper properly. As usual, Sloane undertook the chore. *Honey,* he had said, *I'm going to put you on the chaise longue on the porch, and change your, uh, you know . . . Do you feel like you're backed up down there? Do you want to think about catheterizing?* The words were sympathetic enough, he had broken bad news to her often enough, *Why don't you let me carry you?* or, *Darling, I think this bed will need room for a bedpan now,* or, *Sweetheart, we can't really understand what you're saying very well.* With varying degrees of patience he had said these things, because when he married her, when she was still on the cane, she had had a face like the dimensions of a crystal, all chiseled with wisdom, smarts, heartache, all beautiful like a flock of birds scared up off the cove, all beautiful like the sound of cellos, all beautiful like the morning after a first snowfall, all beautiful with a life fully lived. She was a ravishing older woman, with white hair that she just let fly, didn't tie it off or dye it blue or anything, didn't rouge herself to make it look like she was a goddamned girl, or pluck her eyebrows, she was a woman full of dignity, and she could still reach up to him with her hands, when he married her, and laugh about what a fine time they had had some nights, just the two of them, at the worst restaurant in town, dining out on a twenty-dollar bill, and she didn't even give a damn if he was on a tight budget, a poor man by her standards, didn't give a damn if he had been getting by and not much more, she didn't even mind, and they had been as gentle with her body as if with a fine piece of china in the light of the master bedroom, on that old bed with its draperies, they had been gentle, tested her body and its capacity for giving, and he had found the testing was gentler and sweeter than anything he had any right to expect, and then they had met another time back at his place on the cheap side of town, he tried to tidy it up, make it classy, because the crudity of a younger man's embraces were embarrassing to him, *sure, this is a woman I can take care of,* that's what he had thought, I am here to take care of this poor woman who has a lot of trouble ahead of her, I have waited forty-five years, on my own, for this, to do something generous for a change. *I have waited.* But that was before he had learned to break the bad news. That was before he had watched her fall down and fracture a wrist reaching for a cup of coffee; before he had iodined a bedsore, and looked through it to her very skeleton; before she began sleeping two or three days straight; before she began lapsing into interminable silences; before all that, and before Wednesday night, when he just gave out somehow. You know how these things are, the fuel just runs out. He'd just run out of steam, as though he had been punctured, as though there had been something hidden all these years, and he had suddenly found it, had found it was right in front of his face, right where he was sitting — by his wife, changing her disposable undergarment. This simple news right in front of him. *He didn't have to stay.* It was simple. He left her for a moment, on the chaise longue, just walked past her body, that decrepit packaging, and went outside, back by the pool. The decision had evidently been gathering itself for a long time. It was as if he'd suddenly read a billboard he'd been passing every morning. He knew at once about the nights he'd been awake with the revelation of this thought, standing like a teenager in front of the open refrigerator, sobbing, holding a carton of milk in his hands (missing child pictured upon it), weeping, knowing that his life had jumped its track. The days he'd had the thought at work, walking with his clipboard from steam valve to thermometer to computer screen, checking over what had already been checked over, knowing something was awry, that something had changed. He'd seen it too in the compassionate glances of colleagues, without knowing what it was, at first, without knowing that he could simply lock the door on the way out, that he could entrust her to institutions, to the state, to her accountants, to whoever was responsible for her because of blood affiliation. He'd *known,* and now he understood the sensation. He wasn't guilty for surviving and being vigorous, for wanting to drive long distances by himself, for wanting to watch livestock in some meadow, for wanting to drink coffee from a Styrofoam cup in a silent part of a forest; he wasn't guilty at all. He was just a man up late at night, a man who didn't sleep well any longer, a supervisor in a control room — who had taken a whole slew of night shifts, thinking it through, wondering how things had turned out the way they had, with his feet up on his desk, wiping away the occasional *ocular irritant*. Then Wednesday came. Out there, though, in the backyard, on Wednesday night, there was a grace in the sound of the Atlantic, and he knew it was all right to leave. It would cause havoc, and he was damned scared to do it, but it was all right. He caught his breath. He went back into the house. He changed his wife, toweled her off, hugging her afterward with an unusual tightness, because he loved her, because she had been an angel to him. Then he lifted her into his arms, and she murmured contentedly, and he staggered up the stairs, carrying her, his lungs heaving with the effort, to the master bedroom, where she infrequently slept these days. He set her on the bed, stretched out her limbs, straightened her spastic right arm, and she yelped. Then he removed her clothes, pulled the dress up over her head, got it all wound around her face for a second, and then unsnapped her bra, and went digging around in the drawers for a nightshirt of some kind. Found a lavender slip. But before he put it on her he hoisted himself up on the bed, took off his shoes, untucked his shirt, relaxed a little himself, and then he was kissing her, all across her face — she still had some sensation there, besides the neuralgia. There was still pleasure there. She loved to be kissed, and she was smiling a little bit, or was he guessing that she was smiling, interpreting as a smile what was probably no more than the idea of gratitude, or was she smiling? As he was wiping his own eyes with the corner of the sheet, did she know he was going now to pack? Did she hear him going up to the attic after that? After he kissed her, he thought about making love to her, one last time. *But what good would it do?* He would have to force his way in again, because she couldn't relax those muscles, and he would have to assemble the lotions and creams, it would be circumscribed as always by the good advice of neurologists, sensible cautious exchanges of tenderness, and that's just what he couldn't do anymore, couldn't do it. He was contemptible, he wasn't strong enough when you thought about it, not strong enough or good enough, and he left her there. She was asleep anyway, had fallen asleep without her clothes on, and he tucked her in. And left her there, left her in the house, left most of his things behind, just took these things in the car now, left his aftershave out on the counter in the bathroom, left his dishes in the dishwasher, left a note on her computer, a note with all the wrong words. He was childless, laid off, forced into retirement, and he wouldn't, at his age, work again. He was between situations.

Thus the Tides Motel of Niantic. With its motor court; its penal architecture; its funk of dissipation; its limitless opportunities for the viewing of *porno*; its general policy of discretion and anonymity; its vinyl draperies (closed); its sinister brown ceiling stains; its dog-eared travel brochures for the Bridgeport Water Slide; its continental breakfast of scorched coffee and white toast; all these amenities and more, for the guy leaving his wife. Discreetly charged to Lou's Discover card. After he signs his John Hancock, Lou reaches over the reception desk to give Pranav K. Chanapurthi, the innkeeper, a friendly pat on the shoulder. They have done a lot of business over the years. *Louis,* Pranav says, *have a good P.M. and give the wife a hello for me.* Sloane agrees to do just that. Then Lou heads back to room #3, where he loads his suitcase into the backseat of the Cadillac. The parking lot is empty. He closes the rear car door, gently, and then settles himself behind the wheel. And now to the last afternoon at work — one last impediment before he can really get on the road — an afternoon that will be a chore, Sloane knows, because of *the party.* Unless he misses his guess, the guys in the control room, Reggie Davis, Mac Kowalski, Dorothy Halleran, Ronald Self, and probably some of the fellows in maintenance (he has stuck up for them in the past), the ones who know how much work he put into the place, they'll get him a bottle of champagne, and they'll toast, with mixed feelings, the freedom of late middle age. Honest to God, he hates those parties. Hates being at them and will hate even more being guest of honor. And management will be waiting in the wings, and there will be that creep, Stanford Warren, who's succeeding him, hanging

around, arranging wall photographs in Sloane's office. They'll pad
the party with women from human resources and communications. They'll all sit around pretending to have known him. And
Warren will come up and say, *Oh, by the way, Lou, do you know
who it is over in the legal department that gets copied on the monthly
totals?* (Sloane lowers the electric windows. Look: the sun is balanced on the very spot where sea meets coast.) Lou's a company
man, fifteen years' worth, and will part with this information because he has to, as he was willing to take the fall, when the
corrosion in the lines became a matter of public record. Well,
Sloane himself had authorized it, had authorized the use of sea
water, of *the Atlantic Ocean* as a coolant — there was a hell of a lot
of it, after all, and it was right there, and they desalinated it,
mostly, and Waterford, in spite of the name, was having supply
shortfalls because of drought, and it had been a contingency all
along, and he hadn't done it without alerting management, of
course, and not without consulting Babcock and Wilcox, who designed the plant. Fine, fine, they had said, *fine.* But then it turned
out you had chlorides precipitated by the steam, in the lines leading to the turbine, trace chlorides, residuals, see, and these chlorides had eroded the copper lines badly, lines in, lines out. Salt
water and plumbing — bad combination. It was an experiment
that hadn't worked terribly well, that's all, and Millstone — and all
the other seaboard plants — were better for the experiment. It
would have been ideal, of course, if the difficulties had been kept
quiet. The plant could have replaced the affected materials and
the costs could have been absorbed and they could have adjusted
the safety codes accordingly. It would have been fine, except
that the problem got out. Turned up in the New London papers.
Emissions. This happens with corrosion. Insignificant emissions,
cesium, americium, not much else, dangerous stuff that wasn't hot
for very long, affecting normal background levels by a hundredth
of one percent. For a few months at most. It turned up in the
paper. It didn't matter who did it. Didn't matter. *The real fallout
was in the area of public relations.* The utility wasn't up to
addressing the idea that the local water supply didn't provide
for its needs; they had gotten themselves into a bind, and they

needed to mend their ways. They needed to symbolize their commitment to change. So the CEO of Coastal Power and Light, Spencer Murphy — who played the golf course in Fenwick, who had known Billie's first husband — he broke the news to Lou. Sloane was chauffeured up to New Haven in a limo. *Lou, you know, we all recognize that you have given us a lifetime of devotion to the cause of inexpensive nuclear energy . . . We all recognize that in you we've had an employee of the sort that management always hopes for. A dedicated, no-nonsense type of guy. And we're honestly grateful for that . . . You got into this business, like I did, because of certain kinds of values. Ike said it best, don't you think? "Moving out of the dark chamber and into the light." Do you remember that? I know you do, Lou. And I know you value candor, so I'm not going to beat around the bush. You know as well as I do what we have on our plate up at Millstone. It's a mess. It's unfortunate. But what we want to do today, Lou, is for the two of us to figure out a way to turn the corner on this. I think you know what I'm getting at, Lou. I'm not going to embarrass you. I'm not going to talk down to you. We want to offer you a very generous pension, one of the most generous this utility has ever extended to an employee, including stock options and health benefits for life, for you and your family — Lou, think of what this could mean for Billie — in return for doing this one last service for us.* Specifically, of course, they wanted him to produce the memo in which he had ordered the use of salt water as a coolant. And they wanted him to release it. He saved everything. He had this memorandum on the desk of the publisher of the *New London Day* the next morning. He'd seen it coming, and he'd taken the fall in a way that was unfashionable these days, just as his business was itself unfashionable. He let the society men, the golfers and pleasure boaters, talk him out of his reputation. He'd done it to himself.

The traffic inches along Union Avenue. The kids have gotten out of school for the weekend. They all ease past the pizza place, past the shoe repair, past the bars. There are even a few sailboats on the water, heeling along toward Gardiners Island — as Lou comes to the promontory, to Millstone Rock, where the plant is located. It extends three quarters of a mile out into the harbor, that spit of land, manicured like the gardens of an imperial palace, magnolias, forsythia, red maples, until you come over the hill and the tanks rise up out of the landscaping — not the hourglass containment vessels so familiar from hand-tinted scare photographs, but a pair of large cement tanks holding the two reactors, lifeless and practical, cubical, corrugated (to resist summer storms), three stories high, maybe fifty yards across, the reactors — steam engines with astounding fuel — and then a cluster of subsidiary buildings surrounding them, the red-and-white-striped stack, the waste containment facility, the security checkpoints, restraining walls, cameras everywhere. Vulgar like any practical industrial structure is vulgar. But also sort of beautiful. A large sign on a triangle of grass. *Welcome to Millstone Nuclear Power Plant.* As Sloane passes the main security gate, he waves at the woman in the booth, and slots himself into a spot in the management parking lot. He enters the plant, as he usually likes to do, through the back, through the loading ramp entitled DELIVERIES, where the fuel assemblies arrive, where the waste is carted out. He likes the back entrance, likes to avoid the public relations gadflies, and he isn't afraid of the high-security parts of the product he has delivered for fifteen years. Because Lou worked his way up. Because Lou was in Hyman Rickover's navy, with its nuclear submarines. He was stationed at the Groton sub base, and he did six months under the surface of the gray Atlantic, loading and unloading the payloads, managing their fuel assemblies. He isn't afraid. He'd even been in the *Nautilus* when the first mate plugged a reactor leak with a dozen gallons of automobile antifreeze and they kept right on going — another thirty days. As Sloane ambles through the long corridors, some of the shipping and receiving guys wave at him. He's the outgoing boss, and the boss on his way out is always preferable to the one coming in, the reformer, with his regimes and paperwork. They wave, and Sloane is moved by it. Through these long corridors, he tries to make this last stroll memorable, tries to file away every detail — Thanksgiving decorations on the bulletin boards, the unusually hardy office plants on desks and tables. After going by the showers and the lockers, he comes at last to the elevator, and to the reactor control facility itself. He goes up to the second floor, and arrives at that series of airlocked seals with the multiple, computerized, encoded bolts that lead into the control room. Here he shows his identification badge to Manny from security. They chat for a minute. *Lou, let me tell you about my youngest, the halfback.* Then Lou goes through the airlock. And as he steps through that threshold he is stunned to find that *the place is almost empty.* There are three or four guys, mostly trainees, just kids really, in the main control room, looking nervous and dazed as they pore over the array of video monitors, the five hundred and nineteen illuminator panels, and the annunciators, with their sequences of lamps and gauges — the expanse of computerized bells and whistles that B&W had reinstalled after the public relations scare of 1979. Where the hell are the shift supervisors? Boy, if the paper gets hold of this one! Sloane compulsively checks meters on the way past, the big three: pressurizer, turbine, emergency feed water, he goes up and down the rows of panels, scans printout, and all looks well, of course, no alarms. At the end of one expanse of panels, he finds a *janitor* in the corner, at full attention, in his maintenance greens. A janitor in the control room! He asks where everyone is.

The janitor looks sheepish.

Lou's insides roil for a second, out of habit, as he considers possibilities, contingencies, political schemes, *but then the obvious comes to him.* How could he have forgotten? In fact, he sees now that the janitor is smiling. It's a restrained smile, an amiable smile. And the two of them laugh. It's a *surprise.* A surprise party! The custodian — because he's a hardworking fellow — has almost ruined the surprise!

— Okay, Sloane says. I get it. But I'm still going to bring some of those yo-yos back in here where they belong.

The janitor nods. Why is Lou Sloane talking to him? A custodian? It's 3:21. (Sloane has a digital watch, top of the line, tells your horoscope almost, even has a compass.) He goes back through the airlock. There's this darned party to live through. It's maybe ninety paces down the corridor to his office, to its cartons of memorabilia. Ninety paces to the sad countenances of friends who know that something is up. Why is it always so hard to make conversation at these functions? Sloane passes cubicles, oddly empty offices. He drifts to a stop ten feet or so before the door, frozen for a moment. With sorrow. What if he's doing the wrong thing? At his age? *Maybe he's making an awful mistake.* He begins to clock his pulse. On his fancy wristwatch. But before he can finish the job, he sees Ron Self peek out the door, grinning. Then there are gales of laughter, *Surprise! Surprise!* and Self calls out, *Jesus, Lou, you want to leave us in here for forty-five minutes? Hiding? We can hardly stand each other, you know?* And there is the music of kazoos, and Sloane fakes a smile and rounds the corner and they are all performing "For He's a Jolly Good Fellow." On kazoos. It's pathetic. Plates of sugar cookies spread across manuals and monthly reports and memoranda. The boxes of stuff he's shipping home, though he's not going home. Self and Dorothy Halleran spring the corks on the bubbly. Plastic cups with stems. The activity is brisk. Someone hands him a kazoo: a memento. Under the circumstances, they're all doing a fine impression of collegiality. As you'd expect, Stanford Warren is standing alone in the corner sporting a haggard expression. And Lou, in an instant of affection for friends about to be left behind, can't resist raising his voice over the din of pleasantries: *Stan, you're really gonna leave the control room with that bunch of greenhorns in charge? Jesus, that's taking liberties, isn't it? Is that up to code? Those guys are gonna get cookie crumbs in the plumbing, you ask my opinion.* A few nervous snickers in the crowd, and Warren tries to formulate a politically sensitive reply, *Well, Lou, when you put it that way —*

— I'd keep an eye on it if I were you.

— Well, I'll send Dorothy then . . .

But when Stanford Warren looks around, it dawns on him that Dorothy is an integral part of the celebration. She shoots him a disappointed look. Kowalski, too. So Warren, *that horse's ass*, realizes that it's himself who should do the job. He edges between the overweight bodies in the doorway, and vanishes.

— Okay, good, Mac Kowalski says, — we can let down our hair.

— What? Ron Self cackles, — you mean you still *have* hair?

They have a few good laughs, before one of those party silences sets in. The presence of a scapegoat had organized them. It's evening all at once; the office is bathed in the last autumnal daylight, slanted, crimson, then violet. It's Ron who begins telling the jokes from a dozen years of working together — the guy who used to put his thermos on top of the coolant lines to keep his coffee warm, the woman in communications who scheduled a plant tour for the Wesleyan antinuclear group *during their exams,* the time Kowalski claimed he'd found a lobster halfway down the water intake, a boiled lobster!

— Hey, Lou (Kowalski is in fact *punching him lightly in the kidney* while murmuring), I tried to phone you at home, you know, last night, just to see, you know, and I got the nurse, she said something about you were, uh —

— Yeah, well, Sloane says.

And the two of them understand exactly this weary recognition. Lou will miss Mac. The mirth in the room is short-lived. It's all sympathy now. They're worried. The strangers, the ones he never knew anyway, they work their way to the door, spill out with the stragglers. Just the diehards sipping the last of the cheap champagne. Lou, Ron, Dorothy, Mac, Reggie, three or four others. No one much says anything. And then the janitor from the control room turns up. *The janitor and one of those greenhorns.* They're short of breath. The public address system crackles to life.

6

When I think about my body, I have to remind myself of its condition. Hex watches over her shoulder, squinting, as his mother toggles the joystick arduously, but he can't confine himself long to this posture; he ambles restively around the room, sits first in one vinyl armchair (beige) and then upon the couch — a cloud of dust rising around him. The smell of this room is of dust. He wants to carry his diluted beverage to the bar on the wall (the antique bar with its speckled mirror) — this itch rises in him constantly. He thinks about distance, rate, or about how much noise a trip across the room would make — his black loafers on the parquet — about whether it would distract. He's refreshed himself too often, and he's embarrassed by it. His mother is numbering his drinks. *When I want the truth about my body,* she writes, *I have to open my eyes and look. If my eyes are up to it anyway. To know the location of my hands or my feet. What is the position of my body? How did I leave it? But when I have my eyes closed or when I'm alone, I think of myself as I was twenty years ago, or fifteen, or thirty-five years ago. I'm in a yellow dress, perhaps, walking across a certain field in spring, near a lake, or by the shore, or I'm bouncing you on a knee, or I'm holding your father's hands. I think often about holding your father's hands. And about how curly your hair was. Running my hands through your hair. These are the things I think about. I like to read about gardening now because it reminds me of the way my body felt when I gardened. There was peat moss under my nails. I would like to garden again. I would like to clap erasers together. I would like to play the harp. I would like to chase a neighborhood dog. I would like to polish an antique table. I would like to wear heels and then take them off. I would like to drive up to the front doors along these streets and give the neighbors a piece of my mind. Just for the fun of it. I would like to make love, Dexter, but I will probably never do that again. Not the way I remember it. Louis thought he knew all about my illness. He talked to doctors and they described to him the course of it, and he thought he knew what was in store for him. Louis was aware that I would get to this point. He knew that I would be bedridden, that I would have very little movement, and he accepted it, or so he thought. But when he was finally confronted with the nitty-gritty, well, he was worn-out. I wore him out. I suppose I knew I would. He was a good man, but he wasn't up to it. Who is? I'm not surprised, except by the way he left. He's consoling himself someplace. He's counting on the fact that you're going to step in and take over. That's the only possibility that will let him off the hook. He expects that you'll be willing and able to look after me when Aviva — or the nurse after her — goes home at the end of the day. He expects that you're going to accept this responsibility. But I don't think any such thing, Dexter. I don't expect you to take care of me. I don't want anyone to take care of me. The very idea makes me angry. And that's why I wanted to talk with you today. That is the reason for this note. It's time to get some planning squared away, don't you think? Let's look at the bigger picture. The day is coming, after all, it could be after the very next bath, or the next flu or case of pneumonia, the moment when —*

The time being Friday evening, when Hex Raitliffe, whose profession (to the degree that he has one, having inherited from his father) is *freelance publicist* (in particular the publicity-related specialization that involves mounting parties in society: openings of films, gallery events, backstage fêtes, and the filling of these occasions with people whose photographs will turn up in the papers, on the society pages — though it bears mentioning that Hex Raitliffe is not very effective or diligent at his job, partly because of drinking and stammering) — that hour on Friday night has arrived when Hex usually counts on *an evening out*, on co-hosting an event (*Hex*

Raitliffe invites you and a friend to an evening at BIHAC, 175 W. B'Way) or on turning up at a downtown soirée, talking his way into the VIP rooms of Soho and Tribeca, dressed in his custom-tailored suit, which is to say that *it is the weekend, the kingdom of the weekend is upon him, the biological time clock has suddenly realized it,* and that he now finds himself instead watching three quarters of an hour go by in the drafty living room listening to the sixteenth notes of his mother's joystick, coming up behind her again to look over her shoulder, *Wow, she's even putting in the punctuation,* wiping away a tiny rivulet of saliva tracking down the folds around her jaw, that he should be speed-reading words without under-standing the drift, satisfying himself that this is stuff he wants to dispense with as quickly as possible — *this is an irritation,* a point-less subplot in the drama of his weekend. Friday preempts other programming, right? Even his concern for his mother. So he finds himself, without intending, halfway across the room, on the way to *refilling,* on the way to celebrating, though he can't remember having planned it that way, having planned to cross the room, nor does he know what exactly he intends to celebrate . . .

— *I will be as good as a piece of lumber here on the bed in the living room, and I don't think that you should have to be here looking after me, watching me immobilized, waiting for the lights to go out. I don't want you wasting your time doing that. Honestly, I don't. I don't want anyone — anyone who isn't salaried — watching me petrify. Do you understand? Don't do what you hate. You honestly don't want to spend your life in this house with me, under the circumstances. I know you don't. You are still a relatively young man, and I am expecting great things from you. I am expecting, for example, that you may settle down before too long, that you may have familial responsibilities of your own, and these responsibilities would make it difficult for you to live here in the sticks, taking care of me. You are a city person. You have your life. That's fine. Well then, what would be the best thing to do under the circumstances? That's the important point. There are a couple of possibilities. Let's be frank. First, you could house me in a chronic care ward, where I should think it would be obvious that I will fall in the blink of an eye into a bottomless gloom that all the potions in the world would not alleviate. You remember your father's time in the hospital. Think back on those days. That's what such a place would represent for me. I wouldn't put up with it for a single afternoon. I've grown accustomed to my home, Dexter, I live in this setting — the sound of surf, the smell of New England. And I have my old house here. I will not give up my home and the poplars and the goldfish and the golfers, and the lighthouses of the Sound, I won't give these up. Not to stay six months stiff as a plank in a semiprivate room next to a woman with Alzheimer's. I hope, therefore, that my wishes here are clear. I think we can dispense with this idea, therefore, which leaves only one other —*

The flush of alcohol when it spills over the capacity of enlarged purifying organs to process it! The crimson in the cheeks of the alcoholic! Alcohol as it becomes a routine chemical agent in the lives of human cells! That yearning that is a part of the early arc of an evening's drinks! Burst blood vessels scattered like the freckles across the bridge of the nose, under the thick lenses of spectacles! The perpetual nasal drip! The rheumy eyes! The enlargement, in the mind of the drunk, of the human condition so that the pathos of life is unbearable! Yearning and sentiment adhering to everything! *Yearning* in fact is the word that best describes Hex Raitliffe now, as this warm feeling reaches with its tentacles through his viscera. *Yearning and affection. Yearning and tenderness.* Just for the fact of being here in his mother's house. With his mom! His mom is so great! He empties one tumbler, swallows hard, knowing, suddenly, that an empty glass will not have to be a problem this evening. Go ahead, refill it! Disdain strategies! Be bold! Hex is *aware,* Hex is cognizant that some important familial milestone is taking place in front of him, but for the moment this milestone seems to be manageable, even exciting! It's the good news that this most recent bourbon and water has brought with it. *Difficulties will be dealt with in their time. Good feelings will prevail.* And yet just as he is starting to settle into this complacency, a certain panic also appears in him, concerning *nervous disorders,* where the messages along the CNS, that Autobahn — normally lickety-split, say about 225 mph — those electrical impulses, because of great emotional stress or chemical pollutants, idle down around the speed of a mere Sunday drive, seventy-five or a hundred, no more. Jesus! Hex is on his feet, routed by this irrational alcoholic terror that his own nerves will somehow become like his mother's. Maybe she is contagious. He crosses the room again. He will listen carefully, but perhaps he will also keep the bottle nearby. *Shit, that tastes good.* He tries the wicker chair closest to her. He loves Friday nights, Fridays and distilled beverages and motor vehicles and attractive women, *women with histories.* The radio turned up loud, the incisors of autumn, the windows rolled down . . .

— and I can think of no better way to put it so I'll just say it without ornament. I believe the only recourse in my case, Dexter, is self-explanatory. I would like you to agree, when appropriate, to end my suffering. I'm terribly sorry to bring this up, but what other way can I proceed? I would like you, in the near future, when I'm no longer able to communicate, to undertake to end my life. Through whatever means necessary. I take the exact point at which this would be appropriate to be sometime in the next year when I lose the last bit of limited movement in my hands, and when speech has finally become completely impossible. However, this deadline should be flexible. I'd like you, Dexter, to evaluate my condition frequently and to make your own judgments, in consultation with me. The reason I suggest this course, as opposed to others I've discussed, is, in the first place, symbolic. With my illness, I've lost my liberty, and through this I've lost the ability to make my own decisions about the quality of my life. Louis, for example, felt he could decide things without consulting me. This next act, which I'd like to undertake with your help, would restore my ability to take an aggressive part in my own life, in a way that would both please me and serve as a fitting conclusion to my ordeal. The second reason for your help is practical: I won't tolerate being a personal or financial drain on my loved ones, meaning you, sweetheart. I'd like to leave some money behind, you know, instead of giving it to nursing homes. I would like to leave something for you. So I want you, Dexter, to make a commitment to me. It bears mentioning that, as far as I'm concerned, the point may well have arrived already, the point when we might think about concluding my term. I'm referring especially to the loss of Louis. These last few days have been unpleasant. Of course, I know that

I'm asking a lot of you, and I want you to feel comfortable, or relatively comfortable, with what you'll have to do. I want you to know, however, that I have arrived at this decision deliberately; I know what this means, and I'm not being rash. I intended to extract the same commitment from Louis, but I hesitated over the years because I believed he would turn me down. I don't have the same doubts about you, Dexter. I trust that you will want to think about this and discuss it with me, as you weigh the pros and cons. Remember, at the same time, that mercy is generous. And Christian. You'll come around to my view. It's just sensible. And rest assured that pain will not be a factor, dear. I won't feel a thing.

When she's done, his mother behaves perversely. Uncharacteristically. As she completes her seminal document, her final wishes, *she hits* Go *on her HandiSpeak software* — such that her nemesis, the Microsoft tax collector woman, begins to sing out to the two of them, mother and son, to sing out the sentences lately composed, in the vault of the living room, as if reciting oven-cleaning instructions or do's and don'ts of water safety. Maybe it's the anguish of recent loss or the seriousness of her purpose that leads Billie to do this, to engage the machine. Or maybe it is simply impulsive. Maybe she recognizes *his distraction,* and wants to reiterate her argument. This last unhappy possibility registers clearly in Hex Raitliffe's spiraling consciousness. *This is the technological equivalent of a desperate appeal,* as that voice, that disembodied voice, becomes again a part of the family: *When I think about my body, I have to remind myself of its condition.* Therefore, Hex works hard to stick with things, to commit this baroque example of his mom's reasoning to memory, and as he does so, passages skitter away and he misses them. He misses the introduction, for example, and only catches up again somewhere in the middle, where she's getting to the part about his hair as a kid. He decides to swivel her wheelchair, to turn her from the desk and the computer, so that she's facing him, and in this way, he reorganizes the discussion — the words ringing out into the room, reboant in the undrapered somberness of the space — so that the evening becomes face-to-face, tête-à-tête. Implications rise up out of the drone of that voice: *I think often about holding your father's hands.* A stern sense of obligation overcomes him, like a kind of nausea. Why not quit trying to avoid, avoid, avoid, like some kid? Why not just shut up? Why not listen carefully. *I will never make love again.* His bald contempt for himself surges. Contempt for being ambulatory. Contempt for being disorganized, irresponsible, for not amounting to much. Contempt for awkwardness in love, for awkwardness generally. Maybe bourbon is not the right thing after all, maybe he should change to wine or beer. *Ma,* he starts to say, forgetting, for a moment, his speech defect, *M-m-m-m-mother,* as the voice, that unstoppable voice of HandiSpeak, without *um's* or *ah's* or other pauses of any kind, as that voice drones on, apostrophizes. *M-ma,* he calls out as the voice rolls over him, *who is up to this?,* and Hex knows the answer, he knows the answer, wishes he could slow it down, *C-c-come on, Mom,* he is interrupting, *I'm here, I'm the one who is here, M-mom, and I'm the one who will st-stay around. So we d-d-d-don't* . . . not wanting to hear the rest of it, certain, in a part of him, some fold between the lobes of his brain, where ribbons of dendrites are transmitting sequences of minor chords, somewhere in this part of his brain, the part concerned with loss, he realizes how this is going to turn out, this conversation. He's trying to interrupt it, *We d-d-don't have t-t-t-to* . . . The voice intones, *The day is coming, after all,* and, you know, if such a thing were possible now, he would say that his mother is almost moving, a little bit; her left hand is trembling. Is this interpretation? Is she actually still? *Don't do what you hate.* No, his mother is trembling now, palpably trembling. It's the end of some constellation of nerves in her. It's the CNS plaque forming as he watches, either that or it's some miraculous episode of remission. Or it's simply routine emotion, profound enough to sweep aside medical histories and prognoses.

— Mom, I won't p-p-p-put you in any d-d-damn hospital. I know what y-you're saying. I understand the situation, and you c-can t-t-trust me, you c-can trust me. If I c-can't b-be here by your side one afternoon, I will make sure that somebody is. I will m-make sure. I'm g-g-gonna rise to the occasion. I'm here for the d-duration, M-mom, p-p-p-p-p —

. . . then caught again on the fucking first syllable, the breath going out of him, huffing, his cheeks red, while his mother is rocking and rolling with ataxia, her left hand, the one responsible for composing this dread note, gone all haywire. In the absence of muscle groups that might enable her to smile or frown or grimace, *this expresses her concern,* and he takes it in, desperate himself to say the one word lodged in him, as the voice goes on —

— P-p-please, please, listen, Mom, I would b-b-be honored to t-take c-care of you, p-p-p-please —

. . . *Which leaves us with one other option.* And his mother's trembling rises to a crescendo. The experts say, of course, that with these demyelinating diseases you should *avoid stressful moments,* avoid emotional stresses, which is like suggesting that his mother should steer clear of the whole panorama of life, steer clear of all its events, his dad's death, her second husband's departure, the house falling down, her crumbling body, and Hex himself, the *stuttering alcoholic* who can't seem to hold down a job. She should *avoid emotional stresses?* The lights in the living room halo his mother as her arm trembles and her lips quiver, her eyes oscillate nystagmically, and she's wincing too, as if she has some neuralgic complaint, sharp pain in the cheekbones and the lips and the forehead, like thumbtacks driven into your face; she could fall out of the chair, it's so bad, her trembling is so bad, and then her head falls forward, and the tears spring forth, and that voice, the last voice in the house with any competence to it, the digital voice, arrives at its forbidding conclusion, *and I can think of no better way to put it so I'll just say it without ornament, Dexter, I would like you to agree to end my suffering* — and thus the truth comes to him, what he's already known, the knowledge as clear as shoplifters in chain stores, nothing hidden from him, nothing undisclosed, and he's on his feet again, holding his own bulky head, its ungainly mass, to and fro across the worn imitation Persian carpet, he's circling the room, and his words when they come from him are inadvertent, reflexive, anguished, *No, n-n-no, no way,* at first, and then, *M-m-mom, no way, if you think . . . If you . . . I d-d-don't c-c-care how b-bad it is, I don't care, I'm n-not going to do it, no way, I've never, you know . . . I c-c-c-couldn't hurt anyone, I have n-never b-been the t-type to hurt anyone, I c-couldn't do it, Mom . . .*

I c-couldn't . . . I c-c-couldn't . . . You'll have to find someone else, that's all, you g-get yourself a specialist, I'm sorry, I'm sorry, and anyway, I already said I would stay and I will I will stay . . . I will, I'll c-c-care for you, but the dental assistant, meanwhile, doesn't admit to interruption and continues with boorish single-mindedness, along her journey of fine pronunciations, until Hex is frozen by the last sentences, as his mother vibrates, and who knows what else, suffers with what optic nerve inflammation, what minor personality disturbance, what paresthesia, dysesthesia, spasticity, or urinary hesitancy, until at last: *Mercy is generous . . . I won't feel a thing.* And then his mother slumps forward out of the chair, seems almost to kick it out from under her. (He's got to remember to affix the tray table to the chair.) Rushing across the room, as she goes face down, sprawled on the carpet, dress hiked up her thighs, in dead man's position, a small cloud of dust rising around her as she comes to rest. He eases his arms under her neck. He encircles her in his arms. Lifts her up.

— Are you all right? Do you w-w-want to lie down?

She whispers:

— I want you to . . . print that out . . . so . . . I can sign it.

— Sign it? How are you going to sign it?

— Just . . . do it, please.

— Wh-what if I won't do it? I m-mean, aren't there l-laws about this stuff? Am I aiding and abetting if I p-p-p-p-print it out? W-why d-don't you call a n-n-notary? L-let's get some l-l-lawyers on the case. Or some m-medical ethicists. Wh-what good's it g-gonna d-d-do if I'm here when you sign it?

Her glasses have fallen from her face, and he can see how her eyes are puffy, bright blue — full of life and woeful at the same time.

— You can't . . . *pretend* . . . that these aren't my wishes . . . Dexter . . . You can't pretend —

— Jesus, it's y-y-your life. I'm just the n-night orderly. Do what you want. D-drink h-hemlock. I d-d-don't c-care. Just not on my w-w-w-watch, you know? D-d-don't m-mind m-me. Okay? Sign anything y-you want to sign.

— If you'd just keep . . . an open mind . . . dear.

It's pretty incoherent what she's saying, it's syllabic purée, but the scariest thing is that he understands her now. Perfectly. Couple of drinks and he knows exactly what she's saying. He holds her like a rag doll, lifting her back up into the chair, turning her to face the computer again. And then he works the keyboard. Pulls down the *edit* menu. *Control P.*

— If I let you sign this thing, are we g-g-g-going to go out to g-get something to eat? Will you d-d-do that with m-me, M-m-mother?

A faintest nod.

And the old dusty dot-matrix printer, Lou's printer, the one that he passed along to Hex's mother when he figured out, a year or so ago, that she wasn't going to use the first-rate laser model they'd given her, the secondhand printer lurches into gear. The daisy wheel goes about firing its automatic rounds. Wham, skritch *wham, WHAM.* And when it's done, Hex clears a spot on the blotter (purple) next to the desktop. Which is the appropriate pen here? Fountain pen? All there is at hand is an old Bic ballpoint, yellow hexagonal casing, blue cap, *Millstone Nuclear Power Plant* printed on the side. He puts it in her left hand, because she's left-handed too (because of her disability), and he holds her lovely, elderly, ringless hand in his, and they draw a diagonal on the bottom of the third page and then a perpendicular, her late-model signature:

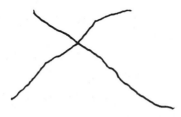

Thank fucking God he can have a hamburger in that hole-in-the-wall with the cavalcade of the past around him *thank God.*

7

But he wants to put it somewhere safe, her son does, that unsettling document. He holds it gingerly, as though there were a danger of spontaneous combustion. He holds it by the corners. He creases it in thirds and sets it carefully on an end table and then ransacks the desk for an envelope, displacing medical bills, statements from her mutual funds, unanswered letters. Louis took care of the paperwork and Louis is gone, with him any system for organizing paperwork, and therefore it's hard to find anything at all. For all Billie Raitliffe knows, it might have been weeks since any bill was paid. She never asked. No envelopes anywhere. A real shortage, she is suddenly aware, of office supplies in general. Her son opens one of the drawers on the lower left side of the rolltop, a drawer of reliquaries, and finds, instead of manila envelopes, a stack of yellowed, flaking historical documents. *She had always been a clipper of newspaper articles.* She used to send things to family and friends. She used to send Hex reams of clippings, week after week, year after year. And though he wants to eat, though the restaurants will stop serving by half past nine, he thumbs these exhibits for a moment. Holds them up, wordlessly: a dinner menu from a Republican fundraiser in New York City, 1956 (they had met Richard Nixon — the entrée had been Dover sole), an article from *Town and Country* about hydroponic vegetable gardens, a number of cheaply printed pamphlets arguing for new, common-sense treatments of neurological complaints that featured almonds, very large doses of vitamin C, and low-fat diets, and then Hex's father's obituary, in multiple copies, from the *New London Day* of December 16, 1963. Her son pauses:

Allen Hamilton Raitliffe of 39 Flager Drive, Fenwick, philanthropist and collector of antiques, died Monday, apparently of cardiac arrest, after a long illness. He was thirty-nine years old. Mr. Raitliffe was born in Concord, Massachusetts, where he attended Concord Academy as a day student until his graduation in 1942. He matriculated at Harvard University, studying Classics, with a minor in Theology. He left the university without a degree, however, to enlist in the United States Army in January 1944. In the services, he attained the rank of lieutenant in the Army Signal Corps. Mr. Raitliffe graduated magna cum laude from Harvard after an honorable discharge. In 1946, Allen Raitliffe married Barbara Ashton Danforth of Boston. Mrs. Raitliffe attended Radcliffe, from which she graduated in 1944. In 1949, the Raitliffes moved to New York City, where, after several years at the Guaranty Trust Company, Mr. Raitliffe founded a trucking and air frieght company, Allied Interstate, from which he retired in 1957. He then moved to the Old Saybrook area, where he began his work on civic projects and the collecting of Revolutionary-era antiques. The people of southeastern Connecticut will long remember Allen Raitliffe's gregarious and unselfish contribution to the region. He was active on the membership committee of Fenwick Country Club and in local politics, he was a generous member of the congregation at Grace Church, and he was an avid hunter, fisherman, and amateur taxidermist. For many years, during the summer, he also served as the Sunday lifeguard at Rocky Point State Park. Mr. Raitliffe is survived by his wife, and by a son, Dexter Allen Ashton Raitliffe.

Beside the article, two columns wide, a picture of Allen, smiling — his enormous head, his conspiratorial smile — threatening to burst from pictorial confinement. Had it not been for the president's assassination some weeks earlier, he might well have commanded more space.

— F-f-forgot how f-full of shit that th-thing is, Hex says, shoving the obituary back into the drawer. He apparently forgets, too, his reason for being here at the desk, as he ignores her *living will* on the end table and rises to his feet, all business, all activity, scuttling around behind her. — D-d-disinformation, you know. He w-w-was g-good at it even b-b-b-b-b —

It goes back many years, their suspicion that Allen had composed the obituary himself, though she couldn't imagine at the time why a man his age, a young man, would have written his own obituary, except from sheer morbidity, and why he would have purposefully lied about his education, his military record, his background, his wife's background, even his own middle name. No reason but perversity. All the same, it was true that after the war he almost never spoke of his work, in the Southwest, as he had also been very private about his later involvement with mining. Allen created and nurtured the idea that he was a *Yankee*, that his roots were entwined with the origins of the nation. But this was just longing. He was from the Midwest, from Minnesota, and when he left the Midwest, he left his parents behind, and when he left the Southwest for New York City, he left his friends there, and when he left New York City, he rarely went back. He died in New England, and had himself cremated, scattered in the Long Island Sound, far from his origins. That's who he was.

— Even b-b-before it was in vogue. He was the original p-p-p-publicist, Hex says. — A liar and a fraud. What c-c-coat do you want to wear? Do you w-want to wear that, uh, p-parka?

Hex glides her to a stop by the closet in the front hall, where the loose hangers chime as the door opens, and in the midst of a plastic-wrapped thicket he manages to find and liberate her port wine, quilted, pleated, full-length winter parka. He holds it aloft.

— G-good enough? D-do you think you c-c-c-could keep the ends of the coat out of the wheels there? It'll g-g-get frayed. You'll have feathers trailing after you —

Stretching out her spastic arm, pulling hard on it, until it goes limp and falls at her side, Hex stuffs this extremity into a sleeve and, reaching down at the cuff for her hand, tugs her fingers through.

She had tried to tell Dexter about the business in New Mexico, about his father's work; she had sat him down one day, after the memorial service, *Dexter, there are some things I need to discuss with you about your dad,* but it had been an oddly fruitless conversation. Her boy had resisted the facts. It hadn't occurred to him that there were gaps in Allen's story. He had never asked about the branches of his family, about his grandparents, about ancestry at all. Not after his father died. He'd contented himself with an annual birthday card from his living grandparents, as he had been content with whatever meager information was parceled out to him over the years.

Similarly, when he was going on ten years old, she had determined that it was time to explain to Hex *the miracle of conception.* But after she gave him a rather technical book on the subject, *Human Propagation,* by the United Christian Publications — *The man and the woman can lie quite comfortably side by side as they prepare for sleep, during which time the man will insert his penis, now fully engorged, into the woman's sheath and thereby christen the ovum, according to nature's will for the procreation of families* — again he'd asked no questions.

It's been a week since she was outdoors. Hex pushes her slowly down the ramp out front. Then into the driveway. Her chair throws gravel. A delightful sound. And there are gulls overhead. Streetlamps bathe Flagler — where the golf carts travel — austere streetlamps with fool's gold illumination. The links are quiet tonight. Summers past, lovers darted in and out of the bushes out here, running across her lawn and the lawns of neighbors, on the way to their escapades on the front nine, but now it's autumn, and they're gone.

— N-nice night, her son offers. — And you've g-g-got great c-c-company. And so what's to c-complain about? Why p-p-pull the p-p-p-p-plug tonight? Why n-not hang around and see how dinner t-turns out? Could be a f-fine evening.

She sighs.

— I don't need your . . . your smart remarks, Dexter . . . Sometimes . . . painful subjects . . . are unavoidable . . . as I think you should know . . . by now.

You see, their past conversations too had faltered along those lines — for example, *Your father was in the war, and he worked in a very secret part of the war effort, which had to do with the making of certain kinds of weapons.* The Limited Test Ban Treaty had been negotiated, oh, she didn't know, three or four months before the assassination, three or four months before this heart-to-heart with the young Hex, and she supposed he must have heard *something* about it (*desiring to put an end to the contamination of man's environment by radioactive substances . . .*) Didn't children absorb these things from the radio or the television? Didn't they learn about them in school? And weren't these discussions especially compelling to young boys? Wasn't this how they settled playground disputes? (*My dad will launch a thermonuclear-tipped ICBM at your dad and blow his stupid head off.*) Not Hex Raitliffe. *At some point you will want to know these things, I imagine, so I think I ought to tell you that your father was involved in some tests where people were hurt, and he regretted it — to his surprise he regretted it — and that was when he left the military. He left because of these things. He didn't want any part of that trouble. Some civilians were hurt and some military men. And when we came east, he stopped talking about this part of life, and about the years when he was in the military and afterward, and I didn't bother him with it. He left all of that behind. And he was exposed to things, more than once in his life. You see, these were important positions of responsibility your dad had, and they were dangerous. He was injured, and we don't know, but it's possible that these incidents from the past affected his health, you know. It's possible.* And here two lines of discussion, the truth of ancestry and the mystery of conception, converged — in the kitchen, in the early sixties, and she went on, *And, after the war, your father, well, was unable to sire children. The two of us could not have children. You understand what that means? Sweetheart? He might have been sterile before the war, darling, but it was unlikely. He believed it had to do with his work. It was the cause of a lot of sadness for him. But just as we were giving up hope of having you, of having our own baby, I became pregnant! It was a miracle! You were a little gift from God. You were unsuspected, and the more so loved for it. Your dad loved you so, Dexter, he loved us both.* The further she went in explicating these events, the less sure she was of the endeavor. What was important about it, after all? There seemed to be only loose ends here, narratives that spun out limitlessly. It was like Allen's own work, his physics, where one theory spawned another without conclusion. The proof was right in front of her: Hex fidgeted at the table in the kitchen. He was too *young* for this. He wanted to talk about anything else. About the New York Yankees. About popular music. He was ten years old, and his father's bone fragments had been scattered in the Long Island Sound, and his mother couldn't stop talking.

— I wanted to . . . be a scientist, too, she offers, as he opens the passenger door of the rented Ford Taurus. — Did you know that? I wanted to study astronomy. But then . . . I just wanted *you*, I wanted a baby . . . that was the thing I was really interested in . . . and you were the answer . . . to a particular set of dreams —

— Sure, he slides his hands under her bottom, groans, lifts. Then she's in his arms and he staggers with her for a moment, her dress billowing. He falls away from the car, catching his balance, his face close to hers, the sky with rippling clouds over her head. The wheelchair, braked by the car door, rolls when he collides with it. It topples over. — Shit. D-do we have to have all these inc-c-credibly heavy c-conversations now? Here's what's on m-my m-mind. I want a *flame-broiled b-b-burger with ch-cheese* and a b-beer and after that I'll t-t-talk about anything, I'll talk about whether y-you have stockpiled enough b-b-barbiturates or about the b-best kinds of nooses or wh-whatever —

He lurches back over by the Taurus, sets her on the hood for a second, rests, and then manages to edge her around the door and into the passenger seat. He smooths her dress. Her left arm is trembling slightly and she's self-conscious about it. She also notices a mild but nonetheless unnerving sensation of urinary urgency, which reminds her:

— Darling . . . I have a feeling . . . that I should have a . . . a *diaper* . . . for the trip . . . and also the catheter. . . . You might want to check . . . in the living room.

— Oh. Sure. Sorry.

She waits.

These mysteries of ancestral history, they render her confused and sleepy. Is there any guarantee that Allen's parents weren't concealing their origins too? Is there any guarantee that they weren't, in fact, from Massachusetts, as Allen had once claimed? Or from the Bay State? Or from the island of Manhattan? Is there any reliable evidence that the name Raitliffe was not as old as the thirteen original colonies, as old as the Puritan vessels that landed on the coastline of Maine, as old as the White Mountains; is there any guarantee that all these Raitliffes did not incline toward some Old World sire, some medieval publican in the candlelight of old Europe? And what about her own family, which seemed to appear and flourish and disappear all in the space of the Great Depression? This investigation doesn't do any more than yield an interpretation of *the person doing the interpreting*. So what will Hex learn by chasing down all these stories? *That when you're an American there's an ocean between yourself and your ancestral home.*

Billie's breath clouds around her head, fogs the windows. She smells new vinyl and regular unleaded. There's a gas reek. Hex returns with coils of transparent medical plastic tubing, an empty IV bag, a diaper. He throws these in the backseat and then folds the wheelchair — tipped onto its side in the driveway — and stores it in back as well. Then he straps himself behind the wheel. He eyes the control panels suspiciously.

— Radio?

The receiver is already tuned to a twenty-four-hour news station. *Keeping you informed of this situation as it develops.* Hex thumbs the search button and the radio goes surfing through morsels, passing over the bombast of contemporary dance music and steel drums of salsa, country and western, until at last he finds what he's looking for, a faint signal on the lower end of the dial, where white noise is indistinguishable from the chanting of Himalayan monks.

As they pull out onto Flagler, crawling, they fall in and out of the beam of the Fenwick Light, sweeping parabolically over the coast. Dozens of luxury homes surround the lighthouse now, so many houses that it shocks her. There's a disparity between the town she remembers, the one in which she settled, and the one she now inhabits. Back then, it was a well-kept secret, a coastal town with a Revolutionary War history, but otherwise neglected, more so than the more glamorous hamlets or fishing villages further east, Mystic, Stonington, Watch Hill, Newport. Fenwick had been *a marsh*, a salt marsh with cattails clogging the harbors and inlets, with shallow waterways impenetrable for anglers and pleasure boaters, a marsh swarming with *stinging flies* and crabs and osprey and heron and sandpipers, all manner of seabirds. Back then, it was the wrong part of the coast, as resorts went. But now the coast is all one resort, there is no relief from the vulgarity of resorts and their short-timers. Old Saybrook and Fenwick are *condominium communities*, Sunset Gables and Pleasant Point and Marshland Estates — and there are motels and motels and motels, and chain stores, and artificial owner's associations to keep out undesirables. Hex makes a right onto 156 and onto the causeway, and there some melancholy in her heart gives way, and she forgets her troubles for a moment, because it was this single reason she moved here, really, this stretch of road, without shoulders, through the marsh, a narrow pavement with a tiny footbridge beside it, three quarters of a mile across the salt marsh to Old Saybrook, right at water level, a part of that living silence, that lovely neglected beauty, and the car, which Hex is driving with the appropriate leisure, weaves a little. They could plunge right in. Across the water, reflected, are the lights of town, the irregular coast of the peninsula, and then around the point on the other side, there is the sea, out toward Old Lyme, and Niantic, and Waterford, and the night is so clear you can make out the lights of Orient Point, on Long Island; this is the spot where river and harbor meet, and all this provisional architecture, this vulgarity of development pales beside the *opening out*. If there were one reason, this would be it, the reason she brought Allen here, away from the city, to this sight, to take in the view, in this two and a half minutes across the causeway, where the best-laid plans of civilization seem contingent, temporary.

— Well, the T-tavern is one p-possibility, Hex says. — Or we c-c-could try P-p-p-p . . . With a gloved hand, he pounds on the steering wheel. — P-p-penelope's P-p-pantry, he mumbles.

— It's up to you . . . dear. I don't . . . know as I . . . will eat much.

And he makes the left off the causeway, at old Fort Saybrook, by the motel there, and they head along Main, past the grand houses in town, the houses of the River Gods, as they used to be called by local tradesmen, those grand houses with their grand porches and their columns and their half acres, along Main past Grace Church, past the Fire Department (the complement of trucks out on a drill), and down through the center of town, where the avenues converge. Hex makes the left onto the Boston Post Road, in Billie's opinion a road of merciless superficiality, where consumers come to get fleeced, and transients hurtle past. It's here that Penelope's Pantry beckons to them, run-down, uninviting, plain.

She should give him the letters, she thinks. What excuse for not having done so already? She should give him all the letters. Some of them are in the very same desk drawer, the very drawer in which he was digging. Not far down in the archaeological layers of that drawer, not far down from the obituary, in the sediment of personal effects:

5/21/46

Dear B:

This is hard to write but I'll do my best. Today there was an accident in the lab. Slotin was doing some last-minute preparations before going south. He was showing off the designs. That guy Hinkley who's taking over the division, he wanted to know a thing or two, so Slotin was taking him around. We'd already packed up trunks and crates to ship off to the Pacific, but Hinkley had some questions about how things were calibrated. So Slotin says come on down we'll take a look. I was also in the lab, with Kline. The boss had that mischievous expression, you know. He knew he shouldn't have been in there at that hour running a reaction for show, but he's the top dog. And the precautions were minimal because he's done it a thousand times before. Didn't make a bit of difference if we hadn't gotten a full night's sleep lately.

They sealed off the lab door. Hinkley was on one side of the table, by the door, Slotin on the other. Slotin had the two halves of this assembly, you know, like grapefruit halves. You fit them together, slot A into slot B, and you have a controlled reaction, just a few particles back and forth, not much. Hooked up to a Geiger counter, you'd read a little energy. You could run your front porch light with it.

But the fact is you have to be careful to fit the pieces together properly, that's the key. And Slotin, while he's trying to fit the top on, he takes out the strip that keeps the halves apart, an eighth-of-an-inch strip, and he's talking to Hinkley the whole time about weather in the Pacific and how the girls in Hawaii are terrific, all that, and then he's about to pick up the stay that secures the top half when he drops the whole thing. I was watching and I still don't know exactly how he did it. He just drops the top piece, simple as dropping a hammer into a tool-box, and the two halves fall together.

The worst part was I knew what had happened. I knew. Slotin did too. It was a prompt burst. There was a glow. I don't know any better way to put it. It was blue at first, anyway, and then a lavender color. The room was lit up. In a fraction of a second. Fast as he could, Slotin — who had wedged his thumb between the two pieces — pried the pieces apart. It didn't matter, though. I heard the Geiger counters peaking before I even recognized what the sound was. I'd never heard them go crazy like that before. Slotin got the pieces apart, and looked up at Hinkley. I could see Hinkley's expression, shaken. And that's when Slotin looked around at me and Kline, "You fellas better telephone the infirmary."

We called the director, too, let the brass know, and then we just waited out in the hall. All four of us. What else could we do? I found a couple of blankets next door — we used to nap in the next lab — and I wrapped a blanket around Slotin. I asked him what he thought the dose was. "I wish I knew," that's what he said. Then he got sick. On the floor. That was the least of his problems. Hinkley was totally ashen. He was close enough, you know, to be contaminated. Any of us was close enough. But this was his first night in New Mexico. He didn't figure on so much trouble.

By the time they got us to the infirmary, Slotin already had burn marks on him. His thumbnail was dead from where he had pried the spheres apart. It looked like he'd picked up a hot skillet. They ran us through the showers. There was a battery of tests. The nurses were wearing protective gear, you know, some kind of protective fabric, while they were walking us through all this. To protect themselves. It was the loneliest feeling I've ever had, Billie, I can tell you that. Nobody knows for sure what the situation is, so we just have to wait. That's where I am now.

The truth is, it looks like Slotin's got the brunt of it. Kline and I were standing on the other side of the lab, so he got the short-range dose. That distance makes a difference. His hands are already twice their size, and the nurses packed them in ice. He's trying to keep his sense of humor, even though he knows. He watched Bowman fall ill just a couple of months ago. They were friends. I guess the doctors were able to run calculations on Slotin, based on the small change in his pocket, the nickles and dimes, and the same with me. Thank God for those denominations. The boss got about 1,000 rads — that's all there is to say about that. I always looked up to him. All the same, I wish I hadn't been working late last night.

I'll call you later. A shoe store's worth of X-rays is what I got, honey, that's what they're telling me. And a good scare. So don't worry too much. I'm going to try to sleep tonight if I can. The censor, who's made an exception here, reminds you to destroy this. Say a little prayer for me. And for Slotin and Hinkley, too. Will you?

Your loving,
Allen.

8

Specialty of the house: seafood. The regional cuisine. Chowders, all manner of chowders, Manhattan and New England. These listed first on the upper left of the laminated menus: beneath *Penelope's Pantry* in a cursive rich with flourishes. Then entrées, including lobster, whitefish — a half-dozen varieties of forgettable whitefish, scrod (breaded, broiled, sautéed), cod, halibut, haddock, flounder — and, for the big spender, a questionable salmon steak recently trucked great lengths on the interstate. Salmon in a state of decay. Or tuna. These broiled with a touch of lemon. In the local style. And for the family — since Penelope's takes pride in being a family restaurant — for the little ones, half-sizes of these seafood platters, or, if they prefer — *Mom, I hate fish!* — there are burgers too, every sort of burger, patties disguised with cheddar and mozzarella and chili and bacon and sauerkraut. It's toward these burgers that Hex Raitliffe races — from the parking lot — because in the consumption of seafood, he waits anxiously through the four to six hours that mark the event horizon of fish- or shellfish-related food poisoning; in the consumption of seafood, he is compelled to imagine *induced projectile-vomiting* and stomach pumps and intravenous feeding. The fish of southeastern Connecticut are radioactive, anyway, what with the nuke plant and the sub base, and so he will not take the risk. No, Hex wants beef. The meat that made America great. He wants to use condiments excessively. He wants to indulge in fats and sodium. And he wants to drink. With great effort, he backs his mother up the three steps out front and leaves her at their summit, just inside the door, holding it open — serving as her own deluxe doorstop — while he hurriedly acquaints himself with the maitre d' — *T-table for t-t-two, p-p-please* — a squeaky-clean teenage girl in corduroys and pink turtleneck sweater whose plastic name tag reads *Jeanine*. She shows him to a booth (there are only booths) in the no-smoking section. Hex hangs his tweed suit coat on the hook there — it's his first moment alone all afternoon — and then, in stage two of the ordeal, he goes back for his mom. She's still holding the door open. A pair of drunks are saluting her on their way to the parking lot. As he wheels his mother into the dining area, the ambient noise in Penelope's Pantry dwindles and the patrons eye Hex and his mother, as they have often done, in the guileless Yankee fashion. The interior of the restaurant is red. The banquettes are red and the faux-velvet wallpaper is red and the fixtures have red bulbs, and the plastic bowls at the salad bar, where there is wilted lettuce and cabbage, are red, and the lobster bibs are white on a red field, and the apron their waitress (Laurie) is wearing is red, as is the bow in her hair. She swabs the table in front of them with an old, pickled rag. Then, in a sort of clown show, Hex begins removing Billie Raitliffe from her wheelchair. Manually, he lifts one of her feet, one orthopedic shoe, from the steel footrest and sets this extremity upon the matted red carpet. Then the other. He hoists his mother up, and with his hip nudges the chair out of the way. So that she won't block Jeanine and the wait staff in the service aisle, he drags her, under the arms, over to the banquette, until her foot becomes hooked around one of the legs of the table and he tries to force this impediment free by thrusting, with one mighty effort, his mother's body into the booth; however, force proves ineffective and his mother falls over on her side — half in, half out of the booth, and he *collapses onto her, shit*, his shoulder mashing into one of her breasts, an elbow lancing her in the pancreas, her head lodged between the seat and backrest portions of the booth's vinyl upholstery, asphyxiating her, her foot still somehow fish-hooked on the table leg, and as he tries to untangle himself from her, and her from the table, he knocks her glasses from her face, and these tumble under the table, skidding distantly across a plastic rug protector. Out of reach. He heaves his mother up straight (at last), pushing her into the interior of the booth, and *crawls down under the table* to look for the glasses. Bangs his head on the underside, on one of the struts, as he goes. Damn. It's like spelunking down here. Petrified chewing gum and hardened snot stucco the underside of the table. He can barely fit. Through deltas of mud and dust and discarded shrink wrap, he reaches for the spectacles, which have come to rest near the chubby ankle (in sagging beige stockings) of a woman from the next booth. He estimates: she's in her sixties. In this light, the ankle looks marbleized. Synthetic. Or maybe it's just that the stockings are leopard-skinned with gravy and slush. As he reaches delicately for the frames, a second ankle swings dangerously close to his face *from out of nowhere!*, and grazes his nose. One orthopedic toe scratches the other ankle protectively. As if aware of an intruder. Nonetheless, Hex eases the frames away from these sentinels without startling the woman. Half an inch at a time. Suppressing his breathing as best he can. *Success!* He is flushed with accomplishment, and retraces his path, banging his head a second time on the transverse, mumbling oaths. Emerging from this dusty recess, at last, he frees the wheelchair from the middle of the service aisle and lays it out on the other banquette. *Are you okay, Mom? Is there a b-b-better way to d-do this stuff?*

There isn't. And it doesn't concern him anyway. He's more concerned with his dinner out. He takes in the interior — the style and dialect of Penelope's. His assessment? Trolling and baiting and gaffing and reeling are not simply locutions from the menu (*The Fisherman's Nets! Chowders and Grogs! Crustacean Cove!*), they are also the language, here, of *the bar*. Which is to say that in a town with no nightlife in the off-season, when the motels are shuttered, and the yacht club is open only on Sundays, and the affluent weekenders come in dwindling numbers — Penelope's bar is the pickup joint by default. On the other side of the salad cart, therefore — just beyond the lobster tank — where the bartender is staring vacantly, arms folded, at a tiny, squeaky television monitor mounted in a recessed shelf, the drunks of Old Saybrook are gathered silently, in a tenebrous light, casting for their catch. They seem as immobilized as the bartender, but Hex knows the way they will turn each to each to whisper their desperations. *When they're good and polluted.* As Hex's eyes grow accustomed to the fish-tank interior of Penelope's, he thinks he begins to recognize these lost souls. In addition to the union guys and contractors, in addition to the indigent, the pensioners, the retirees at Penelope's Pantry, there are also examples of the advantaged, the attractive sons and daughters of the ruling classes, those direct descendants of our founding fathers, sons and daughters who have taken a bad turn. For example, he thinks that the woman in the *suede, fringed jacket* is Jane Ingersoll, the girl he had a crush on in tenth grade. And next to her is Mr. Shaw, the janitor from the ice rink in Old Saybrook, in what looks to be a *purple Ban-Lon shirt.* Then, beside Mr. Shaw, there's Dick Flansburgh, town selectman. In the sixties, if Hex remembers correctly, he was the captain of the fifteen-and-under sailing team at the yacht club. In fact, he's wearing a nautical cap — to cover a bald patch. They're all there, in the pixillating light of the bar television (swirling siren tones). Absently watching the news. If it's not them, well, *close enough.*

Soon, Laurie, their waitress, startles him from philosophies.

— C-c-could you tell us the specials?

— Above your head, Laurie points brusquely. It's true. He has overlooked the chalkboard. It offers minor variations on the regular menu. *Scrod in white wine sauce. Seared, blackened flounder.* The nouvelle preparations are far too ambitious for the operation. — D-d-do you kn-know what you want, Ma?

Billie Raitliffe, whose spirits seem to have ebbed considerably since they emerged from the car, whispers:

— Soup . . .

— Fish chowder, for my mother p-p-p-p —

His expression is importunate as he tries to get the word out. He looks up at Laurie, who with pencil stub in hand awaits the revelation of his choice as if she will score him on it. The interval extends beyond what is tolerable, and his face reddens, and a sheen of perspiration appears on his forehead, until at last he catches a breath: — please, and for myself, a chili b-b-burger, with Monterey Jack cheese, and single-malt scotch on the rocks, thank you, L-laurie —

Before he can even punctuate the thought, she snaps up the menus and is off, gesturing dismissively at the salad bar, mumbling *about Roquefort and all you can eat*. Hex glances forlornly in this direction. What Laurie has interrupted — the projection of certain characters of his youth onto a crew of local barflies — is itself an interruption of a more important exchange taking place between himself and his mother, and as Laurie leaves them there to wait, this dreadful situation seems to hover over the Raitliffes again. He rests one palm flat upon his mother's back; he looks into her wooden features, *K-kind of rude, wasn't she?*, knowing which subject is in the air, denying it at the same time, performing both these actions simultaneously, recognition and concealment, so that as he looks at his mother, he is suddenly terribly worried, and would do anything not to have the responsibility that is now his — *Relax*, he advises himself, *have a drink* — would do anything to avoid this interregnum in his regular old life — *d-d-damn, he forgot to take her coat off* — the interregnum featuring his declining mom and her exhaustion and the chilling suddenness of her mood swings, from cheerful and ebullient to hopeless beyond comfort in fifteen minutes. Her arm is trembling again. He would do anything not to have these responsibilities stretching out in front of him. He's certain, without reservation, *that he's not up to it*, that he won't be able to bear her weight, the cycles of sorrow and neurological dysfunction. He will flee. She's as weak and vulnerable as she believes herself to be and he is too, but before he can get up to leave, *fleeing just like his stepfather* in his late-model domestic Hertz rental with the unusual petroleum leakage, *Qui transtulit sustinet*, this instant passes away, mutates into some related pall, and *he doesn't care*. Doesn't give a damn. He doesn't have to diaper her right now, *at this exact moment*, doesn't have to clean her bedsores, doesn't have to arrange for her autopsy, and so his attention lights on anything else, on the smallish crowd that seems to be gathering around the television at the bar —

— You know? he says to his mother, — I c-c-could swear that that blond woman at the b-bar is Jane Ingersoll, the g-g-girl I had a c-c-crush on in the n-ninth grade. Or tenth.

His mother emerges temporarily from her reverie.

— It's a small town. . . .

— I'm g-g-going to have to g-go in for a closer look. After we eat.

Laurie deposits a drink in front of him.

— Have you b-become upset about something? Mom? You've g-g-gotten kind of quiet. You know, you c-c-can t-tell me, M-mom. If you've b-b-become upset about something.

His mother says nothing. Her eyes, murky, full of judgment, are clotted in their corners with some mucoid solid. She says nothing.

— You kn-know, sometimes you g-get these sudden shifts of mood, M-mom. It c-comes with the turf. With the illness. C-could b-be that you are experiencing one n-now.

She says nothing. Hex reaches with a red cloth napkin, and, lifting her glasses, raises it to wipe her eyes.

— Or maybe you are upset with me b-because of what we've b-been t-t-talking about. Which I can understand. B-but if I'm g-gonna t-try to embrace your p-p-point of view, you can t-t-try to embrace mine, too. You know, like the free exch-ch-ch . . . like the marketplace of ideas. Imagine wh-what's involved for m-me. See what I mean?

Then there's a commotion. At the next booth, as before, there's a party of five, including an elderly woman with hair of regal blue — the woman, in all probability, with the baggy nylons. In small-town form, Jeanine, the maitre d', has seated Hex and his mother *right next to this party*, though there are a half-dozen tables beyond them, all empty and inviting. Hex notices that after several minutes of his private conversation with his mother these locals, the blue-haired woman and her cronies, her bridge partners, suddenly repair to the most distant corner of the dining area. They get up, carrying their salads, their iceberg-and-bacon-bits-with-creamy-Italian salads, and their White Russians, to relocate. Away from the waves of his stammer, the fluctuations of it. It's not unusual.

— Why d-d-don't you just t-t-tell me what you are thinking for a change? he says to Billie Raitliffe. — Wh-why d-don't we just start there? Huh?

She does.

— Don't condescend to me. . . . No wonder . . . that you can't see . . . that the request I've made has . . . its justifications. . . . Furthermore . . . if you think . . . you can leave me . . . sitting out in the parking lot, while you —

— Oh, c-come on. You're just upset, Hex says, — and if *he* hadn't . . . if Lou wasn't a d-d-deadbeat, we wouldn't even be having this c-c-conversation. Let's invite the b-b-background issues up into the foreground, M-ma. Right?

— *You wretched . . . young man!* As his mother proceeds slowly through her exclamation her voice rises in cycles, in volume, up into some glass-shattering frequency, and that party of bridge players, including the elderly woman with the blue hair, stares with alarm and disapproval as Hex tries to calm his mother down, whispers, sips his drink, rubs her back sympathetically. He's perspired clear through his T-shirt and even his vintage dress shirt is beginning to stick to his back.

— J-jesus, Mom —

— Don't patronize . . . me —

— Look, I'm sorry. I d-d-don't mean to . . . judge the guy. But seriously . . . You're p-p-p-piling traumas up right now. You know? I think we should just t-try to have a d-decent supper and not solve all the p-p-p-problems of the world. Let's n-not stray into g-groundbreaking l-legal t-terrain just for a little wh-while. W-we have to g-get used to one another, you know? Let's just t-take a weekend to g-get used to one another's c-c-company. I promise to make affection the order of the d-day. I really do.

But she has begun to cry already, succumbing to choked gasps and wails uncatalogued in the usual range of human expressions (consider the overtaxed muscle groups in her throat, consider the seizing and cramping), and Hex leans into his mother, holds her against his chest; it is all coming out now, the seasons of her frustration are coming out. He can do no better than watch it happen. And he's not the only one watching. All of Penelope's is watching. A hush has fallen over this fine eatery. The sound of an ice cube rolling around the bottom of a highball. Even the televised news has taken second place to the spectacle of the Raitliffes. Hex nervously finishes the last of his scotch. He smiles. By the time Laurie brings the food, his mother has drifted off into mute intransigence. She will not move from where she rests — her head against his collarbone. She will not speak. Even Laurie, who seemed so unpleasant before, sets down the soup and the cheeseburger with an expeditious pity. He looks up at his waitress apologetically. And then points at the drink. *Another, please.*

— Look, Hex says to his mother. — I haven't eaten anything since I h-had some fries on the road this afternoon. I'm g-g-gonna wolf this d-down, and I'm g-going to feed you some of this soup, okay? J-just d-do me a favor and eat something, okay? C-can we just make this easy for now? P-p-please?

He wipes his mother's nose with the red napkin, refixes her glasses, but she doesn't reply. He leans her forcibly back against the banquette, and stirs the seafood chowder. Then he holds up a sample spoonful. *C-c'mon, Mom. Eat.* It's no use. She won't even register the edge of the soupspoon at her lips. And then he realizes. *She's asleep.* That fast. He sighs again. The bar — its attentions are so fickle — has forgotten about him now, too. They are back at the five-alarmer on the television, and he's able to lean Billie Raitliffe in the corner of the booth, to ignore her, to eat in peace. His cheeseburger. A revelation from the inmost sanctum of our double-coupon American culture. Its rareness almost an emergency. A petri dish for *E. coli,* crimson and raw, like a splatter wound. It tastes damn good. It tastes like a thousand bucks. A pride swells in him. Hex feels a sort of pride in his cheeseburger, *how it reaches back to the cattlemen of the West, those libertarians with their traditional values, those survivalist cattlemen, those vigilantes, tamers of nature, his cheeseburger and the Great Plains, those plains and the religious families that rid the West of Native American vermin; his cheeseburger and purple mountains and fruited plains; he loves his cheeseburger; he will eat more than one; he will give himself over to cheeseburgers: eight ounces of premium beef on a toasted bun with onion flakes, iceberg lettuce and rock-hard hothouse tomatoes, artificial cheese food product from an industrial-sized squeezable (recyclable), no-brand ketchup and ballpark mustard, ringed with Tater Tots and ripple-sliced pickles! Save the West! Eat a burger!*

— What's with her, anyway? Laurie says, breaking into his ravenous silence. — If you don't mind my asking.

Hex has devoured his meal breathlessly and has made a serious dent in another drink. The waitress stands with one hip cocked at the edge of the faux-wood-grain tabletop. With her pencil stub, she points at his mother.

— Well, uh . . . he trembles. The sudden responsibilities of conversation. In fact, Hex can feel the hysterical choking in himself already. Because Laurie is attractive, in a seaside way, even if she has a bit too much rouge on, a little too much eyeshadow. Furthermore, she's being friendly, though it's an affability with some sort of purpose behind it. She leans over the table. Gathers up the lukewarm bowl of chowder. *Want me to wrap this up?* Pity is vulgar; it's not an emotion favored in the society Hex was ambitiously bred to resemble. But he's not above the attention. He smiles back.

— She's . . . uh . . . she has wh-what they c-c-call a d-d-d-demyelinating d-d-disease. You know, a n-n-neurological d-disease. Like, uh, m-m-multiple, like, uh, *multiple sclerosis.* Except that MS is sup-p-p-posed to quit p-p-p-progressing in, uh, l-late middle age. Well, y-you, uh . . .

He's liable to tell her the whole story.

— M-m-myelin is a s-sort of a sheath thing, on the n-nerves and —

— Wow, Laurie says.

Hex nods.

— And you know, L-L-lou G-gehrig's d-d-disease, which is —

— On the Yankees. Sure. Hey, is your name, like, *Raitland* or something?

— W-well, yeah. R-R-raitl-l-l —

— Because my friend, Kathleen . . . Here Hex looks over at the bar and sees a woman waving. In fact, *it's the very woman he thought was Jane Ingersoll.* — She says she knew you. Way back when. Or else her sister did or something. That's what she told me.

— It's p-p-p —

Laurie the waitress sits down abruptly in the booth. Shoves the folded wheelchair over and sits on the edge of the banquette.

— Could be, Hex says.

— Kathy Ingersoll, that's my friend's name. Kathleen.

— Oh, well, th-that *is* a c-c-coincidence! That's w-w-wild! B-because when I c-c-c-c . . . when I first c-came in, I thought she w-w-was Jane! I thought she *w-w-was* her sister. You know, it's amazing, b-b-because I haven't b-b-been out here —

— Isn't that cool? Hey, Kathy!

Laurie stands up again, taking with her the soup bowl and the empty scotch (it will cycle back to Hex again as a buy back), and as she heads in that direction, with word of coincidence, toward the lobster tank and beyond, to the bar, heading as though her movement were choreographed with some equal and opposite movement on the part of others, as though *some surpassing perfection of coincidence* has now descended on Hex Raitliffe's weekend, as though coincidence is bound up with other coincidences affecting other lives, *as Laurie heads in that direction, Kathleen Ingersoll herself rises up from her bar stool,* in gray suede mini and fishnets, *wow,* and a pink lacy, frilly low-cut top of some kind, and suede, fringed jacket, and her gait is so enthusiastic and good-natured that Hex can't help theorizing that all bodily movement — all dance steps, all somnambulistic wobbles, all insomniac twisting and turning, even the tics of neuropathology, *the whole history of human kinesthetics* — is simply a series of analogs for the very personal shudder that passes through a body at the moment of erotic transport, well, maybe it's a *guy thing,* but Kathleen's movements are locked into some synchrony with Laurie's movements, and that isn't all, there are even more variables in this balletic instant, because, with *the triple axel* that brings Kathleen from her stool, Kathleen Ingersoll is brought into the gravitational field of *the doorway,* which now swings back to emit into Penelope's another luckless drinker, and as Kathleen is bouncing or even *bounding* in the direction of Laurie and thus in the direction of Hex, in the direction of nostalgia, this *negatively charged drinker,* a small, waifish woman head to toe in black, in black velveteen leggings and black oversized sweater and black denim jacket, with hair dyed black (save for the streaks of green), tangled and unruly, wearing really garish eyeglasses, who is looking at her feet, she *collides* with Kathleen, in the doorway, or rather Kathleen veers close to this *green-haired lesbian* (Hex's prejudice), who then puts up her hands, as if to avoid collision, and *squeaks* incongruously, as between them there is a moment of recognition, a double-take of recognition, perhaps with a dollop of cool at first — cool recalibrated immediately into *superficial tenderness* — and collision thus ends in embrace and the two polaric ions of femininity, the light and dark poles, are joined magnetically, oppositionally, and Kathleen calls out the name of this dark priestess — *Jane!* — as though all of Penelope's will profit from the word, and then they kiss, the two of them, little pecks each on the other's cheek, and they separate, as Laurie is beside them now carrying the scotch, the free scotch, *the buy back,* and the two Ingersoll girls laugh as one — *Wow, it's so funny to see* you *here!* — and Jane also greets Laurie, the waitress, shyly says *hello,* and they are a complex molecule now, these three women, all of them lovely, and then Jane begins to repair to the bar, where she is headed urgently, the molecule fragments, but before she can do so, coincidence shifts — like the back end of a shock wave — in Hex's direction, and Kathleen says, *Hey, you'll never guess who's here in the bar tonight!* And Jane looks in his direction, and he can make out unmistakably — because he's a tuning fork for impending slights — that she both recognizes him and wishes she didn't. *Hex Raitliffe!* She smiles. Noncommittally. Hex waves.

— She must have an out-of-town hairdresser, Laurie says, turning up with the refill. — Don't think they do green streaks over at Hair, There, and Everywhere.

What time is it? After nine? The restaurant has emptied out, it's a frontier outpost, and Hex begins to feel the chill of evening in the provinces. As if the sudden orbit of Jane Ingersoll has stirred some further discontent. *Suddenly, he doesn't want to go home alone.* By his side, Billie Raitliffe is utterly motionless in her sleep. He should carry his mother out into the car, in the dark. Buckle her in. He should go home and watch late-night satellite feed.

He says to Laurie, — D-do you g-g-g-guys kn-know about any p-p-p-p-p-p-parties t-tonight? . . . It would be g-g-great if there w-w-was somewhere to p-p-p-p —

She gestures at the Ingersoll sisters, now fallen into disputatious whispers. Jane pointing at the bar; Kathleen smiling vehemently. — Ask them. I'm on until midnight. Anyway, I never go out. I go home. I just watch infomercials and go to sleep. With this, Laurie passes out of Hex's weekend, though her simulation of kindness will be remembered. She disappears into the kitchen — the double doors close behind her and that's that. Then the Ingersolls suddenly turn up at his table, both of them, the double aspect of womanhood.

— Well, *hello there!* Kathleen shakes his hand — and goes on shaking it for a while. — I'm Kathleen Ingersoll! And this is my sister! *Jane!* I believe you two *know* each other!?

— Yeah. Jane says.

— Oh, yeah, b-b-back during the, uh, LBJ adm-m —

In shorter range, he can see that *she* is older too. Jane is. Like he is. There's wear and tear in her eyes, striations around them, behind the thick lenses of her Eastern Bloc spectacles; and in the black and green work of her colorist there is nonetheless some concealed tinsel; and there are lines on her face for frowns, for disappointments; when she raises her cigarette to her lipsticked frown, he can see that her hands are also crisscrossed with pleats and heaves, signs of hard work; and he can see that she is unmarried too, free of baubles, of silver or gold or crystals. Kathleen, her sister, meanwhile, has the perfect energy of a woman in her early thirties. She's *bouncy.* She's still *young.* That boundary between youth and middle age, so imperceptibly narrow, isn't crossed. Kathleen is Jane *before* this boundary. *But the truth is Hex isn't thinking much about the Ingersoll sisters at all,* nor about wit and repartee, but rather almost entirely about *consonants.* About how to pronounce them. He's trying to think of sentences that have no *d*'s, *t*'s, or *p*'s — *math class,* for example, that idiomatic phrase, is possible, but not easy. *Mrs. Pierce,* meanwhile, name of the math teacher he and Jane shared, is unlikely.

— Your hair wasn't b-b-b . . . your hair wasn't so d-dark in n-ninth g-grade, he stalls.

— Yeah, Jane says, looking away, toward the bar.

— *Hey*, Kathleen says, sliding into the booth, — why don't you come and join us! We're just going to have a *couple of* drinks. She casts a worried glance at Billie Raitliffe. — Is that your *mother*?

— Huh? Oh yeah. She's sleeping for the m-m-m-moment. It's p-p-p-part of . . .

— So come have a quick drink! Kathleen says, — we'll be able to keep an eye on her!

At the mention of a drink, Jane seems to snap out of her ennui.

— W-w-well, Hex says, — I d-d-don't th-think so, b-b-be-cause —

— Well, we won't take no for an answer, Kathleen says. — We'll join you *here!*

Jane Ingersoll, however, precipitously remembers an important call of some kind; she's wandering away from the table, mumbling about *the very important call,* edging away slowly at first, and then more quickly — toward *the top shelf* and its array of mirrors and illuminations and stained glass. Which leaves Kathleen with Hex —

— That's a really *difficult* stammer you have there, Kathleen says, clasping and unclasping her hands. — Have you ever thought about speech therapy? As a little girl, I saw a fine doctor *right here in town,* Dr. Perelli! I could give you his number. I mean, if you like. He's still practicing.

Hex opens his mouth to reply and nothing comes out at all. Then, after a difficult interval:

— It always g-g-g-g-gets w-worse wh-when I t-t-t-t-try to t-t-t-t-talk about it.

— Oh, that's *awful.*

— B-b-b-b-but I h-have n-noticed one thing that h-h-helps a lot in m-m-my c-c-case.

— What's that?

He waves his hands desperately.

— D-d-d-d-d-d —

— Starts with a *d?* Kathleen asks.

— D-d-d-drinking. In m-m-moderation, he manages. And he watches, with a mild triumph, as she listens. — D-drugs t-t-t-too. I'll p-probably be b-better in an hour or so.

Evidently, Kathleen's small-town curiosity thereby turns up a tidbit that's a little more *pungent* than she bargained for. She moves to change the subject.

— Didn't I hear that your father works over at the power plant? At church I guess is where I heard it. (Kathleen gathers up her purse now. A red paper napkin moistened to its side. She begins to retreat politely.)

— Stepfather, actually, Hex says, standing. And then realizing that he is indeed drunk. Wobbling a little, catching the end of the table. Looking back anxiously at his mom.

— He must be working some long hours tonight. With the *accident* and all.

— The what?

Hex's thoughts snap into a sudden, pristine order.

— You didn't *hear?* That's what we've all been watching on television! Emergency reports!

9

Sleep is conferred through grace and sleep is never guaranteed and sleep should be indulged in without reservation, like the intoxication of autumn square dances, and the undigested footage of each grindingly familiar day that scrolls through the commercially interrupted video jukebox of consciousness as it folds into shutdown, this footage is suffered, no way around it, as you take your pleasure, you sleepers with your *cut-and-paste* and your *faux raccord* and your *musique concrète* and your *cinema verité* and your *exquisite corpse,* you sleepers left to struggle, numbering the widow Mrs. Billie Raitliffe among you, in this local restaurant, in the first booth, as gravitation works upon her, and her head slumps down upon her shoulder, *sleep comes and you yield,* arm squashed between one thigh and the faux-paneled wall of Penelope's Pantry, blood pooling in her hand, in her lifeline, in her mound of Venus, in transparent veins, helixes winding around a diaphanous wrist, her last perceptions snuffed out of her, air hissing meagerly from her nose, nylon strand of drool stretching preposterously from a lower lip mashed against the wall, a long straight crease in her forehead at the juncture of two pieces of paneling, the strand of drool now hovering just above her wrist, pendular, and then detaching, congealing in a gob upon her forearm, gluing the fair white hairs to her freckles and pre-cancerous discolorations, fleeting images of testing formula upon her wrist and feeding *baby Dexter, yes, and snatches of gay conversation, distant, in the kitchen,* in this fatigued landscape her old family once tilled, river snaking through it, dust of topsoil swirling, black sun, her mother standing arms folded at a gas stove, her mother? And thistle and bad ground and great storms of topsoil, or the hothouse of summer when she went about in just her dress and nothing underneath, just her dress, not a thing wrong with it anyhow, in summer, they trudged around, all of them, with the men from *the bank inspecting lands to be seized,* the story goes, *sleep such a responsibility she has always said so,* her wrist and its pressure sore, commonly experienced with abridged mobility, the tissue deprived of oxygenation and beginning, however imperceptibly, to rot, she snores her first, a throbbing, comical snore, climbs up through layers of sleep, casts off layers, cocks her ears, *the sounds of mealtime,* their knives and forks, not real silver, nor is the china real, not the sort she has, her mother in the kitchen, *come in now and get cleaned up, you understand?,* then the sound of television broadcasting somewhere, the squall of bad news, malignant waves, carrying him a drink, refresher, that's it, in front of the brand-new Magnavox, carrying *Allen Raitliffe* a drink, her husband, there's singing on the television set, casual and bright tenor singing, this program brought to you by General Electric or Standard Oil of New Jersey, *Ricky Nelson* singing with somebody, with the Four Preps, their voices angelic, their hit of that year, "Big Man," she can still remember the bridge of it, and *Oh Allen, what a rotten couple of days,* his face is constricted with some woe as the Four Preps give way instead to paramedics in a red ambulance, lazy siren rotating on its roof, she had the seizure on the kitchen floor, when they came for her, after her seizure, *Allen, please,* the decades furrowed under, nothing good will grow here, her husband gathers himself up, can't persuade him to stay, *Don't be silly, I have gone through all this hardship . . . I have gone through it alone,* a purple welt begins to form on her wrist at the point at which it is pinioned against the wall, not yet perceptible but forming nonetheless, and her snore hisses in the high part of her, there is plenty of *smoking* at the bar and the sensation in the lower half of her completely concealed from her by *sluggish electrical transmissions,* impossible to know, her bladder nearing capacity has sent the appropriate message to her brain along rutted and pitted central nervous pathways, plaque formation at junctures along her spinal canal, plaque buildup in the very spot within her brain, back-brain plaque formation and myelin degeneration, where this information would originate, *and the broad sweep of the ten thousand lakes and the plains and the squalls of topsoil,* the smell of it on the breeze, *You can't simply leave me like this,* because she's the young blonde in the canary dress, hitching a ride in the rumble seat to a pond outside town, or running behind the trees at dusk, feeling the pleasure simply of a Midwestern girlhood, the carelessness of girl-hood, it's a grand thing, she knows, a girl in an old dress, so worn it's almost transparent, and the pressure of a boy's knee between her own legs, *It's uh a d-d-d-d-demyelinating d-disease,* and remem-ber she had *double vision* for a time and everything was doubled, it's a mathematical disability, you see, two bank tellers at two counters in the bank, two husbands, two sons, *s-sort of a sheath thing,* the urinary pressure increasing incrementally, as the im-ported beer (consumed at approximately 5:14 PM) is converted by the purifying organs into basic dextrose and formaldehyde, is bro-ken down over the course of hours, the bladder stretching uncom-fortably, stretching beyond where it would be tolerable for anyone else, the tissue expanding, a pint and then some, backing up, she rises up again out of the deeper storage of sleep, the other agency in her, the shadow self, the part busy looking after *automatic func-tions* registers, in the secondary waste evacuation, cell-monitoring systems, *socialization breach,* in semiconsciousness, she recog-nizes a repose in the room, a lapse, in which women are dancing, feminine conjurings of desire and sorority, clever and revolution-ary, *I was a strong swimmer, at the back of the town that day, where the pond was, where that river met the pond, I was so happy in the warmest part of summer, the breezes on the plains, and I could swim at dusk, I was a strong swimmer, jumping in the river naked as the day I was born, it was that one time,* holding her baby Dexter now as he has wetted himself, Mercy, and the cloth diapers that they used up so quickly were again at the laundry, *she must have an out-of-town hairdresser,* foghorn sonorities, startling her, language seems to snap into time with it, certain kinds of sounds repeated among sleepers, *I just watch infomercials and go to sleep,* as if it's a command, *the intoxication of autumn square dances,* then Louis wakes her gently, his expression implacable and pitying at once, how it exhausted her that expression; is she actually awake now? or dreaming of waking? *All the feeling goes out of me, just trying to get dressed in the morning, just trying to fasten the button on a blouse,* Louis leaning down over her, taking the button in his own hand, between clumsy forefinger and opposable thumb, or the knee between her legs, that afternoon by the river, the knee between her legs, his skin so pale, like bone china, *Do you know what it's like to learn that your feelings have all vanished?* Louis: *I consulted with a doctor right here in town,* Louis unfastening the button and then lifting her up, her weightless body, her bamboo skeleton, she hears her own frail voice, that plangent song, like Connecticut's dwindling cardinals, Louis carrying her to *the master bath,* burnished porcelain, she has reached a point where the bladder valve mechanism is no longer going to hold effectively these excess wastes, aluminum, trace minerals, trace radionuclides, neptunium, polonium, cesium, bismuth 214, in ammonia solution, to hold this waste admixture longer would be to risk infection or rupture, the body reflexively bent on the prevention of infection, and the prevention of solids in the bladder or kidney areas known as *stone;* she emerges from veils of metaphor, to sound out the indelible words, *emergency reports,* those of you who will go fourteen hours into Saturday and still wake ready for a nap, alertness doesn't last, *Louis's face is charitable* and this is how a man so charitable was once dear to her, *How could she have been expected to do otherwise, when she was in her fifties then, her face caving in, teeth falling out, and could have no other child and no other family except her boy, was she to live alone in her house? Was she to live alone when Dexter went off to school? There was the man in the advertising business and then the sportscaster, because how could she have been expected to do otherwise? But when Louis arrived he was so gentle and carried her to the bath, bringing a split of champagne and bringing stemware,* his face nearing hers, his lips upon hers, in the master bath, as he prepares the bath with floral oils and salts, just to be immersed, as her body decayed, just to be immersed in the bath, in the river, in the pond, immersed in the rains when the rains came, immersed in the rains that dampened the plains at last, immersed in the rains borne upon the great jet stream, immersed in the rains that ended the drought, that ended the agricultural toiling of her family, *of her mom at the stove* and her dad and the men from the banks, ended all that, in this instant of immersion, in the bath, in the river, in the pond, in the rains, in the baptismal pool, held down by this man in the black suit, all wet to the waist, as neighbors applauded, *she was a strong swimmer,* and Hex calls out, calls out vigorously, because her boy has grown up straight and strong, truly an accomplishment that can't be taken from her, *Jesus Christ, that's the asshole right there on the television,* the uninterrupted melody of it, *standing there like some lying government expert,* just how she always *knew* he would overcome the stammer one day, someone says, *Early unconfirmed reports indicate an insignificant leak,* while biological processes work their way out from under the auspices of intention, her bladder reluctantly yielding its responsibilities to gravity and to muscles responsible for periodic evacuation, aforementioned fermented barley and malt and hops converted and transported with radionuclides and other minerals, niacin, thiamin, these ease into her urethra, down along the centimeters of that passageway and *then out,* at first tentatively but then more urgently according simply to the dynamics of liquids, *her poor poor body, her poor body,* Louis, holding her, *What we'd like the public to know at this time is that we have experienced some rupture along the lines responsible both for leakage of waste water and coolant for the storage of spent fuel,* and then in a more intimate tone, whispering in her ear, languorous and erotic nothings, *Do you think you need to catheterize?,* taking the plastic tubing and washing it with extremely hot tap water, coating the end with a water-soluble lubricant to avoid degrading the tubing, saying, *You know that I love you no matter what,* carefully inserting this prosthetic plumbing again, reaching down, inserting the polymer line, finding the opening and inserting, and then dolorous silence, watching it fill, *Oh Lord!,* she shouts, *dammit!,* from the interior, to where the rise-and-shiners are waging their battles, *Dexter!,* Louis sets the plastic bag in her lap, *You'll have to keep an eye on it,* running down, in the restaurant, down her legs, onto the floor, ruining her socks and her shoes, fouling her orthopedic shoes, the sharp stink of it, *Dexter!*, awake, awake, awake, sobbing, all effluences, all liquids, all floods, the body evacuating and corroding and drying and giving itself up to the dust, to the jet stream, blowing west to east, the great desertified breadbasket, lifeless and scorched, as elsewhere oceans rise and batter the coast, *Shit, Mom, I'm sorry, oh shit,* his bar stool toppling as he rushes from the bar, she says, *Well . . . it's too late now . . .* Her eyes open. The light is such an imposition. These voices receding in her and the repetitions and convolutions fading and with this a bereavement at the hard, factual aspect of *red light* and that repulsive corroded lobster tank, the vinyl seat cushions patched with duct tape, the plastic hanging plants, the waitresses reclining at tables smoking and filing their nails, her lips are so chapped and dried, she's so *thirsty,* her face is mashed against the wall, can't move her face, calling out, the corner of her eye where she can just make out the room, it's intolerable, *because she used to run and her legs were strong,* honestly, grief must have originated in the *uncomfortable waking from naps . . .*

— D-d-d-do you n-n-need to go to the bathroom? M-m-mom?

Hex slides into the booth, and pulls her away from the wall, *peels her off,* and there's a moment when he's trying to avoid the damp, the unspeakable damp, but it's in all the crevices of the booth and all over him, puddling and pooling, his mother's brine, can't avoid it, *shit shit shit,* under his breath, pulling her out of the booth, and then calling to someone else, she's shivering, *I d-d-d-dunno, she might have a fever, c-c-can you just reach me the chair,* Billie won't speak, but opens her eyes again, and *this woman* is unfolding the chair, with a brittle expression, pursed lips, little unfriendly face, green hair, for godsakes, *green hair,* this woman unfolds the chair and then takes her, the widow Mrs. Billie Raitliffe, under the arms, Hex carries the legs, the two of them reel toward the chair, drop her into it, *All right, don't sweat it, Mom,* this woman says dully, and they're all watching, all of them in the restaurant, it's a birth or death or marriage or rite of passage, and Billie Raitliffe herself is crying, and there's a blonde dragging bucket and mop, dragging the pail from the kitchen, using the squeegee, wringing out spilled chowder and rehydrated diet soda into this bucket, and this mopper holds open the door to the washroom, they can't get the chair in, the door's too narrow, so Hex and *Jane* are carrying her, again, she is light, like a chickadee, like a girlchild, into the ladies' room. Then in the light of a single uncovered bulb, the fixture swaying from the ceiling, *M-m-mom, you c-c-can't b-b-believe it, Lou was on the t-television.*

10

———————————— I want to emphasize, Stanford Warren says, — that the public is not *now* in any danger, *has not been* in any danger *at any time today,* and will not be in any danger because of this minor emission. This is a minor emission, and not an emergency. There is no cause for alarm or worry of any kind on the part of Coastal Power's customers and neighbors. I want to make this point abundantly clear to the news organizations, so let me reiterate what I've just said. *The public is not now in any danger and has not been in any danger at any time today.* That concludes my statement at this time.

Under Warren's sweaty and desperately friendly talking head there's a title that reads "Millstone Nuclear Power Facility, 5:15 PM," after which the coverage on *Action News Six* cuts away abruptly to staff reporter Samantha Goodman standing on the bridge at Niantic, the occasional hard-luck automobile with creased fender easing into the shot and out again. Samantha's wearing a black-and-white-checked wool suit from Christian Dior ($1,795) and white Giorgio Armani blouse ($225), black Victoria's Secret stockings, pumps by Christian Lacroix Haute Couture, chocolate lipstick, hair by Nicki Finch, at Hair, There, and Everywhere; and behind her, illuminated in the thin mist by spotlights and flickering red air-alert signals, is the grim facade of the Millstone Nuclear Power Plant — in the throes of a Code Two *Unusual Event.* Samantha's hair is lightly windblown (almost as if by an off-camera styling dryer), her jacket is flapping a little, and she's squinting against light precipitation. (Forecast coming right up.) Samantha's report is a *live bulletin,* with the immediacy and authenticity of same. She fixes the microphone just below her chin and looks soberly into the camera as she gestures behind her — sweepingly — at the containment vessel and the ominous buildings of that nuclear edifice.

— Are we ready? Mike? You've just heard from Stanford Warren, acting plant manager here at Millstone Nuclear Power Facility, which you can see directly behind me, concerning the emergency situation that has been developing here since about 4:30 this afternoon. To repeat, the corrosion that had affected, uh, that has affected the main reactor as recently as two months ago has now spread to the more dangerous area of waste storage. That's the portion of the plant where the, uh, high-level waste — the fuel rods — are stored in a large tank, a sort of large-scale swimming pool, Mike. Earlier in the afternoon, the utility had admitted that there had been some spillage of radioactive water into the harbor here in Niantic. They were estimating a hundred gallons or so, over a period of about one hour. According to experts we've spoken with, these emissions will be heavily diluted by tidal activity, and therefore, as Mr. Warren has said, *there is no danger to the public at this time.* That's how it stands now, and we'll be keeping you informed throughout the evening. Back to you, Mike.

In the course of Samantha's reportage, the producer intercuts old weather footage of the plant — ominous violet clouds drifting over the reactors — and file stock of the workers at the plant leaving at the end of a typical business day. As *Action News* anchor Mike Dorman, in charcoal gray single-breasted jacket from Lands' End ($220), pale blue twill shirt ($64.99), and rep tie, takes the introduction from Samantha and prepares to edify the audience a little further, there's a diagram behind him, in the upper right of the screen, of the inside of the plant. Turbine, pressure valves, fuel rods, coolant lines, generators, waste runoff, etc. But before Mike can read his scripted introduction from the TelePrompTer, a technical glitch ensues and instead Samantha is again superimposed above his head. Mike's microphone drops out and we get her voice: — Think it looked okay? Boy, let's get out of here. It's cold! She then assumes a vacuous smile — until producer Ralph Bobker cuts away to a used-car commercial —

— Jesus, Stanford Warren himself shuts off the wall-mounted set and the VCR, looking less heavy, less nervous, more composed in person than on the broadcast, in the staff room on the second floor of the Millstone facility, surrounded by his troops: the public relations guys from the Millstone staff; the public relations guy from the parent company, Coastal Power and Light; the senior operations analyst from CPL (and also Spencer Murphy, the CEO, via a brand-spanking-new ATT ImagePhone 2100, transmitting at 56.6 bps, his face weaving and wobbling in and out of focus in the tiny frame); a squadron of engineers both from the reactor and the waste storage wings of the facility; a hotshot troubleshooter flown in on the Babcock and Wilcox company jet, who has brought along his own dosimeters, Geiger counters, and tool belts; and the Millstone control room gang, both day and night shifts, including Hank Chapin, Mike Kresh, Wallace Hellerstein, Bill Durkee, Reggie Davis, Mac Kowalski, Ron Self, Dot Halleran, and Lou Sloane. Still missing, on his badly timed afternoon off: the onsite inspector for the NRC. They've been in the conference room for hours, arguing, but now that the CEO has shown up — or at least his badly transmitted, baud-degraded likeness has shown up — they've rerun all the reports, they've gone again through all the press coverage, the heavy play on the local networks, the spotty national reports. They were blacked out on FOX, ABC, and CBS. They rated four and a half seconds on CNN, six on NBC, and thirteen very critical seconds on PBS.

— Okay, Spencer, Warren says, — so that's what we've got. I think we're okay for the moment. We have the NRC to contend with — there's going to be paperwork all right, since Stevenson was off getting his tooth pulled, a whole heck of a lot of paperwork — but the code definitely leaves room for us to keep operating the reactors, and to deal with the storage leaks as we can. We're expecting freshly milled parts from B&W imminently. The waste water will be diluted environmentally —

— I agree. (Murphy's snout and spectacles stutter in the little screen in the middle of the conference table.) In the meantime perhaps I can prevail on the engineers to put this in plain English for me again, how we managed to repair the ruptures in the lines, the primary lines, where the salt water carved holes before, *two months ago,* only to find the same problem cropping up elsewhere. And maybe, while we're here hashing this out, *someone* — one of you press relations people — can call up the fire department and make clear that this isn't a first strike, for goshsakes, and we can open the front gate at the facility, get rid of the rest of the non-essential staffers, and hopefully drive off those damn reporters. All right? I think some of your people probably want to go home for the weekend, Stan. Isn't that right?

— Absolutely, Warren says, and turns to the PR men, Aaron Glickes (from Millstone) and Jerry Sykes (from CPL), and they rise from the table, leaving behind a half-dozen coffee cups between them, each perforated with ballpoint-pen holes and filled with cigarette butts. They take up their cell phones and pagers. (There's a pile of telecommunications devices in the middle of the conference table, like a protectorate around Murphy's digital shade, as well as a number of mostly neglected Chinese food cartons.) They head out into the hall. Meanwhile, the specialist from B&W is running calculations on a credit-card-sized calculator and getting ready to deliver his incomprehensible defense of the Babcock and Wilcox insurance position.

— I think we can all agree, Warren says, that it would be nice to have this situation firmly in control so that we can go home. Right? So let's go ahead over these technical issues one more time.

Stanford then again introduces John Wellman, director of product support at B&W. Wellman steps around a few engineers to reach the overhead projector, to scribble a formula or two on the acetate there. He clears his throat theatrically. Of alpha, beta, and gamma radiations, he sings, of their respective particles, of the tendency of neutrons to slow up when conducted through hydrogenous substances, like, say, *salt water,* and of how this can then result in buildups of the transuranic series, and then, in affected metals with a high-resonance cross section, transmutation on a percentage basis, if the neutron induction goes on for too long, or if the bombardment is too intense, *for example in a corrosion-type situation or event when you have iodine or other radionuclides building up in a containment vessel over the course of time, see, the pipes themselves become alpha-emitters in a way never intended by Babcock and Wilcox, at least according to short-term plant usage as defined in chapter twenty-seven bulleted point number three of the management technical packet you all have in front of you.* Lou refuses to put up with it again, though, will not subject himself to the horseshit, will not put up with this physics of *spin*, and anyway he's only here because he can't get the car out of the parking lot — the reporters and the fire trucks are out front, the fire trucks from town, as well as the drab green vehicles from the *fire department emergency training academy* — in case the whole thing should blow sky high, which of course isn't likely or even possible. *This isn't a graphite-moderated reactor, guys,* Lou mumbles on his way out the door, *this isn't the Ukraine,* and that's it for him, because he's done his job for them today, his troubleshooting. He collaborated with Warren and the PR people in blaming the situation on *inadvisable policies of the old management team,* after which he gave simulated off-the-record interviews to the television people admitting that the implications of the salt water–corrosion situation are *only now really becoming apparent,* and what with infrastructural damage this acute you have to expect depreciation of plant, long-term depreciation, bond-financed renovation projects, etc., etc., thus saving Warren's butt, and *reconfiguring the CPL image position,* as one of the PR guys actually said. So when he excuses himself out into the corridor — the featureless corridor — no one stops him. He's going into retirement. Having done his job. Leaving behind $Fs = (ma)(1/2at^2) = 1/2ma^2t^2 = 1/2mv^2$ and the redundancies inherent in dual lead-lined containment tanks and fast-neuron capture as it applies to chain reactions in U^{238}.

Kowalski slips out too. In fact, behind Lou, there's an insurrectional scattering of the day-shift staffers out the door, all of them exhausted and mute, heading like zombies to the parking lot. And probably to a nearby bar. But Kowalski stops to chat. Poor Mac has sweated through his short-sleeved shirt, and the sleeveless tee underneath. He's carrying his wrinkled pullover sweater, must be

clammy as hell, has been all afternoon probably, mopping his big
pink forehead with a faded bandanna as he emerges. Heading for
the water fountain.

— Wonder if this stuff glows yet, Kowalski says, as he gets his
turn at that anemic, fluorinated stream. They chuckle quietly.
Then they observe a respectful moment of silence, watching as
Dot and Reggie Davis and Ron Self all head down the corridor.
Dog tired, all of them. A lot has happened since Mac and Lou first
hustled from the farewell party that afternoon, through the airlock,
into the control room, Sloane running as best he could — in his
loafers — running down the hall, the annunciators bleating, to
find *the high-level storage monitors*, that bank of panels off to the
right (where the additional screens were added when they reno-
vated the control room) — truly redundant since the waste systems were managed simultaneously by another shift in an adjacent
building — flashing like nobody's business. Warren and the trainees stood there looking dumbly at the gauges — in emergency-
induced hypnosis — until someone got smart and hit the
intercom. It was Kowalski, *shift supervisor*, who did it, turned off
the alarms, and called out, all calmness and decorum, over the
intercom:

— Storage, you guys having a problem of some kind? One of
those *bad wiring* days?

— Afraid not, this voice on the intercom replied. — We're registering leaks. That's what it shows here. Multiple leaks.

Mac said, — Uh oh.

Stanford Warren said, — I thought we'd dealt with the leaks
already.

— How many minutes into it? Kowalski interrupts.

The paper was already pouring ceaselessly out of the laser
printer near where they were clustered. The other trainees, on the
other side of the control room, the ones watching the reactor
panels, looked over anxiously at the commotion. It was *Code Two*,
nothing to get excited about, but they were scared anyway. Everyone was scared. *Code Two.*

— Well, initially it was in the storage containment tank itself,
the guy at waste said, — where the coolant lines run out of the

tank. On the seal there, it's a ring sealer. There was leakage. About ten minutes ago.

— Initially? said Kowalski.

— Yeah, that's right. We closed the seal when we found the leak. Most of it was running into the secondary tank, but we closed the seal anyway. Then we opened a second outtake valve, the one that feeds out at the opposite corner, at the northwestern corner, to make sure the level was fine —

— And the valve stuck, Kowalski said.

— *The valve stuck?* Warren repeated.

— Right. The valve stuck. How did you know?

At which point Dot and Ron came in, carrying white cake with marble frosting and plastic forks, shoveling the last bites into their mouths as they stood at the bank of monitors. The tableau: here was the trainee, a young kid with a ponytail and a faint mustache, who was seated in the swivel chair at the computer console; and Mac; and Stanford Warren; and Lou; and now Ron and Dot. Dot spent a minute reading printout, getting a handle on it pretty fast. *It's waste storage.* They all knew about leaks. She asked Ron if he wanted coffee. *We're going to be here a while.* Ron volunteered to go get a half-dozen mugs himself — of that Millstone vending-machine battery acid.

— Certain things you just know, Mac said. — So how big was the overflow? How much gain in the main tank?

— It's not too bad, really, it's around ten gallons an hour of gain. Less than one percent above capacity, I figure. And part of the overflow is running into the secondary tank, that's fine, but there's this leak there, too, and that part is running into a sump that cleans out the secondary tank, and that coolant in turn would be leaking into —

— Groundwater, Lou Sloane said.

Warren sighed deeply.

— Groundwater, the guy on the intercom said. — Yeah, probably. It's leaking around the lines, you know, spilling out of the sump into the fire corridor, and from what we can tell from blueprints there's a *drain* on the floor of the corridor. That's what my guys are telling me. It drains someplace. I don't know if that means groundwater or harbor water. Maybe both. I think it deserves attention either way you slice it —

— Yeah, well, thanks, Chief, Mac said.

At which point, Stanford Warren, panicking visibly, searching the faces in the room desperately, hit upon Lou Sloane, and he took Lou aside, to one side of the control room, the quiet side, the side where all was hunky-dory with the reactors, where the reactors were generating their steam, and the turbines were running, and the houses on the Millstone grid were getting their hot water, and the boys and girls were showering. Stanford said, — Can you make this clearer for me? I'm not even sure about obligations as far as notification goes. Do I call CPL now? And how about the regulatory people? Stevenson's at the dentist. I mean, which of these things should I be doing first? Will you do me a favor and just consult with me for an hour or so here? I understand that you . . . but you have the, uh, you know, reputation, and I —

Lou waved his hands.

— It's an old plant, Lou said, too eager to contribute, too eager to hold it over Warren's head. — Almost twenty-five years old, right? And the corrosion is not, in spite of what they're saying, the problem. The problem is it's twenty-five years old. No one's putting any money into it. Into the plant itself. It's all patches. You know you can sleeve the affected pipes, you know, slide a smaller line into the larger ones, with better, newer materials —

— Of course, Stanford said, — I understand, but what I'm really concerned about is notification.

— That's what I'm trying to tell you. My personal feeling is, it's an old plant, the regulators know it's going to have problems, because they all do; they're decommissioning most of the older models. The NRC is behind that effort. Are you going to be evasive with them? That's going to tie you up a lot. So you have to figure out if that's how you want to spend your workday.

Dot handed them each a cup of coffee, from the tray Self had brought in. There were plastic cups of flat champagne there, too. In case anyone needed it. Stanford asked her impulsively for cigarettes. In fact, Dorothy did have a single, dented, low-tar, ultra-lite flattened in the pocket of her shirt. She generously planted it on

Stanford's kisser. Within range of a dozen *no smoking* postings, Warren whipped out an expensive lighter, torched the crooked smoke, and returned to Lou.

— Well, can we at least keep a tight rein on who's talking? Surely there's got to be a way that you can control the —

— You can try, Sloane said, knowing, as Stanford did himself, that you couldn't. Warren paced, smoking desperately. In the meantime, Mac Kowalski was reviewing the statistics with his intercom pal: *though the valve on the secondary outtake was stuck, the flood had been temporary, and they had halted the intake, pumping the vast majority of the water into the secondary tank.* It was maybe a hundred gallons all told, a little higher than the earlier estimate, not much more, and the situation was stable, except for the leak. Which was slow. On the other hand, the water in the tank would be getting hot, in spite of the casks, the zircon and cadmium casks, because it was old, because they didn't have additional coolant running in there through refrigeration, nope; instead they had a stagnant body of heavy water, water that wasn't being cycled according to the usual protocol. It was sitting in there. This is what the kid said at waste storage — his name was Wayne — and thus there was the one remaining dangerous and unsettling question in the series of questions that Mac had been obliged to ask, which concerned *exactly how hot the water was.* If it wasn't too bad, they could dilute it, they could pump fresh water in, mix heavy and light waters, just keep mixing it until it was, say, five thousand gallons in solution, at which point it would become, according to state and federal regulations, low-level radioactive waste, and you could do anything you wanted with that, you could fill a public swimming pool with it, just about, or you could use it to mass-produce glow-in-the-dark kids' toys. If this were the worst of the imminently dangerous problems, it seemed manageable, and therefore, with a certain amount of wishful thinking, Lou and the other members of the control room staff got acclimated to the emergency situation. To the flashing signals on the panel. They would deal with each indicator in its turn and eventually these lamps would cease from their stroboscopics, and some decision would be made concerning the heavy water; *it just didn't seem all that upsetting,* because every now and then you forgot.

— Well, why bother to dilute it, when there are so many technical hurdles in the way right now? Mac Kowalski called to his new superior.

— Here, here, Ron Self said, sitting at a coolant panel. — Can I propose the obvious? Let's pump the damn stuff into the harbor. That's where it's going, anyway. Let's just cut our losses, get this over with, and take the hit.

—Wait just a darn second, Stanford Warren said, edging up behind Kowalski. — You're suggesting that we —

Warren sucked desperately on the last of his borrowed cigarette. He *already* had an ulcer, Lou had heard. He had been observed chewing away at a wide assortment of antacids and extra-strength digestive medications. He probably had renewable prescriptions for strong sleeping aids. He smoked. No matter what he did in the next hours — and the emergency clock on the main wall counted off the duration above his head, including hundredth parts of seconds — his job was no longer simply speeches about *leadership and excellence and the family values of the corporate community.* He'd been an expert number cruncher at the parent company. But now he had to make decisions.

— Well, how much of a dilution would we be talking about?

— It's not sludge, Self added. — It'd be maybe parts per billion. I wouldn't eat the shellfish in Niantic, myself, but it's worse over in the Thames River with the subs. There you have the commercial fishing capital of the state right next door. There you have tailings and sludge and construction solvents and shit from Electric Boat.

— Well, Kowalski said. — On the other hand —

— Yeah, Dot said.

Stanford looked at them.

— Plutonium, Lou volunteered.

— Right, Mac said. — Some of that stuff is hot for a while. A long while. I mean, it's a slow emission process. Ten, twenty thousand years. (The trainee kid hit the intercom again, as Mac lingered over his desk.) — Listen, Wayne, so how hot is it in there, anyway? Any condensation, or any buildup of that kind?

— Hell, no, Wayne replied.

— Hey, Self called out, perversely. — I got it. Let's *sell* this water. There's probably a market for it. You know, among despots.

— Friend, Stanford Warren said, pointing ominously at Ron, — *that's not particularly amusing right now.*

The intercom crackled again.

— Look, we're going to go ahead and send a man down to look at the seals and the pump. We'll advise after we've taken a look.

And Warren okayed the strategy, and went ahead to call *his* boss, Spencer Murphy, in the privacy of Lou's old office. The lights in the control room flickered mesmerically. The phones began to ring. The pulse tones of emergency signals. *How did the newspapers get the control room number, anyway?* Dot came out of inactivity to answer one of the lines, *no comment, no comment, no comment,* in the next interval, and then Lou Sloane himself decided to go over and take a look at the damage. To troubleshoot at waste. Why not? He hadn't been there in a while. And the decision about dumping had already been made, effectively speaking, or it was being made now, or would be made in the next minutes. They would dump because there was no alternative. Lou Sloane had meanwhile recognized something: in a dim, aching sort of way he was happy. The alert made him happy. He was relevant; he was part of a tussle, part of a contemporary debate. This day would be written about, and when he was sleeping in Stockbridge or Jaffrey or Montpelier, in a log cabin he'd built by hand, in a cabin by the edge of a pond, he would remember this day, and others. He'd held a job where things got done.

The shuttle bus over to storage was an empty, cerulean Econoline, driven by a young black man, Jones, who asked right away if it was true about a leak. Was there a breach? Was there contamination? Was the staff likely to exceed its rated annual dosage? But Lou didn't take the bait. *Haven't heard a thing.* Just another day. Cool as a cucumber. He asked Jones about his wife and children, complimented him on a proffered baby photo, and then climbed out of the van. In the main entrance at storage, he said he was here to perform a spot check and asked for blueprints. They didn't even know who he was. He telephoned Wayne from a wall-mounted emergency handset, pored over the design plans in an empty office, and then descended some three flights of fire stairs, down into that cavern, damp and silent. It was in this substratum that he finally met Wayne, a young man in his thirties with a really stupendous variety of obesity. Wayne surely needed a special extra-large swivel chair at his command post. A sort of a truckbed on which to balance his impressive bulk. Wayne also wheezed asthmatically as he greeted Lou. Together they waited for another man to suit up: a great, burly youngster, no more than twenty-three, who resembled a plumber, with enormous hands and skittery, evasive eyes. This was the kind of employee who was attracted, these days, to nuclear power. Misfits and idiot savants, coveters of weapons-related data, fundamentalists, borderline personalities, pot smokers, people who fell through the cracks of a franchise-fueled economy; these were the guardians of the atomic age. It was an industry-wide problem. This boy couldn't even have held a job as a bill collector, he was so brusque and ill-mannered. And yet he was doing his job here. He got the white suit on, zippered the hood and face mask, attached the breathing apparatus; there was a toolbox at his feet, and soon he hefted it up. Dave McCluskey, his name was, and McCluskey was an employee fully informed about rems and milli-sieverts, right then, no doubt about it. He was rated for fifteen millisieverts annually, no more. The health plan wouldn't cover anything above, wouldn't even cover a stiff neck if he'd taken seventeen (a dose you could conceivably get just walking past the reactor). Still, he went out through the rubber-sealed door, letting in a little blast of contamination, and made his way slowly across the corridor, his flashlight scattering improbable shadows. McCluskey probably had a wife and kids and a powerboat named *Ladykiller*, and was probably hoping to go home to these people and possessions quickly, even if his wife was constantly carping at him; McCluskey probably recognized, in the position he was in, that he was lucky to have a wife and kids, as well as a bunch of pals who would bag that last moose of hunting season with him, these were simple pleasures, these were fine pastimes, looking better and better in fact, as he found himself under the sump pump, under the radioactive shower-massager of the sump pump, waste containment coolant spraying every which way; with his water-resistant flashlight McCluskey indicated this to Lou and Wayne, where they were sealed off in the glassed-in stairwell. The water was being thrown three or four feet, fountaining around McCluskey; they could hear the Geiger counter like a night dense with crickets, and Lou thought, *this was a good kid*; this kid had a keen itch to do his job; he loved his family; he had everything to lose, in the cascade of water, in the geyser, in that tomb, in that corridor; McCluskey had a sort of courage, the sort that Lou believed he possessed himself. Lou came down here with nothing, bereft of everything, and *he* could just as easily have sloshed out into that murky water, harrowed that Hades, that exotic deep-sea exhibit where McCluskey was, with its radioactive fish; like a marine biologist, Lou should have been out there himself, on a hot streak of relevance, but McCluskey came by it naturally. McCluskey pushed on through without any question about the dose, whether it was, say, three hundred microcuries pouring from the sump pump, after which McCluskey would withstand five months in a cement-lined room, fifty-fifty odds of survival, nurses in gas masks all around him, because a good, strong kid like him had honest pluck and an exalted birth, when it was Lou ought to have been doing this chore, a dead man with a heavy conscience, as the drain was draining the heavy water, it was going down the drain, two or three mSvs left in the room, that's all, *because it was draining out to where those fishermen at dusk were hauling in their catch*, McCluskey, on the ladder, dealing with the rivets in the seal, on the valve, with a power tool, and then all the water spilling out, a burst, a torrent of water left in the line, knocking the kid from the ladder, the power drill boomeranging into a puddle, skittering out of reach, the O-ring sealer above him like spaghetti, but he got right back on his feet, *he was tough*, waved at Wayne and Lou, thumbs up, McCluskey was a-okay, the water cascading out of the line, rushing into the drain. Lou wasn't worried about McCluskey, really, Lou was worried about the end of this alert, about *afterward*, when Warren would gather the press up and admit they had dumped the water, at which point there would be no more conceivable reason why he, Lou, former plant manager, would be required on the premises any longer, and he would be obliged to go, imagining the best routes out of town, around a mob of reporters parked in and along 156 — the backup on I-95 now constituting not only the usual late-night volume, the commuters from New London and the road gangs and the flagmen and flagwomen standing nonchalantly in their high-visibility vestments, the traffic snarl probably including now, as well, supernumerary fire trucks and who knew what else, the army, the national guard, the feds, antinuclear demonstrators, and environmentalists. *Jesus, what was he doing?* McCluskey stepped out of the fountain for a second, strode over to the window, held up the rubber sealer, snorting through his breathing apparatus, holding the O-ring, shredded somehow, just completely shredded, and in his white, rubber palm, cracked rivets, before heading back out into the corridor, Wayne shouting after him, through reinforced Plexiglas, *Okay, so just make sure the pipe is clear, and then come on back,* which was when Lou decided it was maybe just palpitations, arrhythmia, this bad feeling, or maybe he was getting sentimental, or maybe he was getting old. He told Wayne he had to go, that he'd carry the message back, whatever the message was; he had to get back to the meeting, the meeting with Murphy, an important meeting, in the conference room, had to go, had to go, *glad to see everything is under control.* He telephoned Warren, updated him, and then detoured, stopped up at the gate, chatted with the reporters about *imminent bond-financed superfund cleanup,* disinforming according to a long-standing interpretation of duty, after which he hustled back to the meeting, the staff meeting, saying nothing, already absent, already retired, already gone, coming to the end of something, and thus finding himself here *with Kowalski,* his stout, sideburned, gin-blossomed subordinate, in conference room B, feet on the table, in the present tense, the two of them, 9:30 at night, drinking *a couple of cold ones,* from the conference room refrigerator, waiting to see if there's anything else they can do when it's obvious, couldn't be more so, that there's *nothing for Lou to do at all*. Which is why Kowalski says,

— What are we still doing here? Shit, what are *you* still doing here? It's your goddamned last day!

Kowalski (from a childhood in Worcester, Mass.) flattening his r's: *gawdamned* last day —

— Hell, I don't care why you're here, he goes on, — you can keep me company.

It's all banter, the helter-skelter of exhausted men in conversation, but it keeps coming around to this question, *where was Lou when Mac called the day before,* and either Mac has heard something or he's making inferences and reading inflections. He has theories and suppositions.

— Well, Sloane says lamely, — my expertise is so priceless, you know? I stuck around. I'm here late today, and I was here late yesterday, and I'd be here late tomorrow if I could. You guys'll have to take me off the premises with security escort. Honest to God.

Nevertheless, he tugs his security badge off now, off his breast, gives it a once-over, stuffs it in a jacket pocket.

— Yeah, well, I don't want to . . . that's your business, you know that. I'm not going to bother you about that. But just I'm concerned is all.

— That's awfully kind of you, Mac.

— So just one more question. It's more along the lines of a friend just asking —

— Well, Lou interrupts, humiliated to find he actually feels like his eyes are going to mist up. He tugs off his glasses, his dark glasses — never did take them off — and busies himself for a while exchanging the dark glasses for the pair in the hard case in the pocket of his windbreaker, and then wiping these down with a handkerchief. — Well, I suppose we ought to just let it drop, if you know what I mean, so I'll just say that I —

Kowalski looks at the beer in his own hand, the domestic beer, cheapest possible beer, and he hoists it to his lips. Their eyes meet for a second, collide, and part.

— The thing I gotta ask then, pal, Mac says, — is if you got a place to stay tonight. Is all.

— It's not really your —

— Because I'm guessing that you're —

— I was staying over at the motel. I can go back there. It's no problem at all. They have a Lou Sloane suite over there, you know. But that's not —

— Well, Louis, you don't want to —

— It's not a problem.

— Don't you think —

— It's nothing, Mac. I'm telling you.

— Look, stay at my place. There's plenty of room. It's not like it's cluttered up. I don't want you living in that Cadillac. I just won't abide a guy lives in his Cadillac. That's putting on airs.

They chortle grimly.

— No, I probably ought to just go over to the motel, I suppose, though you couldn't be kinder. I'll sleep off the, uh, the afternoon and get started in the morning —

— Get started in the morning?

Kowalski pops another beer. The air in the room is recirculated, stale. Constrictive.

— Listen, Lou, if I'm out of line, you tell me, but, uh, I'm honestly not sure, with this being your *last day* and all, that this is the best night for you to be over there by yourself. I mean, it's not like we managed to make the best party for you. I imagine you don't want me saying something like this, and it's none of my business, but let me just offer this observation. You come on over to my place. I'll make you a really fine breakfast tomorrow, steak and eggs or something. If you still don't want to go back home after that, Lou, I'll loan you my damn road atlas. I'll send you on your way.

— Now, listen, Mac, Lou Sloane says, getting edgy. — I can make up my own mind. I'm fifty-four years old. If you knew how things were going, you'd understand. So don't you occupy yourself with other people's troubles —

— You're right, you're right —

— And then on top of everything I come in here and I take the flack for this, waving his hands at the sterile interior, — you know? I *grew up* here.

— I know. I'm sorry.

— So I'll be on my way. And I'll remember how generous you've been.

— As long as you understand that the door's open at my place and that you've got, uh, someone to listen. All that malarkey.

Lou looks over at Kowalski, who eases his running shoes off the table now, and he's not smiling at all, they're each uncomfortable, they're sitting there, and Lou knows his own face is red, there's a throbbing in him — *stroke, apoplexy, thrombosis* — and he's liable to shout, but so far he doesn't —

— I appreciate your input, but you're treading on some damned thin ice.

— Lou, Mac says, I been in there all day too and I personally have swum in that bay on occasion, and I've had a rough damned day, too, Mr. Sloane, and I'm not gonna sit here, watch you act like an idiot. You go to the motel if that's what you're gonna do, or sleep in your car, but don't you make me a part of your selfishness. I'm not Florence damned Nightingale, so don't you make me a do-gooder. That's the end of the discussion, the way I see it, Louis, if that's what you want. I don't care what the hell you do. I'm sorry I ever brought it up.

Mac falls silent. And Lou throws an empty can petulantly at a trash barrel against the wall, like a damn kid, and misses, of course, and an amber foam splatters there, splotches parabolically upon the wall, and right away he regrets it, is really embarrassed, he's on the verge of walking out the door and shouting a few things on the way, in fact, making a few uncharitable remarks, but he can't even do that, and instead the two of them stand up, synchronously, and he drops the can into a recycling bin with others, and in some silent assent they go into the corridor, past other conference rooms, voices there still rising and gathering, debating and obfuscating, *We can run a temporary shunt from the secondary valve over to the primary coolant line and double capacity to take the runoff, and then cycle the waste back secondarily,* and in reverse the two of them wearily duplicate Lou's lunchtime trip up through the front end of the nuclear energy cycle; that is, they go backward through the process, the process for which they labor, from the reactor itself down the hall, wearily, past where the uranium hexa-fluoride is hauled up on forklifts, up from refrigerated tanks, taken to processing, prepared in fuel rods, housed in boron; they go backward through that black magic, Louis and Mac, through the loading dock where the fuel arrives in eighteen-wheelers, until they are free of all this, free of the self-sustaining chain reaction, out into the parking lot, the management lot, no trucks, no load-ing, no uranium, no runoff, no leaks, only one lonely security guy in his booth listening to Christian talk radio on a transistor, *God smites the unsaved*; the mist has turned to rain. It's comfortable in this purgatorial dark. The short tempers and snap decisions of a long afternoon, the voices of Code Two, these have vanished in the rain, the sound of the bay, of waves roiling in the incipient storm, the wind gathering, Sloane's windbreaker flaps like a burgee at fifteen knots. Both of them begin to trot across the parking lot, Kowalski's moth-eaten pullover a spinnaker over his head, as the rain begins to fall. The front gate will be crowded with reporters, for the ten-thirty news, for the eleven o'clock news. Kowalski says, *Gonna follow me?* and Sloane nods, *You know the way in case you get lost?* and Sloane nods, and gets into his Cadillac, next to Kowalski's Tempo, and it starts, and the news radio comes on, *AllNews 660, updating you on the alert at Millstone Nuclear Power Plant,* and Lou checks his dashboard clock, which seems to have stopped, somehow, stopped dead, after five, as though there'd been an electromagnetic pulse while he was busy, as though the after-noon had seen a series of first-strike detonations, the long-anticipated ICBM onslaught, the one that would fry every clock and computer and modem and personal digital assistant and cellu-lar telephone and hi-fi and television and VCR and refrigerator and washer/dryer and electric foot massager and Lava lamp and microwave rotary oven and motorized wheelchair, the first strike that would send them all into their basements, the Yankees of southeastern Connecticut, into a huddle in the basement with cans of peas and cling peaches and fruit cocktail and condensed milk, with shovels and gas masks, bags of cement and fresh earth, lumber and tarps, until the shortest of the half-life durations had come and gone, two or three years, all these families down there, for two or three years, no blossoming of children, no first menstruation, no new romance, all those families and their fantasies of the Cold War, their nightmares of the *binding force*. When Lou raps on the digital clock with a knuckle, with his wedding band, it starts right up.

I I

———————————— To know the life of a man, a frank, unvarnished account of his bedroom is often required: *My understanding is that Billie Raitliffe felt that the house was no longer to her tastes, no longer contemporary enough, this according to Mavis Elsworth, interior designer, and after all she was emerging from her widowhood and starting to feel like herself again. So I was the first to agree that a top-to-bottom redecoration was in order. There was a lot of room for improvement in those old dated interiors! She began by selling off the most traditional pieces in her collection — in order to generate a budget for our renovation projects — and the auction that featured these pieces was well-attended, I can tell you that. Even the preview was a blockbuster. There were cars parked all the way down to Route 156! In any case, since Billie insisted on staying at the Flagler Drive location — a house constructed of stone and in a very traditional architectural idiom — we were really limited as to the range of styles we could apply. We needed things that wouldn't clash with the elegance of the structure itself. Therefore, Billie and I decided in principle on a canny and playful dialogue between old and new. For example, conventional oaks and marbles, the materials of her antique cabinets and desks and tables, would coexist with stylish new objects. There would be reverence for the past as well as a wink in the direction of the future. I like to call the look we came up with Contemporary Eclectic. Although my personal opinion is that a grand house like hers needs to be fully furnished — it's my job, after all — Billie leaned instead toward austerity, toward a kind of pre-Columbian vocabulary, toward black-and-white Berbers and adobe and taupe draperies setting off pale linen wall finishes. She liked rooms that took pleasure in space. You'd have expanses interrupted only by a glass coffee table or by an end table, by an antique hat rack, say, or by the simplest hammock chairs. This was the idea, anyhow, and the only exception to this emerging southwestern palette was to be found in the room we first completed — her son's room.* The kiddy stuff appalled him; he'd shoved the mobiles and the kiddy toys into a closet down the hall, shattering their struts and joists, entangling their strings; he'd gutted a half-dozen stuffed animals, buried toy soldiers in backyard mass graves. All the while begging to do his room over. He'd have done it himself if he had to. He nagged his mother at their mute suppers (frozen foods accompanying the fine wines of Bordeaux), about getting rid of the seafarer mobiles and the dinosaurs on the bedspreads, about getting rid of the bright colors on the walls and moldings, replacing the kiddy toy chest, the kiddy bookends, the kiddy lamps, to make room for the emblems of his burgeoning masculinity. Like crookedly taped posters of baseball players that were already covering over the infantile look and feel of that re-doubt. *This kiddy paradise would give way to the paradise of men,* that is, the paradise of the endocrines, the paradise of growth spurts, the paradise of skin blemishes and skin blemish concealers, the paradise of the objectification of women, the paradise of circle jerks and molestation and homemade explosives, the paradise of BB guns and sexually explicit materials and sudden mood swings and filched drinks. Still, his mother suggested the possibility of *lavender* for the room, over a particular dinner that May, and wouldn't yield, though Dexter (according to Mavis Elsworth, in remarks after the fact) averred that this was the hue of *f-f-f-f-fairies, M-M-mom, h-homos.* He would have nothing to do with it! He'd move into the basement if she went ahead with her schemes! He'd become a runaway! He protested tearfully — because his mother didn't understand, didn't understand, and how could she have understood what was unsaid over processed frozen dinners, *that Hex was one of a handful of truly singular and blessed young people at his private school,* how could she understand that he was a young patriot, a defender of the Constitution, an adherent of the Second Amendment thereto, *guaranteeing the right of the people to keep and bear arms and to raise a militia, and if necessary to mount unpopular police actions in distant nations;* how could she understand him, this dignified young man who, in an era of social ferment, wore bowties and tweed jackets with patches on the elbows and who kept his hair exquisitely combed; how could she have known what it was to be a *Young Republican,* as Hex believed himself, to be recording secretary of that afterschool program, with all the responsibilities that such leadership entailed? She didn't know his special needs, nor understand the forces arrayed against him — *the yawning appetites of puberty* — and thus a battle of the wills ensued over Hex's bedroom. Over color and style, over the arrangement of furniture, over whether or not Dexter would be permitted a deadbolt lock, over wall decorations, over all the details of his life, until Mavis Elsworth herself had to intervene, weighing in unfortunately on Hex's side, at least in the matter of color. (She never understood Billie's thing with lavender.) And thus a blue-gray was instead negotiated. *Blue-gray, as you'd find there now — cracking, graying, peeling, decaying (in spite of the time in the late seventies when Lou Sloane himself did a little touch-up).*

Mavis Elsworth handpicked the team of contractors to perform these initial renovation duties. Therefore Hex and his mother returned home one day, from a seasonal shopping spree in the city of New Haven, to find ladders stacked throughout their house: in the living room, leaning against the bar; in the dining room, lengthwise on the Oriental carpet; roller handles inclining against the shelves in the library; mounds of drop cloths everywhere; a whole unnerving assortment of labor-related fetishes that reached a peak in Hex's room, where these tradesmen — three young men whose invoices referred to their construction company only as *Ascension* — were first to concentrate their energies. There was a rented table saw in the corridor outside his room, and leading into the bedchamber a trail of dusty, portable power tools. In preparation, therefore, that very afternoon, Hex emptied his quarters of most personal effects. He gathered up these cherished items and installed himself in *the rose guest room.*

He was in ninth grade. And as with many boys of that demographic niche there was a girl about whom he fantasized for astonishing amounts of time, hours on end, whole days, weeks at a time, semester after semester, interrupted only occasionally for feeding and hygiene; Hex Raitliffe did occasionally pursue other distractions — conservative dogma and statistical abstracts relating to professional sports, but mostly it was just the girl. This preoccupation with the girl endured even through the earsplitting reports of sledgehammers in his house, as one of the carpenters took out a wall separating his room and the linen closet adjacent, to add twenty-four square feet to the space he had commanded up to that time. (These laborers were chiseling away at plaster and mortar. They sanded and scraped off a half-dozen layers of paint, each with its leads and radioactive pigments.) Theoretically in the midst of exercises on the application of the quadratic formula, Hex imagined instead a private school uniform *clinging to the thighs of this girl* as she rode on her black three-speed down the long straightaway on Glendale that led to the Middletown School, oaks on either side, past a dewy red rubber ball neglected on a perfectly mown lawn, *he was thinking about the way her hips shifted with her weight, side to side,* thinking about the mild perspiration she might generate with such physical effort, until his own cheeks burned. Meanwhile, there was in his room the coat of primer that cloaked a multitude of sins. That is, according to the schedule contained in the contractors' sloppily handwritten bid, they would, next day, be constructing the six-inch raised hardwood platform on which Hex's bunk beds were now going to rest, next to the gabled window so far unscraped, and they needed, if they were to adhere to the schedule, to slap up that coat of primer. Yet, slothfully, one of these contractors sat on the lower of Hex's bunk beds, tuning Hex's own transistor radio to a squelchy FM radio station, WUCN, *this wastrel,* as Billie Raitliffe would say later, *with his unwashed locks and his drug-addled religious pronouncements and his bad beatnik poetry, and his leering remarks about homosexual practices,* picking flecks of primer from his hands while the other renovator grumbled inaudibly about work-related migraines and about how his old man busted his chops, while priming architectural details — the molding and the ceiling ornaments and the French door that was going to lead to *the new linen-closet wing* of Hex's room. They had just accidentally sawed clear through the back of Hex's wicker hamper, and they were kind of sheepish about it. The second guy's ponytail was action-painted with blue-gray latex. In a supervisory capacity, Mavis Elsworth peeked in one day, a fingernail pressed pensively against her lips, but she was so uncomfortable around the two of them, these construction youngsters recommended by a friend at the yacht club, that she couldn't stay. But how could she possibly evaluate their work if she couldn't even talk to them? Billie Raitliffe, on the other hand, was not shy, not timid, and demanded to know *why she should be paying for three of them if only two showed up, and only one of them worked.* She was in an irritable mood that week. Perhaps Billie was troubled by the situational stress related to having men take over her house, men with their nail guns and their barbaric construction dialects, sawing through wicker hampers, sawing through concealed wiring, nailing doors closed, knocking down walls that were supposed to remain standing. These two young men were the worst of the construction lot, these countercultural house painters who barely registered that they were being spoken to, blasting their Vanilla Fudge and Moby Grape and Electric Flag and who knew what else from Hex's tiny transistor radio, these beatniks who turned on a deafening belt sander anytime she tried to assess their progress, and who were always trying to store, in her refrigerator, their repulsive chocolate sodas and meat sticks. Later she would see them trudging up and down the back stairs in search of these jerkies, tracking paint and sawdust with them everywhere they went.

At the same time, Hex was in the guest room looking at a picture from the school newspaper of a girl in a field hockey uniform, her face flushed, the wind blowing blond curls from off her forehead, *feeling that he wanted to protect her from the raised sticks of her opponents,* from the clustering of stick-wielding women in those black-and-white pixels. They wore special sports brassieres. The idea of the brassiere was incendiary to him, brassieres so close to the hearts of girls, so close to the warmth that emanated from them, the flush of their faces, the math of their pulses.

When next, in that week of renovator hordes, Billie Raitliffe went in to demand anew why Denny and Chris weren't finished with Hex's room yet, especially as they seemed to take their time and to break frequently and to leave before 5:00 PM, her demands became even shriller. The other fellow, Ed, their partner, still hadn't turned up, and she was really pitching a fit about it. Where *was* Ed Valentine? And they needed to redo a molding — there was paint clotting at the spot at which the molding met the wall; they should scrape down the window in the gable; they should varnish the platform. *It was shoddy work.* Chris, sitting beside the standing lamp he had recently broken in half and epoxied back together, replied, *Sorry, Mizz Raitliffe, we'll do it over, sure, Eddie's going to get to it himself, tomorrow,* before turning on a jigsaw. A fine mist of fresh pine then fogged the room, driving her coughing from the job site. However, it turned out they *did* redo and improve upon these things. Upon reflection this may have been a strategy in their conspiracy to prolong the occupation, in order to retain their space in her refrigerator, in order to further their proximity to her boy, who at the end of this particular school day was lying in wait for the blond girl of his daydreams (it almost felt as though he knew her), waiting for her on the lawn in front of the Middletown School, on a sun-dappled lawn, and then following her home, first on the bus, later on foot, imagining a conversation in which he impressed her with detailed lectures about amphibious landings and about the Domino Theory and about the importance of parity with Soviet Russia's intercontinental arsenal and about his personal hero, *Edward T-t-t-teller, the Hungarian ph-ph-physicist,* and she was smiling as she asked, *Please, Dexter, could you tell me some more about the size of those Russian payloads?,* following her onto the school bus and then off it, and down along the water — only a mile or so from Flagler Drive to that house overlooking the craggy shore — walking twenty paces behind her, whistling jauntily, throwing a set of house keys high up into the air and then catching them, whistling Rodgers and Hart melodies his mother liked because they seemed cultivated, though the blond girl wasn't slowing, nor was she asking about the Russians, nor bothering even to take the time to tell him to buzz off. But that didn't matter. Because in the week in which his home was overrun by men, that week now stretching into ten days, a late-sixties consciousness was incrementally seizing the residents of 58 Flagler Drive, an enlightenment, and it dawned on him that maybe he didn't have to worry about what she thought, because it just felt good to like her, *It felt groovy,* colloquially speaking, this delirium in which he loved the spot between knee-high socks and the hem of her uniform dress, loved glimpses of her ski-jump nose, loved the way rage and embarrassment looked the same on her — sort of pinkish — loved the way she held her book bag protectively across her breasts, wondering *what she looked like in the latitudes he had never seen,* though this was perhaps not a Young Republican thing to wonder, wondering whether she was as velvety in that nameless region as, for example, a girl's nightgown was, whether the softness of nightgowns mimicked the softness of girls. And after she disappeared into the opaque shadows of her garage, without ever once looking at him, his greatest ecstasy was in wandering home alone embellishing.

Home, where he found that the contractors had taken over! The house was now the command center for their separatist revolution of slothfulness and countercultural values! That afternoon, they were taking a break in the living room, spinning a few LPs on the hi-fi, *when they should have been up in his unfinished bedroom, doing their jobs.* But there they were, instead, reclining on the remaining pieces of furniture, their grimy bare feet upon the side tables. One of them, Chris, was even drinking from a Waterford highball, Billie's crystal, drinking what appeared to be an alcoholic beverage! They had taken over! And they were smoking something, too, some unusual kind of cigarette, hand-rolled, with a bouquet like fermented aftershave and fresh dirt, and Chris even *offered* this homemade cigarette to Hex! *Hey, Tike, take a weight off and do yourself a favor here. Be the first in your neighborhood.* Hex had never felt so threatened! And then Chris *accidentally dropped* the joint on the floor and said, *Bend over and get that, pal, huh?* and the two of them really fell apart laughing. *Bend over!* Of course, Chris himself eventually squatted on the floor to pick it up, and the other, Denny, leapt upon him, simulating, as he cleaved onto Chris's bony lumbar region, *a sort of lower-mammal procreatory posture,* pumping hard against Chris's coccyx. *Bend over!* Needless to say, Dexter was troubled by this display. He refused the cigarette. In fact, Hex fled the house as soon as was polite and walked nervously along the golf course, kicking rocks. He didn't go back until he was sure their panel truck, with its twin-sized mattress in back, was gone for the day.

As the week of home renovation stretched into two weeks, however, *his resolve began to crumble,* to be replaced with a curiosity about the carpenters and their alternative system of ethics. For example, they always referred to minute measurements, say a thirty-second of an inch, as a *pube,* and they were constantly comparing three-quarter-inch plywood to their own fantastic and self-described *Johnsons,* and on occasion they even threatened to expose these parts. Then there was their meaningless shoptalk: *Got any ribbed shank three-pounders? Yeah, over by the pile of three-sixteenths.* Or their disinclination to good old-fashioned work. Partly Hex was fascinated by them because his mother was in a horrible mood every night, complaining about how her house was in disarray and these boys had taken over, and she wouldn't stand for it. They hadn't finished Hex's room and there were expensive tools and scrap wood and sawdust everywhere! And there was something about their calculated slothfulness, their sexual ease, the way they removed their shirts for no reason at all, the way they rarely bathed, their jazz argot, that was frighteningly seductive for a boy who'd lost his dad! But Billie must have recognized that her worry was *too little, too late,* because Hex was already striking up conversations with Denny and Chris. He stood in the doorway to his half-painted room. He listened. He inhaled the paint fumes. Chris said, *Little Man, you're gonna get warpaint all over your fine pullover sweater there you don't watch out,* laughing in his screechy laughter. Hex would ask them things. Trying to seem casual. Maybe he would pose his questions in a general way, *D-d-do you think you c-c-c-could t-t-t-tell me if a girl would ever like a guy like*

*me? D-do you think it would be a g-g-good idea for me to t-try out
for the football t-t-team?* Then, after he stood in the doorway, he
would scuttle back to his room and think about the angles of *her
cheekbones*, that girl's cheekbones, the radii of her breasts, the
amber waves of ringlets. He imagined her coming up to him in
social studies to ask him about the succession of the American
presidency after Speaker of the House. Who was fifth in line? He'd
say, *Hey, maybe we should schedule an extra-help session.*

One afternoon, Chris Knox, the renovator, waited for Billie Raitliffe in the foyer, to give her the bad news: the cupping in the
floorboards in Hex's room, east to west, was worse than he
thought, a half-inch sag, really a bad warp, probably having to do
with the beams or joists, you know, structural stuff, *probably had a
pitch there,* and the platform for the beds was going to rock unless
they built a little something into the platform itself. It would mean
customizing it. *It'll take a couple extra days, probably.* He was ad-
miring a brass candlestick on the front hall table, holding it up,
checking the craftsmanship, while he gave her the news. Their
eyes met. Billie nodded imperceptibly, said nothing, and then
strode with exaggerated dignity up the staircase to the master bedroom, where she slammed the door. And didn't come out. For an
hour, the house lay in astonished silence. Then Chris appeared to
Hex, apparitionally, in the rose guest room, *Listen, we're gonna go
for a little drive and smoke us up some reefers, killer reefers, and we
think you really ought to come along, since we're just about on the
second coat and we think a break is in order, and besides we need to
ask you some questions about your room and stuff, so we can spiff it
up fine for you, you know; so you should really take advantage of
this offer while supplies last,* the blue-gray paint on him, and that
unwashed hippie smell, that musk that would later call up this
initiation as much as anything, *Are you sure you want me to c-c-c-
come?,* to which Chris Knox replied, *C-c-c-c'mon b-b-bro, w-w-w-
would I lie to you?,* cackling as though he were the first person ever
to imitate a stammer.

Though Hex's mother might have emerged from her room at any
moment, from her *mood,* to demand where exactly he thought he
was going, Hex was irritated with his mother. It was obvious there

were profound differences between him and her, areas where there was no Raitliffe familial likeness whatever. He hated, for example, her maroon lipstick. And he felt that she overdressed a little. And her natural hair color was prettier than the fake blond the hairdresser manufactured for her. And all that church stuff was bunk. And she was soft on criminals. And she had this dumb obsession with purple. She said the stupidest things over and over again, like the aphoristic *It wouldn't taste good cold,* or, *If we were all the same, life would be awfully dull.* He himself would never even consider saying things like that. Ever. For these and other parental infractions too numerous to catalogue, Hex Raitliffe took Chris up on his offer. Without a second thought. Without even telling her what time he'd be home.

So: in the panel truck, in May, he smoked his first Jamaican reefer with the original beatnik home-renovators of southeastern Connecticut, weaving along the coastline with the radio on, every song from that trip memorable to him now, for example, "Sad-Eyed Lady of the Lowlands," "Brown Shoes Don't Make It," "Volunteers." And since the biochemical reaction described in this chapter depends on the absorption of a certain critical mass, the beatniks were giggling long before Hex was, at the very serious things he was saying, like *M-my d-d-d-dad was a physicist, b-b-but he p-p-passed away,* or doubled over cackling at his admiration for the first hundred days of the new presidential administration, and as they cackled the radio seemed to get louder and louder, there were the overtone squawks of Pharaoh Sanders and the long deejay monologues in which the personnel were given on obscure live recordings, and Denny reached into the glove compartment, into his cache of inexpensive sweetmeats, Hershey's milk chocolate, Sugar Babies, Three Musketeers, Almond Joys, Chris laughing hysterically, filling his mouth with Sugar Babies, as Hex took another puff upon that home-rolled cigarette and hacked up a caustic, poisonous smoke.

Chris then turned his attentions on Hex, with malice aforethought, to say, *Hey, pal, ever heard of the Vulcan Forge? Know what that is?* Hex shook his head. The term referred to one of the private rituals of Connecticut beatniks. Denny pulled the truck over, beside the water, beside a dilapidated launching dock, and let the van idle. Chris climbed into the back with Hex. *It's like this. What happens is you take this hit and you hold it in for a long time, a really long time, like you're underwater or something, till your lungs are gonna burst, and then when you're letting it out, letting that sweet smoke out, I'm gonna squeeze you around the waist really hard, around the middle, like when you're a kid doing the old spinning-around-until-you-faint thing, just like that, except here, because of the oxygen shortage and stuff, and because of the smoke, it makes a big rush. The biggest rush. It's really hip!* Chris seemed to get a good laugh over the whole thing. His face was pinched and red from the demands of his jokes; but Hex was terrified. Also stricken with wonder. Never mind the dangers of the *Vulcan Forge* — fibrillation, cardiac arrest, collapsed lungs, maybe even coma — he was taking the hit, heedless of dangers, brave and proud, and Chris was *hugging him.* Yes. It happened fast. Hex was holding in the smoke, holding it in, his bronchia like pins and needles, and Chris was hugging him; Chris's arms were tight around him; Hex could see these enormous callused hands and hirsute knuckles clasped around his own front like some tribal belt, the forearms flecked with paint, and then an infinite breath exploded from him, and there was *a ripping sound,* a certain metaphysical tearing that nonetheless expressed itself as an *actual ripping, the rending of the space-time continuum,* and he crumpled, and Hex was a falling body, falling onto the mattress back there, but more properly *falling into colors,* and there were angelic saxophone harmonies, and there was sleep, delirious sleep, at least until he heard Chris laughing, *Man, Denny, did you see that? The tike keels over like a pile of cinder blocks, just keels over,* now up from the netherworlds of Vulcan, up from the crusty, mortuary sadness of that stained mattress, as if his consciousness were floating around the room, and then Hex saw Chris up close, his old torn white T-shirt, his perspiration stains, his coral necklace, the tangles in his viper hair, examining Chris and then Denny, the enormity of pores and oils and pimples and whiskers, *the faces of men,* up there in the front of the van, gazing at their exaggerated features, their monolithic brows, their peculiar smells, the industrial snarl of their voices, those men with their voices *like the g-g-g-guy who p-p-p-played the v-v-v-voice of G-god in The T-ten C-c-c-commandments,* projecting himself astrally into a *lesson* of some sort, though it was unclear what this lesson was or where it ended, or where the ride in the truck ended and where the next day began or the day after or the day after; which day, for example, was the day that Mavis Elsworth peeked in the double doors of the living room while the three of them were sharing the roach, Chris laughing so hard that he couldn't pass the thing? Was it a different day? Those two weeks were all fused together, *the fortnight of renovation,* really closer to three weeks now, marked by clouds of dope smoke and cigarette rolling papers and sandwich baggies, rich parasite grass on an antique table, and a stolen beer or scotch neat in a crystal glass with smudged lip prints on it. *Hey, wh-when's Eddie Valentine t-t-turning up, anyway?* The three of them — Hex and Denny and Chris — had learned the secret joke of youth; those remodelers had trained Hex in this secret joke — behind the glimmer of light at the instant of celestial convergence and interstellar orbit — the joke about the drug heavens behind the regular heavens, with Mavis standing there, a splinter of paranoia lodging in Hex's endocrines, *Oh shit;* it was ten days later, they were high again, and Chris and Denny were laughing even harder, their voices synchronized, or their mouths were moving and sutras were issuing forth, long prayerful chains of syllables, or it was a different day and they were smoking in his room, Hex's unfinished bedroom, blowing smoke out through the screens, one wall partly scraped, the platform for the bunk beds rocking on the warped floor, and they were giggling, the hole separating his room from the old linen closet a big, gaping, ragged hole, the bunk beds covered with drop cloths, Chris and Denny leading him to the rose guest room, laughing and laughing and laughing, *Take a shower, Tike, straighten yourself up before your mom gets home, because we're gonna act scarce now,* and he said, *But w-w-w-wait, w-wait, there's something I n-n-need to ask you g-g-g-guys about g-g-g-g-girls,* the words impossibly long and unpronounceable and he wasn't sure whether he ever really finished the sentence anyway, alone in the house, long after they arrived, weeks after, initiated into the derangement of senses, exactly coincident with the mystery of women, two mysteries once assumed never abandoned, saying out loud at the time, *I'm speaking now, to see what it sounds like,* into the pristine emptiness of the rose guest room, *without stammering.* A miracle! That's how Hex *remodeled himself,* that's how he was when his mother turned up that afternoon — he was high and listening to a jazz show on the transistor, people were reading to some alto sax accompaniment (*During the days when you ate what was dead, you made it alive/Now that you're illumined, what will you do?*) and his mother appeared in her tennis clothes, a sweater wrapped around her shoulders, shivering, her voice, too, shunted into a low frequency, *Hoooonnneeeeeyyyyy, howwwwwwwww wwwwwwaaaaaaassssss yourrrrrrrrrr dayyyyyyyyyyyyyyy,* himself simply grinning, because he could feel every goofy cell in his space suit body, and there were pentatonic melodies to accompany the orbiting stars, and melodies to accompany the atoms and the smaller particles, yeah, everything felt cool, magnolias blossomed nearby, he could smell them, and the promise in the universe was *laughably abundant,* while his mom had a palm pressed to her forehead, she said something about *not feeling too terribly well.* What do you say to people when they say stuff like this? He laughed. *Probably overdid it on the tennis court — my serve was abominable,* his mother said, and it was about the funniest thing he had ever heard, you know, tennis courts, ground strokes, net games, return of service, *Well, let's go take a look at what they accomplished today,* the house in disarray where the team of beatnik renovators had half finished a half-dozen rooms, the house a ruin around them, relic of the lost Eisenhower years, *occupied by a malevolent force of men,* arm in arm they walked down the corridor, to watch the paint dry, the blue-gray flat finish in Hex's room, then by the back stairs, by the banister, on the way to his room, his mother tripped, tripped or fell, no big deal, she just collapsed, really, narrowly missed plunging down the staircase, *That first step is a doozy,* chuckling, and her smile was askew, as she clutched at the banister, that narrow look of concentration riven in her weathered face, and then into the room, a big splotch on one wall, and Billie Raitliffe said, *Well, it's damned exhausting but I guess I'll just have to give them a talking to one more time,* and then she *fell again* and he watched it all in the tranquility of intoxication: her hand reaching out for the doorknob, her legs curling under her, her legs collapsing, her tennis skirt parachuting, a hint of those athletic panties that moms wore when they played tennis, those little socks with the purple pom-poms, all flying apart in sumptuous comedy, all things going out from under her as she fell, parachuted, *cried out,* boy, it was really funny, all things falling, all things flying. And when she came to, she was unable to stand on her own. *Well, you understand that Billie learned of her condition in the middle of the redecoration process* (Mavis Elsworth goes on), *and as a result, we decided to put our plans on hold for a while. And that was really the last I saw of her, because the work never resumed. From what I was told she began to husband her savings a little bit.* Chris and Denny slouched in to collect their tools, three or four days later, to collect their Sears Craftsman table saw and their ladders and spattered drop cloths, their rollers and levels and tape measures and brushes and trays, and they left Hex behind. As their sentry.

Here's how the room looked. The blue-gray covered a couple of walls, incompletely covered them, and there was a big irregular hole on one side, where the room was partly expanded, and the scraping and painting around the gabled window was unfinished (as was the trim around the picture window), and the ceiling hadn't even been primed, nor the moldings, and the platform hadn't been sanded, and the comforter with its happy dinosaurs still decorated the bed, *and that's how it looks still,* though Lou Sloane did repaint two walls in the seventies, for the sake of symmetry. You can still see the scratches and scuffs from the rearrangements of furniture and from Hex's occasional teenaged tantrums — where shelves were overturned or projectiles were embedded in the wall; and there are spots where the masking and cellophane tape have left their black adhesives, and there are tack holes, fingerprints, even the occasional bloodstain. Storm windows that need to be cleaned. Cheap framed lithographs. An old vase. It's a neglected room, a half-finished room, a room full of broken things. But it's still home. The home to which Hex will soon make his way in the company of that girl of whom he often lay here thinking, passing the time. Jane Ingersoll.

12

The barkeep is ADD or ACOA or he's in the up part of a bipolar complaint or maybe he's suffering with irremediable heartbreak. Guys think they can hide their difficulties. But you can find the problems, if you have the key. With this bartender, for example, it's in the way he surfs. He's an artist of TV collage. There's nothing on but trash, anyway, on the wall-mounted bar television, each pulverized sitcom with its lower-middle-class ruffian and his sexy, provocative (not too provocative) honey. The subliminal tonnage of all this romantic comedy, Jane Ingersoll thinks, induces this real-life guy, Hex Raitliffe, the guy next to her, to launch a couple of awkward interpersonal attempts in her direction. (Kathleen Ingersoll, her sister, sits several seats away poring over the latest ish of *Glamour*.) Let's be honest, Jane has no intention of talking to this suitor. And anyway this Raitliffe guy is too self-conscious to identify what any idiot could see — that a menu of prime-time delights isn't for her. He blunders past these signals anyway with his getting-to-know-you cross-examination. He picks and chooses from topics borrowed from his own secret encounters with the women's glossies — probably from the waiting room at the shrink's office. *Q: How d-d-do you f-f-feel about t-t-t-today's women t-t-t-trying to b-balance the demands of f-f-family and workplace? Where d-d-d-do you see yourself in f-f-five years? D-d-d-d-d-d-do you p-p-p-practice the religion of your b-b-b-birth?* When his first lackluster barrage of questions has come to an end — with his stammering it takes a while — she's pretty sure she's given him the right sequence of blowoff codes. Hey, it's not her job to make men feel comfortable! That's why the barkeep has the fifty-four Nutrasweetened channels! Jane mumbles irritably about romance and television and politics, how they're all in bed together (it's like a plot by the Christian Broadcasting Network), but unfortunately this remark encourages Raitliffe. *Where d-d-did you g-g-go t-t-t-to c-c-college, anyway? What was your m-m-major? D-d-do you like f-f-films with subtitles in them? What k-kinds of international c-c-c-cuisine excite your p-p-palate?* The truth is, though, that the look upon Raitliffe's face — the expression behind his extra-strength-legally-blind-can't-see-a-hand-in-front-of-his-face *welding goggles* — bugs her. He's got eyes that are battleship gray. And these long, soft, boyish eyelashes. He's like a chipmunk in the road, in that instant before a professional sleazebag in a Lexus *smushes* the furry little thing. Raitliffe's all sweaty. There's perspiration eddying in the lines and creases of his pained expression; there's perspiration gluing down his scalp flakes and dripping like little stalactites from his unwanted nasal hairs. Like most guys closing on a midlife crisis, he's pretending to be years younger. So she goes on ignoring him, maybe answering one question out of every half-dozen in a noncommittal monotone, *yeah, two kids, two boys.* But she's itchy too. There's nothing worse than vulnerability in a guy. That touchy-feely stuff is a major turnoff. All the magazines tell you so. Still, even though she has a school-of-hard-knocks doctorate in the feminine wiles, Jane does feel a little bit sorry for him. When he struggles with the initial consonants, for example. And then there's his mom. His mom's a rag doll.

The first great commandment of womanhood is *Protect yourself from needy guys.* Right? Jane Ingersoll invokes a voodoo magic, therefore, in an effort to curb her cooperative and sympathetic maternal impulses. Curses, for example, on the part of her that fell for that guy, Nick Flynn — the man who sired her first boy and then left on a cross-country haul; or a curse, maybe, for the one after him, Bob Tracy; or for Jack Goulding or Elvin Herbert (who was black) or for Chris Knox (the union guy). Hey, forget it, how about a curse *on all of them* for the compassion they swindled out of her, for how little of it was returned. And a curse on Dexter Raitliffe, while we're at it, who wore flannel khaki pants all during the Summer of Love — the way she remembers it. Raitliffe, junior Nixonian, thinks he can roll back the decades. A couple of lightning bolts should rain down on him for trying to coax her out of where she is, comfortable and sad. *Q: If you were g-g-g-going to ask a g-g-guy out on a d-d-date after meeting him for the f-f-first time, which of the f-f-f-following w-w-ould be your g-g-g-getting-to-know-him line?* Jane Ingersoll has tried every stratagem to terminate this flirting business in its voluntary phase, in the shallow part of the curve. She's used all the regular old lines on Raitliffe. She's turned away. She's talked to the middle-aged man on her right, the man in the aqua-colored polo shirt and khaki pants and loafers without socks. Old middle-aged Chip.

But just when it seems like Raitliffe might be getting the hint — he's assumed a hurt and letdown expression — just when she realizes that the collar on his jacket has been turned inside out all this time, that he has gin blossoms, that he's a drunk, well, to summarize, that's the moment when the *emergency report* erupts upon the television set. It's one of those commercially-inter-rupted - dozen - headlines - in - less - time - than - it - takes - for - a - com-mercial emergency report, and the top story, what they're calling the emergency, consists of another tale of local businesses hiding their industrial *goop* in the county waterways. Big surprise! They've dumped some Day-Glo red tide in the Sound. They've dumped some acid or some nuclear gunk. Big surprise! She can't really hear the television well but she sure knows the tone. Electric Boat? General Ordnance? A spill from one of those oil tankers out on the Sound? Or maybe they're dredging the rivers again. Maybe they're dredging the Connecticut or the Thames River, and maybe they're going to dump a couple million tons of this dredged-up muck — and its *E. coli* and staphylococcus, or whatever — in some secluded estuary. So what? Same old thing! Everybody knows the shellfish around here causes paralysis! *No danger to the public,* blah blah blah blah, according to this guy standing in front of a thicket of microphones by the gate of the nuclear power plant. And her kids swim in that water, as everybody in Niantic does, at the dock by the marina, or between the lane lines at the public beaches, while the nuclear submarines go by safeguarding our unalienable right to romantic comedy.

Turns out this guy doing the talking is related to Raitliffe somehow, and that Raitliffe has been caterwauling about it for a few minutes, maybe even longer, but the truth is, Jane hasn't exactly been paying attention to him. There's a *kerfuffle* as the other drunks at the bar start to take in the news, and Raitliffe's father, because that's who it evidently is, blunders on about how *the spill made it possible to avert a much larger action, including state-mandated evacuation procedures, emergency fishing restrictions, and a possible adverse effect on the tourist economy.* Though Raitliffe's dad may employ a lot of these local characters, these bar drinkers and fishermen, though he makes it possible that they have health insurance and a subdivision to go home to, and though most of them even think their nuclear-powered hot water is a fine thing, it's pretty clear in this case that he's a lying, middle-management, collaborationist son of a bitch.

At which point, Jane finds that her sister Kathleen is suddenly hovering around her, too, that bloodsucking mosquito of a sister of hers — the meddlesome, 4-H club, small-town sister, her fake-blond-hair-and-pink-toenails-and-matching-eye-shadow-and-Lands'-End-wardrobe sister. Kathleen sidles up to where Jane and Raitliffe are sitting, smiling her expensive smile of childhood braces and retainers, Kathleen with her uncanny timing for whenever there's a scrap worth retelling. She's just waiting for news, as if this strictly temporary warmth between Jane and Raitliffe is because of her powerful instincts for matchmaking. But there's no real chemistry between Jane and Raitliffe anyway. Not the kind that Kathleen needs to get involved in. Nothing there at all, in fact, just the sympathy you feel for a guy who's in a bad spot. Jane tries to shoo her off, but Raitliffe seems to pick up on the friction and begins to pitch his tale of woe to this larger audience —

— The thing is that a c-c-c-couple of d-d-d-days ago — I guess it w-would have b-b-b-been . . . yesterday, or the d-d-day b-b-b-before . . . my stepfather . . . Well, it's sort of an awful story, really.

In the infrared light of the bar, Raitliffe leans in toward the Ingersoll sisters, whispering. It's not a seductive whisper; it's more heartbroken. The place has emptied out, the diners are all gone, and they're all staring emptily across Penelope's, past the lobster tank and salad bar, *at his mother*, the three of them — Jane and Kathleen and Hex Raitliffe — but maybe the others are staring too, these drinking men and women Jane Ingersoll used to look up to. The guy from the post office, the student life counselor from Roger Williams High, the minister from Grace Church. Maybe they're all looking at Raitliffe's mother, wondering what she's dreaming about, while on the thirteen-inch screen, her husband's proclamations are again broadcast to the coast.

— He just left this n-n-n-note, and that's it. I mean, my m-m-m-mother is d-d-disabled, she c-c-can't t-t-take c-c-care of herself, and he j-j-just left this n-n-note, the k-k-k-kind of thing you would n-n-never say to anyone, n-n-never, especially n-not someone who's, you know . . . who's really ill. You know? And I c-c-can't believe now he's standing there b-b-bantering with the reporters, p-pretending everything's okay . . .

Jane's on the point of saying something thoughtful, something sympathetic — because the story starts to sink in — but at the same time she doesn't want to seem like she's encouraging him or pitying him, and she doesn't want his sob story to be a pickup line, she wants it to be *true*. So this opportunity passes, like many opportunities for compassion. And it makes her a little sad. In the meantime, Kathleen muscles in to interject.

— Oh dear, that's awful! Is there something we can do?

— My m-m-mom, Raitliffe says, — she c-c-can't read anymore, you know, she c-c-can't m-m-move the p-p-p-pages. So when I'm h-h-home I read to her — that's how she's able to read. It's important to her. Anyway, Louis b-b-bought this c-c-c-computer for her a c-c-c-couple of years ago, and he p-p-p-put this letter on the c-c-computer for her . . .

Some other stuffed shirt on the television, in an off-the-rack suit, talks earnestly about the leak: they're going to empty some high-level waste into the harbor at Niantic. A *minor emission proto-col*, or some pack of lies. They're going to pour it in there. That's the short version. The report cuts away to a shot of the swimming dock, then back to the reporter, all while Raitliffe is stalled between consonants. Then, on the next station, the public isn't in any danger again. But Jane's companions, the drinkers, have already begun to forget. Because that's how it goes. They forget the news, the names of the poisons, the names of their wives, the names of mistresses, the names of people sitting beside them, the things they're trying to forget, everything goes, that's why she comes here, and when they wake from forgetting, when they realize where they are, they start to forget all over again.

Then *Raitliffe's mom has a seizure.* Or at least Jane thinks it's a seizure. Mrs. Raitliffe's strangulated cry is shrill, uncomplicated as an infant's. Loss, remorse, anger, confusion, impatience, all mixed into one bloodcurdling shriek. Raitliffe knocks his stool over getting up (the barkeep turns up the sound on the television), and the hostess of Penelope's, Jeanine, rushes for the bar phone — *should I call for an ambulance?* As a glass is also overturned somewhere, a shattering, and all the amnesiacs turn and gander, Jane among them, hoping for the swift intervention of trained health care professionals. But Jane, for really inexplicable reasons, gets involved. Who knows why? She's up off her stool reflexively. Because she's a single mother with a thoughtless generosity, the Ingersoll girl who once married a black man and disgraced her family — she's up off of her own stool, following Raitliffe, with no clear idea why. Well, she also dropped out of a nursing program once. They're not like a team, she and Raitliffe, she barely knows the guy, but however it works, they're lifting his mother out of the booth, carrying her legs — she's heavy and slack — they're setting her in the wheelchair, wheeling her into the bathroom, except that the chair won't fit through the door to the ladies' room, there's a reek of urine upon Ma Raitliffe, it's pooling in the wheelchair, pooling underneath, ebbing and flowing like a local salt marsh, still coming, in fact, and upon Jane now too, Jesus, *this woman's pee is on her hands,* lifting, carrying, then wiping down Raitliffe's mother, his disoriented mother, with a dishrag (presented by this girl Jeanine, the maitre d'), his mother who's deaf on top of everything else, or so it seems, gurgling and mumbling nonsensically; and Jane tells Raitliffe he's going to have to take his mother to the ER, but right now they're crammed into this single-occupancy ladies' room, his mom's head inches from the toilet, Jane's butt halfway out the door, they're breathing that stale disinfectant, while his mother is sputtering, *Don't you dare, I will not go there! . . . No hospital, Dexter . . . just a little rest . . .* and it's true, Jane Ingersoll supposes, that Ma Raitliffe is probably beyond artists of scalpel or chiropractors or physical therapists or social workers or round-the-clock nurses, and that's probably why Raitliffe doesn't even argue with her, *Well, I'm g-g-g-going to t-t-t-take you b-b-back to the house, then, and I'm g-g-g-gonna c-c-call what's his n-name,* and the situation seems suddenly under control except that Kathleen and the barkeep are also standing in the door of the ladies' room, looking alarmed, five of them in there now, the door propped open by Hex, the barkeep making it clear that the medical emergency, if that's what it is, would probably be better handled someplace else, where his business wouldn't be hindered, and Kathleen is asking what she should do, *Go mop up, stupid,* Jane says, and that's when Jane and Raitliffe agree between them to put in the catheter, put the thing in Ma Raitliffe, a little plastic bag thing that's designed to prevent the trouble that has just taken place, and there's no way around it, no way around this *intimate moment*, not the kind of intimate moment Raitliffe was hoping for maybe, not the kind featuring the shedding of cottons and the late-night sounds of the Love Unlimited Orchestra, *Imagine you are s-s-stranded on a d-d-desert island with a really ugly g-g-guy, and you have to repopulate our entire civilization, do you (a) m-m-make love with him, but k-k-keep your eyes c-c-closed and p-p-pretend it's really Eddie Doherty, the qu-quarterback; or (b-b) d-d-do you f-f-fling yourself on a b-b-bonfire vowing to p-preserve your d-d-dignity until eng-g-gulfed b-by flames; or do you (c) t-t-try to d-d-discourage him, using c-c-carefully worded arguments about the ch-chemistry b-between the sexes; or do you (d) f-f-find mutual interests in film and p-p-p-p-popular music that might serve as a b-b-b-bridge between the t-t-two of you?* They have the plastic tubing and the bag, and Raitliffe cranks the hot spigot until there's mist on the tarnished mirror, and he does his best to sterilize the tubing, passing it to and fro under that scalding jet, while she's holding Ma Raitliffe's head, stiffly repeating reassurances, *It'll all be okay, it's fine,* and he kneels down beside the two of them, Raitliffe does, beside Jane Ingersoll and his mother, and lubricates the tubing with some stuff, some petrochemical lubricant he has for this purpose, and then having completed these elaborate preparations, Raitliffe just spooks, freezes, he can't make a move, he's terrified, and he looks at her, looks at Jane, imploring. He's glazed with perspiration, he's every inch his age. He doesn't know if he can do it. *I don't know if I* . . . So Jane says, *Shit, just give me the thing,* and wings it according to her abandoned nursing program. Ma Raitliffe is motionless as this exploration takes place; her eyes are averted and running over with tears and the air in the rest room is stale as Jane Ingersoll lifts the hem of Ma Raitliffe's dress, feels up where it's moist. There's the dripping of the sink tap incompletely shut off.

Jane comes to some conclusions during this procedure. In the midst of trying to put her index finger on the urethra of an elderly woman, Jane concludes that this moment is sort of romantic. Like when your husband refuses to carry you up the stairs after you sprain your ankle chasing his kids; or like when your old ball-and-chain sneaks out to a bar with some floozy and comes back to beg for your forgiveness; like when your *cross to bear* calls you to tell you that you were much better to him than his new girlfriend; like when your marriage ends. Bingo. Romance is bad interior lighting, convenience stores, bowling on the league nights, seaside towns in winter, empty main streets. Romance is in the hearts of people who have abandoned romance. It thrives best in rooms like this, single-occupancy ladies' rooms where women give up the ghost.

Thus, Jane Ingersoll finds that Raitliffe's fingers are vines around her own, and the coiling of these vines is in a way *romantic,* and this is what allows them to ease the medical tubing into his mother. *How f-f-far is it supposed to g-g-go? I don't know, an inch, I guess. Is the b-bag filling up? There's nothing to fill it with — it's all over the floor. Wait. Did you feel that? Okay, I think it's all set.* It takes maybe half a minute, all told. Ma Raitliffe doesn't feel anything. Just indignity.

Then they're lifting her back out of the ladies' room, back into the chair. Kathleen is mopping along the passage from the booths to the rest room and of course it's slippery as hell, and stinky, and Jane goes into a skid, trying to set Ma Raitliffe in the chair. How does she get involved in this stuff? Down she goes, carrying Ma Raitliffe's legs, scraping one elbow, landing on her ass. A prosthetic shoe heel bangs her in the forehead. Ma Raitliffe collapses onto her. Hex onto the two of them. And Jane's sister Kathleen doesn't even apologize. Jane dusts herself off, dusts off the smudge on the knee of her leggings, and then goes to fetch Ma Raitliffe's overcoat from the booth. *Say you're doing emergency care with a guy on the b-b-b-b-b-body of his terminally ill parent, (a) d-d-does the experience b-b-bring you c-c-closer? or (b) does it drive you further apart?*

One last glimpse of the television on the way out of Penelope's, into the light rain, the mist, the night, yep, romantic comedies and their romantic couples, standing in front of chintz sofas, in front of their own monstrous television sets, faces red from arguing, shouting jokes that aren't jokes at all, while a voice rumbles in the back of the laugh track, that same laugh track resold from producer to producer, the same laugh track with that voice, the guy who goes *yeah!* on each and every telecast, in the furthermost reaches of the electronically enhanced studio, out across the homes on the prairie, as lovers probe for wounds.

Then a numerical problem presents itself, having to do with automobiles. There's an abundance of vehicles. Because Kathleen came in her teal Japanese subcompact with the balsam-smelling deodorizer in it, and the Raitliffes have their Hertz Taurus, and Jane Ingersoll arrived, as she often does, on her *motorcycle*. A little baby Honda, not much pickup at all, not even chain driven. Good for hurtling through town. The bike, however, is unsafe in the rain. An initial car-pooling proposition would naturally involve Jane going with the Raitliffes in their car and just sending Kathleen home — where she will immediately dial up her friends and gossip about the evening. But Jane doesn't want to be stuck at the Raitliffes' house. She'll see Ma Raitliffe and her stammering boy home, sure, just to be neighborly, just to make certain that Dexter can manage the situation for the night, but that's it. After that she's out of there. She doesn't want to spend her weekend out without the kids — the dads have visitation — being a nurse. Therefore, a second solution presents itself to her.

— Let me drive you home and borrow your car, she says to her sister. They hover by the side of the Honda.

— Then what will *I* drive in the morning?

— What do you mean? I'm gonna bring it right back. I'm gonna help him unload his mom and get them situated and then I'm coming straight back to your place.

— Well, why don't you take your . . .

— You want me to spin out? It's raining!

The two Ingersolls, light and dark, in the midst of their quarrel, each turn to survey the Raitliffes, across the deserted blacktop in front of Penelope's. The Raitliffes, unequipped for the elements, stand by the Taurus. Hex looking up into the skies, as if the rain is punitive somehow. His mother, with her quilted overcoat gathered around her, slumped over in the chair.

— Look, Jane says, let me borrow your car for a couple of hours, and don't be a bitch about it. I'll bring it back.

Kathleen shrugs.

There's a price, of course, which amounts to Jane listening to Kathleen's hot air, her theories and opinions. Tonight's subject? *Codependency.* She read it in the magazines. Codependency: seven troubling warning signs, including irritability and religiosity. You can see the seven troubling warning signs in your man, because certain preoccupations will be distributed throughout his family, drinking, gambling, binging, purging, shopping, fucking around. *Every relationship is codependent, really,* Kathleen says, *and has the potential to be toxic in this way;* in fact, she, *Jane Ingersoll,* Kathleen says, had a codependent relationship with Chris Knox, *thank you very much,* as they both did with their dad, even though their dad didn't drink all that much, and their mother had a religious compulsion, and she was always trying to get them to eat certain foods, and she was always trying to get them to volunteer at the hospital, and on and on and on with this new codependency-related overlay, until Kathleen turns her analysis at last to Hex Raitliffe's stepfather:

— It's when someone gets too reliant on somebody else, you

know? Here he is in a long-term relationship with a crippled woman! No wonder he wants to take some time off! That's what I think.

The worst part is that they're caught on the Baldwin Bridge, the only way across the Connecticut River, the only road. On Friday evenings, the traffic backs up here. In every vehicle, motorists are trapped in conversation, watching the trains race past on the railroad bridge, gazing upriver at the promise of distant forests, the colonies upstream, wondering how far they'll have to drive together, how many thousands of miles, listening to one another's opinions? It takes Jane thirty-five minutes to drop Kathleen home and get to the Raitliffes' house, per Hex's directions, and when she does she finds a note. Taped to the front door. *It's open. Went to get more beer.*

13

———————————————— Moonlight in a break between clouds, and the temporary illumination of drainage valves, a quarter mile offshore, nine feet, fifteen feet, twenty-three and a half feet on your depth finder, at the instant when water at high temperatures begins to course through that valve, pumped out hydraulically into the Sound at Niantic, into the currents. Moonlight on the water, reflection of a reflection, espied by the driver of a rented Taurus, with fuel leakage, following (at some remove) a white Cadillac, in turn following a late-model Ford Tempo.

(The plans for Millstone Reactors One and Two landed on the desks of the Atomic Energy commissioners in 1965, before environmental impact statements affected the business. The back ends of the nuclear process, the daughter products of fission, *the wastes* — chiefly isotopes of iodine and strontium 90 — were, according to these plans, to be tank and pool stored until they decayed to stable levels, usually within a month. More toxic vintages with unimaginable half-lives, which began to accrue over the years because of fuel recycling, were also confined to these sites. Since the coastal region of Connecticut was in 1965 thirsty for industrial jobs, and since the AEC was itself a newly enacted government agency with mixed ambitions, and since civil engineers hadn't yet developed long-term storage contingencies, these disposal and dispersion plans as proposed by Babcock and Wilcox for the Millstone plant were considered appropriate. The AEC, with nominal public oppo-

sition, signed off on the blueprints. Moreover, at the time of the
signing, Millstone's proposed edifice also included shunts that
would pump cleaning solution and rainwater and runoff and anything else that couldn't otherwise be eliminated — including
alphas, betas, gammas, and their fissioning elements — a half mile
out along the floor of the Long Island Sound. In the event of
emergency, these effluents would be moved through lead-lined
pipes to an evacuation point, where they could mix with busy
currents there, in this way diluting the runoff. The AEC also approved of these proposals.)

Hex grapples with the steering wheel. He almost believes the
problem is with the alignment. The Taurus falls into the ecstasy of
oncoming brights, lurches back into the lane. It's like driving a
boat. Having deposited his mother at home, having carried her
upstairs, having toweled her off, changed her housedress, and put
her to bed, having whispered over her invocations to sleep, he then
telephoned her neurologist, Ron Kramms, MD, who wasn't home,
and left word with the service describing in detail her condition —
*inc-c-continence, d-d-disorientation, h-hearing loss, mood swings,
m-m-m-morbid thinking* — and having performed responsibly, he
tried to relax. He awaited the arrival of that spirited young woman
Jane Ingersoll.

What did he figure he was going to do with Jane? What would
he do when she got here? With his mom just down the hall? It
wasn't like his luck was good with the fair sex. There had been a
few scuffles, over the years, women he would meet at parties, as
difficult and troubled as he knew he was himself — like Gillian,
whom he met at some reception. They fell into each other's lives
like an influenza, desperate for what they had each believed themselves to be lacking, dinners and arguments about movies and
even shy, exploratory carnality, and then there was the predictable
disagreement, at the juncture between the second and third
month, wherein she wanted to spend a certain weekend alone, and
he hung up on her, or perhaps he said he wanted to be alone. In
NYC, there was always a reserve of aloneness that preempted
attachment. Most often, Hex recognized that he fastened his infat-
uations onto anyone at hand, girls at ticket counters, women with

lavender nail polish, telephone operators, telemarketers, even Jehovah's Witnesses. They all seemed to have an unspeakable perfection at first. But then he learned, anew, that he was without the passwords, without the signet rings, without the secret handshakes of true love. How would this evening be different? What would he do? *Change his mother's diaper while p-persuading Jane to take off her jeans?* Hex sat in the living room. The lamps there were of low wattage. Their light was unspectacular and sad. There was medical equipment everywhere around him. Gurneys and oxygen tanks and stethoscopes and multiple pairs of ominous rubber gloves. The computer cursor still called out to him with its bad-news compositions. It wasn't a house for seductions. Never had been. Still, Hex wrestled with desire for twenty minutes, with the difficulties of desire. If you're attracted to a person, is it reliable that they are likewise attracted to you? If a date isn't *stated* as a date, is it nonetheless understood as such? So when Jane Ingersoll didn't show (as they often didn't show when he was waiting), he decided to go out for beer. He climbed the stairs, checked his mother. Billie was motionless, eyes closed, hands folded over her chest.

Loneliness and convenience stores are mutually implied. While Hex Raitliffe took a spin around the aisles of Store 24 — nostalgic for his adolescent love of sweets (Hostess Fruit Pies) — he verified, empirically, the faces of loneliness. There were a half-dozen soft, bespectacled, and unshaven guys in sweats preparing their evenings of domestic beer, microwaved hot dogs, potato chips, tattoo magazines, and network programming. This loneliness of convenience stores was also his loneliness. Loneliness was his parking space, his fully furnished studio, loneliness was that apartness that had been a feature of his comings and goings way back into the browned edges of memory, back through his twenties and after-hours drunkenness in NYC; back through the teens; back through the snapshot humiliations of his chubby boyhood; back even unto infancy, loneliness like a foreign tongue, *like an absent dream.* It was the siren call of himself. *There was no appreciable difference between him and the guys buying Narragansett beer, Ridgies, donuts, and* Cheeks *magazine,* and that was what led Hex to pay and bolt, peeling out of the meager parking lot (around self-serve pumps), out onto the interstate, a light rain falling through his open windows, out on I-95, over the clogged Baldwin Bridge, following bulletins on the radio as if the epicenter of broadcasts were Magnetic North — driving recklessly because the feelings that propelled him were reckless, a riptide of concern and apprehension, until, impulsively, he parked at the mom-and-pop filling station across the street from Millstone Nuclear Power Plant and waited. His car smelled like gas. There were barely refrigerated American tallboys on the passenger seat. He popped a warm one. He waited forty minutes for that signifier of cheap nobility, that white Cadillac — Lou Sloane's boxy, white, powder puff of a car — which emerged past the reporters about the time of top-of-the-hour newscasts. These traditional detective techniques were easy to master.

One-fifty-six leads out of Niantic toward Old Lyme, but the Cadillac, which Hex has now concluded is itself following a cheap American subcompact of some description, turns left off the main drag. Soon, they're onto the back roads, the unlit tributaries, adjacent to the coast and then away from it, on tortuous routes, past the cheap residences from the construction boom of the fifties and sixties. Prefab with vinyl or aluminum siding. Every now and then there's a break in the monotony of indigenous maples and half-acre lots, and you can see the harbor and Millstone caught in the crossbeams of spotlights, until the convoy plunges again into enveloping darkness, further into that uncharted area of which Hex knows so little, the lower middle class. When they gain the summit of a hill on the peninsula, it's all tiny quarter-acre water views, with perfectly manicured shrubs, satellite dishes, garages ringed with lobster pots, bikes with training wheels toppled over on the lawns, nameplates on the sides of the houses — *The Kirbys, The Scullys, The McElroys* — yard lights. Hex rechecks the power locks.

To make things more difficult, Sloane's Cadillac slows to a crawl. A posted speed zone. A tightly knit community. The residents turn in early to curl up around the microwaves of their satellite dishes. There's no other traffic on the road. In an effort to preserve his deep cover, then, Hex idles for a while alongside a grove of shad and cherry and densest thorns. The flora of the shore. It must be the last undeveloped lot within miles. When he gets impatient, though, he slowly noses out onto the street, Mariner's Lane, past a half-dozen identical houses, each with its distant view of the power station — blue houses, pale green houses, yellow and lavender houses — only to find that the Cadillac is gone! *Shit, shit.* He backs up surreptitiously, to the empty lot again. He parks. Doesn't want to draw attention. Doesn't want trouble.

He gets out. Unsteadily. With a six-pack.

It's only a half mile from the tip to stern of this overdeveloped neighborhood, the Niantic Shore-Owners Association. Lou has to be in here somewhere. It's a process of elimination, it's scientific, it's a numbers thing. Hex will find the Cadillac. By foot. Pedestrians are harmless. Furthermore, the urgency of his moral purpose forbids poltroonery. Hex Raitliffe hoofs it, and the act of pursuit stanches the feelings from the earlier evening. Who's going to take care of his mom? And how long has he been out driving around now? Why did Jane Ingersoll stand him up? And what will he say to Lou? All this blotted out by his righteous crusade.

He cuts across a lawn at the corner. There's an occasional moonbeam now, and in it he can make out the perfect striations of lawn mower tracks across here, striping the lawn, dew upon them. However, just as Hex congratulates himself on his voluminous knowledge of lawn mower stylings — these are undoubtedly the tracks of *a tractor model* — a vicious barking peals from under the elm at the corner of the property. A rottweiler! America's fearsome and trusted watchdog! Old *Spike* or *Cujo* lunges from the shadows at Hex, desperate to close its jaws around those gelatinous quadriceps, and Hex propels himself — defying gravity — back into the lane. The dog catches on the end of a yard lead and begins to cinch its collar, strangling itself. In the house, a light goes on. The second-story window. A woman's voice — *Leonard? Leonard! Go see what's going on!*

No Cadillac in that driveway.

Hex immediately puts a reliable distance between himself and Spike, at a healthful clip, until, down the block, he's on a bluff above the harbor. Before an arresting view. There are all kinds of trucks and vans over there at the power plant. Spotlights criss-crossing. Bumper to bumper in front of the gate. Or so it seems. Hex goes down over a slope, as the bluff plunges toward the water, cuts across another lawn, tiptoes along shorn topiary that separates the Kirkpatricks from the MacIlvaneys, until he's woolgathering upon somebody's sturdy, cement retaining wall. The harbor just below. The rich, bacterial stink of low tide. The sound of a foghorn. From this angle, in shimmering moonlight, there are also the houses out by the point, where the architecture gets more ambitious. The Shingle style. Landscaping. Hex stays for a while on the retaining wall, pops another beer, sits, guzzles, admires the night, and then shot-puts the empty out to sea. He's struck with the intensity of it all, with the intensity of his *quest* —

Until suddenly he's blinded by an all-weather high-powered deluxe Sears flashlamp, and there's *that voice,* the voice in dreams of persecution, harsh, masculine, repressive, a sort of a dad's voice, *Hey, pal, can I help you with something?,* and Hex makes a completely awkward effort to raise his hands (in one fist the plastic six-pack holder, four cans remaining). He can't make out much about the interrogator, because of the flashlight and the hooded outerwear — but he can tell the guy is a *dad.* Who else gets rousted for such a mission?

— Uh, I was j-j-j-j-j-just . . . I was j-j-j-j-just l-l-l-looking for a f-f-f-f-f-f —

— You got some kind of problem there, pal? You got some reason to be in my yard? Because I'm not sure —

— No, I . . .

The guy closes in. With the flashlight. He's wearing foul-weather gear. Full beard.

— I'm pretty sure whatever you're doing, that it doesn't need to be on *my* property.

— I agree absolutely. I, uh, d-do you want one of these b-b-b-b-b-beers?

The guy draws a blank for a second.

— Look, don't give me any attitude. Don't even try it. Because what I want, pal, is for you to get back on the road in the direction you came. Before I call the cops. Get it?

— No, p-p-p-p —

And Hex, without any intention of capitulating to what the bearded guy asks, nonetheless crosses the yard, back toward Mariner's Lane, while his friend the enforcer, standing at the edge of his patch of American property, trains the beam on him in silence, watching him go. Just when it seems as though Hex's movements are thoroughly prescribed and proscribed and abridged and amended and legislated, though, just when it seems that any notion of an unfettered, dangerous, and ecstatic *liberty* has been wiped out here in southeastern CT, Hex bolts up the lane, toward the point, toward the lighthouse. It's great! A beer escapes from him, toppling from its plastic goggles, pinwheeling along the tarmac, springing a foamy leak. Another goes spinning across a lawn. Hex's lungs heave. He coughs. He starts to laugh. To laugh! Old Ed Driscoll (or whatever his name is), defending his land, calls after, *Hey, this is private property, buster!* So, to confuse, Hex veers preemptively to the right, away from the shore, lurches into a stand of conifers. On the cheap side of the boulevard. No unobstructed water view. It's a dark wood, a folkloric wood, where he stops to rest, where he bushwhacks, where he impales himself on limbs. He knocks his glasses off and falls to his knees, *Not again,* grabbing up handfuls of pine needles (and poison ivy), *where are they,* spinning this way and that, until at last he steps on something, something glass, hears the awful crunch, *oh no,* falls to his knees again, and wearily lifts them, his favorite specs, with one shattered lens, to his face. In the distance, Driscoll calls to a neighbor across the street, *Over there by Van Zandt's,* and Hex goes deeper into the woods, all a blur now, can't tell the direction of the road or the direction of the sea, deprived of the spotlights ricocheting from tree limbs, oriented only by a balsam smell, backward and dead reckoning, until he happens fortuitously into an idyllic backyard. It opens before him. A backyard from the past. From the fifties or sixties. With swingsets and slides all in yellow and red and blue. With a badminton net. With a croquet course. With fruitbearing trees. With a screened porch. And then another dog comes at him. It's a husky. Or a wolf! He can't tell. He hightails it back into the trees. The dog barks itself hoarse. The rottweiler, in the distance, replies. A small chorus of neighborhood hounds then begins, in staccato. The light of flashlights, fragmented by impedimentary tree limbs, hovers over him, sheering off along unpredictable latitudes. Pursued by wild animals and a posse of deputies, Hex can imagine only one course of action. A middle way. Only one hideout. *And so he climbs up into one of the pines.* One limb at a time. Up into the narrowest branches. Twigs score his rutted face. Hex Raitliffe, thirty-eight years old. Up in a tree. The dog, meanwhile, the one pursuing him, comes to the end of the yard and freezes. He must be wearing one of those electroconvulsive stun collars. The collar has electrically induced a seizure of some kind, and now this hound is foaming at the mouth, delirious, immobile.

Much later, up in the tree, Hex's hands are raw from clutching, as the canopy sways — the earth like an undulating tapestry just below him. He sees the flashlights recede down the street. Hex's legs are quivering with exertion. He's afraid he'll fall out of the tree, or that its limbs will give under him, that he'll plunge through the underbrush, shatter vertebrae, rupture something. Branch by branch, cautiously, he lets himself down the tree. Into underbrush. And just when he thinks he's lost them, more footfalls, in the woods, padding through the beds of pine needles.

It's a small boy. A boy in unnaturally baggy jeans and a mass-produced tie-dyed T-shirt and baseball cap (backward), holding what resembles, in the half-light of the distant porch, a water pistol in the shape of a foreign submachine gun. An Uzi. He's maybe ten or eleven. Hex brushes the pine needles from his suit coat, now torn slightly at the elbow.

— I used t-t-t-t-to have a shirt like that, he offers.

— Who are you? the boy says. He gives the trigger a lethal squeeze. The water catches Hex on the chin. The kid laughs huskily.

— Are you g-g-going to c-c-call your n-n-n-n-neighbors? Raitliffe takes off his shattered glasses and wipes them down gently on the hem of his jacket. With the back of a wrist, he dries his chin.

— Whaddya mean . . . ?

— Isn't it p-p-p-p-past your b-b-bedtime?

— What's the big difference, mister?

Hex finds he wants to give the kid something, some advice, some aphoristic morsel — before the police arrive and enclose him into their childproof backseat and take him to the hoosegow. He wants to take advantage of this moment, to warn the kid against lures and snares of contemporary America; he wants to offer his own benevolent friendship. At this strange cusp in his adventures, it seems important. So he starts telling him things, stammering drunkenly, about the luminosity of the night, its moonlight and downpours, about the strategic importance of autumn, about lone-liness and women and before he can stop himself —

— I'm a g-guy who took a *wrong turn* in the middle of town looking for things, see; I'm a g-guy lost in the wrong town; it's like I n-never settled d-down, you know, and I'm no good at my so-c-c-c-called p-p-profession . . . I can't seem to get along with anyone . . . and th-that's the truth . . . So I —

The kid's not registering anything. He sharpshoots at distant targets, boughs of trees, night-dwelling rodents. What parent would leave him out at this hour?

— Did you see any Cadillacs c-c-come this w-way? A white C-c-cadillac maybe? Hex asks. — Kn-know what a C-cadillac l-looks like? B-b-because that's the c-c-c-car —

— What's it to you? the kid says distractedly.

And Hex is stunned by the simplicity of the reply. Even kids think he's a fool. He's exhausted. He's in the worst possible spot.

— It's a long story.

And now Hex violates the unwritten rules of boys approaching puberty, the rules of his woodland host, *that emotion is faggotry or womanliness;* he looks away for a long time, for an interval that would make other adults uncomfortable, and he begins to precipi-tate, and the kid just stands there, like a specter, saying nothing. And having succumbed to this vulnerability, in a fell wood, away from the social conventions of Fenwick, Hex discovers, after all, that the boy is compassionate. Because rather than divulge Hex's location, the location of a fugitive from justice, rather than call out to Niantic lynch mobs combing the area with bloodhounds, the kid just squirts him one more time, between the eyes, cackles, and turns to go back to his house. That is, he turns, with his automatic weapon, and heads into the brush, into the ambiguous night, without commentary. This generosity brings to climax a display of emotion in Hex Raitliffe, a display including gratitude, a surfeit of feeling, and then he falls against a tree trunk, his slot-mouth gaping with a soundless wail, a dollop of mucus tracking down his upper lip. How did he get here? Where is the boy he might have fathered by now? This juvenile delinquent might have been his boy, had Hex not squandered so many years. What's he doing here out in the woods? What is he going to do about his mother? When he finishes this display, it's with the greatest exertion. He's trembling. He's badly underdressed. He's damp. It's cold.

You know, part of this trouble has to do with drinking. Any number of metaphors on the subject of drink wouldn't describe its shape and scale and effect in Hex Raitliffe. Drink brings the music of angels, drink brings the slough of despond. Thus, Hex Raitliffe, shivering and damp, now realizes that somewhere in this wooded acreage he set down the remainder of his six-pack, his tallboys, two of them, and that this beer is gone. This was a trip out for beer. His life would be an unending catalogue of bad luck, if totaled up, except that as he nears the margin of the forest — mumbling a little bit of a prayer, *Hope the c-car is all right, hope the c-car is all right* — he actually *trips* over some beer. It's true! Here in the woods. In the nacreous dark. He reaches down and comes up not with his own beer, tallboys offered up to the woodland druids, but with three or four lukewarm imports that have been carefully left behind for him. Forests, you know, are where the alcoholics come to stow their emergency supplies. In case the little woman has mucked around in the flush tank and thrown out the brandy; in case she has found the pint of rye in the gun case. These long-range planning experts, they come out here to the woods to pursue their regimen of spiritual exercises, and then they go back to their wives or their husbands pretending to calm. Hex feels an immense satisfaction at finding the three warm German beers in the woods. He polishes off the first immediately. He begins calculating with renewed vigor equations of velocity and motion or perhaps indices of refraction or compressibility, as he goes, as he parts a bank of shrubs, goes out into the road, into this quiet beach neighborhood,

over the lip of the next driveway, dappled with moonlight, so joy-
ous, so full of feeling as he sips the next brew that it's hard to
believe — here by the yard of a ranch-style home (painted a fecal
umber). There's a hammock strung between the trees in the front
yard. Maybe this is where he will rest a while. He marches into the
driveway as though he's going to commandeer the place, to find,
parked beside the Tempo, under the basketball net, his quarry. A
Cadillac.

14

——————————————— Throw the bums out, Mac Kowalski says (at seaside), don't encourage them. Limit the terms, cut the salaries. Doesn't matter if they save the sub base, because the rest of the town is a damn mess, the entire Main Street is for rent. And the guy who got elected beds two-dollar hookers in every city on the campaign trail. Every state in the nation, and his frigid wife goes off for five minutes, and he's —

They're on the dock. Mac and Lou. Gazing out. Kowalski's rowboat is bobbing in the troughs, just below. Clouds hurry across the night sky. It's *old guy talk,* old guys and their broadsides, their jeremiads, their outrages. For example, how did they get caught up in this business, anyway, this business of nuclear generation, where they power half the state, fifty goddamn percent of the goddamn state, but everybody *hates* them, like they dropped a ball in the seventh game of the series. Everybody hates them. *Old guy talk,* impotence, memory loss, deafness, bifocals, incontinence. And though, as older guys, they're a blight on the free exchange of ideas, when you really look at them (moon emerging from behind nimbus clouds), you can identify the mechanism of their helplessness. It's in the lapses of the conversation, in which they slide the whole way from politics to the inevitability of sickness and senility. Two older guys standing there, on the dock. Lou with an overnight bag at his feet, Kowalski donning his pullover sweater.

— Nightcap? Kowalski says, clapping an enormous hand on

Lou's shoulder. — Let's stay up late and watch blue movies. Let's solve the problems of the world. I'm not gonna worry about getting in on time tomorrow. Let the regulators run the place.

— Give me a minute.

Lou says he might have left something important in the car, which he hasn't at all. And Kowalski understands. Kowalski starts back across the lawn. There's a garage-mounted security spot that comes on to indicate motion in the driveway, and it suddenly splashes Mac as he ambles (with the methodical progress of a backyard raccoon) toward the porch door. Domesticity — as Lou looks at it from out here — seems unimaginably tender; domesticity is the really inviting porch light. Lou drinks of this tenderness for a long while, this poetry of the ranch-style house on the water with the collapsing dock. It's the poetry of old guys mulling over their solitudes.

In fact, he thinks he might go for a little row. Lou thinks that he might just get in the rowboat, cast off, go for a quick turn around the harbor. The sound of tides. The sea air. He's feeling this compassion. The harbor ebbing, the wind, the night. Rowing is better than your weekly attendance at the damned church coffee hour; rowing at night, drifting down toward the City of New York *is a spiritual act.*

The automatic light on Kowalski's garage snaps off after two minutes, and Lou is bathed in dark. He'll just sit in the boat for a second. He'll just see how he likes it. It's an impulsive idea, rowing, but he's trying to indulge in these impulsive ideas. So he throws the windbreaker on the dock, sets the overnight bag on it, and lowers himself down the ladder on the piling. Into the skiff. Into the puddle in the skiff. *Darn.* His loafers! His socks! It's cold! And yet when he tests the oars, he feels pretty good. Damned good, in fact. The oars are wooden, conservative, none of your lightweight aluminum stuff, good sturdy oars, paint worn from the locks. There's a danger of splinters. He splashes as he hefts these tools. Sea water flecks his glasses. Then Lou casts off boldly, looking back at Kowalski's house; Kowalski, who seems to be pacing around the brightly lit kitchen making some kind of drink with a shaker, something involving ceremony. Lou leans forward and pulls the foreline into the bow. He flings the coiled spring line onto the dock. Then he begins a rolling motion. With his oars.

He runs aground right away. Not hard, just brushes against an outcropping, really. There's a dull, muffled thud. Snailed and barnacled, this rock; but even with no speed at all, even under human power, it could *stave in your rowboat pretty easily.* It protrudes above the swells. Lou's shame at his marine skills is immense. However, he manages to circumnavigate the hazard, *Hard to starboard, Louis,* and is soon thirty yards out into the waterway, under the moonlight, on this Friday night. His stroke has a couple of bad stutters in it, he catches crabs, not like when he was young, when he used to row the river in Groton. On the other hand, there's a dignity in being here, in being an older guy in the harbor, in shirtsleeves, bathed in this night, pursuing the exercise of ancestors, thinking occasionally about the woman you left behind.

Romance is cut short, however, when his ticker starts to complain. Louis is just breaking a sweat. But then the port oar skims the surface, misses the water altogether, and the boat lurches into a spinning motion that sends him into a green marker. All at once, he can't catch his breath. He's wheezing. Lou drops the oars into the bow and checks his watch — his deluxe, light-up-at-any-depth watch — and finds, in fact, that *he can't find his pulse,* not at first. It's a worry he has often indulged, that he will still be conscious, wide awake, when he gives up the ghost — that he will witness the slowing and stagnancy of circulation, that he will feel his brain asphyxiated, that he will be conscious as his last thoughts fade. But just as Lou begins to go into this panic of the hereafter, he locates on his upturned wrist the fits and jerks of his anxious tempo. Tachycardia. Hell, his heartbeat can't possibly be designed this way, with seconds of total silence followed by herky-jerky spikes. Like some monster movie percussion score. *Dammit. Dammit to hell.*

He takes a slow look at the harbor, Niantic harbor; he's seen it from every possible angle, land or sea, during every season, in every light, in every weather. This coast is written on him. He doesn't want to head in, doesn't want to face up to Kowalski, not really, doesn't want to have some heart-to-heart about his foolish plans, doesn't want to talk about them with anyone, favors them silently like a trick knee, but he's also afraid to go further out, too. It would be a shame to pass out into heaven on a childish adventure, to be found twelve hours later, spinning in the currents around Race Rock in Mac Kowalski's rowboat.

And he's exhausted. And he can barely lift the oars. And with the currents running out to sea, he has to do twice the work to make any progress on the way in. In fact, Lou is working at peak capacity *just to stay where he is.* As he fights strenuously to within a stone's throw of the dock, Kowalski's automatic spot goes on again. Lou cranes to see, to wave to Mac, to call out, and as he does so, he drifts back out. Christ. Mac stands there benevolently, on the dock. *I'm a little hung up out here!* He's embarrassed. It's an old guy thing. *No, wait.* It's not Kowalski at all — he notes with adrenaline urgency. He holds fast and squints over his shoulder. *Hang on. It's his stepson.* The prodigal, ne'er-do-well, wastrel stepson. What the hell is the kid doing here? Lou is outraged. His first reaction is plain outrage. He thinks of turning the boat around; he thinks of drifting out into the tall reeds or into the salt marshes, under cover of cattails, waiting for Dexter to leave. Never liked the kid. All the contempt he suppressed out of respect for his wife now has an opportunity for temporary display. But while he's thinking about it he smacks lightly — but with an ominous crunch — against another rock. Is the rowboat taking on water? *Goddammit.* He's sinking! His heart may give out at any moment. Thus do old guys come ashore. He throws his back into a couple strokes, gasping, coughing, ekes out another few yards, until Dexter himself reaches down for the lines, grabs the side of the rowboat, cleats the spring line, guides in the nose, offers a hand. Lou's already struggling up the ladder. Already thanking him exaggeratedly.

— A p-p-p-pleasure, the kid says.

— Almost went down, for godsakes.

They check the cleats one more time. Dexter: fore, Lou: aft. A ritual from years past. Then Lou waits as his pulse subsides into a *lento* passage. Neither of them speaks. Then they move silently away from the dock, away from the house (Lou takes up his overnight bag and leaves it again by the Caddy), up to the mouth of

Kowalski's driveway. Sloane and his stepson measure up one another, figure the spectrum of conversations. Dexter is dressed like hell, not that it's unusual, in a thrift-store suit with a rip on the sleeve, in suit pants muddied and gashed. His crewcut hair looks patchy, and his glasses —

— What happened to the eyeglasses there?

— Stepped on them. In the w-w-woods.

And Dexter is slurring. He's drinking a beer that looks like it spent years buried in the backyard. He's at the spot where the stammering is improved by drink, but the slurring is getting troublesome. The kid is a drunk. As surely as his dad reportedly was.

— Surprised to see you here, Lou says.

Dexter frowns.

— I'm surprised to see you t-too. Although I saw you on t-t-t-t-t-t-television and everything. Wasn't too hard to find you.

— Oh, that, Lou says, rolling his eyes. — That's probably not what you came to talk about.

— No.

A grimacing and twitching is part of the kid's delivery. Lou feels sorry for Billie's son, though he can't stand being with him. Dexter had it rough growing up, *but who didn't?* Whose life story doesn't need a couple of hankies?

— I came d-d-down to t-t-take c-care of Mom today, I mean, she asked me t-t-to —

— What's wrong with Aviva?

— Well, M-mom . . .

— Isn't she showing up?

— Are you . . . just g-g-going to interrupt m-me the whole t-t-time?

Derisively, Lou postures. With folded arms.

— M-mother c-c-called me yesterday evening, or maybe she had Aviva, I don't kn-know . . . Somebody called last night, t-t-telling me to come up. So I c-c-came up. And M-m-mom showed me your l-letter. That was the d-d-drama of the afternoon.

An ugly warmth courses in Sloane at the mention of it.

— I don't see that there's much to discuss.

— W-well, if that's your —

— I can understand why you would want to come to see me about it, but I'm not sure I'd have all that much to say. Not to you.

— I'd rather d-d-d-d —

Dexter gets completely hung up on an initial *d,* and in the interminable bobbing of his ventriloquist dummy chin, Lou turns away. He watches Kowalski. In the house. Kowalski, like a bachelor cooking for his date, lighting candles in the kitchen.

— I'd rather h-have a n-n-n-new *hole* in my h-head than ask you for help in this area, Louis. I m-m-mean, t-talk about falling down on the job. D-d-do you have any idea —

— You have decided to get a little personal about it?

Lou closes on him, a couple of steps.

— I just thought you ought to kn-know how it was going for your w-wife since you left.

— I don't want to hear about this from you. I'm not interested in your point of view, and the situation doesn't really concern you. Except incidentally. If you want to hear how I felt about my marriage, perhaps someday I'll share it with you. But as you can probably understand I haven't had the most terrific week, including a really long day at work, and —

— W-well, that p-pretty m-much sums up m-my —

— So don't go trying to antagonize me because I don't think that's a tactic that you —

They incline toward the conflict, as though they're warming themselves beside it, as though this were an end-of-the-line prairie campfire. Lou could walk away, but he doesn't, and Dexter's face, up close, in the garage security light, is red and determined.

— Well, Dexter says suddenly. — M-maybe *I* haven't always been up to the t-t-task of t-taking c-care of her in the p-p-past . . . Louis, I think it's p-p-probably true . . . that I haven't been up to it, but that doesn't mean —

— Like that time . . . Where were you, for godsakes? When she —

— B-but my attitude is that things are j-just d-d-different now. I really f-f-feel that things are d-different and that w-we . . . I think you and I should agree on this.

— What the hell does *that* mean?

Finger-pointing begins to accompany the dialogue.

— I m-m-mean maybe I wasn't always there . . . b-b-but I'm here n-now. I'm here t-t-today. You should step up to the plate, too.

— Dexter, I mean it. I'm not . . . I can't listen to your holier-than-thou remarks. I lived with her for fifteen years. A lot happens in that time. And there's a reason why things are how they are. I don't have to justify them to you or anyone else.

— Well, I understand, Dexter says. — But I'm her son. That's what I'm t-t-t-trying to tell you.

Sloane says nothing. Impatiently.

— And I don't have anyone else.

— Well, I —

— And . . . I'm not t-t-totally c-confident that she . . . It l-l-looks . . . the situation is really *bad*.

— What do you mean? You've finally noticed? Something is wrong?

— She wr-wrote this, uh . . . well, I'm n-n-not sure I should . . .

They dance in and out of thronging shadows, at the edges of the driveway; they affect casual poses — Dexter unsteadily. It's the way it has always been in these conversations, where the categories of *father* and *son* are more barren than in the conventional formulations. Lou has tried to teach Dexter things, now and then, has tried to instruct, has tried to dispense a paternal wisdom. Once when Dexter wrecked their car. Once when he lost a job. All these conversations, with their dismal results, are suggested by this one.

— I d-don't kn-know, you know, how this is g-g-going to work now . . . I j-j-just think you sh-should c-c-come b-back, Lou. I think you should reconsider.

— Well, I'm not going to take up the slack because other people are unwilling to do their part. What the hell.

— I think you're m-making a mistake. I d-d-don't think you really see what a little f-f-f-f-f . . . what a little p-p-patience would mean to her. She's *d-d-devastated*. I'm n-not any good for her, Lou. She relied on you. And you still —

Dexter breathes. A delay in which he composes himself.

— Well, you still l-love her. Right? And l-life is t-t-too short.

Then Lou Sloane reaches for Dexter's arm. He hasn't even considered what he means by the gesture, whether it's out of conciliation — as when you reach for the arm of another guy to say, *You know, for the male of the species, your company isn't too bad,* or whether he's harboring a little unexpurgated rage. Whichever, Dexter takes a giant step backward, and waves Lou off. He looks as though he'll say more and then he doesn't.

— Look, I'm sorry, Lou says. — Tell me what's going on. Okay. Give me the details. I'm sorry.

However, Dexter's faraway look is fused to a point, and as Lou turns to look, the dull fixity of their conversation, their fixity in their mutual concern for Billie, in which a détente is achieved, this fixity is thrown completely off by Mac Kowalski. Who's coming up the driveway in a low gear, bearing a cocktail. Kowalski is spilling the drink everywhere, so bent is he on the fine entrance, and by the time he's part of their tussle, he has emptied most of his libation on the driveway. Dexter, to all appearances, imagines the worst. So does Lou. There's a febrile *inclemency* about Kowalski.

— Mac, Lou says, — you remember my stepson, Dexter.

Of course, they've met at the occasional company picnic, under the setting sun, under reactor steam clouds; they've eaten mussels on the beach, had ears of fresh corn wrapped in foil, cooked baked potatoes at the edges of bonfires. They've each wandered down the beach at these picnics to drink beer among the rocks. They've each laughed at bad industry jokes. But this is different. Mac's rageful political monologues have given way to an even more sinister philosophy. A rich broth of hormones is stewing in him.

— To what do we owe the pleasure?

— Listen, Mac, Lou says, — I think this is probably a conversation that Dexter and I should be having between us.

— Just trying to look after you, Louis. I thought I saw some commotion, so I figured I'd come out here and lend a hand.

— We can settle this ourselves. Promise.

Mac gives the two of them a sullen, drunken stare — its menace is frank. But when he might leave, just when he might find new distractions for himself in the kitchen, among desserts and main courses, *Dexter pipes up.* Dexter, it turns out, is spoiling for trouble. He's drunk too. Whatever the cause, *he rushes at Mac Kowalski*. Though the other man has a hundred pounds on him. All at once the two of them are like manager and umpire disputing the call.

— H-having a p-p-problem staying out of other p-p-people's affairs?

— Who's asking?

— Fellas, Lou says.

— *Fairy*, Mac says.

— Mac, Lou says.

— Suck on your mom's trust fund a little longer, Mac says. — Maybe that'll set things right.

— L-l-little c-c-concerned about the m-m-m-m-masculinity thing there?

— Watch your damned mouth.

— No w-wonder you g-g-guys are d-dumping that shit into the ocean, j-j-jerks like this —

And Lou is no student of prizefighting, but he knows the pastime includes the *roundhouse punch*, and that idiom pretty well describes the way Mac winds up, at this last provocation, from the left, catching Dexter in midsentence on the plane of his right cheek, between ear and nose, with a comical smacking sound. Dexter's beleaguered eyeglasses go flying, his beer spatters the driveway, and a dismal and heartfelt cry issues forth from Lou's stepson, an anguished cry, arriving expected or predicted somehow, as Dexter rises from the driveway, gravel in his palms, clutching bent eyeglass frames, as Kowalski shouts, *Shit!*, and grabs one fist with the other, massaging it, and Dexter staggers up, doesn't even raise his hands to return the volley, while Kowalski is shouting, *Get up, get up*, swinging at him again, the next punch being (as Lou grabs for Mac) a right uppercut, which a practiced prizefighter might expect after the roundhouse, but the battering goes awry, and Kowalski manages to connect only with Dexter's collarbone and therefore to drive him back several steps, as Lou himself gets into the mêlée, *Mac, for godsakes, this isn't going to solve anything*, Dexter expecting to hit the mat at any moment, solemnity and passivity in him the most expeditious way to get it over with. As

Mac flails, while Lou holds him off, Dexter checks himself. Nose-bleed? He'll have a shiner all right.

— Get off my property, you asshole. Before I fix you up good. You don't know anything —

— I'll handle it, Mac, Lou says, imploringly. — I'll take him back over to Billie's. Go on inside, for goshsakes. Act like an adult.

And Kowalski, still clutching his hand, begins to retreat at last, but with an eye on the situation, retrieving the martini glass from the edge of the lawn, *I don't know how you could ever live in the same house with that cocksucker, Louis.* Meanwhile, there's some strange placidity in his stepson, who likewise begins to recede into the darkened streets.

— Wait, wait a second, Lou starts helplessly. — Look, I'm really sorry . . . He just has a short fuse. It was a horrible day, that's all. You can't imagine.

— I'm g-g-g-going to the p-p-police, Dexter says, and then starts to laugh a sardonic laugh. The convulsive merriment of the perse-cuted. It pours out of him. As if he'd been concealing this mirth for some time.

— Let's keep it between us, Dexter, there's no reason to make a big thing out of this.

Soon they are on a dark stretch of the lane, on Mariner's Lane, heading toward the Niantic Shore-Owners Association. Lou is content to let the conversation rest, to measure the distances with his paces. At least they both seem to know how to leave one another alone, to go about their discrete contemplations. At least they can agree on some things: families are thrown up around the flimsiest of conceits, a day in the Caribbean, a night on the town. You grow closer to whomever you share your house with, as the horse depends on its lost stall mate.

— She's talking about euthanasia, Dexter says at last.

He doesn't even stop walking. (There are flashlights up ahead, swaying merrily.) He's whispering.

— *What?*

— She asked m-m-me t-t-today if I would c-c-consider . . . you know. *No h-h-hospitals* or anything. She's stockpiling sleeping pills.

The conversation is cut short by cries — *There he is!* — and some neighbor of Kowalski's is upon them, threateningly, with a barrage of questions, *What are they doing in the neighborhood? What address are they visiting?* More threats. Citizen's arrest. But Lou Sloane, because he's a manager, immediately begins the discourse of facilitation; he falls into the opaque tone he reserves for team meetings — his son and he are in the middle of a grave medical emergency, etc., and it's only the gravity of their cause that has led them to these expedients, etc., and he hopes that they haven't inconvenienced the neighborhood in their haste, etc. — and soon this guy, the lead vigilante, a bearded guy, softens. Lou sees them all relaxing. Because he knows he can demonstrate to anyone that most of the big ethical and social problems of the day are merely people problems, and though Ed Driscoll tells Dexter that the cops are on their way, it's clear that all of this can be negotiated, and soon Driscoll, and Lou, and some other fellow from up the street (Leonard Van Zandt), and Dexter, are all strolling amiably up the lane talking about fishing and about whether the blues ran as well this summer as in the past, the price of cod versus haddock, and only one last issue hangs in the air, after the locals have slipped away, have barricaded themselves into their private sanctuaries. Lou and Dexter are standing beside the shiny rental Ford. A summons on the windshield.

— Tell me again.

Dexter sighs.

— She m-m-made me help her sign th-this thing with the d-details. How she wants me to do it. You know, Lou, she c-c-cries and then I j-j-just want to d-d-do wh-whatever she says. I'm n-not as strong as I should b-be. I'm not sure I'm up to it.

— Well, you can't let her push you around or make you do anything, Dexter. Because . . . that's just not any way to live. Give her a piece of your mind, that's my advice, stick up for what's —

But Lou can feel the transparency of the argument. Sheepishly, he falls silent.

— More advice. I've only b-been here one day and already I'm exhausted. T-t-t-too much advice. T-t-t-too much stuff to think about.

— Are you going to be able to drive?

And he wouldn't admit it under oath, but Louis Sloane recognizes some feeling in himself, some distinct hydroelectric surge of respect for his awkward stepson. Mightily, he fights off the sentiment. Mightily, he avoids the impulse to console the young man. It's part of the old guy code. Instead, he thumps on the driver's side, on the window, as Dexter buckles himself in. He calls after the exhaust, where he won't be heard, to the old growth of shad and cherry, on that empty lot, to the landscape as it was before, before weekenders corrupted the landscape hereabouts, back when there was nothing in the neighborhood but thorns and Congregationalists. To the vacationing saints of old New England, Lou whispers the secret he has to tell:

— Dexter, I'm going to think about the line you're selling me.

15

———————————— She can't be sure at first if the shade on the footstool is a trick of light or a trick of paralysis — wherein a certain floral slipcover or a love seat or a standing lamp resembles instead her fellow man. There are torsional shadows in her room. Revenants. Well, her glasses are splayed on the bedside table, atop an unopened book. Thus, this guest on the footstool is consubstantial with furnishings, with chairs, draperies, occasional tables. Edgeless and indistinct. A Late Impressionist visitor. And Billie can't slip on her glasses to settle the issue. Instead, she strikes up polite conversation, though she could be talking to a chintz recliner. It comes back to her, however, that indeed there was a woman at the restaurant — at the seafood diner. She sorts through recollections, girlhood in Minnesota, Manhattan steak houses, empty coffee shops of the seashore with their lobster salads and frothy root beers. What was then, what was moments ago. A goulash of consciousness. She can't be sure if the remarks she's made already — *You'll have to excuse me . . . if I'm not a better hostess* — are intentions or remarks, wishes or deeds, especially without a response from this upholstered woman, this interior decoration —

— Not feeling . . . up to giving you . . . the tour of the house. . . . Please accept . . . apologies.

The olfactory sense, the one with its pulleys and engines intact, confirms, moreover, the presence of a lighted cigarette in the boudoir. An act of impropriety that Billie doesn't have the energy to correct. In fact, she's encouraged by the sachet; it suggests a reliability of perceptions. It must be the woman from the restaurant here in the room with her filter cigarettes. Billie intends to ask after Louis, too, to ask the woman if Louis has gone out on some nighttime errand — turning off the lights in the goldfish pond, closing the windows for the rain — so impressionistic is her sense of events, but just as she composes these questions there is the stump of her conjugal amputation, and the polite conversation — in which Billie puts a good face on her own troubles, in which she is charming and indomitable — comes to an end.

— Well, the woman says, — I sure didn't expect a tour.

— Mm . . . , Billie says.

— Can you speak up? Just a little?

A tear runs over Billie's lid, gathers momentum on its shortest possible distance, tracks southerly. She eclipses the next, or does her best. Meanwhile, the woman smokes. A cloud settles above the bed, under the canopy, and when the woman is done smoking (after her nervous stubbing out of that nicotine-delivery system), she comes over to where Billie is prone, this woman comes, the room splitting in half, spilling baubles of color, lambencies. The young woman rises from the footstool, in stocking feet, pads toward the bed, until her face looms over Billie Raitliffe, inflated. She has badly dyed hair, and erosions on her face, flaky patches. Eyeglasses. Her hand parts the angora air around Billie, reaching through to brush back a stray lock; wordlessly, she touches Billie's face, these fingers like a feather duster thereupon, and Billie finds, in spite of all, that she is grateful for any laying on of hands. Even better, the woman then reaches for the spectacles on the side table and settles them upon her charge's nose. Edges are restored.

— What did you . . . could you . . . tell me your name again?

— You don't remember? Jane. Jane Ingersoll.

— Sorry.

— Well, we were in Penelope's, and your son. . . . Well, Dexter and I brought you back over here. More or less.

She tugs at the edge of a comforter. Refolds it, smooths a wrinkle.

— But the thing is I met you before. Way back when I was just a girl. I mean, once or twice, anyway, because Dexter —

The name seems unfamiliar at first — Dexter? Dexter, Dexter — and in the act of forgetting she is freshly alarmed by the stupor of neurotransmitters. Her body responds as through bad phone static. She expunges her motherhood, the only honorable job she ever had. Did Dexter leave the house with Louis? Was Dexter here earlier? Is Dexter home for the weekend? In the repetition of his name, there's a flicker of his melancholy, his naïveté.

— And I came back to meet Hex here and to make sure you were all right, but he seems to have gone out for a minute or something. So I'm just waiting around for him, you know, and I thought I'd come up for a chat.

— How long . . . was I asleep?

This Jane person, by the footstool, performing an almost origami arrangement of bedclothes, seems to concentrate all her attentions on Billie. Listening keenly. Her ministrations are somewhat ridiculous in light of the way she presents herself. Excessive eye penciling — *eye crayon* would be more accurate — skintight black velvet tights, bosom not in the least restrained.

— Asleep? Oh, I don't know. Hour and a half, maybe. Forty-five minutes.

Among Billie's failed biotechnologies is her chronometrical sense. Her days are of shifting durations and equinoxes. Three eight-hour days, each with two and a half hours of shut-eye, or one seventy-two-hour-long night, or an Alaskan summer with scarcely a quarter hour of unconsciousness. Any nap or respite in the evening leaves her wide awake and solitary through the black hours of earliest morning.

Jane Ingersoll disappears into the master bath, with its capacious tub, its aluminum railings, its ten thousand prescriptions — the bathroom of a cruise liner, a trans-Caribbean gerontological bathroom — and Billie can hear her mufflings and paddings, filling a glass, setting aside some beauty potion. Jane distractedly makes an observation about how short the days are getting, like scrap paper in a gale, they seem, and then turns up at bedside with a glass of water and, improbably, a loopy childish straw, a glow-in-the-dark straw with a half hitch or sheepshank or love knot in it, bobbing in opaque tap water.

— Left over from Halloween, Jane says, amused with her ridiculous surprise. — My kids love these things. They take them everywhere. Evan wanted to take it to the speech therapist with him. I had to take it away from him.

Jane holds the glass while Billie sips from it, while Billie is engaged in her effort to avoid choking. Choking would require advanced nursing, and this would be inhospitable. When a last tablespoon of the water, making its passage through the faintly glowing straw, spills out upon Billie's dress (she can't remember why she's still wearing her dress), Jane whisks away the glass and sets it on the beside table. Without a coaster.

— In the drawer, Billie gasps.

— Oh, sorry . . .

Coastal Power and Light, a pad. She slides it under the glass.

— How old . . . are your children?

To which Jane offers a number of lengthy anecdotes about boys and the trouble they get into, their tendency to get really messy head wounds (*Evan ran down into the basement, smack into a girder!*), clothes that are outgrown in days (*One time I swear I could actually see him growing*), how they fall out of trees and fall off of bicycles and fall in and out of love with you. They go into your room and rummage through your drawers. They read the love letters you leave on your desk. This is the sudden, open landscape into which their conversation flees, the landscape of boys. Wild animals, with grass-stained trousers; boys shooting at woodland mammals with slingshots and pellet guns, boys naked with the neighbor's girls, boys groping their Little League pals, their friends and relations; boys and their mothers. Jane, according to Billie's sense of it, expands as her torrents of motherhood spill into the room; Jane begins to smile, a guilty smile, as if motherhood shouldn't be as rewarding as it is. It's a fine conversation for a time. Until Jane arrives at a dead stop.

— You know, she says, — you kind of got yourself into a mess at the restaurant earlier, and it might be a good idea if we were to maybe sponge you off.

— Well, you know . . . , Billie says, there's a little difficulty —

— I mean, I don't want to cause any trouble, but —

— Unfortunately . . . there's a sort of a . . . practical problem . . . it's awful . . . but I get muscle cramps . . . that sort of thing . . . in the tub. It's . . . unpleasant for guests.

— You what?

— Also, pains . . .

Jane composes a lazily sympathetic expression.

— On the other hand, Billie says, — you know . . . if you . . . if the water is . . .

— Excuse me?

— If you keep the water cool . . . if it's body temperature.

— Well, I don't know if that's such a hot idea. Maybe when Hex gets back —

— Hot idea? Billie says dryly.

— He's had more practice.

— Perhaps you could run it . . . with some bubble bath? The smell of a bath . . . is lovely.

Jane is cornered. The Widow Raitliffe is compelled, these days, into interpersonal politics. She is implacable, determined. She provides no alternatives. Jane therefore paces the bathroom, trying to decide, hands on hips, brushing back split ends, straightening things, relaxing into a carelessness. *Whatever,* she thinks. Whatever. For the second time that day, then, a bath is to be prepared for Billie, who is aware, as Jane is not, of the peril. *But with Louis's farewell like a billboard upon her,* safety is the least of her concerns. So Jane draws the bath (the sound of running water elemental and curative) and lights a honey-scented votive candle (on the counter, beside Billie's ornamental brushes). The bubble bath has an evocative perfume, lilac and church incense, and the light in the master suite is ocher, autumnal.

— Where . . . did you say . . . Dexter went? Billie calls, but Jane doesn't hear (or doesn't reply), and Billie has to repeat herself. It's a referendum on her very ability to communicate, and she's doing her best to shout. *Why does this Jane person have to leave her alone in the bedroom?* At last, Jane emerges, having stripped down to her tank top, her blouse tied in a knot around her waist; elsewhere the spout gushes into the tub; steam begins to cloud the bathroom, to billow through the doorway.

— He went to get some take-out.

— You don't need to . . .

— Said he'd be right back —

— Drinking, probably, Billie pronounces.

Jane is busy with practical questions. She scans the room, disappears briefly out into the hall, in search of the wheelchair.

— How should I cart you in here?

However, Jane Ingersoll must be used to carrying kids around, carrying small boys under her arms, their toes and feet wiggling like pennants as they steal from the shelves of the supermarkets. Jane Ingersoll must be used to it. Her arms are sinewy, with *biceps and lats*, or whatever they're called, the hillocks and knolls of youthful anatomy. Jane throws back the blankets that drape the Widow Raitliffe, and the two of them get a good look at that body, its twigs. The artist who would draw Billie Raitliffe would be accused of the mere suggestion of figure. Billie suspects that Jane is shocked, because Jane speaks of her every intention gently, *I'm going to just pull back the sheets here . . . I'm going to pull you over to the edge of the bed.* And then she begins to pluck Billie's housedress from her, very hesitantly. Billie's cavities and concavities are like those of a prisoner, or vagrant, a personage shivering and dispossessed and naked, except, that is, for the disposable and absorbent adult undergarment. *Better be careful about . . . taking that off.* Her body hairless, defoliated, goose-bumped. Jane un-Velcros the diaper, and with that diaper full of ammonia and chamomile, she does the etiquette-class walk into the bathroom, to avoid spilling somehow. Upon returning, she plunges her hands under Billie's bony hips, her fold-up skeleton, puts her lower back into it, and launches Billie up into the air, and into a change of scene, rising up over the edge of the bed, unsteadily, her head tumbling against the breast of this younger woman, older mother in younger mother's arms; *mothers make this world habitable, mothers arrive to ease your anguish, mothers remain afterward to sort out your mess;* from this angle Billie's own feet depress her; her feet are gray and lifeless; the flesh almost green underneath her nails; she was pretty once, too, but who will believe that now, though there must be auburn photos that will tell the tale. Jane sets Billie on the throw rug in front of the tub, removes her antique spectacles again, and then reaches to slip a hand under the undulant bubbles. When she's satisfied about the lukewarmth of the bath, she does some more heavy lifting, this naked old woman, slipping Billie's toes in first, as though she were about to be honey-dipped, and then the rest of her under that fabulous blanket. Jane Ingersoll's face, as she lowers Billie into the tub, somehow becomes bearded with bubbles — perfumed in lavender, bearded in white. *First time in a month of Sundays that Billie has felt the urge, for a moment, to laugh.*

The water hardly eddies in this peace, of course, because Billie doesn't stir, seated on the aluminum brace that holds her there, keeps her from drowning. In the silence, Billie loses Jane Ingersoll to some daydream, no doubt of her own mother, Mrs. Ingersoll. Why else would Jane bother with the Widow Raitliffe, had there not been a Mrs. Ingersoll who listened to the diatribes of the young Jane with her beatnik dresses and her motorcycle-driving boyfriends and who knew what else? The steam in the room induces the past, the Ingersoll past, the Raitliffe past, especially after Jane nudges the door shut. To forestall draft.

— Is the water too hot?

The widow doesn't reply. Nervously, Jane Ingersoll rouses herself, directs the conversation back to the study of sons. There's a quarter inch of water on the tiled floor now, the throw rug is soaked through. Jane splashes while scrubbing Billie's back. She goes at the job eagerly. — What was Dexter like as a kid? What does he do in the city?

Billie says, — Sensitive . . . sensitive to a fault . . .

The questions generate more questions. *Did he get into trouble in college? Were his grades good? Did he come home for the holidays? Did he expect you always to do the laundry? Was he a difficult teenager? Did you find you were stricter than you'd expected to be? Did you find discipline was hard to administer? Were there things that Dexter refused, on principle, to eat? Do you always think of yourself as a mother now? When do boys begin to resist their mothers*

*for good? Did you ever find that your training as a mom was finally
over?* It's nervous chatter as she sponges under Billie's arms and
lathers her hair, and it prompts Billie's monologue, in reply a tem-
pest of verbiage — entirely misunderstood because of her poor
speech skills — but one that extends well into the next few minutes, notwithstanding the occasional interruption, binding together the two mothers, in a sort of prolegomenon to any future
discussion of sons:

— When they're teenagers . . . they always get into some business . . . with music. . . . I didn't much understand it. . . . Even if
you like . . . foolish music . . . or liked it . . . when you were that
age . . . the noise they're fond of . . . is worse. . . . It goes without
saying. . . . That's when you first know that they're going . . .
through puberty. . . . When Dexter was very young . . . he liked
what I liked. . . . Then he changed . . . but if you haven't had the
. . . experience with the youngsters . . . you think it's you that
caused . . . whatever difficulties they get into. . . . Well, for example . . . his grades started to go bad . . . at the end of high school.
. . . He seemed distracted. . . . There's probably a . . . special curve
. . . for the grades of adolescent boys . . . or some such. . . . He
surely wasn't going out of the house much . . . and then later he
got the draft deferment . . . went off to college . . . studying God
knows what. . . . Your boys will study what . . . they think will most
upset their parents. . . . So he was taking *Eastern religions* . . . and
Marx and Nietzsche and the philosophers. . . . Allen would have
had a coronary, honestly. . . . Still, you know . . . when he finished
a candy bar . . . I would reach out for the wrapper . . . and when
he was having . . . trouble with the classes . . . I would read the
textbooks. . . . When I had to stop the car short . . . back when I
drove . . . I would reach over to keep him from hitting the dash . . .
and when he wanted to break the crystal goblets in the pantry . . . I
swept up the pieces. . . . If I saw he was aching . . . then I ached
. . . and if I saw he was happy . . . then I felt happier. . . . I had
raised this happy man . . . I thought, and so . . . I noticed I didn't
mind . . . doing these things . . . and of course I knew . . . that
other people would . . . shake their heads . . . what shabby clothes
is he wearing? . . . When I went to visit him when . . . he was in

the college infirmary . . . Dexter took . . . some pills of some kind . . . got very sick . . . they pumped his stomach. . . . I was on the canes then. . . . Anyhow, when you are a mother . . . you love your boy . . . the way God loves him . . . you don't see the awful haircut . . . you don't see the dalliances . . . you see the part shining up . . . the healthiest part . . . and you never stint on affection . . . you never know how to do otherwise . . . do I love him still? . . . without hesitation? . . . Well, yes . . . I have my concerns. . . . That money he has. . . . It's enough to put off . . . growing up. . . . You let your boys manage things . . . at a certain age. . . . You declare them adults . . . whether they want to be or not. . . . The ones that don't get pushed out of the nest . . . love you most . . . and hurt you worst . . . leave you anyway . . . and you'll get used to the . . . stretches of loneliness . . . and that's when you know you don't want to be merely a mother . . . though a mother is the best thing you have been . . .

— Want a cup of tea or something, Mrs. Raitliffe? Jane interrupts when the declarations become unintelligible. — Sometimes it's nice to have a cup of tea with a bath.

— A cup of tea . . . might be lovely —

Jane selects a pale blue towel from the rack. For drying the widow. When Billie's child-rearing manual sputters out once and for all. The younger woman gives the cold water a boost, from the tap. And stirs her cauldron with the scrub brush. She smiles at Billie again, generously — she must have had braces as a girl — and Billie feels a sense of accomplishment, as if she has passed down the wisdom, preserved the legacy. Then Jane heads out to fetch the tea (*spearmint, please,* the widow calls). *Rigidification occurs then.* As if fine-tuned for her solitude. In her sternum. Her chest knots, and then there's an incision that races through her abdomen, answered by a blow in the lumbar. Theme and its variation. Front and the rear. The complementaries of pain. Billie groans. These transient throes, the sensate zones of her innards, are then followed by the predictable neuralgia, darts in her face, stippling her forehead, her scalp, each to a pore, all before she might even register any accounting of pains, and then the most ridiculous variant on the whole thing, *pains in her teeth,* for God's sake, which are mostly capped or cemented in, anyway, after a half-dozen root canal therapies — and she shrieks, and the stitches flicker and feint. Just as she is trying to cope with the menu so far, her eyes begin to go dark, first at the margin, a chiaroscuro, a clair-obscure blindness, in which she can make out the sink, the blue towel, the shimmering bubbles, but the door is gone, draperied in gray, and then the mirror and the lamp have dimmed, and there's something stabbing in the roof of her mouth, as if she's chewing on pushpins, and her eyes are extinguished, and she is bobbing in the water, in this silence, with screws on all her swollen joints, the muscles coiled and helixed, her breaths shallow, the rolling thunder of spasms wiping out even the autonomous functions, *what if her breathing goes before her thinking does, Jane, Jane,* the calls are so frangible, so brittle, and her legs do their involuntary dance, their spasmodic dance, the water churning, a balled fist percussing against the side of the tub, and she's thirsty on top of everything else, if she could just slip her tongue down and lap up some, if she could organize herself to slide under the surface; the pains dart from front to back, she's impaled, lanced, disemboweled by her agonies, and her jaw seals shut now too, *Jane Jane, please,* if she could slip under the meniscus of the tub, as the bright light erupts, recognizable after the fact, only after its hangover, the bright light of haphazard wiring, memories stacked indistinctly into one vacuum-packed memory, burst of light, burst of memory, folded back onto itself, a yearning, a hankering in an instant and then consciousness folded sideways, an envelope of love, of the love of mothers and sons. Her mouth begins to foam.

16

I'm talking on a dial phone, an old dial phone, five pounds' worth, and this kitchen is bigger than my entire apartment. You could park trucks in here, or feed an army, and the refrigerator, one of those enormous serial killer refrigerators, you wouldn't even have to cut off the arms, just go ahead and throw victims in whole. The house is so big I got lost coming downstairs to make tea. I don't know where I ended up — there's a living room the size of a tennis court, library just as enormous, except it all looks like they got bored with home improvement back around disco. And there's space junk everywhere, lasers-and-infrared-electronics-holds-off-cardiac-arrest-while-you-wait-for-paramedics stuff. On the other hand, there's paint peeling off the walls, chairs with slipcovers all worn down and cotton spilling out. Breaks your heart. So I'm wandering around getting totally confused about where the kitchen is because I came down the front stairs and overlooked the back staircase for the servants — it's this house-of-the-seven-gables staircase that leads straight into the pantry where there are a thousand glass cases full of china and crystal and gravy boats and samovars, foot lockers for the silver. I mean I could live in the pantry, no kidding, the kids and I could live in the pantry, easy. Anyway, I've been here I don't know how long, waiting for the brat of the mansion to get back. He just disappeared. I mean, I've been stood up before, but not like this — no, no, it's not a date, it's not, I mean date like a metaphor, okay, like a simile, whatever, I'm just lending a helping *hand, I don't really care if you think it's a bad reason. But it doesn't matter anyway because I'm in the house and he's not and there's no one here. I was looking at the old big band records in the living room, trying out every piece of furniture and stuff, but it was kind of spooky so I went looking for his mom. It was either that or wait in the car, you know, and it was getting kind of cold. Then I go upstairs and she's there all right, half asleep, but otherwise fine, no one would believe that stuff happened earlier, and I'm up there, and we're talking about Evan and Bobby and it's all going fine, except that she sort of smells bad,* Jane whispers this, *well, she didn't smell like roses and I was worried, you know, is it unhygienic or something? Did he bathe her? Or maybe she wet the bed? I don't know. I didn't worry exactly, but I just figured, you know, if she's my responsibility for the time being I'm making sure she's okay — wait, wait, listen, let me finish. Of course I took her clothes off, what am I supposed to do, put her in the tub in her dress? Of course, I took off her clothes. I mean, if he's supposed to be a care provider, or whatever, it's a bad situation. So I just took charge, and you know she's a tough old chick, not ashamed at all, must be used to it, so she just floats in the tub, giving me all this advice thing about what I'm supposed to do with Evan and Bobby, boys are divine, boys are varmints, boys are this or that, I don't know, it was adorable in a battle-ax sort of way, and now I'm having a cigarette down here, letting the tea steep, maybe she'll nod off again or something. Look, I don't know when I'm bringing the car back. I'm sorry about that, I'll bring it back, I promise, I just don't know when. Give me a break, are you going out? Are you going on a date at this hour? What is it, like eleven? You're not going anywhere. I promise it'll be in your driveway when you go to the gym or whatever, tomorrow. Where are you going anyway? Forget it, I'll bring it back when I bring it back, don't be a shrew. Stay in. Clean your apartment, watch figure skating on TV. How should I know? He'll show up any minute, anyway, unless he wrapped his car around a tree. Do you think he was that trashed? Maybe I should call the cops. You're friends with all the cops. I'll tell them I know you, give them a little work.* A giddy feeling, like a good movie trailer, just from doing a little good. Normally, Jane Ingersoll can't stand other people's parents — Bob Tracy's mom

ordered her out of the house once (bad language); Chris Knox's
dad called her a strumpet. But Jane Ingersoll finds that she kind of
likes Ma Raitliffe, with her old-fashioned ornery ways, her sub-
junctives, her politesse, and when she gets off the phone with
Kathleen, she feels the prick of accomplishment. She has stuck it
out here at the Raitliffe compound. Ma Raitliffe can't stay awake
much longer. She's barely awake anyway. Out the kitchen window,
night like ink. The teapot throws off a floral cologne. Jane will have
a cup herself. She'll take the tea up, sit by the side of the tub,
dribble spearmint on Ma Raitliffe's chin, and worry occasionally
about the delinquent Hex later. Touring the pantry, Jane finds the
rest of the tea service, the matched Sèvres or Dresden or Limoges
cups and sugar bowl and creamer — the *backup* tea service — and
organizes the tray so that she might carry it up the back stairs. But
since she's still in her pink bobby sox (only clean pair), damp from
the bathroom floor, she loses her balance on the first hairpin of
that flight, and *drops one of the teacups.* They'd been stacked according to an early training in food services. For a second, she's a
juggler, the cup hovers in the air, then it spontaneously disas-
sembles, followed by the cruel amputation of the teapot spout. The
teapot slides off one side of the tray while she's watching the rest
of the mishap, and lands with an alarming crunch. The *infusion de
menthe,* begins to leak, down the stairs, onto the linoleum. A real
mess. Five hundred dollars' worth of china there, maybe. A whole
week's salary at the Old Saybrook Historical Society. Evan and
Bobby's spring wardrobe. She can't afford a broken fingernail, or
torn nylons, much less the replacement of heirlooms. There's not
enough light on the damn stairs either. Jane swears, alliteratively,
euphonically, enthusiastically. Maybe she could glue it. Glue the
teapot. Hide it at the back of the shelf. Spout facing away. There
must be epoxy someplace. *No, no, she makes the honorable decision. She'll confess. She'll come clean, accept responsibility for her
actions, whatever the cost. Fuck.* Meanwhile, the minute hand
sweeps around the kitchen clock, traditional Westclox with its
ebony perimeter and Palatino numerals. Jane searches through the
pantry closet. Locates the whisk broom. Then she takes up the rag
blanketing the kitchen faucet — recently used to clean up some

microbrewery grog. It hasn't been wrung out. She sops up the tea, scours the floor. She sweeps. Then Jane finds a strainer and, to be safe, strains the tea from the one-armed teapot into a pair of coffee mugs (eggplants pictured on pastel fields). It's an exacting process. One mug passes the test, is uncompromised by sediment from the ancient ceramicists of Europe. In the other, however, a sliver of Limoges drifts among the tea leaves. It's predicting something, to be sure. She tries to fish out the splinter with a teaspoon, but it scoots around the perimeter. Forget it. She'll take the mugs up, anyhow. She'll make do. In preparation for the ascent, she takes her socks off, and leaves them, like pink fillets, on a chair at the breakfast table. The trip this time is more methodical. Jane avoids further expense. She begins calling out to Ma Raitliffe as soon as she hits the landing, coming down the hall, spinning out a disclaimer. *Oh, Mrs. Raitliffe,* she says, rounding the corner into the master bedroom, *I'm really sorry I took so long. I had a little mishap on the staircase. It was kind of dark. But it was really my fault. I'll be happy to pay.* The door to the bathroom is open six inches. There's a warm light inside, an intimation of ritual hygiene. Jane's almost laughing at the bad spot she's in. It's a hassle, but it's comic too. The little things go wrong; you're trying to help but you make things worse. She pushes back the door, *I'm walking chaos, can't take me anywhere,* and sees the water on the floor, the room filling up. It's equatorial in there, like in one of those decorated fish tanks, *and that's a manatee there,* the body in the tub assembling itself, limb by limb, into significance. She can't even look at first, because she knows — *Wait, that's Ma Raitliffe's shoulder blade, and those are her hands,* distorted by the water, distorted by bubble bath petrocolors, distorted by the dim overhead lamp. *That halo is her gray bun,* come untied somehow. Jane drops the mugs into the sink, where they topple and spill. There's the report of their shattering. Then, notwithstanding black velveteen leggings, Jane launches herself into the tub, sloshes into it, all the horror film imagery of bathrooms upon her now, Arkansas toothpicks, rapes, bloodlust of every kind, bloated floating bodies, trying to get a purchase on Ma Raitliffe, trying to hang on to her, under the arms. The widow is slippery, of course, bobs from side to side, is waterlogged, and Jane, who has already decided on the worst, can't lift her at all. She's strategizing, kicking at the side of the tub distractedly, then she's *submerging herself,* actually getting down under Ma Raitliffe, the soap stinging her eyes. Jane levers the body, drenched herself, holding on to the handicapped railing, *the lightweight aluminum convenience bench* furrowing a canal in the back of her neck, the straps of her tank top slipping from her shoulders, and her hair tangling around Ma Raitliffe's wrists. She works the leg press, until, with a dam burst, an emptying of the tub, the other woman flops, like an uninflated pool toy, onto the bath mat. Jane stumbles out of the tub after her. Ma Raitliffe's eyes have rolled all the way into her head. There are only the whites. She's a lower aquatic mammal, Jane's hysterical breaths remarkable in the silence, unanswered by other breathing. Ma Raitliffe isn't breathing at all. *You killed her, you killed her, you walk into a house and people start dropping dead.* Jane Ingersoll would give herself over to sobbing except that there isn't time. It's happening in parts of seconds. She hurdles the widow's body, into the master bedroom, tracking the bubble bath to the phone, the cordless phone, hits the three digits, jams it between her ear and shoulder. Back into the bathroom, to Ma Raitliffe, pale like china, naked sagging belly, pensile breasts, demure and elegant c-u-n-t, hair matted around her gray face. Jane presses down Mrs. Raitliffe's jaw with one palm, and the sound of the operator comes over a great expanse. *Yeah, I'm on, uh, I'm on Flagler Drive, I don't know the number, fifty-two, in Fenwick, it's a big stone house, listen, the owner is, I don't know her first name, and she's — can you just hurry, please? No, I don't know, she fell over in the tub, I don't know, maybe ten minutes ago, look, I don't know the number, there's an aqua Honda in the driveway. A Honda. Just hurry up, I'm the only one here.* She flings the portable phone away, it skitters through the doorway, comes to rest under the master bed. Then without hesitation Jane tastes Ma Raitliffe's lips, starts her stertorous huffing and puffing, pinching closed the nostrils, forcing her reserves into Ma Raitliffe. Jane is pounding on her chest (making bruises, probably), pressing her ear between breasts, thinking she hears some faint dial tone there, unless it's her own thundering.

She pushes a knee into Ma Raitliffe's clavicle, just above the gelatinous breasts, to keep her head from toppling over to the side. Everything is quiet. The clocks have all stopped, the traffic is observing an emergency ban, the zoo animals tremble silently in their cages, there's a general strike — every endeavor in southeastern CT given over to this suspiration, this breath of God. Jane hears pleas in her head. She hears bargaining. A minute has passed or two minutes have passed. Ma Raitliffe's dendrites have frayed, suffocated, and Jane Ingersoll crumbles, in the bathroom, into a fetal slump, from which she uncurls herself almost immediately only to slap Ma Raitliffe, to cry out, to bury her face on the older woman's shoulder. She's always late, *she took too long with her stupid telephone call to Kathleen,* and now Ma Raitliffe is gone. And just when Jane has accepted her manslaughter, the dark months of remorse ahead of her, just when she has accepted Evan and Bobby's semesters of ostracism from public school, just when she has moved them all to a remote trailer park in northwestern Rhode Island and changed her surname to Hearne or Connelly, a fountain of bathwater erupts from Ma Raitliffe's bereaved lungs, water and bilious tissue or internal rot or disjecta, a mulch, and Ma Raitliffe gives a single desolate sigh, and then nothing. *Again? She stops breathing again?* Jane Ingersoll, helpless with panic, with shock, bangs on Ma Raitliffe's chest again, until her fists are tingling, and falls into long illiberal kisses, stares into Ma Raitliffe's eyes, as if with some language of gazes she might beckon Ma Raitliffe hence, and in fact the eyes do seem to roll down from their heavenward fixation, and Jane can see not only sclera but cornea, pigmented iris, undilated pupil, clear back to the retina of Ma Raitliffe's arctic blues, window of the soul. How much of the old gal is left? How much stored in the lobes? How much is the vegetative basics now, functioning of the organs, nothing more? Jane desperately pinches Ma Raitliffe's cheek. *Come on, please, just a little air, please. They'll be here any second. Don't leave your son like this,* and an eternity passes and a couple more eternities, a half-dozen of them in all, featuring enough anxiety to power local generating facilities, *and then another sigh,* symphonic crescendo, *forte, forte,* and Jane is so happy about it, even if it's followed by a third dread void. Still there's a flicker of consciousness in that body on the drenched bath mat. She's sure of it, enough so that she doesn't hear, at first, *the calls,* incalculably vivid, no voice ever more welcome. From downstairs. *Hello?* It's like she's always been here, closeted with Ma Raitliffe, mired in dramas of life and death. *Did she try to clear any throat obstructions before she began the mouth-to-mouth procedure?* Then she registers the sound of the voice. From downstairs! *Oh shit, up here, second floor, bathroom, thank God, thank God,* and the cast doubles, the EMTs crowd around her on the floor. They push her to the edge, *at last,* two *extremely handsome* black guys in uniform, they crowd into that grotto of moistures and femininities and begin firing requests at her, *get us a blanket,* while rigging up the respirator, the defibrillator, devices and monitors, until Jane is actually crowded out into the master bedroom, where she watches from the sidelines, as they restore her breathing almost casually — *Did you clear the tongue?* — and attach her to some rack of electronic junk. One of the guys gets on shortwave to the dispatcher, the other disappearing, doing the main staircase in 10^{-24}, to return with gurney, and Jane Ingersoll slinks out of the bedroom, *at last,* collapses into an armchair next door in the *rose guest room,* head between her knees, holding tight on to her exposed ankles, *she lost her own mom,* five years since (adenocarcinoma), never had the wisdom to straighten that out, never got it figured out. The stories of reconciliation and understanding with dead people, bedside reconciliations and expressions of fealty, serial narratives with refoldable seals, with genetically engineered fruits and hothouse blooms and fat-free chocolates, *these stories of eleventh-hour reunions are to lead you back to the people who know you, the people who forgive you here — don't wake to find them gone.*

Then Hex Raitliffe turns up. Of course. Her date. Shouting up the main staircase, *Mom, M-mom?* He has seen the ambulance in the driveway, or maybe he has followed it, over the causeway, winding out of Old Saybrook, his insides shifting as the ambulance takes the left turn, *toward his house,* its siren lamentation scaring up seabirds. Hex races past the rose guest room, down the hall. Following the sounds of modern medicine — the gurney as it is unfolded and assembled — he comes upon the scene with a yelp, but any reaction is immediately smothered in the language of calamity, *release forms, next of kin, post-traumatic observation, possible oral-airway line induction.* Hex's devastated gasps commingle with empiricist talk. Jane would comfort him, but she goes in and out of her own convexity of panic. She's pretty sure that if Hex has any of the beers he went out to get that she will indeed drink one, maybe more than one. But soon her attentions fix on a woman's voice, wheezing like an old harmonium, above the bass and baritone racket. Ma Raitliffe herself, with her refrain —

— No hospitals! No hospitals!

Bent out of shape about it. But that's just tough luck, because she's muffled by the professionals instantly. The EMTs take no chances. They are to transport Ma Raitliffe *alive.* It's their job. They brook no interference. (Jane Ingersoll ascends from her flamingo armchair.) The EMTs, while venturing rash clinical diagnoses to Dexter — *could be stroke, could be aneurysm* — gag Ma with an oxygen mask, muttering about *endotracheal intubation* as though the patient were not even there. As Jane watches from the hall, Ma Raitliffe, countenance fogged in the mask, executes another bloodcurdling wail, her last chance at civil disobedience. Her swan song. After which she wilts. Which is all that Hex has to hear from her for tonight: *I don't care if you d-d-don't want to g-g-go, you're g-g-going. I don't care. This is t-t-too c-c-complicated for me to manage, all right? I know you're upset and f-f-frightened, I'm frightened t-too, but I'm not leaving you in the house, not if there's something really wrong.* Ma Raitliffe murmurs something about promises Hex has made to her. Betrayals of confidence, betrayals of filial responsibilities, etc. But the words dwindle, and the EMTs strap her in, and soon she's rolling down the hall.

— D-don't forget that she's taking b-b-b-beta interferon, Hex says, — for the n-n-neurological thing and maybe p-p-p-p- (he's chasing them to the top of the stairs) . . . *prednisolone,* some cortico-steroid or other, and nitroglycerin, antidepressants. MAO inhibitors. I'm right behind you. I'm getting in the c-c-car, right now.

The technicians, with their impeccably shaved heads, their smart uniforms, their dour expressions, are wordless. They scarcely acknowledge him. But Hex follows them to the front door, anyway, throwing on his suit coat, as the gurney rolls over the gravel in the turnaround. He attaches subparagraphs of advice — about spastic limbs, about nystagmus — until they slam the panel doors on the back of the ambulance. He's still stuttering in the rosy glow of taillights.

Then on the step, under the lamp on the front step, Jane Ingersoll finally gets a good look at her date. As the siren issues its call. Wow. His clothes are all torn. There's a rip in the elbow of the jacket, his collar is ringed with mud, there's a tear in his slacks. He's grass-stained entirely, like he just played touch football with teenagers. Even worse, he has a wicked shiner. The right eye. Jane pulls him back into the foyer, tugs at his arm, the better to see in the light, to see the dark pastel of his wound — Mars Violet on the old acrylic color wheel, *the color of war*. His lip is split, his nose caked with clots.

She says, — You look like shit.

— Yeah, I know. (Then with some irritation.) — Why d-d-d-don't you t-tell me what the hell happened?

— Oh, boy, she says, — she wanted a bath so I gave her a bath. Then she wanted some tea, so I went to get her some. And when I came back upstairs, she'd fallen in somehow. I should never have left her.

Jane begins to cry, in an acute, childish way, not with refined adult stiflings, in an anguished free fall. Gasping. The abandon of it feels unending, even more awkward because Jane doesn't feel like she knows him very well.

— It's my fault, I got on the phone, I didn't know where you were, I was worried, and then I dropped the teapot, and I didn't know. I got everything all screwed up, and I'm really sorry, I don't know what to say —

Hex gapes curiously, standing aside, arms crossed, but then he does what earlier in the evening might have seemed like knavery, *he gathers her toward him*. She sees him coming like an old, eccentric uncle, not like a guy on the make, and she doesn't stop him, doesn't avoid it, succumbs to this gravitation, and his arms in secondhand rags are soft, gentle, tender, not in peak condition by any means, wobbly, timid. The two of them, from the awkwardness of it, from the surprise of it, *from the delight of embracing*, fall back against the table in the front hall, where the portraits have been replaced by an old mirror, and they're under the influence of a *magic looking glass*. They topple a candlestick. All their reversals look like opportunities. Jane Ingersoll emerges temporarily from the tunneling of middle age, breaks intermittently away from kids, taxes, utilities, deaths, divorces, aches and pains, into the grove of embraces. It's a meadow, it's a greenhouse. Maybe she likes it too well to bother about who it is she's embracing, maybe she likes it better than what comes later, *but right now it feels like paradise*, and she sees the two of them, over his shoulder, in that looking glass of necromancy, and she doesn't see the drenched tank top and the disordered hair, the running makeup, the leggings clammy like a wet suit, doesn't remember how cold she is, doesn't see the demarcations of the fistfight upon Hex Raitliffe, or his shredded suit jacket, his stooped posture. *It's like coming out of the bridge and into the second chorus. It's like coming out of the sermon and into the Eucharist. It's like coming over a crest with the river below and the village all in lights.*

— W-well, I should p-probably —

— Hang on, she says, — don't blow it.

Her cheek on his shoulder, his chin against her forehead. She doesn't want to be the one who pulls out. She doesn't want to be the one who overlooks possibility. But Hex squeezes her once hard and begins to unwind himself.

— Well, it's not your f-f-fault. I should have b-been here.

— Yeah, so where were you, anyway? she says. — I was here an hour and a half. Alone with her.

She turns to the mirror to deal with her hair.

— You wouldn't b-b-b-believe me if I told you.

He's starting toward the door.

— I'll come along. If you want.

Raitliffe looks like she just agreed to have his baby, or to wait for his return from the Pacific War. Of course, there are logistical negotiations, *because there's the Taurus, and if they stop to get the bike, then they're going to have to ride her bike, so it turns out she'll*

*get her bike back, but Kathleen's car will have to stay in the Rait-
liffes' driveway for part of the night, or else they have to ride the
bike all night, and leave the Taurus at Penelope's.* Raitliffe handles
this with aplomb. His manners are good.

Then she's back in the bathroom, in jaundiced light, and her
blouse is draped over the wicker chair in the corner. In the time
since her ministering, the whole sequence has diminished to actual size, to mortal scale. She falls to her knees, with a piety,
mops at the slick floor, uses the blue towel she never used on Ma
Raitliffe's limbs, until this towel is sodden and rank. Four fingers of
water remain in the tub. Last bubbles effervescing. She pulls the
plug. Watches it go. When she's done, wet through again, Jane
hangs the blue towel to dry, and goes into the master bedroom to
pull tight the sheets, to straighten and fold back the comforter. All
this time, stepping around the place where his mother lay. Where
did she leave her boots?

17

At about 11:28 PM, the patient, Barbara Ashton Danforth Raitliffe, age 70 (4/5/22), Caucasian, approximately 100 lbs., suffering from chronic relapsing MS, or ALS, Guillain-Barré, or other neurological dysfunction, and secondary hypertension, 160/80, systole/diastole, major depression and anxiety-depression disorder, angina pectoris, colitis, irritable bowel syndrome, urinary urgency, osteoporosis, psoriasis, in conjunction with accidental suffocation, possible grand mal seizure, possible cardiac arrest, possible stroke, possible drug- or drug-interaction-related loss of consciousness or coma, carbamazepine, captopril, MAO inhibitors, diazepam and/or other benzodiazepines, Prednisolone, etc., in trace amounts, revived with cardiopulmonary resuscitation, thereafter considered alert, given oxygen and vircuronium to inhibit vocalizations, transported by ambulance (Old Saybrook FD) to New London General, by drivers and paramedics, Reginald Banks and Michael F. Miller, Jr., admitted 11:40 PM, to semiprivate room, for observation. 11:32 PM, patient's closest relation, a son, Dexter Allen Ashton Raitliffe, 38 (9/30/54), Caucasian, 180 lbs., 5'9", early indication of alcoholism (pancreatitis and slightly enlarged liver), early indication of Halcion addiction, multiple cranial and facial hematomas, history of stutter/stammer speech pathology, in a condition of increased blood flow to scrotal and related tissue, having consumed four jiggers of distilled hundred-proof alcohol (scotch whiskey, blended, and/or sour mash),

185

and eight sixteen-ounce distilled malt beverages since 5:00 PM EST, reaches, by means of several small intermediary footsteps, across a space of approximately one meter, for Janet Sally Ingersoll, of Old Saybook, part-time administrative asst, also 38 (8/11/54), able-bodied (weight unknown), Dexter Raitliffe, with only minimal muscular dysfunction from aforementioned intoxication, reaches, while experiencing feelings of heightened well-being, possibly al-cohol-related, the resultant embrace lasting approximately twenty-five seconds, during which, by virtue of proximity, nose to scalp, there's the olfactory impression of wheatgrass and sea vegetables, also of body oils — diluted by immersions and lavations — sandal-wood and lilac. They are standing in front of an antique mirror purchased at auction in Lakeville, CT, by patient Barbara Raitliffe in 1973, wobbling on an Oriental carpet, the embrace enduring until, according to norms and mores, D.A.A. Raitliffe removes his left hand from its resting place on the exposed "small" or lumbar region of Janet Sally Ingersoll's back, fingertips just touching also upon the swell of the right lobe of the gluteus maximus, or funda-ment; he removes his left hand as well as his right (patting lightly against the spot where there might have been the clasp of a bras-siere), mildly irritated at the brevity of the embrace, a brevity Raitliffe does not mention. 12:01 AM, having parked a 1992 Ford Taurus with 232 miles on its odometer (NYS plate #HCE 810) in the designated emergency room parking area of New London General, 1300 Broad St., leaving the lights on momentarily, as, beside him, a Honda motorcycle (belt-driven) shudders to a halt in the parking slip adjacent, Dexter Raitliffe has a sudden mnemonic experience of unknown cortical origin, involving the eastern face of the hospital, a humdrum and utilitarian piece of public architec-ture designed by students of Louis Skidmore, somewhat in the style of Skidmore's celebrated Atomic Energy Commission build-ing, fashioned in ecru of case-hardened steel and reinforced con-crete, and this memory inaugurates certain endocrinological events, releases natural steroids, natural opiates, reactions having to do with the sudden wash of memory, such that Dexter Raitliffe, at 12:05 AM, beholds: *this is the hospital where the old man died,* an observation promptly repeated to J. S. Ingersoll. The worst of news. She is in the process of removing her red metallic motorcycle helmet — it complies with State of Connecticut regulations. She is shaking loose her locks. For the purposes of this account, it suffices to note that Raitliffe's remark about New London General Hospital is somewhat inhibited by respiratory abnormality (c.f., stammer/stutter speech pathology, as described above), causing in turn the repetition of certain sounds, particularly hard consonants.

12:10 AM. D.A.A. Raitliffe telephones patient Barbara Raitliffe's consulting physician, Ronald Kramms, MD, specialist in neurology and pediatric neurology for the shore region, but fails to make contact, reaching instead Kramms's answering service, with whom he leaves the number of a pay phone in the Emergency Room of New London General Hospital. This call contributes further to Raitliffe's pre-ulcerous gastric lesions; to the burning in his pyloric sphincter, to the inflammation at the spot at which sphincter opens into duodenum; this call contributes to the perturbation and churning of Raitliffe's abdominal cavity, exacerbated likewise by the mnemonic coincidence aforementioned, exacerbated by concern about the condition of the patient, exacerbated by a related but less significant worry that J. S. Ingersoll — sitting on a blue plastic bench, reading a copy of *Highlights* magazine with particular attention to the word search puzzles at the rear of *Highlights* — will become bored in the waiting room, bored of his company, that J. S. Ingersoll will realize in him the unmistakable imposture that is, in his view, his only memorable personal characteristic. 12:13 AM. Ronald Kramms, MD, calls the Emergency Room of the hospital on its main line. Raitliffe is summoned to the admitting desk by secretary Arlene Margaret Perrin (age 28, 141 lbs., obsessivecompulsive disorder with specific indication of hand washing and germ phobia, as well as bulimia and depression), who transfers the call to a nearby courtesy phone, *I've already spoken with the guys on call and their feeling, with which I concur, is that your mother has suffered a recurrence of chronic symptoms, probably due to the bath, or maybe the humid conditions in the bathroom. I think I've explained to you before to be careful with the bath. Anyhow, they've done a preliminary EEG and it's not at all conclusive, but that's the feeling. There's really no danger tonight. Do yourself a favor, get a good night's sleep.* After which a doctor on the premises, specialist in internal medicine Martin O'Brien, MD, with carefully trimmed salt-and-pepper beard and male pattern baldness (early subject in clinical trials of the Rogaine™ hair-loss treatment), appears in the lobby, asking for a Mr. Raitliffe, and, locating him, Dr. O'Brien reiterates, in the vague language that comes naturally to consultants on the Barbara Raitliffe case, the diagnosis of Ronald Kramms, MD, while smoothing nervously the thinning curls upon his head. Thereafter, Dexter Raitliffe and his companion, J. S. Ingersoll, are given leave by O'Brien to speak briefly with the patient, Barbara Raitliffe, in the examining room, before her relocation by gurney to semiprivate accommodation, before Dexter Raitliffe goes through the lengthy and inhumane business of establishing that there is indeed a large financially strapped insurer willing to underwrite this hospitalization — according to the benefits package of the Connecticut Power and Light Utility, whose employee, Louis Sloane, by virtue of fifteen years' valued service to said company, is insured virtually without limit. Before completing this interrogation by the bulimic woman in the glassed-in cubicle, Dexter Raitliffe, at approximately 12:22 AM, takes his mother's right hand (while J. S. Ingersoll stands at the foot of the bed, playing with a rubber reflex mallet), in an examining room the shade of cudbear or perhaps amethyst, and says, *Hey, how are you f-f-feeling?* experiencing, at this moment, a dervishing of finches or chickadees in his abdominal cavity, because of the confluence of hospital rooms, because of the mnemonic confluence of past and present hospital rooms, because of memory, because of his pre-ulcerous condition, because of his *globus hystericus* (swallowing impeded by imagined throat obstruction), because of his cold sweat, because of his magical thinking, such that Raitliffe knows with complete certainty the next remark to issue forth from his mom, the remark his father would have uttered when he too was unconscious in this very room (actually two floors above and down the hall to the right), the sentence he too will murmur when bedridden and close to death, *I'd be a whole lot better off . . . if you hadn't . . . put me in . . . this darned hospital . . .* Raitliffe, with impressive rudeness, makes an effort to interrupt the following broadside, mumbling about hospital food and good drugs, partly in order to spare J. S. Ingersoll the full force of his mother's tirade, partly because he lacks at this hour the strength for philosophical combat. However, Barbara Raitliffe continues in spite of interruption, *If you are trying to dispatch . . . me in the slowest . . . most painful . . . way possible . . . you are doing . . . a fine job.* D.A.A. Raitliffe, for whom this very theme is a quagmire, is now speechless, looking first beseechingly at Jane Ingersoll (tapping on her elbow, seven-eight time, with reflex mallet), whose features are composed sympathetically — there's an arcing of eyebrows and a carefully monitored upsurge, at her lower lids, of saline precipitate — looking next back at his mother, trying to speak but finding words and consonants utterly blocked by his condition. Instead, he holds his mother's hand, unclenches her fist, straightens the fingers, holds this hand flat between his own hands and warms it, while a woman behind the *corrugated polyurethane examining room divider* speaks in a whisper to a daughter or niece or granddaughter or other unidentified but selfless girl relative, of the merits of certain kinds of traditional confections, e.g., peanut butter cookies, sugar cookies, Rice Krispie treats, triple-decker Jell-O desserts, the best ways to prepare these confections, the necessity of pastry bags and double boilers and molds which will sustain the maraschino cherries, green grapes, cling peaches, canned pears, raisins, cashews, other additives, likewise of certain knitting stitches and their difficulties, and of the ways to pay the bills that her husband has never learned to pay, and of all the things that will have to be made orderly when she's no longer around. It seems to Dexter Raitliffe, in his silence, that this woman, this dying woman (his diagnosis), speaks with the dignity of regular Americans; this woman speaks with a feeling neither he nor his mother can ever muster at bedside or even on a good day, even with his inheritance and his fine schooling and his illustrious background and his electronic gizmos and his expensive therapies, even with these advantages Dexter Raitliffe finds that the only words that come easily to him, when you get right down to it, are words of apology. Raitliffe hypothesizes, while studying the back of his mother's hand, that his first word as a pudgy and apprehensive boy, before *Mom,* before

Dad, before even the name of his nanny, was probably *sorry* —
which also had the advantage of being relatively pronounceable, in
terms of his handicap. *Sorry* for things he did and things he didn't
do, *sorry* when appropriate, *sorry* when inappropriate, *sorry* for all
occasions, *sorry* for everything including some first inadvertent
failure, some crime much more acute than the Edenic sins of the
Old Testament geeks with their apples or tomatoes, *some failure so
inestimable that language was invented to try to justify it,* so that, at
12:37 AM, with nurses and orderlies standing by, ready to wheel the
patient (Barbara Raitliffe) upstairs, as they also wheel away the
dying woman on the other side of the room divider, Dexter now
formulates the few predictable lines, *L-l-look, M-ma, this just isn't
the time t-t-t-to t-t-talk about it. They're g-g-going to watch you
overnight and I'll c-c-c-come b-back in the morning to spring you,
to t-t-take you back to the house and we'll t-t-talk then. That's all I
can do. I'm sorry.* Therefore, with vital signs stable at 1:00 AM, as
shown by third-floor night nurse Ellen Mary Harrison, African-
American, 63, with hammer toe, mild bursitis, and insomnia, the
patient (Barbara Raitliffe), in the absence of next of kin (Dexter
Raitliffe now busy with insurance questions), is given intravenously a mild sedative (Versed), and at 1:15, she is, according to
records, sleeping comfortably.

To the consternation of D.A.A. Raitliffe, his companion, Jane
Ingersoll — with whom he is now intent on spending some hours
unencumbered by attenuations of family — begins at 1:08 AM an
unsolicited conversation with an ambulance driver, John Edward
England, 28, African-American, able-bodied, USAF veteran of the
Gulf War, just outside the egress of the emergency room entrance
of New London General Hospital. John England at the time of this
conversation is smoking a Marlboro brand tobacco cigarette while
leaning against the side of his spit-polished GMC ambulance,
which, because of earlier rain, has a fine gleam upon it, in which is
England's reflection. Though Raitliffe strolls purposefully away
from this conversation, with a casual step that belies his rended
sexual pride, he inadvertently hears enough to know that the conversation initially concerns recently enacted antismoking legislation in the State of Connecticut, and how (as he would digest it)

this legislation is an abridgment of the rugged individualism at the core of American transcendental values — *a person is responsible for knowing themselves and their own damn vices* — how this legislation marginalizes smokers and their friends, is plain un-American, *probably thought up by communists or some shit.* The exchange between Ingersoll and England is brief, touches only glancingly on the life and impeccable service record of recent vice-presidential candidate Adm. James B. Stockdale, and is appended to this account merely to point out the careening or haphazard nature of Raitliffe's psychology at this particular hour of Saturday morning, as he stands in front of the east face of the hospital *where the old man died.* In addition to physiological complaints already described, Raitliffe is particularly tired of watching any and all of his contemporaries pairing off as though it were prearranged, men or women, wherever, in nightclubs, in night school, in public places, on buses, subways, trains, at street corners, in lines for bathrooms, hitting it off in conversations that would take him a good twenty minutes, *Hi there, I couldn't help overhearing your remarks on reforestation in Katmandu and it really struck a chord in me,* pretexts time-tested and approved by *1001 Ways to Meet Single Women,* all of these conversations of lonely hearts, prose of lovers skydiving into one another's arms, hastening from beds to the aisles of churches. But not Dexter Raitliffe. Under the constellations in the parking lot of New London General, at 1:04 AM, Dexter Raitliffe resolves that this Janet Sally Ingersoll will not shake herself free from him, he will open up the plum-colored bruise of his personality, he will exhume its somewhat decomposed contents, because tomorrow his mother will be out of the hospital, and therefore now is the time, if not now, when, young Raitliffe! Now is the time to speak words no ear has heard! 1:05 AM; from a nonchalant and imitative reclining posture against the rear driver's side door of his rented Taurus, he therefore approaches Jane Ingersoll, presently trotting down a handicapped-access ramp from the emergency room loading dock, smiling infectiously in the light of streetlamps; Raitliffe approaches her wordlessly, forcefully, ex cathedra, a man of action, takes her by the wrist, lightly but firmly, her delicate wrist, leads her to the bike, the motorcycle, the steed. *Your car smells like gas,* she says. *There's some p-p-p-problem with it,* he says. The tank on the motorcycle is nearly empty. There is no additional helmet. The bike is misfiring. She has not cleaned the points. And the roads are still glazed with a dangerous precipitation. But, undeterred, Raitliffe says, *G-g-give me a ride on your b-b-b-bike, Jane, let's g-g-go for a ride,* and, after an interval, Ingersoll says, *Uh, sure,* coming to the conclusion, Raitliffe supposes, that this, indeed, is the very last rock-and-roll-misspent-youth-checkered-past motorcycle romp ever to take place in his mass transportation life, because, in the morning, Jane's bike will have turned into an eight-year-old boy or a Chevy Cavalier or a quarterly estimated income tax chit, and there is just enough time to stick up a bank or kill a man or to be a lover on the run. As follows: Ingersoll straddles the motorcycle, approaching it from the left (bike as palomino), settling herself there embarrassedly, hopping up and down on the starter, until the engine turns over. She then signals to Raitliffe, and he mounts the passenger space at the rear, his pubic bone and detumescent penis mashed snugly against the cleft between the hemispheres of her slim posterior, no way around it, and though at first a natural Episcopalian shyness leads him to suppose that he might hang on to the storage rack on the back of the motorcyle rather than grab around Jane Ingersoll's back, once she shifts gears and leans in as they arc out onto Broad, he can scarcely keep his mount and — foreseeing his halved skull spilling its sweetbreads onto the avenue — he therefore clutches her fast to him, around the waist, his hands like a belt buckle in front of her, while beneath he feels the shuddering, throbbing heart of that engine. Acceleration being the drug of choice under the circumstances, Jane Ingersoll races out of town, shaking the scorched leaves from the autumnal trees, past the old, ramshackle Victorians where the seafarers of New London once put into port, those old rooming houses on the hill, lately inhabited by the hard-luck underclasses of Connecticut's crumbling cities, gang kids and their terrorized parents, the unemployed, the elderly, until they're out by the chain stores, the auto dealerships, thirty or forty miles an hour *above posted limits,* until Dexter and Jane Ingersoll are rocketing along the swerve of the shore, passing sta-

tion wagons on the left, panel trucks on the right, failing to signal
in the centrifugal thrust of their turns, the squeal of their tires,
beside the great rail beds of the northeastern corridor and along
old mariners' bars, following the course of the Thames River, back
from the mouth of the harbor, watching the mesmeric lights of the
port reflect upon the river, until Jane Ingersoll doglegs to the right
at the railroad station, past the army recruitment center, bounces
over the tracks, grazes a shingle on an empty guardhouse at the
edge of a parking lot — and guns it onto the public pier of New
London. Out onto the pier! With the bridge span above them,
where the after-hours scofflaws aim for Boston before closing
time. Raitliffe finally tumbles off the back of the Honda, skinning
a palm. Across the rippling currents, now, is the backdrop to this
contemporary romance, monument to all that's great in Americans, *Electric Boat, a division of the General Dynamics Corporation,* where, in the dry docks, in show business spotlights, for all to
see, are constructed *Polaris* submarines. Cranes poised about them
like industrial handmaidens, tawny abominations, the pride of
southeastern Connecticut, where New London's remaining working men and women — excepting the ones behind the counters at
the adult bookshops and the package stores — clock in to build
weapons of destruction. *J-j-j-jesus, they are ugly,* Hex Raitliffe says,
and Jane nods, because the bike's still idling. To this indelible
sentiment she then adds, *In the winter, the kids fishtail their cars
out here, at the end of the pier, to see who can get closest to driving
into the river,* and Hex says, *I w-w-want to k-k-k-k-k-k . . . I w-w-
want to k-k-k-k-kiss you,* and Jane laughs. She shuts off the bike,
kicks the kickstand. On the pier, against the stage set of ferryboats
and dredging barges and Coast Guard vessels, with wharf rats
slipping in and out of view, Jane pulls off her helmet. *I feel like a
kid again,* Raitliffe says. She draws nigh. In the sandblasted and
sea-worn red brick of New London with the nuclear-equipped
fishing vessels of the millennium, in the city of fissioning Yankees,
Hex Raitliffe — cramping from the cold, fighting off postnasal drip
— kisses his beloved. A fishing pole, with an eel wriggling on its
end, appears at the edge of his field of vision, drifts past, carried by
some unseen insomniac. Her mouth tastes like low tide, New

England ports, cigarettes, drink, experience. He's too shy to poke his tongue around. They soon break apart sheepishly. *You want to drive?* Jane says. Raitliffe shakes his head. *Come b-b-b-back to my house,* he ventures. *Let's g-get warm.* And Jane doesn't say anything at first, but starts the Japanese motorcycle, and he waits for a reply. Meanwhile: up the hill again, past Eugene O'Neill's statue and past O'Neill's house, where his Irish family wrestled and fought, past the auto dealerships, past the strip malls, until they're in the parking lot of the hospital, no closer to sleep than they were a half hour prior — 1:52 AM, and Jane Ingersoll is still unclear on her plans, her inclinations, but Raitliffe proceeds anyway, at a conservative fifty-five over the Baldwin Bridge, in the Taurus, followed by the bike, leading her into the turnaround at 52 Flagler Drive. She parks the motorcycle. She takes off the helmet.

The house, reputedly brought west from a Dutch castle or a German castle, stone by stone, *as all affluent residents of the coast say of their houses,* doesn't heat well. Indoors, D.A.A. Raitliffe is concerned about heat. Through the mortar, through the tiles on the roof, the chill, the disappointment of waste energy. Janet Sally Ingersoll has incipient hypothermia, digital frostbite, and/or seasonal flu in the incubation phase — lightweight jacket, damp leggings, boots without socks — but like colonial settlers the two of them begin to make a fire in the nearly habitable fireplace. Jane knots up the last few scraps of newspaper, and shoves them under a few split logs. — She seemed okay. Your ma.

— Sure, sure, Raitliffe says. Scotch?

She holds up a moldy scrap of newsprint, an old television section insert from the *New London Day.*

— Need more paper? Okay, I'll g-g-go get some in the k-kitchen. Use that . . . whatever that thing is on the t-table there —

— What? This?

Typescript. Maybe three or four pages.

— Yeah, yeah, he says. — Use that.

— Yeah, does it . . . will it work in the fireplace?

Then, back toward the kitchen, through unlit chambers, vaults, rummaging in the recycling bin in the pantry, gathering up a stack of newspapers, finding a box of deluxe blue-tip matches — he emerges into the light, to sit with her before the impeccably laid firebed. He strikes the match on the stones of old Europe. They arrange themselves, with throw pillows, on the area rug, to watch the enthusiastic part of the fire as it consumes his mother's living will. Unconsumed hunks of ash drift lazily up the chimney.

18

Your partner comes with a set of specifications he or she is obliged to offer to you, before proceeding with the mating ritual. For example, Jane might say to Hex Raitliffe — as combustion begins in the enormous fireplace — *I was ten and it was Kathleen's birthday and I was jealous so I ate the entire tube of cake-decorating stuff. It was emerald-colored. I puked for hours.* In shorthand, she unearths decades of child development. The bulleted points in her or any amorous guidebook have their own tendentious movement. They start with small, not terribly salacious revelations and then move on to more advanced chapters and appendices, troubleshooting advice, culminating in the removal of outer garments. Hex Raitliffe says, *I'd just c-c-come into my inheritance and I b-b-booked first-class t-tickets for me and a c-c-couple of friends to g-go to San Francisco for one night, to see this b-b-band, b-b-but I t-t-took so many Quaaludes that I c-c-couldn't remember anything about the show or where I stayed and I d-d-didn't wake till I was on the p-plane home.*

However, Jane Ingersoll has had some second thoughts. Because of her surroundings. There are the really menacing shadows that you get from firelight and piles of medical equipment. It's like some creepy Victorian-era sex fantasy in the Raitliffe household; she expects cast-iron chastity garments, beakers full of vermilion opiates. Jane watches Hex Raitliffe's mouth move, watches the stutter happen. He's telling her about the trip to the West Coast or later he's telling her about his twenties (*I p-practically lived at the Mudd C-c-c-club*), but all she can see is an aspect of him that must be specific to firelight. His wistfulness. The stories, in firelight, uniformly feature reversals; *he wakes up crying, she dies, they part.* Why did Jane come back here anyway? Why did she agree to go with him to the hospital? Why doesn't she just get in Kathleen's car and cruise back across the river? She should place the call, secure the rescue. *Come quick, the guy's a werewolf!*

On the other hand, she's not offering much. And when she does — *I never went to college, and my friends from high school, they mostly went off to make their fortunes and I was just hanging around going to the beach in the off-season and working as a secretary* — she feels somewhat comfortable. The ice cubes rattle in their glasses; the stories ebb and start anew. Jane pours the next round herself, dancing into the draft at the back of the room. She doesn't have the equation you need to figure how many drinks you're supposed to have in an evening, *the number of hours minus your body weight plus the temperature divided by the square of the proof of the beverage times the half-life of the rare earth metals at absolute zero or something,* so she just keeps drinking. But while performing mixology, she starts to shiver. There's a chill. At fireside, she reaches for the patchwork quilt on the couch, hauls it down, wraps it around herself, tucks her nail-polished toes underneath its hem.

Hex Raitliffe, of course, has *profound identification* with her troubled autobiography, nodding vigorously at stories of beach-combing for lobster pots, pot smoking at the quarries, middle-of-the-night trips to the empty mall outside of town. Amid these tales, he puts a new log on the fire. A perfectly truncated birch limb. His shiner has swollen. He smiles, he's raccoonlike, and before she can even stop herself or think it through or enumerate her reservations she reaches out for it, for his wounded profile. As he kneels beside her, her fingertips graze the surface of his cheek and he gets all shy, fumbling with the edge of the quilt as though its patches are fraying, *B-b-black eye as a k-k-k-kid was a b-b-badge of honor.* Grazing his cheek with her fingers (she removes his battered glasses) repairs something in her, cloaks her own loneliness so it's out of reach, fixes the shock of things; grazing Raitliffe's cheek fires up a great, benevolent silence in her; it's a radiant silence that lasts for the entire duration of touching him, like the music of late-night jazz ballads. She does it some more. She has second thoughts about her second thoughts.

— I had a boyfriend once who would never kiss me.

— What? Raitliffe says.

She touches him some more. She's trying various caresses. She samples the confectionery certainty of her body, of her glands, of her skin, of her fingertips. Her body moves toward Raitliffe on its own, in spite of objections, while Raitliffe organizes the quilt. Soon the quilt is around the two of them, they are conjoined by it, and she's telling him all about the guy, Chris, the one who wouldn't kiss her: *Chris crept up on her when the bedroom lights were off, Chris would never make love in the light, like the light would convict him of something, Chris wouldn't talk about sex under any circumstances.*

Raitliffe says with amazement:

— I would n-n-never t-t-treat a woman like that.

And she believes that Raitliffe believes that he would never do something like that, although she's pretty sure in the morning that this demurral will seem like an instance of degraded or excessive romantic language. It will pale during sleep. Raitliffe doesn't stop there, though, he moves on to elaborate a whole theory of kissing, *K-k-k-kissing, you know, is like a renunciation of d-d-devouring,* he's dead serious, he's a sociologist, *it's the height of g-g-generosity,* and this remark, of course, engenders a string of kisses, instantaneous, underneath the blanket. Fire crackling, drinks dwindling, wind in the flue. And since she hasn't kissed anyone in weeks, except maybe her boys, Evan and Bobby (who both think kisses are gross), she is willing to examine the entire practice, to try out many of the contemporary forms, e.g., *snow flurries,* five or ten faint kisses, lightly applied, upon the brow, upper cheek, eyelid, or other above-the-neck planes; or *finger painting,* in which glottis, used with a digital facility, travels over the Adam's apple of the recipient, and up underneath the jawbone; *overcranking,* which involves the almost totally motionless lateral movement upon the lips of the victim, similar but not identical to *the asthmatic kiss,* in which, again nearly motionless, lips slightly parted and imperceptibly touching, you *pant,* as though in need of one of those plastic inhalers, a style often followed quickly by the popular *lamprey,* named for its resemblance to the feeding practices of certain bottom-dwelling species who will attach themselves orally to the other fish; or archery, which also follows the gentler, more tender kisses. Raitliffe himself introduces *the archer's instrument here,* aims his tongue at her uvula, to probe for that swaying esophageal appendage, pausing on the way to scour out the spaces between her rear molars, and to touch upon, if possible, her bridgework, her gum lines, her caps, while holding tightly on to the back of her head. This kiss prompts a fresh autobiographical revelation from her, *I'm a demon for flossing,* the words unfortunately garbled in this context; Jane then closes her lips around his tongue and sucks indelicately on it in a style known in some rural communities as the *chicken frank.* Finally, to end with the sublime, Jane and Hex tackle the kiss honorifically entitled *From Here to Eternity* (1953, d. Fred Zinnemann) for the sea-drenched necking of Burt Lancaster and Deborah Kerr. Here the participants recline themselves with nervous laughter, stacking their bodies horizontally, fixing the quilt over themselves, torso to torso. *I love to kiss,* Jane Ingersoll says, rubbing her hands on the AstroTurf where Raitliffe's crewcut is thinnest, the back of his neck. His hands hover at the bend of her waist as it flares out toward hips, and they await the enveloping of the wave, as did Lancaster and Kerr, until, *indicating his perfect sense of delay as an amorous deployment,* Raitliffe suddenly unhinges himself and sits up. He fixes his attention somberly on the smoldering in the fireplace.

— I haven't b-been with a woman in three months. Last time was Gillian. It (Raitliffe's expression genuinely anguished.) B-before that it w-was almost t-t-t-two years.

Of course, she's supposed to gently touch the shoulder blade — there's a six- or eight-inch span that's acceptable for the conciliatory gesture. She's intended to reassure. Certain templates have been preformatted for the moment. *It doesn't matter to me. It's you I care about. This moment is so special.* Your generous older woman would say these things — after forty a woman wouldn't even hesitate — but Jane Ingersoll doesn't feel like it. She faces away sipping her drink, watching the firelight dapple the far wall. Actually, Raitliffe's hesitation raises some thorny questions. *Why hasn't he been with a woman? Why has it been so long?* Or even some of the following: *Does he surreptitiously cruise the gay bars? Does he pick up guys through the personal ads? Does he shoot harder drugs? Does he have small, painful ulcerations on the side of his penis? Does he have tiny hives of warts, visible only with considerable magnification?* She's thinking like an insurance company. She's thinking like a mom. She should call Kathleen, right now. But it's probably three in the morning. She can't call Kathleen. Unless it's an emergency.

— You aren't diseased or anything, are you? You aren't a high-risk partner, are you? Anything you should be telling me?

— Jesus, no. This is an excess of g-good news, he says. His speech has a liquid grace. Must be the drinking. — I have a big sentimental streak. I'm afraid of needles. I cry at movie trailers. I c-c-c-c-cry at sunsets. I hug other people's kids. Good news isn't my d-d-daily fare.

— Well, Jane says, — just because I'm here doesn't mean I'm easy. I'm a single mother. I feel good about family as a concept. But it's not unusual to want to have a few decent memories, you know? Before my cheeks cave in?

— Sure, he says. Emptying a glass.

Thus, she pulls him backward away from the fire, kissing him hard on the lips; she unclasps the topmost button on his dress shirt, his French-cuffed dress shirt — it has been untucked and multiply creased through the better part of the evening; she puts a fingertip on his lips, forbidding lengthy speeches, except for really important tactical bulletins, *You have to let me do everything, if I want your help I'll ask for it* — shifting, ahead of schedule, to the removal of outerwear, to the removal again of her own black blouse, which comes off easily, flapping over her head like a waterbird, and then there are his pants, grass-stained and faded, which she winches over his hips, as she would do with Evan or Bobby (trying to get their jeans into the washing machine), and then, in a presumptuous gesture, she begins to ease up her tank top, finding suddenly that his hands are there too, like the hands of a fisherman, short, stubby, massive, sliding up underneath the Lycra-and-cotton blend. Then the tank top is like a booster segment from the old Apollo missions flying away, and her breasts are exposed to the drafty air and with a little yelp she sneaks down under the quilt, peels off her leggings to expose the trembling boughs underneath, and here she is with this brokenhearted guy and she's wearing nothing but a mulberry-colored string bikini, grateful for the half-light, in which stretch marks are the elegant cross-hatchings of some pen-and-ink. Raitliffe has on oxford-cloth boxer shorts. They begin, again, to kiss. Her breasts feel bulky, as they always do in the company of others, but this plexus of nourishment is the region to which Raitliffe slithers under the margin of the quilt. All she can see of him is his scalp. *The orbit of his tongue around her there isn't half bad,* she supposes, not quite as good as Evan was as a baby, but it will do the trick (her attention drifts up toward the ceiling). A back rub wouldn't be bad either if performed correctly, *gentle is best;* Raitliffe winds her mulberry lingerie around her knees, over her ankles, and off. The rustle of his boxers coming off. There they are, like primates, anthropoids, prosimians, protohominids.

Has he bathed? She begins morbidly to look for sympathies between bodies of mother and son. She nudges back the quilt to get a better look at Hex Raitliffe, the hillock around the waist, and the prairie growth on his chest — an integument of fur, white and gray, which halts, thank God, before the shoulders and the back. Except for his belly, he's actually sort of twiggy, like his mom. Probably disdains food, purposefully starves, fasts, mortifies the flesh. But before she can complete the compare/contrast with a good long full-frontal close-up of his stylus, Raitliffe's head, like some oblate gymnasium ball, lodges itself between her legs. She learns from the feeling first — from the rolling through her, through her stomach, through her vertebrae, up toward the back of her neck. He's addressing himself to sheath and hood. She sinks onto her back, sighs. Certain ecstasies have to seem dainty lest you should spook the delicate sensibilities of men. Her swells come in twos and threes, always from the south, sweeping through tarsals and naviculars and metatarsals, tibia, femur, pelvis, rib cage, *skull,* back around, toward her wrists. The flood of circular impulses crowds out the valves and organs; the whole of her gives over to some part where she's undistractable; she's made of crystal; she's made of precious metals; silk flowers, rice paper, dusk in summer, *chamber music, night swimming, penny candy,* then Raitliffe lays off again,

— Boy, you are p-p-p-p-pretty, Jane, b-b-boy, this is special, this is a special moment for me, b-b-but I have this p-p-problem, I hate to b-b-bring it up, really, b-b-but I c-c-c-can't . . . this just isn't . . . it's not a g-g-g-good location for me, I just d-d-d-don't feel . . . I wonder . . . uh . . . b-b-because of the hospital c-c-cot and all, the medical stuff everywhere — it's just not g-going to work for me, b-b-because it's . . . it's . . . like d-doing it in her room, or something, would it b-b-be okay if we change venues? Is that okay with you?

— You sure picked an interesting moment.

— My room. Let's g-g-go up to my room.

— Well . . .

He leaps back into his boxer shorts, forestalling again her anatomical studies. Is he maimed down there? She leaves the clothes everywhere on the floor. She strides down the hall nakedly, breath still misting her insides, a slickness, a mildly erotic sway in her gait, a sort of pride. She doesn't want to get cold, though, so she's not dawdling or anything. Raitliffe, in his boxer shorts, drags the patchwork quilt behind them — it's a middle-European cape — laughing as, on the stairs, he tries to wrap it around her, tripping on the edge of the quilt, tumbling down a couple of steps, grabbing for the banister, barely averting a series of somersaults; then, on the second floor, as she parades past Lou Sloane's room, past the master bedroom (averts her gaze), Raitliffe catches up with her, wraps the blanket around her once and for all, cocoons her with it, kisses her against the wall by the *rose guest room,* and then jogs past — it's embarrassing — to prepare the marriage bed. He's doing the once-over in his room, housekeeper-style. By the time Jane makes her entrance, in her country gown, he has already peeled back the sheets on the bunk bed, turned up the mood lighting — an old light-up desk globe. On the bunk bed! She's going to make it with Raitliffe on the bunk bed! The walls are peeling. Everything is covered with dust.

— I'm p-p-pretty sure they washed the sheets since I was in c-college.

But she's still in a thrall, in the riptide, because, in spite of the terrible elusiveness of the female orgasm — you're there, you're there, and then you think about laundry, about pretreating a coffee stain, and you have to start all over again — *there's only the one direct route through the maze, if you want to be really personal about it,* guys can pound away at her for hours, above or below, front or back, and it feels okay, but nothing happens. Coitus is robust, theologically sound, the protein course of sexuality, but it's not enough for Jane Ingersoll. *She likes the tongue,* its velar, retroflex, cacuminal performances, its papillae, its mucoid membranes, its linguals and glossals, its Indo- and proto-Indo-European roots. So that when Raitliffe, crammed at the end of the bunk bed, spilling off on a cascade of quilts and bedding, picks up the task he left off, she hardly complains. His stutter makes him especially gifted in certain ways. He warms the spot which has only slightly cooled, holding onto her hip, cupping the underside of her ass, and the first electrical storm passes through her at once, like a break in the clouds, like alliterative quatrains, like wind chimes, freshly mown grass, goat cheese, new car interiors, church choirs, grand slams. Then the aftershocks, and she hisses, mumbles, the sound pried from her whether or not appropriate. *Ouch, ouch, ouch.* And Raitliffe stifles a laugh, and climbs up on top of her.

— Okay, she catches her breath. — I'm going to contribute. Let me contribute. Tell me what you like. And while she's composing a sample list, none of it true, *I like doing it on other people's lawns, I like public places, I like the empty back rows of airplanes, or on buses, I like boys half my age, I like foods, maybe milk or honey or cake frosting, I like guys in uniforms, especially when they take off their uniforms, I like guys who aren't gentle at all, although sometimes I like the gentlest guys of all, I like to put a finger in myself while making important telephone calls for example to the accountant* . . . she's separating Raitliffe from his boxer shorts, coming finally to gaze upon his *manhood,* which has a sort of doughy quality. She takes it into her hands, begins to knead. Penises are the ugliest anatomical part there is, next to goiters, and if you had one, firing its curds everywhere, you'd probably have your moods too. Guys and their dicks, like New England weather. Unpredictable. So Jane Ingersoll gives Raitliffe's homunculus the best hand job she can muster, thoughtful, patient, generous; she spits in her palm and applies the elixir. When that doesn't work she puts it in her mouth.

In the light of Raitliffe's desk globe, she can't really make out that much about his physiognomy, whether he's wart-covered or ribboned with ropy veins, but he's obviously slim enough. His testicles are little cashews, not those asteroids some of her boyfriends have unveiled to her. He's circumcised. His thatch of curls is appropriately pruned. Raitliffe tastes okay, too, no low-tide funk.

Jane Ingersoll has been *assured* during twenty-odd years of experience that she can give a blow job that will do the trick under most circumstances. She likes having things in her mouth. No special stratagem is applied, no tonguing of the glans, no overriding the gag reflex, none of those sideshow skills that guys take from sexually explicit publications and force upon their mates. *She just likes having it in her mouth sometimes* and when she likes a guy she can worry over him for a long time without being too bored. Still, for all the attention she lavishes on Raitliffe, there are no tangible results. He's tense. Can't unwind. He lies back, he sits up, he rolls around, he doesn't caress her hair, doesn't try to turn her around. Nope, Raitliffe is late for an appointment. Raitliffe is preoccupied with some routine moral conundrum. After a while, Jane sits up. She takes his left foot in her hand. She massages the sole. His foot, a crabbed, barnacled *claw*, is truly ugly.

— Okay, what's up?

— I really really like you, you know. I do . . .

— That's sweet of you to say. (She moves from the heel up to the yellowed talons, squeezes them one by one.) Worried about something? Anything you want to talk about?

— It's n-n-n-not that . . .

— A lot of men have trouble, you know. Part of life. It's nothing to be ashamed of.

She can barely bring herself to say all this supportive stuff. She must have said these things a thousand times by now. Raitliffe removes the left foot from her grip and thrusts the other at her.

— I'm not a perfect physical specimen, she offers. — I know —

— You're really b-b-b-beautiful. You're t-t-totally b-b-b-beautiful.

— Oh, I get it, Jane says, — you're running for office.

— Really, Raitliffe says. — If I had any idea when I was younger that I would b-be as lucky as I am right now, I c-c-c-could have made it through the next ten years happy as a c-clam.

— I should have been able to predict.

— I mean, maybe it's m-my mother. I don't know. I g-g-gave her a bath this afternoon too and that always b-b-b-bothers me a little, I mean —

— You gave her a bath too?

Raitliffe nods.

— She didn't tell me.

Jane Ingersoll presses her thumb deep into the sole of Hex's right foot.

— And this afternoon you know she also t-t-tried to p-p-p-persuade me to p-p-p-p-p-p-p-p-p —

There's a long strained silence, and then she watches Raitliffe dislodge the sound. With a tap upon his cheek.

— *P-p-p-pull the p-p-plug,* he says. — Give her the b-b-barbiturates, or whatever it is she wants. I don't know.

— What? You mean like a . . .

The news deserves a respectful space. She sets his foot down on the rippling bedspread.

— B-b-b-but that's not it, that's not the p-p-p-problem. There's something else I should t-tell you. I should —

His expression is solicitous.

— There's no b-b-bad news. I mean, I should say I really liked . . . I liked what you were doing, I like b-b-being around you, very much, it's not that . . .

They're like vines now. They're getting comfortable. She settles between his legs, her head resting on his thigh. She stares up at the underside of the top bunk, the bunching of sheets tucked into it.

— There is one position I k-k-kind of . . .

— So let's hear it —

— D-d-d-d-d-d-d-d-d —

— You won't hurt my feelings.

— D-d-don't interrupt me. I'll never finish.

— Sorry, Jane says. — I'm sorry.

Then, with mild irritation, Raitliffe blurts out the request.

— D-d-d-did you ever let anyone . . . *restrain* you?

— What?

— You know, like —

— Tie me up?

— Well, I mean . . . I'm not g-g-going to —

— Tie me to the . . . to the bedposts or something?

— Well . . .

And of course she's a modern woman, an adventuress, who has endured many contemporary *variations, poses,* the guys who want you to stand motionless in the window under the moon wearing only ballet slippers; the guys who want you to wear cloth diapers; the guys who themselves want to wear your panty hose; the guys who want to hit you with things, or the guys who want you to hit them, and, of course, the guys who want to tie you up. Missionary style is old as oatmeal.

— I was living behind the mall with this one man and he used to like to do that. He liked to tie me up and then go watch the television. It wasn't about sex. I'd be in there for half an hour. *Nick? What are you watching? Do you think you could at least bring the radio in here if you're going to leave me for a while? You know?* He'd drink a six-pack, call a few friends. He liked to watch ice hockey while I was tied up.

Jane Ingersoll is polite enough, or queasy enough, not to mention the symbolism of Raitliffe's request, but she's alert to it. Your bracing truths of the sexual battlefield are usually right out in the open. When she looks at Raitliffe — who's helixed halfway around an uncomfortable foam pillow — she knows that he knows that she knows. She'll be immobilized. Paralyzed.

— Look, you're not going to tie me up and apply red-hot fire irons, are you? You're not going to gag me, or set the house on fire and leave me, or do any bodily harm, right? Promise?

Raitliffe pauses with a drama that unfortunately suggests to Jane Ingersoll that he's had the conversation before. — It's the only way I c-c-c-c-c —

A calculated, performative stutter.

— It's more c-c-comfortable for me this way.

— Well, then I guess it's okay. I guess it has to be okay.

So she gets to the innermost layer of Raitliffe, to Raitliffe as he is known only to selected intimates. It's the last issue to explore, the most advanced chapter in his user's manual. Or so it seems. Almost immediately he produces fuchsia velvet binds from under the pillows, bowlines one of them around the bedpost, and takes hold of her wrist. Left wrist first. A knot in name only, since she could pull it off right away. But in the spirit of adventure, she doesn't pull it off. The best she can do — because he wants her facedown — is to kick against the mattress. Emblematic resistance. Eventually, she gives this up too, gives up her feet, lets him fix the ankles. Her thighs are enough apart that she feels especially vulnerable, like he might come at her with a speculum.

— Pull a blanket over us will you?

Instead, he gives her the back rub. Some American amalgam of the disciplines of the North and the East, Asian and Netherland-ish, involving both a reverence for the female body, for the luxury of curves, for the elegance of her back, thumbs probing along her spine, up under her hairline; he has a eucalyptus unguent that he pours on her. She imagines she can see it from a great height, from the ceiling, her body the way it was when she was a teenager, when she was like an ideal of beauty, in the plaid skirts of private school, ribbons in her hair, dope or stolen pills in her ridiculous patent leather purse, digits furrowing under the knots in her back, moving down to the swell of her, in cars and on living room couches, in some epiphenomenal terrain, how Nicky gave her a back rub once before they were married, under the worst of circumstances, his dad in the hospital with a stroke, Nicky's tears upon her back, best back rub she ever had, or the music teacher in the public high school, he'd tried to give her a back rub, or a neck rub, after school, probably why she gave up the violin, the guy was a creep with horrible dandruff, or after she wrecked Kathleen's car, Kathleen's Datsun, she had whiplash, went for physical therapy or whatever you call it, and the women there would say all the nicest stuff to her, how pretty she was as they worked on her back, though she was past pretty by then and full of worries but maybe still a little bit attractive, from which basement of reflections she emerges to notice that lips are now being gently applied to her spine, one kiss per vertebra, the twenty-first, the eighteenth, like an inchworm making its progress along her, Raitliffe climbs onto her, kisses her cheek, facing away, kisses her neck, kisses her arms, glides up to her fingers, and daintily puts the fourth finger of her left hand (loosely suspended in its velvet restraint) in his mouth, sucks on it, at which point, because he's beside her head, she can see that there is indeed some progress at last in his *primary sex organ thing,* standing out in front, well, horizontal is better than a sag — and soon he lies upon her backside, and his hands tunnel their way down under her, grab onto her breasts, so that he has secured himself, she guesses, and then he starts like he's just going to insert the thing, she reminds him to *Use protection, if you please,* and he says, *Oh, of c-c-course, sorry,* and whips out the condom, as if he has a supply of all these accoutrements, velvet ribbons, massage oil, condoms, and bourbon, it turns out, a flask from which he takes a slug, stashed underneath the bed. What other stuff must be under there? He unfurls the condom, rolls it onto himself, with a snap. Meanwhile, it's not exactly like a rain forest down there, inside of her, it's not exactly equatorial, since he hasn't been attending, so he's obliged to do preparation, lapping from behind, *You know, it's entirely possible that there might be a second note-worthy development here,* happy to report, she's falling through the cracks, murmuring vowel sounds, pulling at the velvet bonds, grinding into the sheets, when Raitliffe, athwart her, attempts to introduce the sergeant-at-arms, it fills her for a second, and then he's entirely still, bangs his head awkwardly on the upper bunk bed, seconds pass, the fullness of him, and then some infinitesimal movement, movement like no movement at all, folded into minutiae, *Come on, Come on, Come on.* How little you can get away with! He grabs her hips and works his way between them, and then stops again, still as a camouflaged bird, maybe she's getting a little dizzy, maybe there's an oxygen shortage or something, the way her face is mushed up against a foam rubber pillow, she turns the other way, not much better there, folds of the blanket impeding the passage of air. What are the symptoms of oxygen deprivation, tracers, vapor trails, haloes around the lights, sudden revelations, religiosity of the Hindu, Buddhist, or Presbyterian variety? *I am inventing my own gospels, I proclaim love is about motionlessness and haste;* see, there's stuff you only learn when you are willing to be this still, until everything in you is angry, which is when Raitliffe sheathes himself again, and sighs morosely, and then nothing, she can feel condensation, tidal movement, buoys tolling, the foghorn, the tides sweeping through a narrow channel, Raitliffe pulls out of her entirely, she can't tell what's happening, he disappears off into the room, she hears the flask getting tipped over on the floor, he curses, she's grinding as best she can against the sheets, against some bunching of sheets and blankets underneath her, thinking of the moment when the straps come off, *she doesn't need Raitliffe,* with a token effort she fights against the bonds, love is change of scenery, love is the exhaustion of options, *love is the people left over,* your middle-aged eccentrics, and she says forcefully, in contralto, *Oh man,* and comes, and yanks her right hand free, to put a knuckle in her mouth, shredding the velvet ribbon, a dark shadow passes over her, no idea what Raitliffe is doing at all, except that as she travels up through the skeins of sensation, she sees that he is actually sitting on the floor watching her, *jerking off,* Raitliffe is just handling himself, desultorily, fidgeting, in a feckless retreat from the pleasures of intercourse, and when he sees that her hand is free, that she's beginning, naturally, to untie the other wrist, he gets agitated, leaps up onto her, holds down the free hand, until she gives up again, *D-d-don't move, just for a second, d-d-don't move,* and there's the sound of him doing it, holding down her one wrist with his right hand, with his left doing whatever it is he's doing, puttering, groaning, and then he clamps his hand over her mouth, not so that she can't breathe, *Shh shh,* not to frighten her, but so that she will hear his next stupendous declaration, the language of purely glandular secretions, *I love you I love you I love you I love you.* That old business, that refuge of liars. Which coincides with a sudden spattering upon her back.

— Oh shit, Raitliffe says, his horror following upon fluency. He disappears out of his bedroom. It's the only thing he's forgotten to calculate in his preparation for this union: spillage.

And he's lost the condom somewhere, too, in the middle of his travails. It's lying in the center of the floor, as though molted. She frees her other hand, but waits politely until he's returned, waits as he sandpapers her back with an old faded washcloth. He's trying to erase every trace of his seminal goo from her back, from his own chest, from the sheets, and in erasing, he overlooks that Jane Ingersoll isn't exactly *unhappy*, is sitting up on the bed now, untying her ankles. *You know, I don't like the way it tastes, it tastes horrible, like toothpaste with a soy sauce chaser, that's the really bad thing about it,* expostulating in the flush of freedom from bondage. Raitliffe misses these reassurances from her, in his scrubbing and scraping. After which he slumps onto the floor, lost in interpretations.

— I'm ashamed, he says. — I'm so sorry I subjected you t-t-t-to that.

— Don't get bent out of shape, Jane says. — You didn't subject me to anything. It's no big deal. It was theoretically interesting. Aren't you cold? Get under here.

He's drinking, taking a long pull at the flask, but eventually, shivering desperately, he climbs into the bed with her, and they lock arms and thereby indulge in comforting, but, because she's wide awake now, because some postcoital adrenaline is released into her, Jane Ingersoll isn't content to just lie there, or to let Dexter Raitliffe doze off. She mulls it over, discounts the *I love you* part as the patter of lonely people, realizes, by deduction, that she's not lonely actually, not so lonely as she might have said earlier in the evening. In fact, from this angle it looks like she has a lot of friends, a whole shoreline's worth, no matter what trouble she's gotten into, friends all over the sorrel-colored desk globe, and there are her two adorable boys who have made life more tolerable, and her sister. In fact, if she's being honest, she can even count herself a member of that heretical society, that Masonic cult that permeates all the Americas and Western Europe and the newly democratized Eastern Bloc countries and even the poverty-stricken developing nations (she holds Raitliffe tightly against her), that parallel but backward civilization that spawns fairy tales and folk dances and all the wisdom passed orally from woman to woman, *the society of fine moods.* Covetously, she holds their ancient traditions in her heart; covetously, she whispers litanically to herself: *things are pretty good.*

— Hey, Raitliffe, she says. — Let's go dancing.

19

Lou, Lou. You awake? Kowalski calls from the doorway. Incandescence haloing his squat, boxy figure. The sound of Lou's name summons him uneasily from nightmares (a squad of young below-the-waist amputees, on skateboards), he hears his voice, comfortable with emergency — *What's the problem?* — dismay seizes him, and he begins to stir. What room is this, where has he been, a little twin-sized bed with fossilized pillow, wall-to-wall carpeting, electric blanket, the wheezing of a rickety humidifier? Where's his wife? Startled, groaning.

— Lou?

— I'm up, I'm up, Sloane mumbles. — What time you have?

The nausea of uneasy dreaming takes up its housing, somewhere just behind financial anxieties, disgust at the prospects for the next twenty-four hours, fear of bodily catastrophes, where it will dog him for the rest of the day. He reaches for his glasses, on the bedside table. Except that there isn't a bedside table.

— I can't sleep, Kowalski says. — I'm rolling around in there feeling just awful, Lou. I thought you might be up too. I'm trying to find a way to explain how I handled your son, Lou. You know? I just feel awful about it.

— Not *my* son.

— Listen, I'm godawful sorry, Louis. Godawful sorry. I don't know what got into me.

— Dexter had a few himself. He knew what he had coming.

Lou waves Kowalski in, sits up in bed. Mac makes a beeline for the glasses — on the old steamer trunk across the room. Carries the frames over, stems first. Lou experiments with fittings until they're just right, and then draws up his knees, mountaintops, under the covers of the chastity bed.

— I really clocked the kid one.

Kowalski sprawls in the plaid recliner.

— Well, you landed a left, Lou says, — but I think Dexter had a sort of rope-a-dope strategy. He's more talented as a prizefighter than we had any reason to expect.

Mac laughs politely.

— I mean, he got out of the way of the next couple. You couldn't really connect after the first blow. If it was a twelve-rounder, I'm not so sure, Mac. He's younger.

— Yeah, well, Kowalski says.

— Headache?

— Bad one. Couldn't sleep. Headache along with upset stomach. It's a bad stew.

Kowalski massages himself at the temples, as if the approach will somehow repair the mass poisoning of brain cells. Thus, the discussion of hangover remedies: vitamin B, vitamin C, the entire antioxidant series, prayers, hot milk, yoga, televised sports, Scrabble, cold shower, the company of dogs, weeping, raw oysters, iodine. Mac's conclusion, *that a hangover is really an expression of personal responsibility* and thus ought to be endured proudly, resolutely, is endorsed vigorously by both men.

— Lou, you think I ought to go over there and apologize to him?

— Who? Dexter? Lou reads the digital alarm clock. — Not at 2:37.

— Tomorrow. I mean tomorrow.

— Well —

— I just can't live with myself sometimes. I just can't figure out why I do what I do.

— I know just what you mean, Lou Sloane says.

Sleeplessness, the fatigue behind Lou's eyes, feels blue. The torpor, the listlessness. Now that he has time to think, now that he's in possession of the facts, whatever they may be, sleep will never come. On the other hand, he can hardly imagine getting out of bed.

— Well, he's asleep now, your boy. That's what you're saying.

— Mac, leave it alone. Look, I'm going to turn the light on. Is that all right?

Lou's goalpost legs protrude from under bedclothes. He switches on the old standing lamp beside him, a flea market model, a pink bonnet of stained glass at its zenith.

— You'll excuse me a moment, pal? Lou says.

— No problem.

However, when Lou, in flannel boxer shorts and sleeveless white tee, goes across the hall to empty himself, into the mildewed and meagerly appointed bathroom (New England Patriots towels, matching set), the door of which will not entirely close, Kowalski follows. He stands outside, hollering self-lacerations over the hiss of tap water: *I get the jungle juice in me, Lou, and I'm going to get in some trouble, some altercation, it's been going on for twenty-five years, I'm really getting too old for it, I am. I'm going to have to stick to beer or wine.* Lou is more concerned about prostatic enlargement. The impoverished flow, the drip, and the occasional piercing, skewering pain down there. Hopefully, the faucet disguises the sound. Jesus, he's getting paunchy too. And his teeth are a mess. He has cowlicks. When Lou emerges from the bathroom Kowalski is still rattling on. He follows Lou back across the hall, oblivious, as Sloane starts pulling on clothes.

— You want to eat? Mac says. — Should we just go ahead and eat?

— It's not even three.

— Breakfast, Lou, my favorite time of the day.

— I'm not really sure I —

— I'm sorry for waking you up. Really.

— I was doing a little tossing and turning myself. It's fine.

— I'm going to skillet up a special recipe. Might sleep better on a full stomach. You never know.

— Big glass of orange juice, that'll do the trick.

— Should I get some?

— No, I . . .

From the kitchen, where the view is best — a whole wall of glass — Lou can make out the expanse of the sea, a spangling of moonlight on swells. He gives up scrimmaging with Kowalski, accepts the cup of coffee, what the hell, and loses himself in the broth of dark beyond the house. Kowalski is enveloped in rites of cuisine. The griddle is heated to *high* so that the eggs (*dash hot sauce, 1 tbsp. bacon bits, pinch onion salt, diced sausage, lightly browned, season to taste*), with a flash of steam, scramble on contact.

— Medium? Well?

— Scorched, Lou says. — Desiccated. Lifeless.

Kowalski, with potholders, bears forth the warmed plates, with sprigs of parsley, sections of orange, raisin toast, mounds of eggs, arterial cloggers, three or four eggs for each of them, a feast for autumn. Lou is concerned about his ticker, of course, but he figures the polite thing to do is to dig in anyhow, in spite of the cholesterol profile of the meal. So he does. And he has to admit that the eggs are *zesty, tasty, savory.* It's Kowalski who breaks the silence finally, having worked his way around to his raisin toast with homemade preserves.

— I think we made a big mistake at the plant.

Lou chews contemplatively.

— Probably right.

— Not just the ruptures in the coolant lines, either, or whatever. Surge line, containment. Not just that.

Lou Sloane gets up with his plate and his juice glass — they're finished inside of ten minutes — and begins stacking (a smear of raspberry jam on Kowalski's saucer), but Mac physically blocks Lou's access to the sink, takes the plates by force. The guy's a linebacker.

— I'm in charge of the cleanup. Guests have no rights whatsoever.

Kowalski and the pressurized spray gun at the sink (single basin, moldering drying rack), Kowalski shouting over it:

— I'm worried about ruptures, but what I'm really thinking about is currents, Lou. I'm thinking about the currents in the mouth of the harbor.

Steel wool pad from the brightly colored box.

— Okay, he says, — you have the water coming in across Race Point, from three directions, essentially. You got the water at the other end of Block Island, just as turbulent, also coming in. You got the Thames River running out, southerly. You got Two Tree Channel, runs southwesterly, into the Sound. All this water heading into crowds. That's what I'm worrying about.

— So the runoff —

— It's going to sit right there, in Long Island Sound. Right? I mean, where the hell else is it going to drain to? Staten Island? It sure isn't going to Portugal.

Lou brings over his mug. Drains the last.

— I think the B&W theory, the design theory, is just the opposite. Around Fishers, Watch Hill, you have tide running out past Montauk, Block Island. Open water there. It's tidal. Coming in, going out. There's room. It's all going out someplace. I mean, the navy has been dumping out there for years. They're getting ready to dump there again. Tailings from the sub plant, sludge from the river. Like Ron was saying. It's never hurt commercial fishing in the region. Not that I know of. Never has.

— But how far out does that line go. From the plant. Half a mile, tops?

— You're saying there's not enough current to disperse this stuff? I'm just not sure I buy it. You should have seen me trying to row in the rowboat earlier. I barely made it.

Kowalski takes up an old rag, an old T-shirt. Dries the plates methodically.

— By the way, it's got a leak in it, Lou says, — the rowboat. I hit a rock, I think. I don't know, I might have made it worse. It slipped my mind. Really sorry about that.

— Not at all. There was a hole already, Kowalski says. — I tried to patch it a couple of weeks ago. Let's go take a look.

— You want to go out and look at the rowboat?

— Well, if it's sunk, I want to know —

Then, in the kitchen, Kowalski gets his idea. Lou can actually see the idea dawn in Mac's cuboid visage. There's some unfastening of obsessions, some shunting off of nervous energy onto it: *this idea will occupy them for some time,* this will give them an activity in their sleeplessness, a positive outlet for the fixations of old guys. Maybe it'll even hold them until 6:30, until sunrise, when Lou will begin his trek to Lake Sacandaga, NY, or White River Junction, VT, or Truro, MA, or wherever:

— Yeah, we could look at the rowboat, Kowalski says, — and then we could go out and check the waste-water pump.

— Check the what?

— The waste-water pump. Out in the channel.

— You're pulling my leg, right? What kind of running lights on your boat? You have a G-M tube?

— Lou, what am I? I'm a shift supervisor. Maybe I'm a little tardy returning equipment, but I happen to have here in my house a Geiger counter, a portable proportional counter, gauss meter, rate meter. I have headphones. Cell phones. Everything. I packed it all together in a shipping container earlier in the evening, in case it'd come in handy.

— I think it's the middle of the night and you're having night sweats. Or you're halfway between drunkenness and a hangover. That's not a good time for major decisions. You're going to submerge the company's equipment in the harbor outside of Waterford? You'll probably damage the diodes or get condensation in this stuff, rust it out. We won't be able to see anything. And anyhow you don't have a long enough cord, thirty yards of cord, say.

— Actually, forty-two.

— Not to mention getting out there. You want to take your boat out there in the dark? I hit a rock in the first thirty seconds I was rowing.

Kowalski, with simmering irritation:

— Lou, I was born here. Back when it was still a beautiful place to live. I grew up in Niantic. This is my home. I've been here ever since I was a kid. Never lived anyplace else. If I'm gonna wake up in the middle of the night worrying about what's in the water — cesium in the water, thorium, or neptunium, for godsakes — I'm doing it as a native son worrying about his neighbors. I think that's justification. I'm not going to endanger my job or the plant. You know I'm not. You want to come along, you can come along. Or you can go back to bed.

— Suit yourself.

— But say the neptunium, or whatever it is, settles two towns over, the channel deposits it in Madison. Just a few million particles swallowed by the shellfish. Or say it drifts over to Bridgeport maybe. Say we can make sure the currents carry it to Bridgeport, where we stick the blacks with it. For about a million years, 2.2×10^6 years, I think that might be the number. I went along with the suggestion because the situation was dangerous this afternoon and I was doing the best I could. But now I'm thinking about it I don't like it. And I don't really give a damn if the whole thing looks bad for Stan Warren. I want to know what's what.

— I can't believe I'm having this conversation with you at this hour. And you're using exponents.

In this ballet of pliés, développés, pas de chat, pointes, grands jetés, this ballet of policy, the two of them advance in a certain direction without completing the debate. They're moving toward the back door. They're by the coat rack. Where, after a silence, Lou capitulates.

— Well, truth is, I don't really have an opinion. I don't even work for the damn place. I've got other things on my mind. But I'm going out on the boat, Mac, strictly because I can't sleep, and because it would be dangerous for you to try to operate the boat alone under the circumstances. But you're going to have to loan me a sweater.

There's a UConn Huskies sweatshirt on a peg. A hooded sweatshirt with a marsupial pouch. There's a nine-volt flashlight on the shelf. Lou pulls on the sweatshirt, puts his windbreaker over it. He finds a synthetic ski cap, navy blue, just in case, clamps this on his head. Kowalski, the loner, the bachelor, is in foul-weather coveralls, bright yellow, and an Irish-knit sweater. He carries the packing crate with the gadgets in it. They lock up behind themselves and pass under the boughs of an old elm. Lou shines the flashlight. In spite of its obsolete design it has fresh batteries. Kowalski goes down the ladder and into the rowboat. It sags beneath the weight. Lou hands him down the card-board box.

— How far out are you moored?

By which he refers to Kowalski's Mako with twin Mercury one-fifty-horse outboard engines, a vessel designed especially for the high-speed pursuit and destruction of dwindling coastal sport fish. Or for outrunning Coast Guard patrols. The *Barracuda*, as it is named, is twenty-one feet, with a canopy over the helm and a tiny cabin, fore, for storage space. Kowalski periodically invites the day shift out on the boat. Lazy afternoons in summer in which few fish are caught and much beer is consumed. Everybody wears zinc oxide on their noses. Everybody eats BBQ chips or sour cream 'n onion.

— Just beyond the rocks there.

The bow of the dinghy, with its cargo of plump older guys, is just fingers above the waves. Lou's loafers are soaked through. The flashlight, when he inadvertently shines it into the hull of the rowboat, actually disturbs a small school of minnows gathered around Kowalski's feet. The wind has picked up considerably, and the moon (three quarters, waning) is everywhere reflected. Coming in and out of the clouds. It's just after low tide. The safety issue still troubles Sloane, but when he brings it up — the safety of taking the boat across the harbor, outside the shipping lanes, at three in the morning — Kowalski gives him a predictable lecture. *It's a quarter mile across the channel, not much more, and then around the peninsula there, by the back side of the plant, I've done it a million times, drunker than a skunk, in heavy fog, and the boat is fine down to seven feet, anyway. I can take it in that close, as long as we're going slowly.* Kowalski's strokes are long and graceful and he doesn't bother to look over his shoulder. He knows the route. While he begins to tie their drenched bowline onto the puce-colored beach ball that marks his mooring, Mac directs Lou Sloane — who's dragging himself and the box full of nuclear con-diments up and over the stern of the *Barracuda* — to get to know the depth finder. It will be his responsibility. They'll leave the bumpers attached; they'll do a radio test. Safety first. The engines turn over. A nearby gaggle of cormorants is startled by the noise.

Dislodged from the surface of their dank rocks, they skim the surface of the harbor, in and out of Sloane's flashlight.

— You're sober enough? Lou says.

— Soberer than I am out here most of the time.

Lou climbs up on the bow, unfetters the mooring. They glide into deeper water. Behind, the rowboat orbits around the beach ball, up and over the oscillations of their wake. Lou sits on the bow with the flashlight, calling out the lobster pots and buoys, *Clorox bottle, ten o'clock,* while Kowalski consults the charts, the radar. He has all the navigation equipment, compass and sextant and loran, a guy with charts for every harbor or inlet or strait within a hundred miles. The course is already plotted. When Lou Sloane gets cold up top, he retreats under the canopy, behind the windscreen, with Mac, where he continues faithfully to aim the flashlight out across the bow, in search of hazards. The beacon mounted just over their heads also casts a diffuse light. They're doing a couple of knots, nothing more.

— I snagged a lobster trap like this, one night, Mac says. — I'm minding my own business about sunset, and I see the pot, pink and green. It goes under the bow. When it comes out from under, it's trailing me. Following. A horrible sight. There's a shuddering, you know, and the boat slows down. All of a sudden I'm dragging a couple hundred pounds, around one prop. The engines are groaning. Luckily, I wasn't far from the dock. This was in Old Saybrook. I towed it in. Hauled up the trap, hand over hand, like the lobstermen of old. It was maybe fifty, seventy-five feet of line on there, and it was heavy as hell. Turned out the trap was full of lobsters. Full of them. I left the trap on the dock, but I swiped the lobsters, a half-dozen anyhow. I got a couple of gourmet dinners out of it. Surf and turf. After that, I had the guys at the marina take the boat out of the water to look at that prop. It was twisted up like a coat hanger.

Mac's eyes are fixed on the water. He keeps a tight grip on the helm.

— So we're out here on the water, Lou. We got a couple of beers, it's pretty quiet. So what's going on with your wife? What's going on at home?

— Oh, hell, Mac. You didn't drag me out here to —

— You don't have to talk about it, if you don't want to. Fine with me.

— You're going to be my marriage counselor? Coach me through crisis management or some garbage?

— No way, nohow, Kowalski says. — Keep that flashlight up. The way things have turned out for me, I couldn't persuade a woman to run out of a burning building.

Lou sets the lamp down on Mac's navigator's table, and goes rummaging forward in the cooler for *a cold one.* It's not that his resolve has been shaken loose, exactly, since the conversation with Dexter. Resolve isn't what he thought it was. Airtight, reliable, complete. In the middle of the night, when he had exhausted his left side, his right side, his stomach, his back, when he couldn't come up with a *fifth sleeping posture,* that lost chord of unconsciousness, *the decision, the resolution, the plan* spontaneously unglued. He was looking at six weeks alone up north, wearing high-visibility clothes eating at the last-chance White Mountain Pizza shack next to guys with missing arms, guys on probation, putting up in trailer parks, locking himself into motels, watching the Weather Channel twenty-four hours a day, listening to Christian radio, driving around in a rented RV; in the middle of the night, at Mac's, he told himself he had already made up his mind, and that was that, but soon he found he had not, soon he was thinking that Billie wouldn't be around much longer, and if she died like Dexter said she was going to die, swallowing the tablets, inhaling the carbon monoxide, if she passed on like that and he didn't get to talk to her, didn't get a chance to make her laugh, didn't get to hear her unrestrained cackle, didn't get to see contentment sweep across her troubled face that way it did sometimes — like a rainbow — if he missed the chance, he knew, he would live out his days miserably. He wouldn't be able to wake in the Knotty Pine Cabins of Orford, NH, and look at himself in the mirror. What was out of reach in Billie was still back there someplace, in deep storage, all the things he had loved about her, the things he had brought out in her. Good things. What a strong woman she was, what a wise woman, wiser than he, and more generous.

— Beer? he calls to Kowalski.

— No thanks, I'm driving.

— How far?

— Ten minutes maybe. See the red marker yet?

Lou swallows greedily from the can. He can hardly believe it when it starts coming out, the language of his marriage, a ten-foot swell of regret, past the mechanisms that stifle talk, all *that dirty laundry*, the ups and downs. It's himself he's talking to, in the dark, enveloped in dark, with the sea all around him. He doesn't look at Kowalski while it starts to leach from him, and he speaks so low, *I get afraid, Mac, I must just be a damn coward, or weak or something, I'm afraid all the time, in the middle of the night imagining I'm thinking things, calamities, thinking I'm hearing some disaster, she's choking, she's having a heart attack, and what if I don't wake up, I'm waking up thinking these things, I mean when we got married and I knew she was sick I didn't care, because she was so beautiful and sweet and everything, and I didn't care if she was sick, because I thought I could take it, and it would happen slowly and it would happen with a whole lot of good cheer and good times and great memories and all of that, a dignified illness, price of love, that's what I thought, but what I didn't expect was that I'd get hit so hard with each bit of bad news, just like she did, until I was just uncomfortable enough to feel like things were going to get a lot worse instead of better, that she was going to hurt terribly, that she was going to be anguished, that she was going to die, just die off in front of me, I had never even thought of her dying before, I knew but I hadn't really thought about it, and now I was thinking about it a lot, she was going to die in pain and I was going to have to watch, and the boost I'd always gotten as a happy person, I lost all of that, bit by bit, after a while I never even remembered I lived like that, that I'd been a happy guy, and I started to feel like it was all bad news, Mac, all bad luck, and I had to brace myself every day for the next bad thing, and I needed to feel I could do something for myself because of the clouds I was seeing on the horizon, because I was giving up hope, that I wouldn't just holler at her to put on her own damn diaper, feed yourself, for godsakes, I gave up hope, Mac, because she gave up hope, and the only way I could still live with her was to be insulated, and I had nowhere to go with it, and what would happen to me if I left, I had no family anymore, Mac, that's all the family I had left, in that house, in that wheelchair, all the family I had left, and how the hell was I supposed to live after that, anyhow, after what I knew of Billie when she was younger, and then on top of everything else, I got the news at the plant, it was the last straw, I never even told her, never could bring myself to tell her, because what was she going to say about that, when she was facing what she had, and I thought I was having a heart attack, every night just about, piling up more worries, what do I do if tonight's the night I find her dead, what do I do if tomorrow's the morning I find her body cold in the bedroom, I was so tired and so scared, not like a man ought to be, not like a man who has any self-respect, but like a child, Mac, a little child. So I decided to go.*

As they draw near the point, the end of the peninsula, off to port, Mac concentrates on navigation, gives Lou a wide berth. There's the smokestack (striped like a barber pole), the reactor tanks, the radio tower, all in spotlights, red signals blinking on the radio tower. No steam. Millstone disappears to stern, inch by inch; Kowalski noses further into the harbor. Here and there, a bedroom light on the lazy arc of the next cove. Insomniacs.

Mac says, — You got yourself a hell of a problem there, I'd be the first to admit it. I didn't realize it was that bad. I should have realized, I guess.

— Well, I —

— I'm glad you felt you could get it off your chest.

Sloane finishes the beer, slips the can back into the cooler. Meanwhile, Kowalski throttles back the *Barracuda* — they're just drifting for a moment — and takes up the neglected flashlight. In the beam, he picks up a piece of driftwood, a very large piece of lumber, flecked with eggshell primer, a whole plank, eight or ten feet long, the flotsam the harbor carries with it, a piece of somebody's house, a piece of somebody's homeowner dream. With a gaff he keeps for *deep-sea expeditions*, for marlin and for giant tuna, Mac fends it off. It goes lazily drifting toward the coast.

— If you can't live with her, you can't live with her. I guess that's the lesson there. What are you going to do?

— That's my predicament, I guess. I wish it were simple, Mac. I wish I had it all figured all out.

— Of course.

Now, Kowalski points at the red channel marker, just to port, a half mile off the point. The foghorns, in their idiosyncratic intervals, wail. There are the two lighthouses from this spot. The two beacons. One is *a schoolhouse,* Lou knows, a little red-brick affair, like a New England schoolhouse. Right in the middle of the Sound. All this water, in tonnages, running down past the estuaries and tidal pools. Past the schoolhouse. This is where the waste water from Millstone empties out. Only a little further to go. Kowalski has marked a probable site, in red pencil, on his chart.

— Of course, if you're still living with her, then that's a different thing, right? If you're going to be married to her no matter what, if you're going to be stuck with her wherever you live, whether you buy a mud hut out in Nevada or something, whether you live in Iceland, if you're still living with her then, thinking about her day and night, then what's the difference? You might as well go back and shack up. You're married.

— Don't get condescending about this, Mac. I swear.

Kowalski puts down his red pencil, upon the bisected and trisected chart of Niantic Harbor, in order *to violate the time-honored masculine tradition of avoiding looking another guy affectionately in the eyes.* With the free hand, he claps Sloane on the shoulder.

— Lou, that's the last thing I want to do. You do what you want to do with her. I'm telling you what you're telling me. What you're saying to me is that you're still thinking about her. Well, that's obvious. Maybe you still love your wife. That's what anyone would tell you, anyone you know. Even someone like me can see the obvious things.

— Bunk, Sloane says, and repairs to the stern.

— Whatever you say. Forget about it. I'll never bring it up again. You know I won't.

From the trolling chair at the stern, Lou reluctantly carries over the crate of monitoring equipment. He pulls out coils of wire. Kowalski must have been up for hours preparing this spaghetti, wrapping the lines in bulky layers of electrical tape. Poor-man's waterproofing. Speaker wire? Telephone cord? Lou tests the batteries, just to make sure, unwinds the coils. Kowalski, hovering from task to task, puts the boat in neutral, and goes up to the bow, to anchor.

— How deep? he calls.

— Forty-one. Lou is holding the tube, with almost fifty yards of wire uncoiling around his feet.

— Another hundred yards, it'd be too deep. Maybe we'll hit the damn pipe right on the head, just hook the anchor right around it. You okay, Louis?

— This is a fine specialization for me, he says. Arranging the diagnostic tools.

Sloane's hands are raw and red. When they're really cold, he puts them in the hand-warming pouch of his x-large sweatshirt, but first he takes the hem of that borrowed robe, and, removing his glasses, wipes his face, with attention to the eyes, glad to be out of Kowalski's line of sight. Then, after the respite, back to work. The Geiger counter is one of the industrial-strength standard models, *without the thin window that might allow for short-range or weak radiant particles, etc.* It's industrial as well as *sexy* — not like the Erector set contraptions from the early days. A black steel alloy houses the glass tube and electrode, the tube filled with pressurized gas. In theory, it encounters an *ionizing event,* such that the ions pass through the housing and disturb the pressurized material inside, knocking loose the secondary electrons, which, in this case, will travel along forty-two yards of electrical cable to a rate meter, battery operated, in a sleek black plastic case, which in turn will pick up the pulse of current in the form of an old-fashioned *click,* a click signal that will automatically decay because of the circuitry in the rate meter, shunted off to an amplifier and thereby to the headphones (lightweight, with orange foam ear guards), to be followed by the next. A good thing this particular Geiger counter doesn't have the porous alpha radiation screen either, since it would just leak. Of course, *your G-M tube always registers cosmic rays* — even here, in the empty mouth of the harbor at Waterford in the thick of night, without submarine, nor barge, nor tanker, nor pleasure boat upon the seas. Even here *the surface of Lou Sloane's troubled earth is bombarded with cosmic rays from the furthest reaches of space* — and that's how Lou Sloane tests the Geiger counter. It should give on the order of sixty or eighty clicks a minute, like a human pulse, say, from the background radiation, the cosmic rays, and so it does, in the pristine silence. About the time Kowalski's anchor hits bottom and Mac climbs back, midships, to shut off the engine, Lou Sloane has the apparatus set to go.

— Wouldn't have believed it, Lou says.

— I love that sound, Kowalski says.

The ticks in the tiny speaker on the rate meter. Their call of the wild. Kowalski checks the needle, pulls off the headphones.

— You know, I never did honestly think we'd get this far.

It's what's under the surface, unknowable, that's so beguiling, the kind of stuff that's routine at the plant — imperceptibles; everything they don't know and are in danger of not knowing through the whole of their lives; why the guys in the social classes above them control all the money and influence; why there are the demonic impulses just outside of consciousness, murderous rages and inconsolable sadnesses; why there is illness and affection that goes awry. That's what men fish for, that's what guys dive for, that's why the oil companies drill into the trenches of plate tectonics; that's the mineral in the volcanic eruptions of magma; *guys conquer nature to figure out their own backyards*; they take to the ocean in the same way they shave. *Radiation is like alchemy,* Lou thinks. It tells you more about the physicists looking for it than it will ever tell you about the elementary particles, and it's this that leads to Mac Kowalski winding up with the tube, harpoon style, giving it a good fling; it goes out about twenty or thirty feet, coils of cable chasing after. It breaks the surface of the harbor, like a bluefish at dusk, vanishes.

Because salt water muffles slightly the free movement of radiation, it's not a surprise when the sixty or eighty clicks per minute dwindle to fifteen. It's not even a surprise when the clicks stop altogether. They wait a few minutes. There's a static charge, picked up on the amplifier, in the headphones, some unrelated noise. Kowalski pops a beer.

— Reel her in, Mac says. Maybe the water has ruined the tube. See if it works in the air.

Lou hauls in the line.

— You're sure we're in the right spot?

— We don't have to be in the right spot, Kowalski says. — We have to be close.

When the tube comes up the side (Lou's hands have gone numb at the fingertips), Kowalski gaffs it. It's scarved by lengths of kelp, a tan strip of something that resembles lasagna. Mac peels it off.

— What's it read?

The clicking resumes, as though it never stopped. Like a college experiment. *Say you had an electron gun and a wall with two evenly sized holes in it and a detector on a further wall. Why can't we say with any certainty that a given electron will go through either hole x or hole y?* It's designed to trip you up. This experiment. It binds together experimenter and experiment, until the two are indistinguishable, adjoined.

Lou says, — If it's still registering the background, we can't have ruined the tube. Maybe it's the salt.

Kowalski scratches his thinning scalp. They try again. Same technique, a sort of baton twirl. Lou gives out coils of line, yawning. It's really dark.

— Can I stay in the house for a few hours while you work? Lou asks.

— Stay all week, if you want, Kowalski says. — Stay a month.

After an interval like the last, they find that there is no clicking from Kowalski's experimental apparatus, *though there is the same unusual static.* It was there before. They didn't notice, didn't think much of it, the sound of the waves, what with the sound of foghorns, the background noise of their respective personal travails. They discounted the static.

— Well, it's making some sort of noise, Lou says, looking at the rate meter. Kowalski, who's staring thoughtfully out at the plant, wondering — as Lou himself had been wondering earlier, *why no steam, why no steam?* — mumbles a response without listening. Lou says again, — I don't know if this is anything or not, but what would you think if the needle were off the scale?

— What's that?

— The needle's off the scale, Mac. Off the scale.

Kowalski trips over the packing crate on his way to Lou's side. In the flashlight, he gazes over Mac's shoulder. Clamps the orange foam headphones onto his head, falls into the trolling chair.

— Can't be, Mac says.

— I agree, Lou says. — Maybe if we landed the thing exactly at the mouth of the pipe, but what are the chances, and even then. That stuff is diluted. Those drums aren't supposed to leak like that. In containment. There's no way. That would be a major spill. I was down there today, where it was leaking, and it didn't sound like this, and they were picking up all the activity. We could be a hundred yards off, or fifty yards off. We could be on the wrong side of the plant altogether. It's ridiculous.

— Right, Mac says. — Let's pull it in. I have another idea.

— Water sample, Lou says. — We could take it into the office.

— No, wait. Kowalski disappears into the storage cabin up front. Lou hauls in the G-M tube, which again starts to meter the smorgasbord of background nutrients, protons, neutrons, mesons, gamma particles. He dries off the tube on his sweatshirt. Too bad they didn't bring film badges, or some less complicated technology. You could drop them over the side. In the meantime, Kowalski turns up with a first-rate surf-casting rod. An expensive spinning reel on there.

— Just because we're frustrated, Lou Sloane says, — doesn't mean you should start fishing.

— Don't impugn my record as a sportsman, Kowalski says. — I was thinking we could bait this with a thermometer.

He sets the rod down and comes back with his toolbox.

— We can see if they're throwing off heat. The runoff lines.

Lou searches his groggy identity for an opinion, but at this hour, it's empty in there. Lazily, he ponders the strategy, while with pliers and electrical tape he meanwhile manages to perform simple mechanical tasks, as Mac Kowalski prepares to affix a three-dollar thermometer to the multiply barbed, glittering, psychedelic, facsimile baitfish on the end of the surf caster. *Sure this thing isn't radioactive already?* When this chore is accomplished, Kowalski, with impressive form (he really gets his back into it), floats the thermometer a few feet beyond where the last missile broke the water's surface. The reel trills as it feeds out, into some union of moonlight and horizon. The lure dips with a subdued splash. They wait. *Anymore beers?* Yes. Lou and Mac split the last, passing it back and forth. *What's the water temperature?* Fifty-three. *What do you figure plant runoff will do to the temperature?* Depends how close the boat is to the evacuation point. *How long will it take to register on the thermometer?* Ten minutes. Kowalski has gone into his professional disguise, stern, remote. Minutes pass. The confinement that Lou Sloane experiences on boats, left over from his tour in Rickover's submarine fleet, finds its expression in a time like this. Boats, however small, with however few occupants — beer-swilling guys in Hawaiian print shirts, Japanese whalers, navy enlistees, Greenpeace hippies — boats are a microcosm of the society of dry land. A little floating emblem of civilization in a vast, multifarious unknown. *Thus your need for restrictive shipboard command structure,* for your specializations of tasks and chores, lashing of main sheets, swabbing of decks. Until you dock.

Kowalski turns the trolling chair to port, holsters the rod in the cup holder on the armrest and begins hastily — against the advice of anglers — to reel in indiscriminately, without concern for slack, without keeping up a pressure on the prey. The reel sounds like a Geiger counter. He whistles a tuneless melody while he fishes. He makes short work of it. They are each of them, Lou and Mac, expectant, wanting not to know as well as to know, as the thermometer, still attached to its gaudy lure, clatters against the side of the *Barracuda.*

— Damn, Kowalski says. — Watch it doesn't scratch my fiberglass.

Lou goes to lay hold of the thermometer, pendular above their heads, but as he reaches it swings out of reach, swooping around him so that he feels the multiple barbs close to the back of his neck; Mac, coming belatedly to understand the need to subdue the rod and its fully armed lure, tries to set it back in the trolling holster but this creates a whole new arc and trajectory. He stumbles slightly as the boat pitches in a wave, and the hooks on the lure loft in and out of the flashlight — it's dive-bombing them — until Lou makes one last desperate grab, courageously endangering his right hand, the fleshy part of it, entrapping conclusively, without impaling himself, the *facsimile baitfish*.

— A lot of fight to that son of a bitch.

Kowalski, however, addresses himself immediately to the thermometer, looking for an angle that will enable him to read it.

— Well?

The light is awful.

— What's it say?

He experiments with the flashlight.

— Sixty-eight, Mac says. — I think that's what it says.

Kowalski carries the thermometer over to the running light on the stern — next to the furled American stars and bars. He checks the figure again. Hands the thermometer to Lou Sloane. Lou stares at it for a while, rubs his sleepy eyes.

— Sixty-eight seems awfully high, Lou says. — Really unlikely. If it's from storage, the water should only be, what, body temperature? A hundred, if they're having trouble with the coolant? A hundred and ten on a really bad day. But it would still be diluted by the channel. You'd get nothing. Maybe a degree or two. There's no way.

— Absolutely, Mac Kowalski says, heading again to the bow. — It has to be the thermometer. Want to go tie up at the plant for an hour or so?

— At the plant?

— Must be something going on over there, right? It's worth a look.

Kowalski groans as he hoists the anchor.

The thought formulates itself slowly in the sleepless Lou Sloane:

Because the top end for a BWR is 600–650 degrees; that's about what your primary coolant runs, 575–600 degrees, and, therefore, if primary coolant was leaking, you'd get a higher temperature in the

harbor, and because if there's primary coolant leakage, you have a
serious high-temperature situation —

— There's another rupture? Lou says.

— Wouldn't want to overstate the possibility, Mac says,
— wouldn't want to understate it either.

The dock by Millstone is for entertaining, for the use of Millstone employees and their families, and it has become a sort of
Millstone tradition that the top brass, the NRC regulator (good to
give the government people a few perks), some of the shift supervisors, plant manager, are all permitted to tie up there without notice. Otherwise, it goes unused. It was a preexisting feature of the
compound, and it has been kept up mainly by private pool among
the Millstone family of employees, rather than with the tax dollars
of CPL customers. It abuts three pleasantly landscaped acres at
the edge of the Millstone peninsula. Since Lou Sloane doesn't boat
like he did when he was younger, he has never much used the slip.
When he gamely leaps from the bow to the dock, therefore, and
ropes in the *Barracuda* like it's a steer, it's the first time he's set foot
there in months. The stern bumper collides with a piling. Kowalski
hoists his black Mercury outboards.

Next, the security guard, a nightwatchman neither of them
knows by face or name, won't let Mac Kowalski in the fuel-
handling entrance of the plant. Not without a security badge. He
doesn't care if Kowalski is the governor of the state. Doesn't care if
he's from the NRC. Doesn't care if he's from the National Guard.
Mac takes it well. Millstone is on high security. There have been
difficulties throughout the day. *A Code Two unusual event,* for
example.

— You don't know who we are? Kowalski asks.

— No sir, I'm afraid not.

— You don't know who your own plant manager is?

Lou, on the other hand, happens to have his badge. He's been
wearing the same windbreaker for almost twenty-four hours now.
It's filled with wearisome personal effects. Reminders of the past.
The nightwatchman nervously gives the proffered badge the once-
over. A walkie-talkie in the booth squeals with activity.

— Could you remove your ski cap? he says to Lou. Compares

the photo with the security badge. But then, coming upon the flaw in the badge, as though it announced a sort of a conspiracy: — Sir, this badge is expired. This badge expired yesterday.

— Young man, Lou starts in, — we have a serious business here, and this gentleman with me here is the day-shift supervisor and I would like your permission to —

— Can't let you in. I'm sorry.

— Give me your phone, Mac barks.

— Can't do that. Sorry.

— I'm going to call the damn control room. Then you'll let us in the damn door.

— Wait, Mac, wait a second, Lou says.

That's when he gets tired of removing mountains, of fixing stuff that was broken from the start. Lou does. When it becomes clear that Kowalski will be admitted, as he should, but that Lou's request for a day pass is about to get bumped up to corporate communications, where they'll ask why Lou wants to be admitted, if he has an appointment, if he is here on official business, the nature of the business, before they promise to send somebody down *just as soon as they have a free moment.* Lou is, more or less, about to be escorted from the premises.

— Mac, I'm going back to your place. I'm tired as hell. I'm not thinking clearly. I'm not sure I'll be an asset. You go ahead and tackle this one. You're a good man. You're a good friend and I'm lucky to have you, I sure am. Go on in and run this thing by the books.

They're standing in parking lot C. The clouds have all blown off. Stars mottle the sky. The places of his life. The reactor service building. Steam boiler. Screen well. Switch gear. Turbo-generator. Nuclear energy. Kowalski doesn't say anything. Doesn't bother to persuade him otherwise. They know, in a way, how it's going to turn out, the drama of narrow misses and evasions that don't address the problems of such a complex enterprise, the paperwork, the coverage by cub reporters. The attenuated versions of the truth. By sunrise, Kowalski's concerns will have been muted but not eliminated. He'll take his boat home, hose it off, like usual, at the public dock.

Mac asks if he wants to phone for a cab from the security booth.

— Nope, Lou says. — I'm going to walk a little.

— Sure?

At which point Ron Self's pickup pulls into the lot next to them. Ron, tall, narrow, with a stylish crewcut and graying mustache, tonight wearing a high-visibility pullover sweater. He isn't his usual sidesplitting, backslapping, life-of-the-party Self, though. They exchange somber greetings.

— Did you guys hear?

The breeze blows stiffly through the parking lot, spiraling.

— Hear?

That the NRC is parked out front in a military convoy, that the main coolant line ruptured just after two AM; that the emergency core coolant line failed because the filters were all gummed up; that the primary coolant was diverted into the waste-water line; that several thousand gallons of radioactive coolant were pumped into the Two Tree Channel; that the NRC ordered a shutdown; that the reactors, one and two, were powered down to 35 percent of capacity; that there was a near miss in the void coefficient an hour later when they didn't lower the control rods properly; that the utility was going to try to pick up half of the lost megawatts from the other reactors upriver; that the NRC then dispatched inspectors to those plants as well; that these plants turned up violations promptly; that the utility made plans to purchase additional energy from CANUS; that, because of a freak storm in Montreal, also sweeping over the Great Lakes, the system was having trouble providing the necessary power; that the Consolidated Edison Corporation of New York could not make up the difference; that the Long Island Lighting Corporation could not make up the difference; that the state legislature will convene in the morning to discuss the situation, to vote in a rate increase effective immediately; that the storage rupture hadn't been sleeved yet; that shifts have all been called in; that front gate is locked.

By then Lou is already on his way out, away, far from the debate, from the argot of atomic energy, blanket pressurizers and in-pile tests and leach liquor and maximum permissible doses and pinch effects and shim rods. The two of them are calling after him, Self is calling, *Need a ride?*, but he has already started up the service road on foot, the sound of this foreign tongue behind him like Old English. This is some bygone epoch in him now, as he walks up the service road with a certain jauntiness; the cars that come up the lane lean on their horns as they pass, the drivers lean out the windows and wave, one offers to drive him home, until he puts up the hood on his *UConn Huskies* sweatshirt, bundles his windbreaker and leaves it by the side of the road complete with expired security badge, and doesn't stop until he is expelled through the gate and reaches the pizza restaurant across the street from the plant, the all-night pizza restaurant. Indeed, he sits at the counter next to a man with one arm, light of heart, not at all distressed about the utilities of the Northeast, with their megawattages ebbing and flowing, happy about leaving all of that to Mac and Stan and Ron and the others, as he orders a small pie with pepperoni and mushroom and green pepper, *hell, the works,* Lou Sloane, sleepless, practically hallucinatory, Lou Sloane, absconder, in affable conversation with the lone unwashed eighteen-year-old overnight pizza maker, *A lot of trouble over there last night, really good for business, reporters in here all night, all trying to buy slices but I told them, whole pies, only whole pies,* and then as the boy pulls on the draft to fill a sixteen-ounce glass with a cola made famous in these United States, and the lights in the restaurant dim, just for a second, and the streetlamps twinkle, the dialysis machines gasp, the VCRs all across the Northeast blink 12:00, 12:00, 12:00, computers hiccup and gobble their random access memories, house alarms go off, heart monitors flat-line, children's nightlights fail, the systemic brownout flickers across the whole of the northeast corridor, once, twice, three times, and the boy chef of the all-night pizza joint says, *What the fuck,* the oven resets, the tap on the cola machine goes out, and the jukebox — caught irreducibly on a recording by R.E.O. Speedwagon — shuts off its monotonous display of colors and then promptly begins anew with a swelling of pianistic abominations, in the midst of this demonstration of the *before and after of energy* and all that flourishes in it, this intimation of energy-related omnipotence, before Chicago agrees to sell Montreal the three hundred megawatts, so that Montreal won't have to ask Rochester for the power, won't have to bother Chicago (in the middle of its lake-effect blizzard), so that Rochester-Syracuse can sell five hundred megawatts to CPL, who will in turn charge the cost of these watts to the people of southeastern Connecticut, after the state legislature fresh from election-year triumphs and awash in utility industry PAC funds votes in the rate increase, so that the people of Connecticut can heat their homes and run their televisions and explore their brand-new Internet linkages and keep the lights on for their errant children, Lou begins with gusto his pie with the works and extra cheese, picking off a scalding morsel of sausage, plotting his route home to his wife, through a system of cab rides and footpaths and cautious reconnaissance missions, by strategy and stealth, to Billie, to repair the damage, to offer his heart, to win her back.

20

———————————————— He's had these spells, in the beer-shellacked interiors of bars, howling, stuttering at strangers, spinning out hypotheses about *the thrust of metaphysics,* your early Christian Church, second to fourth centuries (in which the Valentinians are flayed), or about how *Reagan was the b-b-best g-g-g-goddamned p-p-p-p-president this c-c-country ever had,* green olive speared on the end of a martini saber, flecks of his spittle on the lapels of strangers, misting the faces of gin-blossomed barflies, wiping his mouth on his sleeve, pushing an empty back across the bar, one last important point, *It's all about the Mormons . . .*

Waking on the floor, *if waking is the right way to describe it,* or between the bumpers of parallel-parked cars, with particles of gravel embedded in the planes of his face, waking on the subway at the end of the IND line, picked clean of his valuables. If just one time he could wake at home, not in the stairwell, not on the welcome mat, not in the elevator, *but enveloped by bedsheets,* if just one time he could show a little respect for his shelter — $925 a month — a little respect for his neighbors, for his thousand square feet and doorman access, for the prohibitive co-op board and the shriveled, bejeweled harridans from the penthouses north and south who control it, if he could show a little respect . . .

*   *   *

She's saying something. Giddily, sloppily. Or this is simply when he tunes in, takes note of the conversation, *wait a second,* Jane Ingersoll, so wonderful, so charming; all of his life a rehearsal for the entrance of Jane Ingersoll, personification of feminine kindness; *they mesh in these perfect ways,* Dexter and Jane; they're the right heights for one another; she has the right kind of disdain for small-town life; she has kids, and he just loves kids. He would like to lavish his surfeit of feelings on her adorable little naysayers, would love to be called *Dad* by some moppet who refuses to do any kind of chores. Furthermore, Jane Ingersoll knows French, she knows words for Gallic amorous practices, for the names of night-shades, *aubergine.* Probably read the Existentialists in the original. He's got his shoes off, his feet up on the dash, breathing deep of the new-car smell, leaning his head out the window. She says, *We need gas.* He says, *Imp-p-p-p-possible. C-c-came full from the rental agency . . .*

When the depressant effects of the drinks begin to settle in for good, the interval in which he usually looks for other drugs, there's an inadequacy that overtakes him. It comes at a certain point. You're driving through New London, say, there are unemployed guys throwing rocks at your car, or you turn a corner and cruise a long patch of trailer parks and planned communities, miles and miles of these provisional edifices. In this silence you glancingly address the truth about yourself. You confront, for example, the fact that one day in three you actually *shit blood,* a stream of reddish brown goo that makes you want to lean over and vomit into the sink at the same time, a hydroelectric jet of undigestibles pouring out of your ass under considerable pressure. You have tremors. You have paroxysms of anxiety. Stabbing pains in the major organs. You wake in unusual places with little memory of the past. You say aloud things no human being should say. You sob.

There are rules Hex Raitliffe should be observing. Handed down by experience. Good, solid, dependable rules. He should send Jane Ingersoll home. He should call her in three days. He should wait for the third date. He should slow down on the drink. They shouldn't be going out late like this when they've just met. Or reunited. He shouldn't be thinking about sleeping with her, not if he respects her, *Wait a second, he's already slept with her. Jesus, he forgot all about it.* A surplus of remorse at this movie trailer of his recollections: not being able to get it up, tying her extremities to his bunk beds. Luckily he didn't execute the leg shot: *sometimes it happens before he's even got his slacks off.* A globule on his own shin. *Flask please.* Jane passes it laterally. On top of everything else he's having blackouts. He should turn the car around, he should seize the wheel, jump the lane divider. Home by dawn . . .

— I already told you, Jane says . . .

Something about the *nightshades?* What is it exactly that she already told him about? *Outside of Groton.* What was she talking about? Is there a conversation in midstream?

— Where are we g-g-going anyhow?

— Aren't you listening? Outside of Groton in an old church, an old Congregationalist church or something.

He mumbles, — You have my und-d-d-d . . . my full attention.

He makes plans involving kissing her on the straightaways, *on each and every straightaway.* He would like to bank a few kisses in anticipation of his next dry spell. As it is, he just finishes one kiss as the next begins to call to him. He presses his whiskey-moistened lips against the indentation of her temple, brushing back strands of hair for easy access. They take a slow curve by the tri-county beer distributors. He waits for the next straightaway, for a long, dull patch clear to the horizon.

He quit drinking once on advice of a urologist, when his . . . his *plumbing* wasn't working properly. (Over the Thames, past an unobstructed view of Groton's nuclear submarines.) Quit once because his liver was swollen and painful. Quit at the behest of a GP. The stoppages amounting to a week per. Once he quit as a New Year's resolution. He drank by nightfall. Once he quit for love. He recognizes in his hull that he should take the pledge. He has made forecasts, over the years, as to the date by which he should quit. By age thirty, by thirty-five, by forty. But gradually he seems to have put aside this notion of quitting.

— It's a gay club, Jane Ingersoll says, — I mean, mostly a gay club anyhow. You're not bothered by that are you? Raitliffe? Not bothered by a few gay men, are you?

Swarming over the premises in highway patrolman outfits?

— It's just a dance club, really, but a lot of gay men go there. Plenty of other people go there too, because the music is really great to dance to. It's the best around.

Near the sub base. In the shadow of the American nuclear arsenal. Forty-five MIRVs per boat. Sailors, at the club, cadets, in their starchy uniforms. A gay club with actual sailors.

— No p-p-p-problem with that. That's just fine.

Taking up the flask.

On the hills above the Thames, on their way to this club named for a legume in the nightshade family. Jane Ingersoll isn't kidding when she tells him it's a deconsecrated church. Hex Raitliffe wakes from a sort of catnap in the Taurus to find that they are parked in front of a New England Congregationalist church. Early-nineteenth-century, classic oblong horizontal design with single white spire, black shutters, shingle roof. Without adornment of any kind. Unpaved parking lot. Cars and motorcycles parked every which way. A hundred and forty-four souls inside, he expects, or thereabouts. In excess of the fire code.

Jane Ingersoll, to whom he will pledge his troth, to whom he will cleave, for good or ill; Jane, who will bear his children; Jane, helpmeet, perfect sundered half of him, at his side. *This is the club I told you about, the dance club.* Beyond the reach of the local sheriff and his men, those early-to-bed-early-to-rise guys. They would come by for harassment and kickbacks, but it's the middle of the night. Jane Ingersoll helps Dexter from the car, prises him out of the seat, hefts him up, until a surge of pride makes it impossible for him to tolerate further aid. Thereafter, he lurches across the parking lot under his own steam, according to faulty directional impulses, veering toward the filling station next door, Anderson's Gulf. She calls out, and the sound of her voice brings him back. He turns, waves, topples against a parked car . . .

Deconsecrated. Larger in the interior than a church has any right to be. A main room with bar and dance floor and stairs leading down, down into the grim subconscious of the place where there will be linemen from Electric Boat, union welders and riveters, suspended by steel cables above dominatrixes (women in tutus or feather boas, in gold lamé or rhinestones or double-knits), or cadets from the submarine fleet, or nuclear engineers, in leather policemen's clothes and pith helmets, chased by women with riding crops. Downstairs. Meanwhile, on the dance floor, pairs of guys swaying in perfectly synchronized waves — on the twos and the fours — to an approximation of the club noise that took hold in the city back a few years ago — confabulated, anonymous synthesizer squawks organized on turntable and digital interface by faceless deejays. Techno-junk, with maybe the occasional number by the artist formerly known as Prince, perfect for the Groton area with its high-tech and military economic depressions.

A few heterosexual dyads, if that's what they are, lounging on bar stools. There's even a straight couple getting down on *the floor,* in street clothes, jeans and T-shirts, wriggling to ambient tides.

— A drink? Jane says.

Has he ever refused? He doesn't want her to leave him here, in the vault of dancing militarists, the gay military subculture, among handlebar mustaches and degrees in nuclear engineering, among launchers of payloads, but his desire for drink outweighs reservations. She comes back with the specialty of the house — half price on weekends — the Blue Boy, looks to be made out of vodka and Windex. It's blue. It's a blue drink. Maybe a hint of lavender. It foams. Tastes great. Good for your windshield too. Tilts it back and . . .

*   *   *

— What are you trying to say? Jane Ingersoll says. Her face close on his. They're at a table at the margin of the dance floor; she has come back with drinks. Hex Raitliffe's behavior is falling below the minimum expected for a first date. A gentle, ministerial tone marks the way Jane Ingersoll talks to him, but Dexter sweeps past this. He is reminding her *not to leave him alone for too long;* his tone is getting more shrill. He can tell. The text of the remarks is muddy. He can still reckon with a particular law of falling bodies: *the more he tries to keep her within range, the more he drives her off,* but he can't derive, in his low-functioning state, the broad ramifications of the law.

The interior, of course, *is aubergine.* Or maybe heliotrope, or amethyst, or damson, or perhaps purpure, or something along the lines of archil, or mauve, or rather magenta, amaranth, mulberry, murrey, violaceous, or perhaps even fuchsia. It's the color of monarchs, of the gods, the color used to trip up Agamemnon. The mirror ball spangled above them, with the tinted lights reflected and refracted upon it, picks up aspects of the violet draperies and purple vinyl booths and repeats them, until the room doubles, then quadruples.

Tears of gratitude in Dexter Raitliffe's eyes when Jane Ingersoll pops the question, *Raitliffe, want to cut the rug? Up for a little dancing?* Rarely involved in the intensely intimate experience of modern dance, rarer still with a woman so calibrated to his needs: Jane Ingersoll, whom he loved all the way back to the eighth or ninth grade, *who is therefore fated to love him.* However, notwithstanding lessons as a child, *Raitliffe can't dance.* In spite of an early facility with the cha-cha, the waltz, the fox-trot, the jitterbug, the pony, a reasonable facsimile of the lindy, he can barely make a go of it now, even with the simplest steps. The only dancing that really suits him, according to inclination and to style, is *the pogo,* a short-lived and scarcely remembered precursor to the moshing favored these days by the kids. This dance, of course, involves a simple up-and-down *hopping.* Striking your neighbors on the way by is also encouraged.

*   *   *

He's an amazing dancer, of course, a brilliant dancer, a white guy with a preternatural amount of funk and exhibitionism, who can shake his money maker with the best of them, a guy who regularly won all the dance contests as a boy, who found that pounding out the steps in dance class, the threes and fives and double times, the sambas, the sarabandes, was the one talent with which he was really blessed. The kids all stared, as all the gay men stare now, all gazing at him, giving him the once-over. Their heads swivel as Dexter Raitliffe crisscrosses in and out of the spotlight. He's surprised to find that he doesn't mind terribly having the attention. He dips Jane Ingersoll and plants a kiss on her exposed throat. A rivulet of perspiration breaking across his brow. It's great. All the dwindling strands of the national counterculture are present here on the dance floor: there's a kid in a Native American headdress, maybe a refugee from the casino across town; there are men dressed as women; there are women dressed as men; there are molecules of all the sexual preferences and all the races, black, white, Asian, Hispanic; all there, parting as Dexter Raitliffe, white male oppressor, begins a short history of tap, ornamented with a few steps borrowed from the golden age of disco, a thrust of the hip, head cocked to the side, *the land of a thousand dances* . . .

He can barely stand up straight on the dance floor, so drunk, has the spins, in danger of puking the chowder from dinner, that's what it tastes like anyhow, his stomach rumbling ominously, he lurches against the wall, stopping to catch his breath; if Jane Ingersoll wasn't appalled by his company before, she will be now. She dances solitarily across the floor, isolated, walled-off, laser-illuminated, in a go-go cage. Her corkscrew undulations. He calls out, *Honey, you g-go ahead and d-d-dance and I'll just watch, it's all right, I'm fine, I'm not very g-g-g-good c-company t-t-t-tonight, it's that stuff I've b-b-b-been through t-today, it's just too much, so I'll g-go sit d-d-down and you just d-d-dance with whomever, d-d-don't worry about me,* shouts over the synthetic industrial music, sheet metal in the rear of the mix, she nods and smiles, not clear if she has heard him at all.

He wakes, slumped sideways on a bench. He starts, as always when coming out of lapses, out of washes of unconsciousness. Checks for his wallet. It's still there, warming a spot on his hip. Oh, Connecticut. *Qui transtulit sustinet.* You come from good families, you dancers and lovers of Connecticut. You wouldn't rob him. You might take his cash, but you'd leave the credit cards and his driver's license and his social security card. He's in the spin cycle. He feels like shit. He looks for Jane Ingersoll, casts his lackluster gaze around the room. She's not in the cages. She's not upon the plinths. His head throbs. A fresh Blue Boy in front of him, can't remember asking for it or paying for it, etc. Drinks greedily, though a voice of moderation in him, one of his *committee of ethical supervisors,* politely advises against, lest slurred speech should give way to complete derogation of bodily function. But the advice is belated. *God, he hates churches. Who would have brought him to this church?*

How could she dance with *another guy?* How could she do that? Through the ominous clouds of dry ice, through the monster-movie simulations of the fog machine, he can see the woman he loves, the woman with whom he is destined to live out his days, with whom he will grow old and forgetful, *dancing with another guy.* The interloper is vaguely familiar, a black guy in a uniform. They're moving around the floor as if the movements were blocked out, premeditatedly choreographed for Dexter's benefit, for his viewing delectation, doing *the hustle* or is it *the bus stop,* one of those suggestive urban dances. The black guy is dignified, however, solemn, almost pious. Hex gets up and crosses the floor, protoplasmically, as though he too is part of the intricate steps of their performance, past the bar, past the faithful at the bar, the dry-ice fog and the lights of the mirror ball spattering him, adorning him. But he gets caught behind this waiter who's hauling a tray full of Blue Boys and sweet drinks with parasols or plastic kitschy submarines in them, and his way is blocked off. No access in any direction. The waiter himself executes, in the process, a perfect homage to Gene Kelly: a good-natured leap and a kick of the heels, a smile pasted on his mug, using the tray, the booths, and the bar itself as props. He croons, in a boyish tenor. Dancers to the left and right of Raitliffe, dancers like a congregation of parishioners, duplicating Gene Kelly's steps, as the black guy in the uniform begins, with considerable charm, the national dance of Argentina.

— Raitliffe, someone I want to introduce you to.

Sacked out on a bench, he wakes to find Jane Ingersoll standing over him. She's close enough to check his pupils. Just behind her is the black guy from the hospital, *the ambulance driver.*

— John England. Met him back at the hospital. He's an ambulance driver from the —

Raitliffe says, — P-p-p-p-p-p —

Hex's talk is like some Indo-European gibberish. Stuttering, gasping, groaning. Nonetheless, England gives him a distracted stare, pumps his hand. A firm handshake!

— Nice to m-make your acquaintance. C-c-c-c-come here often?

England doesn't answer. Smiles.

Jane Ingersoll says, — Want to dance with us?

Meaning she and England. Meaning would he like to dance with this couple as they perfect their own arrangement of bodies, their cuckolding? Their elimination of him?

— What do you mean? Jane Ingersoll says. — A few minutes ago you said you were going to sit out for a while and I should just go ahead —

— I d-d-didn't mean that —

— Maybe you and I need to have a conversation, Jane Ingersoll says. — Or you could go rest in the car and I'll drive you home in twenty minutes. I mean, what is it you're getting at, Dexter? It's not like we are engaged or anything. We just met.

Over her shoulder John England stands nonchalantly, watching the action in the club.

— You ought to sleep it off, she says. — You're all edgy. You're making things up. And, anyway, John here is . . . Well, if you don't know, I can't explain it to you. He's . . . he's batting from the other side.

*   *   *

Then he has a vision, *spiritus contra spiritus*, a religious ecstasy, in this church, this beauty in a wedding gown, *this drop-dead fox*, in a sort of modified wedding gown anyhow. Shredded at the bottom, so that he can see her bare feet, her lavender toenail polish. She has enough mobility to dance. There seems to be a white garter belt and stockings, white veil, flounces. All in white. A virgin of the deconsecrated church of the gay men, sitting on the end of the bench. It's not clear at first if she's a waitress, if she might be bringing him replenishment for his empty glass, or if her motives are otherwise. She asks if he's there by himself, and he says, *Yes, I mean, no, I mean my date has b-b-b-been, uh, d-d-d-detained for a minute or two, right over there, but she's* . . . and this vision straddles the end of the bench, in her torn wedding skirt, quite a bit of makeup too, swirls of color upon her face; that's what he can make out behind the white veil — and Raitliffe tells her, *I'm in reduced circumstances —*

She simply wants to be treated like a lady. Her name is Florence — Flo, for short — and she asks if he wants to dance, but he confesses that he's too drunk to dance, and she asks if he wants maybe *to explore a few other options, like they might secret themselves in a dark corner or in a closet or a confession booth, one of the wonders of Congregational architecture,* though he knows well that among the old Protestants there is no such booth, and so he passes up these kindly suggestions as well, and then she asks how he got *the awful shiner, and how did his clothes get in such unfortunate condition,* and Raitliffe admits that these injuries are part of his reduced circumstances, *part of the welter of d-d-d-difficulties that has b-brought him to this d-d-dark p-p-place,* Florence's expression dispassionate, disengaged, *My dad d-d-d-d-died in a church, see, and that's why I'm n-n-not a g-g-guy who g-g-goes into churches as a matter of b-b-belief. So I'm awfully surprised that you b-b-b-brought me —*

Where another girl might have expressed some terrible shock at Dexter Raitliffe's woeful imagery, might have reached out to comfort him, to offer support, to enfold him in simple caresses, Florence is noteworthy mainly for her ennui. She could conceivably file her nails at any moment. Her impersonation of womanhood is incomplete therefore; she says nothing at all, bestows upon his forehead a single kiss, sweeping aside her white veil to do so, leaving there a lipstick of such deep maroon as to be in the hematoma family, after which Dexter himself reaches out, arms extended, to put his head upon her breast, *the foam rubber prostheses*, because if she's seraphic, as he supposes, it's because seraphs are exempt from the riot of gender. Whereupon Jane Ingersoll and her inamorato return from the floor —

— Excuse me, Jane says, — you two busy?

— Who? Dexter Raitliffe says, — What?

Before he can even begin to catalogue in a friendly partisan way Flo's angelic spirit, her warmth, her sympathies, her steadfastness, her tenderness, her selflessness, *Florence has vanished*, has disappeared into an agglomeration of like-minded worshipers, a clot of tantric yogis, gnostic libertines —

— Did you get her number?

— What are you t-t-talking about? Raitliffe says.

Jane reaches for his face, to wipe away the imprinting of lips.

— Are you some kind of freak or something, Raitliffe? I mean, maybe we should just get that part straightened out right here —

— I was . . . just . . .

Then there are three short blackouts affecting the juice at Aubergine, the first lasting a few seconds only, such that the expensive state-of-the-art sound system slows — an LP spins down into a sixteen-rotations-per-minute approximation of the voice of God — and then drops out. There's a roaring in Hex's ears, of silence, of ultra-high-frequency hiss, which quickly merges with the dissonance of frightened voices and with the overturning of bottles and glasses, a hundred and forty-four surges of worry, while at the same time there is that minutest of seeds, *excitement*. The only gay club between here and Hartford now plunged into dark, darkness and hysteria and expectancy, a hundred and forty-four guys and girls who think, just for a second, that *the submarines are launched* or that the counterforce has struck or that the sound of their own panic is a flourishing of air-raid sirens, and so they make for the man or the woman that they always liked from afar, or they make for the doors, for some final possibility of relief.

The lights come on. A brief, sardonic titter. A collective giggle. And then the club plunges into penumbra. It's some stroboscopic effect among other dance floor lighting clichés. Before the deejays can wind up their turntables, it's back. Darkness. In the frame just prior, Hex Raitliffe spots Jane Ingersoll, working her way toward him, against one wall, and he heads blindly for her, his cinematic lover, except that he succumbs to *a massive head butt* on the way, a spike, in the solar plexus, probably from a former varsity football player who has just discovered his sexuality, and Hex goes backward over a bench, his legs giving out beneath him, in the dark, sailing through space, arms and legs weightless, stars going around his head, that dead stop of blackness; he can hear earnest appeals as he goes down, *Excuse me, are those my dark glasses?* and *Nancy! Nancy! Let's adopt!* and then someone plants a cowboy boot on his head and he —

The last brownout. Hex Raitliffe cradled in the arms of Jane Ingersoll. Or is he cradling her? As best he can. A hundred and forty-four bodies crowded at the exit, trampling not only Raitliffe, but others, six or seven other men and women with their arms over their heads, whimpering, rolled like fresh lumber to the margins of the dance floor. In the emergency lighting, the black lights, the reflective tape, Raitliffe thinks he sees Florence, in her wedding gown — like Marilyn Monroe wrestling with her skirt over the subway grating — levitating, ghostly above the exit, pointing the way to the weary men and women of the church as they file out to safety, streaming into the parking lot, the sound of motorcycles revving outside, as the lights come up at last, as the lights shimmer and stabilize, and Raitliffe says to Jane Ingersoll,
    — B-b-boy, I have gotten into a lot of t-t-t-trouble tonight —
    Jane says, — Let's get out of here. Let's get some sleep.
    — G-g-give me five minutes.

*   *   *

The stairs down into the antechambers of erotic torture turn out to have a far simpler explanation: rest rooms. Raitliffe weaves his way against the tide, finishing the last of a Blue Boy, and he discovers on the way that even though there are no private rooms for sado-masochistic fantasies and group encounters, it's creepy anyhow. *Das unheimlich.* As he goes down the stairs, there are familiarly exposed ducts, cinder block walls, and even — as though this were a staple of church interiors across America — a series of old file cabinets on one wall. What's fearsome here, really, is memory, the gap into which nonsecular omnipotence pours its perceptible limits, illness and suffering, human cruelty, *ethnic cleansing, crusades, jihad.* His dad's name is among those names inscribed in the filing cabinets of church basements, or on the rest-room walls. Lost friends, condemned to earth. Wandering souls. No wonder there are guys here cruising. They are going with the tide of restlessness. They saunter past Raitliffe and the others in the row of urinals; they empty and occupy the stalls. The circulation of desire is brisk and desperate. From the urinal to Raitliffe's left, a guy in pressed denims mumbles, *C'mon, guys, there's a world health emergency,* while zipping. Hex Raitliffe, meanwhile, experiences urinary hesitation. Can't make it happen.

With John England, suave consumer of American tobacco products, Hex and Jane eventually take their leave of those lilac interiors. Though Raitliffe is embarrassed to admit it, he is still unnerved by the presence of the ambulance driver. England clenches an unlit Marlboro between his lips while simultaneously managing to excoriate the local utilities, *Probably going to pass the costs on to us.* Outdoors, it's colder. Trees articulate, in the breezes, postures of human distress. The stars are vivid. Raitliffe's torn suit and dress shirt aren't nearly adequate. He and Jane and John head for the rented Ford Taurus, which, by coincidence, is parked exactly next to England's customized '72 Mustang. *Where's your p-p-professional vehicle?* Raitliffe asks.

The Ford Taurus is parked a couple of cars down *from England's ambulance.* What is the ambulance doing out here? He could have sworn England just pointed out his *car.* Is there an emergency? Are our ambulance drivers thrillseekers, danger junkies, cruising the clubs on duty, taking needless risks? Raitliffe lurches through the parking lot, steadied on the left by England, on the right by Jane Ingersoll. All are shivering. Hex raves about his father, about ghosts in church basements, about weird architectural conjunctions of theocratic design and fate. A *freemasonic plot of some kind.* Then he becomes hung up on his mother, the interventions of doctors, the technologies of mercy. He's raving. He's hallucinating. A gnashing of teeth, a beating of the breast. It's unattractive, and it gives way, again, to excessive apologies, *You should just leave me here. I'll sleep it off.* There's urine trickling down the front of his pants. He can't walk.

— You guys smell gas? Jane Ingersoll says.

A discussion of fumes takes place, to which Hex Raitliffe has not added much. As before, John England with Marlboro clamped between lips. England takes from the breast pocket of his starchy white uniform a lavender box of matches bearing the logo of the club. From which box he extracts a wooden match and prepares to strike it. The inadvisability of such a procedure in the presence of inflammable high-octane fumes doesn't occur to any of them, not initially. Though it is not clear where exactly the fumes are coming from, Jane Ingersoll, always a pragmatist, seems to reach across Raitliffe, mumbling a warning, a caveat, as England, with hubristic cool, flicks the lit match to the sandy basin of the parking lot, intending to stamp it out with his impeccably shined loafer.

The match goes end over end through the air, toward the Taurus. Raitliffe — with special perceptive skills acquired through excess of drink, with an instantaneous shame that will long mark this crisis — begins to understand what's in store. At the instant of inception. *As in dreams.* Like a little *Olympic torch.* Like a flaming high school baton. Toward the Taurus, toward the pooling leak underneath, toward the underside of the carriage of the Taurus. Jane Ingersoll's belated cry. She reaches clamorously across Raitliffe for England's arm, a look of irritation frozen on the black man's face, the match going end over end, unextinguished in spite of the breeze, in a gravitational parabola. To earth. The Taurus acts as a temporary shelter for the spark, the gnostic flame, the manifestation of the glow, of the first cause. It lands underneath the car. Raitliffe, displaying the courage of drunks and children, whips off his suit coat, his secondhand suit coat, tailored to himself exactly, and prepares to muffle what is to come.

The Taurus gives an exhausted *thunk*. The sound of your boiler coming on. The unleaded regular ignites. In the parking lot. Scraps of weeds underneath scorched, old browned dandelions, a half-dozen of them, blackened. Raitliffe falls on the conflagration, with his suit coat. He starts at one end. There is this knee-high *underbrush of flame*. The suit coat, the tweed, burns well. Hex has to let go of it. He is depilated of his left eyebrow. He has a bald patch on the side of his crewcut. He doesn't feel these things. John England, however, schooled in emergency, grabs ahold of Raitliffe and, without comment, drives him back a few feet, as the fire begins to digest, more thoroughly, its automotive fuel.

The rental car engulfed in flames. A medieval bonfire, really, instantaneously. It's the bonfire whereupon, in some past autumn, the witches of the Northeast were once consumed. It's the ritual purgative for New England's Congregationalists, who have evidently given up their churches to drunkards and fornicators. Damnation and hellfire. And it's like *the high school bonfires of old.* (John England reminds them that the gas tank could yet explode. They drag Raitliffe back behind a tree to watch. With the other bystanders.) It's like *the bonfire before the big game.* Hex watched them all from afar, those intramural contests, the guys and girls in their letter sweaters and tartans, their tweeds, their cheeks the color of crabapples from the chill. In the tangerine light. He watched them all, searching for the edge of his apartness. The moment in which his apartness was once and for all explained. *What is the hidden meaning of heat that it so overpowering in its spectacle? Heat is about teen love!*

*   *   *

With a crowd, a couple dozen, they watch as the Taurus explodes. It's a little bit of a letdown, really. Nothing like on the cop shows. The Taurus should be airborne, should be executing rolls, scattering smoky fragments. Instead, as the gas tank combusts, the windows shatter, almost demurely, and a black noxious smoke begins to trail above the scene. A guy next to Raitliffe with a motorcycle jacket wheezes asthmatically. The air bags erupt in the dash, like time-lapse blossoms. All in seconds. But the really incredible thing about the whole mess is that *it sobers Raitliffe up.* He could touch his fingertip to his nose.

The license plates begin to char. The tags. And the parking lot begins to empty. The night dwellers make preparations before the first light.

— I have a cellular phone in the Mustang, England says.

— Mustang? Raitliffe says, I thought you were d-d-driving your —

— What do you want to do? Jane Ingersoll asks. — You want to —

— I just d-d-don't know, Hex says. — I'm c-c-confused.

— You ought to call them.

— C-c-call who?

— The rental agency? It's a rental, right?

— In the morning, Hex says. — I c-c-can't d-deal with it. I'll c-c-call in the morning.

— Don't be stupid.

The tires burst. The amber ringlets of flame lick the front and rear windshields, craggy with remaining glass. The employees of the club appear before them, shaking their heads. The blackened hulk of the Taurus. It's been a long night.

— They have a roadside assistance program, Raitliffe, she says. — I bet you just call and they'll come pick the thing up and drop you off another. It's not like —

— I d-d-don't want to d-d-do it, he says, nudging her off a

couple of feet. — I'm really c-c-c-cold, and I want to know if you . . . love me.

Jane's face lights up. Blazes.

The firetrucks or is it the paramedics or the police, roused from their beds, come up the street from the opposite direction. Hex Raitliffe recognizes now the intermittencies of those sirens and the lamps behind them, because, after all, they are leaving the scene in John England's ambulance — because what else would he be driving? — which England drives like a maniac. What's the emergency? Hex holds his cheek against Jane Ingersoll's face, all the way across the Baldwin Bridge, all along the vacillations of the coastline. A hundred different shades of trouble fore and aft. By the time they are back in Fenwick, John England is a stranger. They get out of the ambulance, the two of them, to repair to the beds of the rose-colored guest room, where Hex Raitliffe once pored over Jane Ingersoll's photograph. This is some temporary consolation, this warmth. *Tomorrow,* he thinks, *I'll take a furlough from the b-b-b-booze.*

21

A sleepless night, in which Billie Raitliffe eschews the traditional sheep-counting in favor of occurrences of gun-related violence in the State of Connecticut, these incidents drifting into her consciousness in fragments, via the hall radio at the nurses station: Lionel H. Everson, father of four, Little League coach, contractor, of Norwich, walks into his boys' bedroom with a .38, places the barrel to their heads, sequentially, muzzle to temple. His boys. In the hospital bed, where they have strapped down Billie Raitliffe because of tremors, she has had ample time to consider Mr. Everson's plight — every twenty minutes, twenty and forty minutes past the hour, from about 3:00 AM, when she woke for the night. Every twenty minutes, a restatement or an embellishment. *Kept pretty much to himself,* the neighbors opine. At 4:20, Everson's crime begins to be replaced on the all-news radio station by a series of gang-related shootings up near Hartford, *apparently gang-related,* they say. Hartford's second most high-profile business, after insurance. Strapped into a hospital bed, after a life of much adventure, Billie listens as Duane Collins, 19, and his brother, Louis, *fire Magnum machine pistols with armor-piercing bullets (forty-five rounds per clip) from a Ford Explorer into a party of high school students from a rival athletic team, three dead, six injured,* from which she moves next (4:40) to the late-breaking story of Gail Schramm of Glastonbury, a most uncommon American, *the woman who kills.* Gail is operating a computer modem hookup at the time her alleged assailant enters her house through a porch door; Gail is typing to a friend on the Romance Connection of her newfangled online service, *Hearing strange noises in the house be right back;* her correspondent then uses his p.c. to hack the phone books for the Windsor Locks authorities, who arrive just as Miss Schramm, equipped with a sport gun, a 4-10 given her by her brother, pumps the second barrel into the chest of a neighbor rustling around in Gail's hedge looking for a house cat. A whole catalogue on the all-news radio of these relationships with nine millimeters, forty-fours, three-fifty-sevens, twenty-five automatics (pearl-handled), thirty-ought-sixes, assault weapons, antiaircraft missile launchers, as well as, at eleven minutes past the hour, the weather, *clear and cooler.* She is strapped down so that she won't fall out of her bed.

About dawn, or in the tenebrosities just before, the radio falls silent. Shuts off. Billie can't be sure she isn't imagining it. Can't be sure her proximity to the hereafter isn't such that the little annoyances of life — the oxygen line in her nose, the stink of her own urine — aren't simply beginning to fall away from her. Silence is glorious and absolute. Even her uneasy hospital roommate has given herself over to a somnolence. The monitors at the side of Billie's cot skip out on their jagged but relentless heartbeats. Billie is resolute and dignified as she abandons this earthly shrink-wrap once and for all. *A purple corridor, and deceased members of her family are waiting for her there, wordlessly, with outstretched hands* . . . But, no, the radio crackles again, thrumming with megahertz. Connecticut is busy with its carnage, its 5.1 annual murders per hundred thousand citizens, 26.9 rapes, 252.5 aggravated assaults. Thirty seconds, and then again she's in the silent purgatorial chambers of *kingdom come,* no radio, nor roommate, nor nurses with their expressions of fatigued concern, just a slurry of perceptions — bad hearing, worse eyesight — and then, disappointingly, the radio waves again, *Transmission difficulties at Connecticut Power and Light due to load management failures and problems at the utility's nuclear reactors . . . Sporadic statewide brownouts.* The ache she feels at the invocation of nuclear anything. Why couldn't she have hankered after men who were in businesses free of complications, agriculture, say, the practice of small-town law.

A consternation of night nurses rises to some crisis, drowning out the signal of the all-news station, and the hospital lights stutter once again, after which the generator must come on for good, or so Billie guesses — so that the ICU patients, attached to their technologies, can avoid trouble. A gruff voice, affecting calm, eddies over the intercom, asking for *available nurses* from some floor, and Billie's roommate stirs, rolls over onto her pancreatic tumor; the night nurses rush past their room, hastening to the dramas.

The hour before dawn is not the time to essay these thorny theological questions. What to do next? How to proceed? Desire, memory, religion, taxes, the worst playground disputes of grade school (Billie Raitliffe the jumper of ropes, the hopscotcher), such things nonetheless seem to come up at this time of night. What else is there for her to think about? But as the conundrums begin to amass, like long strings of binary code, the night nurse, the angel who charts the afflictions of Gentile sufferers, comes bearing food. Begging Billie Raitliffe to eat. *So that they won't have to feed her intravenously.*

— Come on, honey, you don't want us to have to call the doctor. You don't want us to go through all that rigmarole.

The spoon, fresh from its sanitary plastic baggy. The night nurse reaches up with this utensil, and when it finds no avenue of ingress, she attempts to force apart Billie Raitliffe's lips. Billie keeps them shut tightly. Billie Raitliffe repels the food for some time, but then, in contemplation of dawn, just now breaking, she accidentally opens her mouth for the merest second, and the nurse, powerful and experienced, takes the opportunity to induce the spoon into her, with its nutrients, which Billie Raitliffe then elects to cough up and spit upon her hospital gown. This struggle continues in silence for some minutes, the nurse working the spoon between the widow's teeth (dislodging, temporarily, her bridgework), scraping off its contents on her uppers, laying hold of Billie's chin and holding this chin shut, waiting out the autonomous swallowing mechanism, until a fit of coughing seizes Billie and she eliminates the mouthful of especially pulpy oatmeal. Bulbs of hot cereal gather in the folds of her bedclothes.

The nurse remarks that *the doctor will be along any minute.* Therefore, she's going to prepare the intravenous tube. That is, she is going to perforate Billie's arm, tape it down, pending authorization. There's a recriminatory dimension here, and Billie shrieks to draw attention to recrimination. A long open vowel, like the warm-up exercises for a difficult aria. She even wakes the woman with the pancreatic cancer, who sits up, cries out, *Who's there?* and then seems to fall again into morphine semisleep. Billie's screech likewise brings a couple of other staff nurses, including a few from the morning shift. All stare as the avenging angel tightens the elastic around Billie's arm and begins her needle work. The widow boils.

— Should be ashamed of yourself, a woman of your age.

— Don't you . . . speak that way to me . . .

— And how are your bedsores? the nurse soon asks disingenuously, as though she'd been working in this direction all along. Having introduced the feeding tube, she begins unstrapping Billie's extremities. — Might as well look after them while we're waiting.

With an accomplice from her shift, the night nurse rolls Billie over like a coiled piece of carpeting, and then pulls wide the flaps of her hospital gown — so that the Raitliffe skeleton breathes freely of the rubbing alcohol and ether and manifold germs in that recirculated atmosphere. The professionals busy themselves with a fetid wound in one of her buttocks. The night nurse points out the features of this pressure sore to her less experienced colleague —

— This one here is pretty bad. Almost stringy when you start to clean out the . . . Right. Like that.

The mozzarella of bedsores. The room is rank with disinfectants and the sweetness of decay. After some cleaning, with some industrial alcohols, the night nurse cheerily attempts to set things right.

— Sorry if I was a little short with you.

She gathers up her biohazardous rags.

— Maybe you'll try having a little more breakfast now?

In the next hour, Billie gives in to fury, her heart stinging as her mottled flesh might have. She, of course, refuses all sustenance. Various narratives of revenge occupy her, and thus the hour passes, much quicker than any hour should pass. Then the cast enlarges. Her boy, Dexter, and her neurologist, Ronald Kramms, and a staff doctor gather around her bed, feigning concern. They help her on with her glasses. They placate and calm. The night nurse, torturer, is gone. It's unclear, really, if she were *ever present at all*. No one will believe Billie when she attempts to catalogue offenses of the nursing staff.

— They're telling me, Kramms interrupts with a line of commentary apparently in progress, — that you've refused food since you arrived, Mrs. Raitliffe. Now, we can't stay strong if we're not going to eat. Right? Do you have to make this so difficult? If you won't eat, I'm going to have to leave you in here for a few more days, and I will authorize feeding you, if that's consonant with your family's wishes. Good nutrition, of course, is integral to what we're trying to accomplish. Remission, containment of symptoms.

— I'll eat . . . when I get back . . . to the house . . .

Kramms waves his hands exasperatedly.

— In the meantime, you understand about the hot baths? I don't know how many times I have to repeat myself here. It's just not going to work. You're not going to respond well to the high temperatures. It's going to exacerbate the symptoms. That should be abundantly clear at this point. It's a trauma. Do you understand?

She doesn't bother with a reply.

— Let's move on then to the issue of antidepressants. Are you in touch with the psychopharmacologist I recommended? I really think you're going to find that this new drug yields results. They're doing amazing things with the, uh, re-uptake inhibitors. Dramatic results. Can't you have your husband or your son here secure the antidepressants for you? I'm telling you, in my opinion, it's worth the effort. Now, I'm willing to write this most recent incident off as a close call, but only as long as you get serious about the medication. The next time I'll keep you in here for a week. All right? Dexter, are you up to the —

— G-g-g-got it under control. Fine.

Dexter, however, looks run-down. Even she can see this. He has a black eye, a *contusion* of some sort. He has singed an eyebrow. Or has shaved it off and also the left side of his skull. And he's wearing an awful pair of flannel slacks that he almost certainly borrowed from *Lou's closet*. Why? The slacks don't look like anything Dexter would wear. They don't fit properly; they bag around his ankles almost like those awful bell-bottoms or some equally ridiculous style. He has also appropriated a mauve-colored golf sweater. He's spectral. Ghostly. Upset. Her concern about this, her maternal concern, interferes with other practical issues. Her nostalgia for the simple movement of embracing is keen, and her melancholy at having lost *this privilege of comforting* is, therefore, the worst disability of all. Meanwhile, the nurses have taken leave, as have Dr. Kramms and the staff doctor, with their expensive advice. Thus, with the Mylar curtain drawn across the room, it's just the two of them again. Mother and child. Dexter will be in charge, again, of dressing her.

— D-d-d-do you want me to take this Band-Aid off here? From the IV t-t-t-tube.

— What's wrong with your face?

— I'll t-t-tell you later.

— Don't worry about . . . the dressings.

Hex unlaces the hospital gown in the rear, leaving it draped for a moment. Then he retreats into the bathroom, where her bathrobe hangs. It was all the EMTs had time to wrap around her last night. Dexter, averting his eyes, begins timidly to enrobe her with this garment. His eyes dart around. He gets her arms entangled, as usual, in the sleeves. He tries to put her head through the sleeve.

— Something . . . bothering you?

— Later, he says.

He goes out into the hall to flag down a wheelchair.

Mobility, with its suggestion of self-propulsion, lightens her spirits considerably. The change of scenery. Just to see doors and closets and nurses stations and to pass them at a clip. The desperately ill, the temporarily ill, they go in and out of her stereopticon. The comings and goings of events. The elevator with its descending numerals. The waiting rooms. Operating amphitheaters. The wheelchair careens through the automatic doors at the front of the hospital. There's the satisfying sound of the rubber tires on rubber matting. Tires warbling. A taxi idles out front. In the sun-dappled AM. A taxi? As Dexter begins the arduous process of unloading and reloading, he thanks the cabby for waiting. He forks Billie out of the chair and folds her into a sort of a ball, small enough that he can *mush her* through the rear door. Into the backseat. An orderly turns up, swipes the empty chair, is gone.

— What happened . . . to the car? she asks as Hex Raitliffe climbs in on the far side. He straps her in. He leans forward to give the driver the address. And then:

— G-g-g-got into a sort of a fracas with your husband last night. Or at least with . . . his . . . his second in c-c-command —

— You saw . . . Louis?

— Dexter's mouth hollows out. His face takes on the exaggerated stylings of a player's mask. Gripped by some hyperbolic feeling. — Mom, I'm having a really b-b-bad d-d-day. I don't know. D-d-do you really want to hear about all this? I know you have a lot on your own mind —

— Tell your mom . . .

— I'm worried I'm having a . . . I don't know . . . a nervous b-b-breakdown or something. I d-d-don't know what's g-g-g-going on, Ma. I c-c-can't slow down long enough to b-b-breathe, and I . . .

Dexter's eyes meet the eyes of the driver, in the mirror. Polish or Czech, or otherwise Balkan. His eyes are locked on them, trained on the rearview.

— I c-c-crashed up the rental c-c-car —

— Oh, no. Darling.

— Or it c-c-caught on fire or something. I d-d-don't remember. I wrecked the car and left it b-b-behind. I g-g-got in a fight, I went t-t-to talk t-t-t-to Louis, to t-t-try to t-t-talk to Louis —

— Dexter, I'm touched that you . . . but you know . . . you —

— And I t-t-t-t-trespassed out on some g-g-guy's p-p-p-property . . . or at least that's what I remember . . . and then Louis's friend from the plant, he p-p-p-p —

— Someone hit you?

— And then I wound up at some nightclub —

— Dexter, you can't . . .

It's some arcane dialect, their idiomatic eccentricities, the expressions and tics spoken alone by this dwindling tribe, ancestral Puritans, dwellers on this continent for three hundred years, *dialect of rectitude and virtue* nonetheless concealing a history of shame and regret, all implicit in silences and church attendance and problems with drink and indirection in speech and manner.

— You're . . . going to . . . have to . . . apologize . . . of course.

— I kn-know, he says, — I know.

He sighs.

— How d-d-do other people manage this? How do they manage to grow old stylishly and settle down?

The taxi accelerates onto the Baldwin Bridge. The railroad bridge just parallel is in the open position so that some schooner, some ship of fools from the last century, can tack with its cargo of affluent tourists into the Connecticut River. *Here, on I-95, when it was brand-new, was where she and Louis had a blowout one night. Twenty years ago perhaps. And here's where they had to stop, on a cross-county scavenger hunt organized by the country club. And here's where Allen and she looked at a house once, when the parcels of land were acre upon acre. Apple orchards and dairy farms. Subdivided and subdivided since.* The light is crisp upon the sea, mottling the ripples. The boats will be in the water for just a few more weeks. The anglers will squeeze in a last fishing outing before springtime. All this letting go of things. When was the last time Billie was on a boat? When was the last time she listened to water tickling a hull? A decade ago? When Louis took her out in the rowboat among the tidal marshes looking for horseshoe crabs? She thumbed a field guide to local birds. He kissed her when they saw a blue heron rising up out of the mud almost casually, wings the color of the skies. When?

They're not even out of the car, but nevertheless she begins her tactful effort at persuasion.

— We've got something . . . to discuss.

Dexter is paying. Rooting through the pockets of borrowed trousers for balled-up denominations, a half-dozen twenties, wadded like spitballs. His hands tremble. He can barely smooth out the scraps of legal tender to find the appropriate markings. Nor can he hold still while accepting change or counting back the tip. Still, he manages, reddening with embarrassment. And then he lopes toward the house to fetch her chariot. Then they are perfumed with taxi exhaust. She settles into the chair. They start across the crushed stone to the front door.

— Let's g-go down to the water, he says.

— We have . . . to have a . . . conversation . . .

— I need a few minutes.

— I'm tired . . . I'd like to go . . . inside . . .

— C-can't you indulge me, Mom?

— No, I cannot . . . what we have . . . to discuss —

By the front door now, pushing back the door. Into chilly interiors. He stumbles on the step.

— That's just p-plain self-d-d-d — . . . What you're d-d-doing. In the t-t-tub last night. At the hospital. How am I supposed to look after you? I mean —

— Don't you —

Her shrill alarums.

— I d-d-don't really c-c-care if you're upset, Mom. You're acting like a kid. Sometimes, I feel like I c-c-can understand why Lou felt he had to go. When you're b-behaving like this . . .

The remark is so perfectly incisive that it silences her. Her eyelids fall like theatrical curtains on the conversation. Dew rises in her. Her head slumps onto her chest. In the meantime, Hex hangs his borrowed cardigan sweater, with grass-stained elbows, in the front hall closet. He smooths it once to eliminate creases.

— If I'm g-g-going to c-c-come here and look after you, if that's what you expect me to b-b-b-be d-d-doing, then there are g-g-going to b-b-be a few changes. There are g-g-going to b-be a few rules. If you want me to just p-p-pull up stakes.

The gears and their teeth mesh, the satellite locks into its perpetual tumble, and she whispers that she *doesn't want to live, doesn't want to live, doesn't want to live, doesn't want him to have to do it, but she doesn't want to live out her days, what's the point, no point, what earthly point is there, she wants him to do something about it, she wants him to take care of it, if he were a son, a real son who recognized the sacrifices she had made for him, then he would make this sacrifice himself, he would do what she asked of him, he would take care of this difficulty, he would take care of it, however hard it is, it's too painful now, and only going to get worse, today's monosyllable, tomorrow's strained silence, today's wheelchair, tomorrow's bedpan and bedsore and dementia and pneumonia and mummification, the money will all get used up, and he'll have to sell the house and sell the stocks and cash in the mutual funds, until there's nothing left, day after day, no insurance, astronomical bills, and she doesn't want him to know these things, she wants to leave some things private, a woman should be able to die with her head held up and if those muscles don't work, the ones that used to hold up her head, then she shouldn't have to suffer, she shouldn't have to suffer.*

— D-d-d-damn it. I d-d-don't want to listen to this —

He stamps trying to get the words out. And just then the telephone rings. A blessing. She can't remember the last time she heard the telephone ring. She fixes on the detail. Who could possibly be calling? At this hour? First thing in the morning? Who'd call? Dexter cocks an ear, though the answering machine is out in the living room. It's enough time to rethink the pitch of their rancor.

— You said you were t-t-tired. Are you still t-t-tired? Why don't you t-t-take a nap. We'll t-talk more about this. I'll t-t-try to t-t-talk about it if that's what you want. After you rest.

— I'm not interested in . . . discussing it.

— I know. I know. B-b-but you're g-g-going to have to make d-d-do with me right now, b-b-because that's all you've got until Monday morning. I'll bet that was Kramms on the phone just now, and I'm g-g-going to c-c-call him and t-t-tell him what you're telling me, what you've been talking about all day. And then you and I will d-d-discuss it further. After I t-talk to him.

— You don't understand.

— Sure, I do.

He lifts her into his arms, at the foot of the stairs, and begins, unsteadily, to climb. Her feet protrude out over the banister. As her eyes wobble in her head, the floor and its carpets spin kaleidoscopically. The first floor recedes. He could drop her here, she thinks.

How easy it would be. He could just drop her over the landing. He could loft her out of the window across the hall, out onto the wrought iron fence surrounding the old rose bed, or she could go headfirst on the flagstone, or he could plunge her into the goldfish pond, he could carry her there and make still her heart. It would take no time at all. The gravity of the situation. There would be no struggle.

— I love you, you know. Mom.

No nerve impulses in her wrist or very few. The phantom pains she has, the phantoms of her illness, would mask the slash of a goodly blade, shaving razor, or vegetable dicer; same could be said of the arteries in her neck, fine as angel-hair pasta. Easily severed. Dexter could give her head a good twist, jiggle the vertebrae out of line, no more demanding than ripping open a breast of chicken for its delectable viands. This violence would be gracious. Instead, he carries her to bed, as though she never left, sepulchral bed, mortuary bed, memorable only for varieties of repose. The movement from one bed to another, the relentless progress of bed rest and bedside entertainment. *She's in bed again,* in the same soiled robe she has worn for years, wore it to the hospital and back, and it's true that she's tired, that her head flickers with hypnogogic images and familial battles, for example, here's Allen Raitliffe, holding aloft a bouquet of roses, a peace offering, inbred roses from the backyard, *very kind of you, let's not quarrel, there's something I want to show you here about the mathematics of the stars,* differential equations, she looks through a telescope in the desert, Allen shows her the soup of the galaxies and describes to her the weightlessness of interstellar space, she is weightless there, *drifting off,* amazed at how small is the eyepiece of that magnificent tool, they invite her to come back anytime, glad to meet her, her boy draws back the curtains, pulls open the windows a crack, chill breeze, *November,* ample sunlight, she should have done more than she did, and Allen and the telescope and the roses and the mathematics and the sun and the earth in the backyard when you turn it over with a trowel the fertilizer . . .

She finds him by her side. On the bed. Actually sitting on the other side of the bed, as though it were his own. With his shoes.

It's *the way you recognize a person, by their shoes, you see, shoes are a measure of the man,* work shoes from the thirties — badly in need of repair, with burnished leather, resoled — or wingtips, or sandals, *sandals with socks,* or tennis shoes, *or Wellington boots eaten away by decades of salt water,* a great burden relieved by the fact of him sitting on the bed, shoes or not. She's not alone. She's relieved to find that people will manage to put up with your floundering. They'll still be available. It's the very kind of reliability that occasions this chitinous shell of sleep . . .

Dexter holds out a cup of water when she shakes off the dreams. He's touching her on the shoulder, holding out the cup, Dexter. In a valley beside her legs, where the hills of the bedding empty out in a lowland glen, there are the half-dozen vials of potions, various sleep promoters, though she can hardly seem to stay awake, and her son is speaking to her, offering some accounting of entelechies, here's why he's doing it, the reason for his reversal, *You understand, I d-d-don't want to, that's the truth, and I d-d-don't know what I'm g-g-going to d-d-do later,* and he's shuffling the mound of scrips looking for a most potent, unexpired jar, the phenobarbital maybe, turning the child-proof caps, *What's going to happen to me?,* shaking out a half-dozen of the pills, setting them to one side, MAO inhibitors, *Don't eat any cheeses with these,* maybe a little cheese, therefore, some Camembert or a Brie wheel to hasten the sorcery, some Xanax, some diazepam (generic), some triazolam, some haloperidol (inhibits drug-interaction hallucinations), *D-d-d-do you think you c-c-can swallow these?* Her preternatural exhaustion, her complete willingness not to have to combat particular events, good-bye bedpan, farewell to catheterization, *au revoir* to the kindness of strangers, but she's frightened nonetheless, doesn't know if she *can* swallow these medicines, doesn't know if she wants to take her leave, after all, isn't that a surprise, and so she's glad he's beside her on the bed, as he begins to open the jars into the glass of water, spilling the color wheel of the capsules, crushing the tranquilizers with a fingernail file so that they'll be easier to get down, *a straw,* there on the bedside table, the curlicue straw from the night before, the lovely childlike ornament that Jane Ingersoll brought, *There's the straw right . . . there,* and he nods, and then returns to the project, crushing the larger fragments in his palm, his hands trembling badly. He stabs himself with the sharp end of the file, draws a vermilion bead from himself, and this corpuscular additive gets mixed up with the sleep pellets, transported into the glass with its murky liquid, little vaporous trails of pink and blue drifting down into the glass, tiny particles from the capsules, *Are you sure this is what you want to d-d-do? D-d-d-don't say you want to d-d-do it for me, because I'll stay here as long as you need me to stay, Mom. I'll put aside whatever there is for me to p-p-p-p-put aside. Mom, I'd d-d-do anything so that you c-c-could stay. I'll t-t-turn over a new leaf, I p-p-promise I will.* With the volition she has left, she tries to execute the common American nod, now that she has waked enough to understand the ramifications, in spite of fear, she reaches for the common American *okey-doke, yup, allrightey,* and much time passes, maybe *years* in the subjective time of old widows, as she tries to manipulate the muscles in there, tries to make them do their job, and perhaps she does, *yes, she's sure of it,* there's a sort of a nod there for her son to see, a small tottering in the neck, an indication of a certain dignity, at least given the signal loss due to neurological illness. It's almost forceful, really. So he reaches across her for the straw and dips it into the glass. The time it takes him to put the glass beneath her chin, the time to reach across the gulf between idea and deed, is minimal. The opportunities to scuttle this plan, it seems, are back a ways, back twenty years ago when she was on the cane, when Louis used to drive her around in a golf cart, back then she might have thought twice, but she has hidden away all the photographs from then, all the good memories, as she begins to use the swallowing muscles, esophageal and alimentary, as she uses these remaining muscle groups to drink from that fountain, from that fresh water, that spring water of the Green Mountains or White Mountains or the Sangre de Cristo Mountains, that unpolluted ambrosia, that H_2O. She is thirsty. The glass is empty. He takes hold of her hand. It's closer even than the marriage bed. She sleeps.

She can scarcely wake to tell if it's the blinds or if it's lights in her that are dim, if day has come and gone; she can't remember which day and what was the forecast — mixed clouds and sun — and he comes to her bearing *a plastic bag.* Yes, she remembers now but doesn't say anything, he comes with a plastic bag from the pharmacy, must be a pharmacy, she did so much business with them, must have been a great number of pharmacy bags in the house, Duane Reade, or CVS, or Rite Aid. His expression is so sad, she wishes he could see that it is no trouble at all, not to be troubled on her account. *This is an experiment . . . I've been meaning to undertake . . . I don't know how I got . . . so busy . . . when I'd be better off spending time with you, darling,* and the pharmacy bag descends over her head. Like a snood. Perhaps she is going to be bathed now; she loves to be bathed; perhaps she is going to make a trip through the car wash. Gosh, the straps around the chin are a little tight, there's a sort of a knot, a double bow perhaps, there's some awful condensation in this room, the edges have become gray, isn't it possible to open a window, doesn't feel up to it herself exactly, but perhaps Allen or Dexter will open the window, and she would like to take a little walk, after all, she has things to do, calls to make, plants to plant, invitations to extend, kindnesses to bestow, is there time for a walk?

22

The fall from the cot in the living room is long; he's backward; he's upside-down; he is back in time; his stocking feet, grimy and rank, are where the pillow is; his head is at the hospital corners; he's still wearing his glasses; he has *slept* with the cracked glasses on; his clothes are repulsive; his body is coated in pungencies from the night before; in the buffet of human archetypes, he is, as he falls, like *week-old macaroni-and-cheese or cold Chinese take-out.* Sensation returns to his extremities discretely, as with switches thrown; it's dawn and there's an ominous citrinity to the sheets and to his clothes, and as this leakage starts to command his attention, starts to flood him the way the tidal soup of the Sound, for example, ebbs back into the salt marshes of Old Saybrook, Hex Raitliffe begins to panic, throws himself sideways off the hospital cot — *the hospital cot in the living room?* — understanding thereby that he is not in his bedroom, *can't remember why,* buttery socks slightly elevated on the pillow; he needs to attend to certain bodily functions *if he means to avoid further mortification,* pitches sideways off the bed, misjudging the distance, misjudging the narrowness of the cot, into the ceremonial vault of the living room, headfirst, somersaulting, flailing, crying out. He lands curled on the rug. Like a fetus.

Raitliffe himself would emphasize the panic in the present situation. An unwarranted perturbation, a disquiet, though there are few bodily threats on the horizon. He's a guy at his mother's plush country house for the weekend, taking it easy on a Saturday morning, relaxing. *Why then this feeling that the world is the color of over-the-counter anti-diarrheal remedies? Why amid the acupunctural lancings at his temples, in his liver, in his pancreas, does he have a certainty of really bad things to come?* There are any number of urgent issues, each of which would merit a little concern, at least they would merit concern after he's had buttered toast and a cup of Joe out on the terrace, watching the sailboats get an early start out. Yet he feels like he swallowed a hummingbird.

Raitliffe kicks off his trousers on the way to the half-bath in the foyer. He gets the pants off of one leg, *hopping,* and then trots with this unshed layer cuffing his right ankle. His boxers are damp. His shirt is ripped and torn and smudged variously with some fecal stuff. He's like the three-legged dogs of his old neighborhood, their stubby tails wagging. The kids stoned these dogs. He gazes upon his own face in the poorly lit vanity mirror in the half-bath. *Oh, man.* His eye is swollen and purple, his face is scratched, his eyebrow is practically gone. There's a bald patch over his left ear. His lip is split and crusty with some clotting mica. There are little soapy patches at the corners of his mouth. His teeth are green enough to photosynthesize. He sinks backward onto the toilet.

Once he was a sweet kid, he could swear it, with an easy smile and a good humor, chasing after ice cream trucks, scaring up Canada geese, stopping to look at puppies, longing for siblings and for three-hanky endings. He was an innocent kid, or mostly innocent anyhow, and there are people who would testify to this over drinks or late at night.

His breathing races. A blood-pressure exam would show it up. His constitution, in general, is idling around *the initial levels of emergency* as he begins to remember, for example, that Jane Ingersoll came home with him. *That girl he loved in ninth grade.* Punk rock siren. She came home with him, and there were protestations of ceaseless affection, the sort of protestations impossible to live up to with a hangover. And then she was gone. *Was it good?*

Raitliffe weaves unsteadily out of the john. He slams the bathroom door with unnecessary violence. The toilet runs. Forgot to jiggle the handle. With the abbreviated attention span of his predicament, the attention span that is a symptom of his *toxic with-drawal*, Hex Raitliffe then tarries in the front hall, opens the door to verify the situation with respect to the car, to reacquaint himself, to attempt some state-specific perceptions from a mostly sober vantage point. His motives are obscure. There's some piece of information missing: it has to do with cars. This information will make the morning more difficult. As the great front door swings back, to illustrate the point, it brings with it a blast of dawn's early light that drives him, cowering, into the living room, where the draperies are already drawn. He gets only an initial picture of the driveway. *There are no cars at all.* Maybe he parked the rental somewhere else. Wouldn't be the first time. He has searched all of Greenwich Village for parked cars. He has asked beseechingly at parking lots: *I think it's sort of a cerise color. Late model. American. I may have p-p-parked it here last night.*

Must be after seven already. The excruciating light. First metaphor for how panic will express itself, how it will flower: he's shaky in the light, in any light, on the way into the kitchen, *Some caffeine wouldn't hurt at all,* a little caffeine. *Did he bring his sunglasses with him?* Raitliffe gets sidetracked drawing closed the curtains and drapes, trying to keep out the insolent sun. He has an actual throb in his frontal lobes. When he runs out of steam, it's in the dining room — where the glimmer of sunlight illuminating the hems of faded drapes is still too much.

Practical issues beckon to him. *His mom is in the hospital, he has a job he's supposed to do for some foundation, middle of the week, somebody has to feed the goldfish, he has to contact Aviva and settle on her schedule for the next weekend.* Driving himself forward, into the kitchen, scouring the shelves for the beans, for the grinder of beans, getting preoccupied with the grinder. It's a sexy piece of machinery when you think about it, sleek, white, columnar. *Ought to call the hospital,* ought to call and see when visitor's hours begin. Ruminating about the coffee machine. How full to fill it? The sound of the grinder is violent. He reaches up into the cabinet for a mug with an artichoke embossed upon it. He turns on the old radio over the sink. The news. *More trouble at Millstone. Man shoots three in Windsor Locks.* Shuts it off immediately. In the sink, there is an open jar of applesauce, a soupspoon still buried in the remainder. He digs in, though the Macintosh pabulum has been watered down by a drip from the tap. A couple of spoonfuls, before he begins to feel like it's a bad idea, that he might not be able to keep it down. Hey, wait, he's still in his boxer shorts. Raitliffe peels off the torn shirt, trudges up the back stairs in search of other clothes, becomes lost on the second floor.

Passes by his own room, which doesn't have a stitch in it anyway, maybe a sweatshirt that his mother gave him for Christmas twenty years ago still hanging in the closet. He never liked any of the stuff she gave him; she was always wasting her money on the most laughable clothes, trying to affect his wardrobe long after it was feasible, well into his thirties. By chance, or by inclination, he turns up instead in Lou Sloane's room, top of the front stairs, and steals the first pair of trousers he finds hanging in the closet. Flannels. Baggy in the cuff. He belts the slacks pretty tight too. They bunch. He also swipes a striped short-sleeved polyester shirt and a cardigan sweater. Back down the front stairs. Past the foyer bathroom: his own discarded trousers there, like a molted skin.

Coffee. He has to have coffee. As he's finishing the preparation of coffee, he gets an idea to call Jane Ingersoll. Before the advent of coffee. Before he forgets about the coffee. It's kind of early, but by the time he dials the numbers, he's forgotten how early. She's not home. Jane's out somewhere. He begins to worry. Where did he leave her exactly? To her machine: *Hello, Jane . . . um, D-d-d-d-d-d-d-d-d-d* — his stutter worse than expected — *It's me, Hex Raitliffe. I think . . . I uh, we were t-t-together last night, and I just wanted to say, I uh, I had a g-g-g-good t-t-t-t-time, at least, well, we had a g-g-great t-t-time last night, I think, it was really g-g-great to see you, and I wanted to thank you for it, b-b-b-b-b-because, I might have said, it's not all that often that . . . and I was wondering if you c-c-c-could . . .*

There's a muffled thud, something toppling over, and then a ragged voice, husky with drink and cigarettes.

— Oh, shit . . .

— Jane? Jane?

— Jesus, Raitliffe —

— Did I call too early?

— Raitliffe, what time is it? Didn't I just see you like an hour ago or something? . . .

— Oh, right —

— Couldn't I sleep for a couple of hours before we talk again?

— Of course. Sure. I'm really sorry. I've just —

— The kids are coming home soon, like in a few hours or something. Look, I'm sorry I left without leaving a note or anything, but I —

— Well, that's no b-b-b —

— It's just that —

— Forget about it. No p-p-p-p —

— Hey, you should call about the car. Did you call them? The car people?

— The car. Yeah, in fact, I was wondering, if you —

The coffee machine respires, across the kitchen. It's a digital model. Has a memory chip in there. He can smell the elixir starting to achieve its scorched and sludgy intensity.

— I was wondering, Raitliffe starts again, — if you c-c-c-c- could t-t-tell me exactly where the c-c-c-car is?

— You don't remember?

The words are a mounting struggle, and not just in the usual way. They are viscous and gray, and they seem composed of some abject muck, of some material that will reflect badly on him, and he is practically unable to get the questions out. He wishes, more and more, that he had never picked up the receiver in the first place.

— Well, sure I remember. Of c-c-c-course. I just c-c-c-c-c —

She waits for him. Her staccato breathing.

— I'm just not sure, you know, where we p-p-p-p —

— Raitliffe, she says, — maybe you don't want to know. Maybe we'll just wait on the car thing for a couple of hours. Look, I have to get some more sleep. I can't even think straight. You want me to come over there and take you to the hospital? You know your mother is in the hospital, right?

— I . . .

A reflex in him strikes.

— I'll come pick you up, Jane says, — don't go anywhere.

A seizure of rectitude, perhaps a sort of *petit mal* seizure, abnormal EEG tracings, voltage spikes, you know, almost like a real seizure —

— Listen, I'll c-c-c-call you later, I . . .

— Don't be silly.

— Just remembered something I have to d-d-do. I'll t-t-take c-c-care of the hospital situation. I'll c-c-call you later in the d-d-day.

— Wait a second. I'll tell you about the car.

— G-g-gotta go.

— Raitliffe.

— Thanks . . .

He slots the wall phone back in its holster by the breakfast table, where, coincidentally, a pair of pink socks — must be Jane's — are laid out on a chair. Instinctively, he takes up one of these and holds it to his forehead. Should he call her back? Which of his many repentances should he undertake first? The socks are grayish on the soles, threadbare at the heels. Jane Ingersoll apparently doesn't take care with her underlayers. Her garment drives Raitliffe back to the night before, to their *jujitsu* in front of the fireplace. Like other fragmentary recollections, he finds that this one has a merry upper layer which conceals some core disappointment or loss, and in this way his perturbation gets even more insistent, more physiognomic in its dimensions. *Coffee, above all, coffee, with its amphetamine properties.* His pulse skitters, and he pours the coffee unsteadily, coming to realize indeed that his hands are trembling, pours the extra-strength drug into the artichoke cup, his breathing coursing as though he's doing some sort of 10K road race, he takes the coffee, spilling it all the way across the kitchen, as he slumps in one of the chairs at the breakfast table, and dials the hospital. *His mother has had a seizure.* Visiting hours at —

As the coffee starts to perform its time-honored chemistry, his preoccupation with the incandescent lights in the house, daylight, fluorescence, halogen — begins to make him squirm. The lights are a problem. He shuts off the dim, offensive bulbs remaining from the night before, the hall fixtures, the rheostats, the switches, the dials, and then he gets an even finer idea, goes down the staircase to the basement — by the back door, by the washer and dryer at the service entrance — still carrying the cup of coffee, urgent in his haste, *to shut off the main circuit breaker.* He stumbles along one wall, tripping on terra-cotta planters and antique bicycle parts, the atavistic basement-orienting skills of childhood, using these techniques for divining and reckoning, to stumble promptly upon *the fuse box,* its sleek metallic surface, his palm upon it. He throws the master switch. It has an authoritative snap. The boiler and the coffee and the stereo and the computer, all the Raitliffe guzzlers of power, shut down, the clocks go off, and in the dark of the basement he feels ephemerally secure.

Back upstairs. Proteins. Call the cab. To the hospital. He has to spring his mother. He has to do something about his car. He has to call his answering machine at home. *There's a philosophical hesitation in him, one that he can hardly bring himself to examine.* It resembles marijuana angst, or test anxiety. Just when the prayer-like repetitions — *Relax, you'll be okay, take it easy, breathe, it's just the hangover, relax* — begin to seem effective, the anxiety subdivides or reproduces, bringing with it the next desperate argument for a treatment, which floats like a nimbus cloud into his field of vision: *Shit, Hex, have a little nip, a shot, a splash, a hair of the proverbial dog, a swig off the top. This will clear all the nastiness right up. Just a little bit.* It'd actually be good for him. Opens up the blood vessels, promotes corpuscular flow. Cardiologists report that it's a regimen for well-being.

However, he's taken the pledge, at least until lunchtime, to clean out the system, do the liver a good turn. Let things run their course. Until he figures out what to do about his mom. Nevertheless, Hex goes out into the pantry. (Wasn't there something about *the preparation of food* he was considering? Wasn't there something he was going to eat?) Behind impeccable though dusty glass cabinets are the dozens of bottles, shelved according to their cachet. The liqueurs, the good stuff, the collectible wines. He discounts the single malts, the sour mashes, but gets as far as taking out a bottle of brandy. *Hey, it's just an after-dinner drink. Have one. Go ahead. Don't be an altar boy.* He actually opens the bottle and breathes of its sugary sweetness, its gravitational allure. *The finest perfume.* And then Raitliffe reels, hustles out of the pantry, leaving the coffee cup behind him there, leaving the bottle teetering behind him, to collapse again at the dining room table.

Then there's this ontological snag as Raitliffe confronts the fact of distilled spirits in his mother's house and *the relationship between distilled spirits and his present state;* in this snag, *Hex begins to worry about his worrying,* to look on his emotions with a panicky critical distance, which leads to worry about this distance itself, about the second- or third-order status of worry, *worry about worry about worry,* that is, spinning off in metastases of panic that have as additional aspects their shamefulness, such that not only is he engaged in the traditional seductive compulsions of morbid thinking, suicidal ideation, etc., but now also worry and shame and worry about shame and shame about worry, and he knows that this thinking is erroneous, comical, out of place, embarrassingly familiar, and he is therefore disinclined to really address it openly. But he has to call somebody. He has to try Jane Ingersoll again. Or his therapist. Or his high school history teacher. Or Jane Ingersoll's sister. Somebody.

— Raitliffe? Is that you again?

— Yeah, I . . .

— What the hell is wrong? I'm never going to get any sleep. Is there something you need help with? At this exact second? Otherwise could you let me sleep?

— I don't know, I . . .

— What's up?

— I think I'm . . .

— What's the problem? Look, is there really something wrong? Do you want me to come over now?

— Uh . . .

— Okay, okay. Look. Raitliffe. I'm going to take a shower and eat some food. Did you eat anything? Maybe if you try eating something. I'm going to eat and call my sister about her car, and then I'll be over. In a couple of hours. All right? Can you sit tight for a couple of hours? I mean, doesn't your mother have an entire discount pharmacy up in her medicine cabinet? Why don't you take a

Valium, Raitliffe? Don't be stupid. You're not hefting the entire globe. It'll all work out.

He struggles to get out the next word, a mere word of thanks, but the syllables are so misshapen as to be incomprehensible, and then the line is dead, and he falls to the floor in the kitchen where one of Jane's pink socks has also drifted like a ghostly footfall, an imprint of the lost confreres that have strode through this old house, and he sits there on the tile floor for a while, before falling to his side to hold his head between his palms, the sock balled before him.

His mother's medicine cabinet should be a matter for the FBI, or for the fashionable legal wing of the Catholic church, or for the local teenage garbage heads — the derelicts treading the path he treads himself. His mother could arm a whole chapter of the Hemlock Society. As he begins inspecting the contents, though, he sees that it's mostly out of date, that Billie's refusal to medicate herself over the years, to deal *proactively* with her decline, has adversely affected any planning for this moment. Raitliffe has trouble holding the containers steady enough to read them. He's pretty sure that one with the blue pills is Valium. He used to buy it at the clubs, to dull the serrated edges of some buzz. Valium. It's like fluorine. The kids in the clubs use it, the addicts in the ghettos, the housewives in their homes, the elderly, the sleepless, the catchers in the big leagues, the politicians. Five milligrams, ten, fifteen. Hex doesn't use a cup. He dunks his right profile under the tap. The water courses down his face. He heaves a sigh of relief. He looks again at his features. It's true: he feels a little better. Well enough to travel.

But by the time they are disembarked from the hospital, by the time he and his mother are home and he has her in her chair, he's feeling again like he's being devoured by extra-large vermilion aphids, or that his skin is plastic — while they are standing in the doorway (she's chittering away about how he's supposed to finish her off), while the phone is ringing, and a cold sweat breaks out upon him all at once, and he's not even listening, and he formulates some distracted replies that don't have to do with anything; he'll say anything; he'll do anything to keep her quiet. The lights are awful. With the last bit of energy he has, he carries her to her room. He draws the blinds, pulls up the covers over her breasts. He whispers endearments, desperately, *She's the only person who ever treated him well, he's turned over a new leaf, really has, this time it's different, he's really not going to drink, he's really going to stick around, and he's going to stay alert, well, for a while at any rate, he's going to give generously, the way she gave to him, he's going to love what family he has now,* but it's clear that she hasn't heard. (A sleeping mother is the best kind to offer your endearments to.) His skin crawls. His failures are stashed and secreted now wherever he looks. He hasn't listened to one thing his mother has said to him, never has, he can't understand her half of the time, he never listens, he never listens to anyone, as he never once listened to Gillian or to Jane Ingersoll the night before; in his hands now are the charred edges of the typewriter paper, sooty and fragmentary; so Hex Raitliffe prays the Great American Prayer, the American psalm, the prayer of infants, though to whom he prays is unclear — Anglican New Testament God of the church of his parents? Interdenominational and mostly secular god of his liberal arts education? More likely, as with his fellow Americans, he supplicates now to a provisionally devised personal deity, made up on the spot, reasonably all-powerful, completely generous, adapted from Hollywood and rock and roll and moonlight on water. He prays to this God, with burnt offering, *G-g-get me out of this, get me out of this one fix, I'll do anything.*

Now he hangs in the doorjamb of his mother's room. In or out? His eyes hollowed like caves. He climbs onto the empty side of the bed. He tries to sleep. Next to his mother. She snores. The air goes in but doesn't emerge. Raitliffe falls in and out of vertigo. Every breath is her last. After a few sequences from the cutting room floor of nightmares, he allows himself suddenly to think the unthinkable, and he finds it has been an insistent signal, an encoded message beneath all of this, like the beacons of radio towers or industrial stacks. He just hasn't tuned the station. Now it crowds out the other frequencies. *He might do something to relieve her of this.* In troubled dreams, trying to nap beside his mother — he used to sneak into her room, his parents' room, at night, and crawl into the crook of her arm — he holds the pillow over his mother's face, or bears a cleaver up from the kitchen and hacks at her neck. He lurches up out of these dreams, with a cry, to find that his mother's eyes are open but drifting shut again. He can't sleep. He can't wake. He hears things. He hears sirens. He drifts off. Takes her life again. That's how the decision is made. *He relinquishes himself.* He asks if this is what she really wants, *Is this what you really want?* He could swear she actually nods.

Thus, Hex Raitliffe feeds her those comestibles. Death, the sixth food group. His mother swallows. There is an appropriately fancy straw that she has gotten somewhere. On the bedside table. She knows. She wants what she has said she wants. Before he's finished making the decision, though, before he has even ironed out the wrinkles in the decision, felt secure about it, she has swallowed the pills that he's ground up with trembling hands, and in the silence, she falls again to sleep. Immediately, he worries. Haven't there been moments when he has felt angry about her illness, angry enough to wish her dead? *Yep.* Haven't there been times when he hated her enough, her intractability, her manipulations, her pride, that he wanted to finish her off? *There have been times like this.* Haven't there been days when he has really indulged in the simplicity that would result from her passing away? *Sure, there have been these kinds of days.* Hasn't her condition, her immobility, her powerlessness been to his advantage? Hasn't he profited by it at times? *He has.* He takes her hand as she sleeps and he holds it in his own. His hands tremble. He's a murderer. He's a pacifist. He'd never hurt anybody. He's enraged. He's sadder than he has ever been.

He circles the premises, the old stone homestead, goes rifling the drawers of the desk some more, sifting through the memorabilia, a mound of it out of a drawer, a college paper he wrote on the Dead Sea Scrolls, yellowed newspaper clippings. He remembers about the telephone ringing, about the answering machine, and reaches behind the desk to unplug the digital machine and to carry it down to the basement, where, for a moment he restores power, to locate a grounded outlet nearby. He depresses the *new messages* button, *Mike Schlosser from Roadside Assistance at Hertz, we're calling for Mr. Dexter Raitliffe, as regards the rental from the, uh, 40th Street Manhattan location, uh, of a Ford Taurus, New York license plate HCE 810, please call us at your earliest convenience.* A second message, more urgent, also from Mike, regarding a *police report from Groton, Connecticut, and a 1992 Ford Taurus, rented to you,* and Raitliffe's pulse begins to race anew, and he considers barricading himself in the broom closet in the pantry. It would be quiet in there, it would be dark. He could take a little time — with the pool cues and flashlights and hip waders — to think all of this through.

He beats on the answering machine with a rusty garden trowel until the casing shatters. An hour has passed. His mother's breathing, when he goes to look in on her, has grown no shallower, and there's no evidence at all that her controlled-substance stockpile is doing what it is designed to do, and he begins to shout, *You c-c-can't even do this right, you c-c-can't even d-d-die with a little d-d-dignity, you've had the wretchedest life I've ever heard of, if you won the lottery t-t-t-tomorrow, your house would be d-d-destroyed by hurricane b-b-before nightfall and the lottery agency would go b-b-belly up,* and this misguided attack enables him to go into the linen closet in the hall and fetch the plastic bag, his jaw locked, as with infection. It's a continuous action, in which he ties the plastic bag around her face thoughtlessly, the logo of the national chain of pharmacies over her eyes. The logo covers her eyes so that he doesn't have to look at them. He holds the bag tight to her face, waiting for the breathing to cease, but it doesn't, it's like the ticking of some foolproof digital timepiece. He holds her nose shut, through the bag, but it's no good, the west wind of which she breathes leaks from the spaces between her lips — he would kiss them, but instead he tries to hold them closed. Seduction and euthanasia, pretty close together. Kneeling beside her on the bed, pinching closed the nostrils and with the left hand trying to hold shut her mouth. At the critical instant, though, *he can't do it, can't do it,* can't seem to make himself. Too complicated. He takes one of the goose-down pillows, an old one, leaking feathers, leans her back against the mattress and holds the pillow across her face, her Rite Aid Pharmacy face, the gray-white wisps of her hair protruding underneath the margins of the plastic bag, wiping out her face, wiping out the face of his mother, her torso, her immobilized claws, powerless to do anything about it. He holds the pillow over her for a minute or two or three, for five minutes, five endless minutes, the stink of his own flesh dripping on the pillow, sweat and tears, until he releases the pillow, and gazes wildly at his hands, not believing that they have done what they have done, *P-p-p-p-p-p-p-p-p-p-p-p-please please please*, he says, *t-t-t-tell me I d-d-d-didn't, t-tell me I d-d-d-didn't.* He peels back the pillow, and unties the plastic bag. She's still breathing.

He goes to fetch the gun. There's just the one left here, the bequest, the one Lou Sloane was unable to sell off, Winchester Model 21, prewar, original stock still on it. It's in Hex's closet. In the bedroom. And there's the gun-cleaning kit, too. Before he can use the gun he has to clean it. It's part of the tradition, part of the legacy. First remove the stock from the barrel. Break the piece. Then, with felt ball and brass brush, with the patches affixed to the cleaning rod, wipe away the gray particulate accumulations in the barrel. Then the Browning ultra-fine oil, with it petroleum distillates. Lubricate the barrel. (It's ten or fifteen years since he fired it. There's corrosion.) *The greatest enemy of the firearm is the sweaty hand.* Then, remove the chrome snap caps, and load the firearm with the green plastic Remingtons. Some buckshot. Some number six shells. High brass and low brass. One of each. Number six in the right. In case he misses. With the unregistered hunting weapon, this sport gun, Hex Raitliffe strides back down the hall toward his mother's room. Wearing the face of mercy.

23

Not a footloose guy, really, Lou Sloane nonetheless strikes out from the all-night pizza restaurant in the first light of dawn like a hitchhiker. The sedimentary past of Connecticut is the landscape he traverses, Waterford to Niantic, east to west, like a damn hippie. Along the waterfront he goes, toward Kowalski's house, to fetch his personal effects. He's groggy like he can't remember having been. The morning is coming in sunny.

Here's the marina — between two shuttered taverns and a half-dozen beer neons — where the Freeds, Dan and Stan, used to have their fishing boat. An aquamarine lobstering vessel with the classic square cab. She always needed another paint job. She was always peeling down to an underlayer of anemic yellow. The Freeds had hands like swollen mittens. They were drunks. Lou can remember somebody telling him — Kowalski, perhaps — that the Freeds' own father was still lobstering in this harbor in a rowboat. Pulling the traps by hand, on weekends. Moonlighting. Probably carried a flask in the boat. Next: the hardware store — a dozen lightweight metal traps stacked in front of it. The surly owner, Kenny Driscoll, used to supply them occasionally over at the plant. Driscoll moved to Florida, sold out to a retired detective from New Jersey who gouged the local guys. Beside Driscoll's: the auto parts store.

Lou makes slow progress along the depressed Niantic harbor, facing traffic. He would accept that ride now, if it came along.

One-fifty-six weaves away from the shore, from the houses on the bay, and with it, after half an hour, Lou disappears into stands of birch and maple, past an elementary school, past a nursery, up the hill to the *Niantic Shore-Owners Association.*

He frets about how to present the case to his wife, how to phrase his lengthy apology and explanation. *Honey, I've made a terrible mistake. Let me try to tell you what has happened.* Amid these worries, Sloane tries to get by one house, on the corner, past a sunny patch of impeccable lawn, where a sleeping rottweiler keeps his watch. The hound wakes and makes a beeline for Lou, to the edge of the tarmac. *Lou's mission is good and true,* though, and he therefore speaks a New England plainspeech to the hound, *Attaboy. Sit. Attaboy.* Because what if the dog is the impediment that keeps him from making his *full and entire restitution?* Methodically, he starts back down the lazy hill, past aluminum siding, past lawn jockeys, and then makes another attempt. The dog, flopped over on his side for some fellatio, scrambles up. It menaces. It lunges. *Just in time to avert tragedy,* however, the paunchy owner of the canine, wearing nautical cap and navy Bermuda shorts, skips down the winding flagstone — a screen door hisses shut behind him — to restrain his devoted companion, *Trigger, down. Trigger, down. Sorry about that, real sorry. Down. Down. He likes to meet new people.* Lou has the unpleasant sensation that he's about to be sold insurance: yep, it's Leonard Van Zandt, Aetna Life and Casualty. Leonard fits his pipe between his lips. *Have we met before?* But Lou pleads haste — and continues through a copse of evergreens, to the end of the road.

Again, at Mac Kowalski's ranch house, there are delays. In the kitchen. He avails himself of juice, of a piece of cold, leftover bacon, quilted in plastic wrap. A respite from all the walking. Where the night seemed forbidding with its rain and high winds, the day is like grace — light breezes, bright sunshine, the call of gulls over the roof. Grackles. *What will he say? Why go back now?* No reason to suppose things will improve, as the symptoms of Billie's melodrama will find ever more baroque ways of torturing her physique, *I can imagine you are surprised to see me, Billie.* All he has to do now is load the overnight bag into the Cadillac; all he has to do is strap himself into the driver's seat, fit the key in the ignition; all he has to do is to drive, to ford the mouth of the mighty Connecticut. But, instead, Lou goes back into Kowalski's guest room. *Sure is quiet.* He lies down on the extra bed to think about the situation. His eyes are splintered with sleep, with incomplete dreams. As soon as he closes them — provisionally, just for a moment, he's unconscious. And yet some strategizing precinct continues its efforts. Sloane's nap is like imprisonment. It features torture imagery. *He is constrained by nautical lines. He is shackled and chained.* He decides he will have a cup of coffee, one cup — Billie won't be up yet anyhow. Then he'll go. Really. He reclines again. An hour passes.

Finally, from a light sleep, Lou blunders into Kowalski's paneled recreation room with bumper pool table. In a somnambulistic stagger. He tries Billie's phone number. His own phone number. At Flagler Drive. Remotely, the machine begins to answer. The computerized voice. He stifles a sob. He hangs up. He dials back. Hangs up again. *Billie, darling, I know some things about myself now, some dark things, and I think I want to try to share them with you, in the hopes that I can explain to you why I did what I did and why I've come back.* Then, in the recreation room, in one last mighty effort at procrastination, Lou composes, with a desiccated magic marker, a letter of thanks to his lifelong friend, Mac Kowalski. On a legal pad. This note is about *the indivisible bond of true friendship. We meet only a very few people who are so generous, Mac, so devoted, that they can see us at our very worst and still stand by us. They offer us the great human gift of forgiveness. When we see them we know that we are loved, and we learn that the responsibility of friendship is something we leap into eagerly.* Lou signs his name to this document and masking-tapes it to the refrigerator in the kitchen. In the instant of this gesture he realizes that he has also written his own manifesto, or words in the direction of *a manifesto, one that would apply just as well to his wife.* He doesn't know where he gets these commonplaces, these psychologies. *Billie, I think I know now about the indivisible bond of true love, how we meet a very few people who are so generous, so devoted, that they can see us at our very worst . . .*

Emboldened, therefore, Lou buckles himself at last into the driver's seat of his Cadillac. He tunes the oldies station. He sings nervously along with Motown antiques that combine the spiritual with the profane — guitars and pennywhistles. Lou's *basso*, half-step afoul of the melody, rings across crests and dales of the *Niantic Shore-Owners Association*. He has only to pass through Old Lyme now, that municipality famous for deer ticks, along the mouth of the river, and then over it, stopping additionally at an eponymously named package store, Olde Lyme Ales and Spirits, where he settles on a fine champagne. He will produce this bottle and some of Billie's stemware at an opportune moment. If all goes well. He also stops to *check the oil*. He examines his dipstick with a blackened rag. Then, in the men's room, he thoroughly washes his hands. He is haggard and unshaven. He looks sad. Perhaps this is the mien with which to beg for forgiveness on a Saturday morning. In the meager fluorescent bulb of the men's room at the Getty station of Old Lyme, Lou Sloane despairs. This is preposterously hard. His life is no circuit diagram or blueprint for lives. It's not tidy.

Across the Baldwin Bridge, he is entranced by difficulties. He goes down the main drag of Old Saybrook, the avenue of summer houses, to where the peninsula empties out at the Econo-Lodge. Across from the war monument. A hundred yards off, in the harbor, a rock with a half-dozen pines upon it. A little isle. Lou goes perpendicularly onto the causeway, and parks there temporarily to gaze. And then he takes the county road into Fenwick. The road home. The great beauty of this low, marshy boulevard wrings a nostalgia from him. He turns onto that spit of land, Fenwick, the country club and environs, where his wife lives, and nearly rams a golf cart, wiping his eyes. It's Justin Grant and his second wife, Laurie. They're dressed in bright pastels. They wave convivially as they cut off Lou's Cadillac. They shout halloos.

The police car appears in his rearview about this time. No sirens, no official haste. Just there, crawling up the lane, with a sort of forced nonchalance, as with all small-town authorities. Though Lou Sloane is an admirer of the men who have the hard job of keeping the public peace, he feels a concern at this black-and-white mirroring the Cadillac, bend for bend, curve for curve; he makes a right onto Flagler, it follows; he mounts the hill, it follows — so that as he rises up over the water, to see sunshine sparkling there, the black-and-white does so too. The day is clear. Fishers Island, all in green. A ferryboat halfway across. Montauk, its bluffs like a chimera.

The police cruiser slows to a halt behind him in the turnaround. At the edge of the lawn, a motorcycle is tipped over on its side. In desperation, following a procedure long-standing among Millstone employees, Lou Sloane removes his car keys, reaches out the open driver's-side window, and places them upon the roof. In this way, municipal and state workers communicate their fraternity. *I won't flee.*

— Mr. Raitliffe? The cop in his mirror, peripherally in his ken.

The name, in this context, surprises Lou. His first thought, of course, is that he has committed a crime. He doesn't know how to answer. He throws up his hands. — Well, uh, I suppose. No. Well . . . my wife's husband has been dead for some time. I'm Louis Sloane, I'm the current Mr. Raitliffe, if that's what you mean, I suppose.

He thrusts a paw out the window. To shake. The cop stares at it hesitantly.

— License and registration?

— Certainly. After an interval: — Could you tell me the offense? Is there a violation of some kind that I should know about?

— No, sir, says the patrolman. — I sure hope that bottle is not open, though. (Pointing to the passenger seat.) He then retires to his vehicle without further conversation. The hiss and hum of two-way radio traffic breaks out amid birdcalls of the shoreline, finches and jays, robins and mourning doves. Lou sits in the Cadillac, gazing distractedly at the house. Every blind is drawn. The place looks neglected, as if *his Herculean presence alone* held off disorder and decline. Or maybe it's just the fresh perspective he brings, this perspective of remorse, that makes it possible to see the house as it really is. Dispirited. In the midst of Lou's rumination, the patrolman, in squeaky black shoes, returns.

— We're looking for a Mr. Dexter A. A. Raitliffe.

— That would be my stepson, Lou says. — All right if I get out of the car now?

The cop nods.

— Would it be possible, Lou inquires, scrabbling to collect his keys, — for me to ask exactly what the nature of the problem is?

— Afraid that's something I'm better off discussing with Mr. Raitliffe personally.

— I saw him last night. I should probably tell you.

The cop, like a mannequin in the driveway, begins to show a mild interest. He produces a notepad.

— And where was that?

— I was staying with a friend in Niantic. We were —

Even the ballpoint has a holster on that utility belt. The guy must be a rookie, twenty-four or twenty-five tops, and Lou surmises that the rookie is hot on the trail of his first big arrest. A major drug ring on the Connecticut coast. White-collar crime. Scofflaws. Parking violations.

— Night fishing, Lou says.

— You were night fishing with your stepson?

— With a friend. I just ran into him. My stepson. On the way in. On the road out by my friend's house.

— Ran . . . into . . . him.

Scrawling it all down.

— On the street, Lou says. — He was —

— And do you know whether he returned to the house? Did he come back to . . . (Checking his notes.) — Flagler Drive?

They look at the front door of the house, each of them.

— Well, Lou says hesitantly, with the politeness of a home-owner: — Would you like to come in?

— I'd like to speak with him, yessir, if Mr. Raitliffe is here.

They start across the gravel toward the house, the oddly silent house, to knit up the remaining strands of the conversation, but just as Lou is rummaging in his pockets for his jumble of house keys, *a third car pulls up the drive at the 52 Flagler residence. A* Japanese subcompact. Since the house, as Officer Brian Reilly might term it, *is to all intents and purposes apparently empty, without the perpetrator or other inhabitants residing therein,* they turn their attention to this Japanese vehicle, which shudders to a halt just behind the cruiser, in spite of Officer Reilly's attempt to wave it around the perimeter of the driveway, *Miss, Miss? Could you please park your vehicle around the other side?* Cupping hands around his utility-infielder mustache. And Jane Ingersoll — though Lou Sloane doesn't know yet that this is the name of the woman with the cabbage-colored hair — complies, with a fair amount of gear shifting. She then climbs out of the Japanese subcompact and heads for the front door as though Lou and the police officer were not even there.

— Excuse me, Lou Sloane says, *as the Caucasian woman with the bleach-spattered denims, approximately 5′4″*, walks familiarly to the front door. — Excuse me?

— Going to visit a friend, Jane mumbles nervously.

Lou interrupts, — I'm afraid that I don't know you, and this is my —

The Caucasian woman thereupon puts two and two together. She flutters, trembles, with new information. Moreover, she recognizes intuitively the difficulty of having a police officer on the scene — especially when the aforementioned officer, *because of intensive training in acuities of psychology and criminal behavior back at the academy*, begins to see a pattern emerge in Jane Ingersoll's demeanor and begins to pester her with unresolved questions himself, *Do you know a Dexter A. A. Raitliffe? Have you seen Mr. Raitliffe in the last twenty-four hours? Are you aware of Mr. Raitliffe's whereabouts at the present time? Can you tell me if you saw a Dexter A. A. Raitliffe driving a rental vehicle at any time in the last twenty-four hours? Can you identify the owner of that motorcycle?*

Jane Ingersoll replies, — I'm not really sure where you're going with all of this.

Thereafter the officer and Lou Sloane both inquire into the name of *this unknown Caucasian female* and Jane gives them the biographical specifics in an abbreviated form and then the great door to the dilapidated Raitliffe manse swings back and lets the daylight into its aquatic interior and the three of them, Officer Brian Reilly, Lou Sloane, and Jane Ingersoll, form a sort of bundle, and this bundle proceeds in Indian file across the foyer, where a pair of pants, knotted and inside-out, lie neglectedly, and into the main floor of the house. It is Lou Sloane who calls out into this vault, in his falsely cheerful bass-baritone, *Anybody home? Dexter? Billie?* Officer Brian Reilly meanwhile heads counterclockwise, *having begun his secret but nonetheless full-fledged investigation of the premises, away from the stepfather of the alleged scofflaw, who may be covering up certain activities,* while Jane Ingersoll waits in the front hall, as if she didn't know in her heart exactly where to go. This Caucasian resident of Old Saybrook, this single mother and administrative assistant, then heads up the stairs, pulling off her boots so that she can proceed softly, leaving the *black Justin cowboy boots with rounded, worn heels* on the stairs.

Officer Brian Reilly meanwhile encounters, in the kitchen, a single pink sock in woman's size on a vinyl-covered chair at the breakfast table. He hypothesizes, therefore, as to *illicit sexual activity taking place here, could be a high-priced call girl ring or a sexual cult of some kind, maybe even Satanic.* He then seizes the sock as evidence, but, realizing the murky legal terrain in which he is operating here, he carefully replaces the threadbare pale pink nylon athletic sock in its approximate former location. In the pantry, an open bottle of cognac. Later, in the dining room, he notes palm prints, in dust, on the antique table. It then occurs to him that the electricity is off. He scrawls this on his pad. Lou Sloane, at the same time, in the living room — where there are tangled bedsheets on the vacant hospital cot — stalls in front of his own words, his own idiomatic expressions, in hard copy, on the desk. The shock of his language arrests him. *Your poverty has tired me out.* He can see with a sudden clarity that it is his confusions that have led to the shrouds of silence here. There is a rubble of paper and artifacts on the floor. The Raitliffes have been searching the past for explanations. He rustles through these fragments, too. Letters from Allen, a parking ticket from the last decade, a seed catalogue open to varieties of corn.

Lou goes out the French doors onto the patio. He invites in daylight. The languor of the patio is more austere than pleasant, and as he's taking in this austerity his eyes pass over the window of

Billie's bedroom. The window is open; the blinds are fluttering against the screen. This interior calls to him. The room calls to him. Thus, he does the old guy jog, back into the house, where he encounters Officer Brian Reilly, and in an unspoken acclamation, a unison of community standards, they head up the front stairs together. Their step is suddenly fleet.

In the meantime, Jane Ingersoll brushes past the occasional table in the second-floor hallway, overturning an empty vase, and is therefore the first to see the scene as it is being enacted, the first to find that Hex Raitliffe *has a gun of some kind, a rifle or shotgun, trained on his mother,* asleep in her bed, peacefully unconscious. Who knows how long he's been this way? The barrel of the gun trembles as Raitliffe attempts to keep it steady. (The bed separates him from Jane.) The muzzle of the weapon is four or five feet from his mother's head. It's the only exposed target. Raitliffe's mother is under blankets. Jane's *hiss of surprise,* her alarm, gives her away. *As the assailant learns that he is observed, he begins to shuffle uncomfortably with the 12-gauge side-by-side firearm.* He blanches. Jane locks eyes with Raitliffe and though she feels only apprehension, she's aware that the gaze they share is most like a carnal gaze. He frees himself from this transaction, however, to concentrate on his *target.* Jane falls out of the doorway, carried away by primitive instincts. She rushes into the hall, ducks behind a closet door, halfway open. And listens. Plugs her ears, takes her fingers out, hums, listens, weeps briefly, curses herself for weeping. Hears nothing. Then footfalls. *Oh shit.* Jane Ingersoll is caught between the desire to rat out the assailant, to betray Raitliffe to the authorities, to get it over with, and the contrary need, to warn him about upcoming events. *He tried to pick her up in some restaurant. She couldn't have had any idea.* Jane ponders options, pros and cons, but the scene is moving rapidly and before she arrives at any conclusion she can see Lou Sloane and the cop moving in. So she breaks free of her redoubt at last and calls to Hex Raitliffe, calls, as she hurries from the closet, into the master bedroom, heedless of bodily harm — *Put it away, just throw it under the bed. Just throw it under there now. They're coming. Come on. Do it. Stash it. Under there.* These seconds scarcely pass. The seconds in which Raitliffe *signals to her,* stutters, waves her off. *B-b-b-beat it!* He doesn't want to wake his mother. He doesn't want her to wake, except in the hereafter. Jane's voice upsets the delicate silence that will be ended only by the blast.

— G-g-g-go on, he says. Pleading. — Out.

— But, Dexter —

It's the last parley on the subject, their last parley, because immediately, Jane is joined in the doorway by Raitliffe's stepfather and by the mustached rookie. The bellow that erupts from Lou Sloane is elephantine, a sound from the world of primitive communications. It's desperate. Lou and the cop collide, elbowing into the room, as in some silent reel, and then the interior is crowded with participants, the *dramatis personae,* soundless in their idiosyncratic ways, motionless. (Elsewhere, Hertz corporate detectives are bearing down on this address and Jane Ingersoll's sons are standing, shivering, out front of her locked house.) All is still, at least, until Lou Sloane makes a brave attempt to gain control of the situation. Pulse thundering arrhythmically, he takes a step in the direction of Raitliffe, who then, according to the rules of gun-related imbroglios, *points the weapon at him.*

— Dexter, Lou says, — what the hell?

— I d-d-don't have to d-d-discuss anything with you, Hex says. His voice quavers. — This is b-b-b-b —

— Raitliffe, Jane Ingersoll interjects, — the cop is here only because of the car. Just put the gun away. We'll get this squared away.

His wavering barrel trained on Lou Sloane.

— D-d-don't interrupt me, Raitliffe says. — I hate b-b-b-being interrupted.

— Drop the weapon now, the cop says, using his advanced psychological weapons and tactics. But Raitliffe *d-d-doesn't seem to c-c-care to hear the c-c-cop's p-p-position on the situation.* Rivulets of perspiration trace his forehead. With an awkward gesture, during which the gun arcs dangerously around the room, he wipes his face on the sleeve of his cardigan sweater.

— Dexter, Lou begins again, — I know you're under a fair amount of pressure about this. I know she's put a lot of pressure on you, but that's no reason to do anything so drastic. The situation is changed, that's what I'm trying to tell you. I've thought about what you said last night. That's why I'm here. The officer just happened to be here in the driveway, I didn't bring him, I can promise you that. Nobody's going to make this hard on you. If you just put the gun away. Give it here. Let's try and get this sorted out as a family. Let's make a start of it.

Jane Ingersoll refrains, — Do what he says.

— Jesus, Raitliffe addresses the beloved, — you're g-g-going to c-c-c-collude with this g-g-guy, you d-d-d-don't know what he's like.

— Pal, Officer Brian Reilly says, — think about the mess you're getting into.

Hard to tell, if it's rivers of sweat or what, Jane Ingersoll thinks, as Raitliffe waves the shotgun around again while toweling his face with his sleeve, and the rookie slips into the hall to radio for backup, and then, *per instructions from the dispatcher* — because he is a rookie — this protector of the common good takes the stairs two or three at a time, down the front staircase, landing badly in the foyer — after tripping on somebody's cowboy boot — so that he twists his ankle rather painfully. Could even be a sprain or a chip fracture. He limps to the squad car — *he injured himself as part of the struggle to subdue the assailant* — and takes up his two-way radio; then he waits in the car, weapon drawn; waits for the captain with the bullhorn, waits for the nail-biting, hair-raising standoff; waits, like they do these days, for the guys holed up with the crates of weapons and quotations from the book of Revelation: *he was probably a radical environmentalist or something, probably had been stockpiling armor-piercing ammo or automatic weapons up there for months, wanted to return the golf course to its natural state.*

Raitliffe's hands are trembling. He's beginning to feel the heat. When Jane Ingersoll slips across the room to attempt to lift Ma Raitliffe out of the bed, to carry her to safety, to nurse her, Hex Raitliffe really begins to panic. Jane moves slowly, hands raised, with a feminine gentleness. Nevertheless, *he turns the gun on her.*

— Come on, Dexter, Jane says, poised by the bed, — put it down.

— Shut the hell up, Raitliffe says, and marking the seriousness of the moment, he decides at last to switch off the safety on the weapon. His concentration on this simple technology — a small switch on the stock — provides Lou Sloane with the diversion he needs, and Raitliffe's stepfather again starts toward him, with one last mighty paternal effort; the truth, unfortunately, is that Raitliffe is more educated in weaponry than anyone could expect. He is finding he *can* handle the gun adequately, and he manages to get the safety off, to raise the weapon up against his unshaven cheek even as Lou is crossing the room. He takes aim, using the upper body — probably the vascular organs — as his target, and without further delay, without deliberation or forethought *he squeezes the trigger,* laying claim, thereby, to much suppressed rage and grief, maybe even generations of it, in the rank fog of sulfur and salt-peter. Unmuffled by the decoration and ornamentation of the interior, the report of the blast frightens Jane terribly, the permanence of it, the report of shot passing very near to human physique and through a lampshade in the corner before blowing a large hole in the plaster wall, passing near on the way to *Lou Sloane's head,* leaving a faint powder burn upon Sloane's face, which the step-father of the assailant herewith crouches to touch with his pillowy fingers. The whole *philosophy of blast* is startling in a way Jane has never felt, the way in which things tumble, sunder, and disas-semble. The recoil from the gunfire drives the unprepared Raitliffe back off of his feet and sideways over an armchair. Sloane, cursing, renews his sortie, except that Raitliffe has summoned the agility necessary to turn on Lou, fully now, with a madness in him, such that Jane rushes forward to try to stop Dexter A. A. Raitliffe, too. He is risen and is standing over Sloane now, and Lou is reaching for the barrel, and Jane Ingersoll is crying out a liquid vowel, anything that might arrest Dexter, but there's another blast, and then a sort of tinkling as the corpuscular geyser begins to fountain from Lou's right hand, mostly grazed but still blasted almost clean away. His thumb exposed in a way no such digital attachment should be. Shimmering. Raitliffe breaks the hinge on the shotgun. Two empty plastic cartridges are ejected clean. A sulfurous vapor again tails away from the weapon. A hunk of the floor is gone.

The noise wakes Ma Raitliffe. Her eyelids flutter. She mumbles. Lou Sloane similarly groans and rolls upon the Oriental carpet, clutching the one hand with the other. Raitliffe steps over him. *To reload.* There are several extra shells at the foot of the bed. Jane Ingersoll clutches the bedpost nearest the door. The elderly Widow Raitliffe whispers, *What . . . on . . . earth,* coming back to consciousness to find her ambitions scuttled. To find her boy with his gun, striding menacingly across the room. And Lou Sloane, at the sound of her slim, distress-call of a voice, himself cries out, *Billie, honey, I'm home. I'm never going to leave again.*

Jane Ingersoll evacuates. As Raitliffe gathers up the new shells, he reaches out for her. The image will come back to her later, the way he holds the gun broken over his arm, the way he reaches out his free hand. But Jane turns and flees, out into the hall, down the front stairs out into the driveway, deaf to his calls — as he follows her, several paces behind, to the front door — deaf to her own agitation, deaf to the cop in the squad car, not hearing any of it. Her tires screech as she pulls out, there's a general screeching and wailing. Jane is gone.

What Dexter Raitliffe has looked for, meanwhile, has come to pass, and he doesn't know it. Here's what happens. Carrying the shotgun, *the assailant* goes purposefully into the living room, and from there onto the patio, and thereby into the Raitliffes' backyard, past the goldfish pond, past the empty swimming pool. When he reaches the edge of the property, he then trespasses onto the Firths' lawn, which of course abuts the golf course, and from there *he commences his futile escape.* What he has looked for, therefore, is in the squad cars, performing their arias on the causeway; what he has looked for is in the day, crisp and clear, into which he thrusts himself, wearing his stepdad's clothes; what he has looked for is in the way the men, with slippered drivers, stand beside idling golf carts as he traverses the first and then the third fairways, those upwardly sloping holes; it's in his nascent detoxification — the way his own skin reeks like Wild Turkey; it's in the way that he realizes he is still carrying the shotgun, and determines that he might now part with it, his father's gun, in the trap on the fifth; in the way that the sunlight on the water, a hundred yards distant, seems to smooth over his worst excesses; it's in the way he misses Jane Ingersoll already, the worse for having scared her; it's in the fact that he has not hurt his mother; it's in the way he pulls off his cardigan sweater, stippled with his stepfather's blood, and leaves it on the bench by the green; in the way he pulls off the flannel slacks, not caring any longer who should see him, the Armstrongs, for example, who are passing in a cart and gawking; in the way, in boxer shorts and stolen shirt, he walks through the underbrush at the end of the fairway and emerges onto the ring of yellowed grass around the lighthouse and pauses to watch the sailboats tacking across the Sound; in the way he tiptoes his way across the rocks on the point, rocks thrown up by some glacial juggernaut; in the way, in stocking feet, he wades down, over blue crabs and snails and barnacles into the water; in the way he pulls off his socks and his shirt; in the way the police, having ascertained the direction of his escape, give chase, *weapons drawn*; in the way he dunks himself in the frigid headwaters of the great Connecticut River still wearing broken eyeglasses; in the way he begins, in the style of earliest swimming lessons, a leisurely breast stroke, in spite of the chilly temperatures; in the way he hugs the shore, doing a lap. He would never injure his mother. Mall franchises, mercy killings, sudden deaths, white supremacists, antigovernment militias, single mothers, new viruses. It's all here. What harried and preoccupied divinities would preside over and even *love* a naked felon swimming in the irradiated waters of the Long Island Sound one Saturday in November just after dawn? Who could love the kind of guy who would shoot at his own family? Those with ears will hear.

24

8/11/46

Dear B,

I'm getting this down now, in the hopes that it'll explain a thing or two later on. I'll just put it aside for a rainy day. I didn't want to come down for this Charlie business. But that's my job, right? The flight was bumpy over to Hawaii and the same southwest. We're staying in Kwaj, the phosphorus capital of the world. It's just a barracks, really, and darned warm. Not a fan anywhere, except in the mess tent. After the guys from the lab got the equipment constructed on the battleships — they were going to detonate over a small fleet again, this time with lab animals tethered on board — we relaxed on the ship, played cards, and so forth. The test was supposed to be at dawn, like before. The Baker shot pretty well swamped an entire coral reef or that's what the boys say. It's just gone. This time we were on the open sea. There was a new trigger apparatus on the design that was supposed to make it work better. It has to be used lickety-split. A mixed core, a composite. Anyhow, these weren't the things on my mind. I don't know why. The other guys, they were anxious about this because it's important for the Super program, or they were anxious because the second shot missed entirely. My heart just went out of the work, probably when they shipped home Slotin.

There was grub in the early morning, and then the bombers took off from the airstrip on the island. We listened to the radio reports. With Baker, there were navigational miscalculations, so they were cautious about measuring the distances. The bomber was closing in for hours, it seemed like. You couldn't see the atoll. It was over the lip of the horizon. We were all preoccupied with the weather. The wind had shifted a little and it could just as well have blown the whole mess in our direction. The military didn't train for fallout, but we did.

At five, they were above the target, and we'd donned the film badges. The radio operator counted down the last seconds over the loudspeakers.

Like I say, it was a predawn shot, underwater. Pretty complicated. The first thing I noticed was how quiet it was. I was sure we'd botched it. All that for nothing, the Communists in our backyard, that's what they'd be saying. But you forget in the moment that the sound wave doesn't arrive right away.

No one has any idea what that flash looks like. Even if they say they do. It depends where you're standing. I don't think there's even a name yet for that kind of light. The stupid idea I had was that I should watch for a few seconds. I took off the goggles after the flash, because I just wanted to know what I'd gotten myself into. It was bright blue at the beginning. There was a boiling in the sky, a boiling of lights and clouds and sea. This is what you get with your underwater shot. A lot of boiling.

We plugged our ears.

The cloud unfurled kind of like a morning glory, with shapes I'm not sure I would have been able to forecast, even with all the number-crunching machines in the world. Then the sun started to peek over the horizon. It was second fiddle by comparison. The sky was luminous and gray and violet while all this swept over us. We were fifty miles away with the whole sky the color of purple. The shock wave reached us by then — this was in parts of seconds — and we had to hold on to whatever was loose. Hats and papers, it all went into the drink. The wind was so hot, a sirocco. We hung on, and this bruise in the sky enveloped us. I had to remind myself to breathe.

We were steaming into the target area. Not very fast, of course, but in that direction. It took a whole morning, but soon we were there, checking on the goats and sheep. They had the flash burns, intestinal problems, all of that. I kept to myself. The water in the archipelago, when we got there, was marshy green. Oily where the smaller ships had vaporized, sunk to the bottom. The fleet that was a mile out was all twisted up, like by heavy incendiary bombing.

They were feeling good about it. The brass. They hit the target. The composite core worked. It was on to the next problem for them, the hydrogen fuse. This was how we completed the last of the regular A-bomb tests. The guys got drunk as skunks when we got back to Kwaj. They celebrated. They woke with hangovers, but I'm not sure it was from the drinking.

When I get done with writing up the results at the end of the month I'm going back to the university. I don't want to do it anymore, Billie. I want to get as far from the Pacific as I can. I want to get out of this business. I want to spend time with you. I want to drink Irish coffee on the porch. I want to visit amusement parks. I want to get rid of our radio. I want a daughter or a son. Will you be my partner in all these crimes?

Always yours,
A.